WHEN SHE WAS GONE

BOOKS BY
SARA FOSTER

Come Back to Me
Beneath the Shadows
Shallow Breath
All That Is Lost Between Us
The Hidden Hours
You Don't Know Me
The Hush
The Deceit
When She Was Gone

WHEN SHE WAS GONE

SARA FOSTER

BLACK STONE PUBLISHING

Printed in the United States of America

First edition: 2025
ISBN 978-1-0940-9405-2
Fiction / Thrillers / Psychological

Version 1

Blackstone Publishing
31 Mistletoe Rd.
Ashland, OR 97520

www.BlackstonePublishing.com

For my daughters—and all daughters,
who make everything worth fighting for.

PROLOGUE

LONDON, 2002

When the call came in, the neighbor reported screaming, but by the time Rose and Tristan pull up, number 39 is silent and dark. They had been the closest team available, just finishing a routine welfare check a few streets away, so they'd hurried over, keeping the sirens off.

On the surface, nothing appears out of the ordinary. The suburban street features a row of nondescript terraced houses with drab, redbrick facades, architectural leftovers from the seventies that no one has yet had the good sense to knock down. Each one has a small front garden with a path and a gate, the hip-high walls a clear designation of boundaries but a feeble barricade to the outside world.

Only last week Rose had visited this address with another constable, after a complaint about a screaming row, but Joseph Burns's wife, Natalie, had refused to make a report. She'd sat on a cheap, sagging gray sofa feeding her baby, her eyes downcast as though that might avoid Rose seeing the one that was purple and swollen, or the dirty bruising across her neck. However, without a witness, if she was unwilling to make a statement there was nothing they could do. So they'd left her and the baby, a sweet nine-month-old boy called Dax who had gurgled and grinned at them. They'd known that it would probably not be their last visit, but had been unaware of how quickly things would escalate. And now, here they are.

"I can't believe social haven't been here and collected this kid yet," Tristan grumbles as they get out of the car. In the darkness of the early evening, rain is falling, but so gently that Rose can hardly see it, except for a shimmer of misting droplets visible beneath the orb of the single streetlight. Her face is damp, and a steady wind presses the cold of the encroaching winter firmly against her skin.

Tristan is hungry and irritable, and Rose understands why. As an experienced constable he should have been back at the station doing paperwork. He's only out here because the early flu season means half the station is off sick. Rose is grateful for his experience on this particular house call, since she's still getting back into the job after an unexpected maternity leave. She thinks of Louisa now, tucked up in bed with her grandma watching over her, waiting until Henry and Rose come home from work. A lucky girl, born into a different world than the poor little mite inside this house.

It's not easy to leave baby Lou for the long periods of shift work, but Rose has wanted to be a police officer for as long as she can remember. It's her way of trying to make a difference in the world. Tristan understands. He has three young boys at home, and he'd spent their shift asking about her baby and regaling her with horror stories of toddlers that left her chuckling nervously.

Joseph Burns is well known to them. He'd joined the army as a teen and seen one tour in the Gulf before being thrown out. He took to fighting in the street instead, making his money from drugs and stolen goods. The time he'd spent in prison had only made him harsher, with better criminal connections. Natalie is a quiet, sweet woman as far as Rose can discern, but a wife and kid haven't managed to subdue Joseph's dark temper.

As they approach the front door, they realize it's slightly open. There are no lights on inside, and Tristan makes a gesture to Rose to go slowly and carefully, before he pushes back the door and calls, "Hello?"

No reply. There's a crackle of energy running through the stillness.

Rose senses there are people watching from behind curtains and doorways. She can feel the pulse of their adrenaline alongside her own.

The corridor is dark, but once inside they hear the baby wailing upstairs. Tristan indicates that Rose should go up, and he hangs back by the doorway. She climbs steadily to the second-floor landing, finding all the rooms unlit except one, which has stars and moons projected on the walls, whirling slowly around as a nursery rhyme plays.

She inches forward until she can see inside.

Natalie is lying face down, motionless, blood pooled around her head. The baby has pulled himself to a stand in the crib. He clutches at the bars, wearing only a nappy despite the cold, his face a mess of snot and tears. He is screaming while somehow managing to keep his pacifier from slipping out of his mouth. When Rose comes in, his eyes remain fixed on his mother.

Rose moves fast, checking for a pulse she knows she won't find. She depresses the orange button on her jacket, automatically silencing other radios so all officers in the area can hear her.

"Urgent assistance. This is three five nine tango x-ray. Backup required at thirty-nine Amersham Street."

She scoops up the baby and runs down the stairs, toward the front door, instinctively looking around as she does so, surprised that Tristan hasn't come to find her.

"Stop!"

The voice comes from the darkness behind her, cold and commanding. She turns.

Joseph's hand is gripping Tristan's shoulder, a large kitchen knife pressed to the constable's neck. Tristan stands motionless in the dimly lit corridor, his arms in the air in surrender. His eyes are white with fear.

"Give me my kid," Joseph yells.

Tristan keeps his eyes trained on Rose, and gives a small shake of the head.

"Give me my fucking kid!"

"I can't do that until you put the knife down, Joseph," Rose says steadily.

She sees the gratitude in Tristan's eyes, knows that it was exactly the right thing to say. Sirens wail in the distance, swiftly closing in. Joseph hesitates, and Tristan lunges. The two men wrestle as Rose stares in horror, clutching the child, holding his little face against the crescent of her neck to shield him as much as she can.

Tristan frees himself and stumbles forward toward Rose, as Joseph raises the knife. Rose glimpses a large tattoo shaped like an hourglass on Joseph's forearm, gone in a flash as he brings his fist down hard. There's an arc of blood and Tristan falls to the ground face-first, his body limp by the time he hits the floor.

Rose screams.

Joseph looks up and meets her eyes, stepping over Tristan, the knife dripping crimson in his hand. She moves the child around further on her hip, trying to protect him, but the baby writhes, pummeling Rose with his tiny fists. Joseph's attention snags on his son, as Dax lets out one long, furious wail.

The sirens are getting louder.

The strike is so fast she doesn't see it coming. She reels backward from the punch, choking as her nose fills with blood, the baby ripped from her arms. Her knees start to buckle as she watches Joseph and Dax disappear into one of the darkened rooms at the back of the house.

Tristan is motionless, blood pooling beneath his abdomen. Rose collapses to the floor, kneeling in front of her friend, trembling as she reaches for his pulse, searching for life in his clouded eyes, his slack and ashen face.

CHAPTER ONE
LOUISA

"Nineteen . . . eighteen . . . seventeen . . ."

Honey's pudgy little hands are over her eyes as she counts, but Lou isn't concentrating. She's staring at the path that leads away through the bushland on the beach's southern side, wishing Fabien would come back. She's furious with him for spoiling everything when the week had been so perfect. His secret visits to see her each morning had felt deliciously wicked, not least because she knew her bosses would be outraged, and she hates them both right now.

It's obvious that Kyle and Frannie think they own her. They are as bad as each other, and their fight last night had terrified her: the two of them screeching and growling like wildcats, insults and accusations flying, threatening to kill one another. It had been such a relief to get the little ones down to the beach early this morning, and she really doesn't want to go back to the house. Every day she thinks about quitting, but whenever she looks at these two small children, the thought of never seeing them again—of abandoning them to their toxic parents—is awful. It's hard enough to leave at the end of a nannying contract, even when the parents aren't a pair of vindictive arseholes. She'd been devastated on her last job when she'd had to say goodbye to baby Luca. They'd glossed over that part in the nanny training.

This early-morning beach time has become an essential part of Lou's routine. It's picture perfect here, the gentle arc of the coastline sheltering it from much of the harsher weather and strong winds that Western Australia is known for. The sun is soft at this hour, the air crisp and clean. The water laps quietly at the shore, its shallows a bright, clear turquoise, perfect for little legs to wade in while shoals of tiny fish, almost invisible against the sand, skitter and skim at their heels. Further out the ocean surface darkens; occasionally they glimpse a flash of a dolphin's silver fin.

Lou always wishes she had her camera—the light is incredible—but she'd restrained herself, knowing she couldn't focus properly on taking photographs and watching the kids at the same time. Anyway, it's good just to breathe and relax without anyone nagging or giving her a task. Spending time here helps her hold off the brooding thoughts that gather like storm clouds later in the day, when she's tired of wrangling the kids while Kyle and Frannie shout their orders from the pool deck. Not to mention all the extra jobs they dole out to her—loads of washing and serving drinks and anything else they care to come up with. As soon as she'd started working for them, they wouldn't let her take any time off unless they had another nanny on hand for the children, and they'd demanded she pause all social media and use a different phone, which had pretty much cut off her contact with the outside world. At first she'd respected their rules, understanding the restrictions as a desire for privacy, but now she sees these orders as part of their narcissistic need for control. This week she's also been expected to look after two older children, belonging to Kyle and Frannie's closest friends, while the four adults drink themselves into a stupor. Luckily the older kids don't like getting up early, otherwise she would have had to bring them down here too—and that would have blown her secret trysts with Fabien.

She'd been desperate to see him. Until they hatched this plan, they hadn't spent time together for nearly six months. Fabien could only snatch a few days of leave, and there was no question of Lou getting time off, so they'd decided he would have to sneak in to see her. She'd checked out the beach on her last visit here a couple of months ago, and found the path that ran through the bushland to the road. The whole thing had worked like a charm, since Kyle and Frannie rarely got up before eleven. Fabien would hang out on the beach with Lou for a couple of hours each morning, then he'd head off to surf with his friends in nearby Yallingup and she would continue her day with the kids.

However, today, before she could even tell him about last night, he'd tried to persuade her to quit.

"You hate this job, Lou." He'd sat close to her, stretching his deeply tanned legs out against the soft sand, running a hand through his dark-brown hair, pushing it away from his light-green eyes. He was so handsome that she melted a little each time he looked at her.

"I know." She'd kept her eyes on the children. "But I have to work. I have no savings and I can't stay in the country without a visa. Besides, the kids really need me. They're so little."

"Really? So you're going to work here until they're eighteen?" He'd laughed at her, shaking his head. "You can't help them, Lou. They're not yours to save. And you'll find another job."

"You don't understand," she'd insisted, angry with him for making her feel silly, even though she knew he was speaking the truth.

He'd thrown his hands up in response. They'd stopped talking, watching the kids play until Fabien said he had to go. She'd kissed him on the cheek and then he'd walked away, rubbing the back of his head as though pained. She'd wanted to chase after him, but she couldn't leave the kids.

Damn, she thinks now. *Why couldn't he just be understanding?* But if he doesn't come back, she might not see him again for months. Can they part on a quarrel for that long, or is it over? There's a lump in her throat at the thought.

Honey opens her eyes. "You didn't hide him," she cries, snatching the bear from Lou's hand with a frown. Lou can see the tantrum brewing, the little girl's right foot lifting off the ground, ready to stomp her frustration into the sand.

"Sorry, I got distracted," Lou says, quickly grabbing the scruffy blue teddy. As Honey counts again, she heads across to the jetty and tucks Valentine into one of the deeper crevices. The little girl never tires of this game, racing up and down on the soft white sand, shrieking with delight as she finds her favorite toy. There aren't too many places to hide Valentine on the open expanse of beach, so Lou is forced to get ever more inventive, while baby Kai sometimes gives the game away by pointing and giggling from his lofty position on Lou's hip, particularly now he's learned that this makes his sister scowl.

Sometimes Lou imagines running away and taking the kids with her, to a quiet island where she'd teach them to enjoy simple, earthy pleasures rather than becoming the spoiled little shits they're destined to be with parents like Kyle and Frannie. It's disappointing, seeing the kids' open, trusting faces turning toward wariness around their parents, their soft hearts hardening each day, aware of what is happening around them even when the grown-ups are too drunk to notice. Honey already runs to Lou when she's hurt, despite the fact it makes Frannie's face darken. The child's small, spongy brain has absorbed the unspoken dangers of her mother, although fortunately Honey is usually in bed by the time Frannie's drunkenness turns sarcastic and maudlin. It's Kyle who receives most of Frannie's spite, and he rises to every bit of the bait. There's a pent-up fury in him that Lou has come to fear; his fists and jaw clenching ever tighter as the weeks go by. She prays she won't be around when he finally unleashes, and she's learned to get out of the way pretty fast, but no amount of pillows over the head can smother the sound of the couple's furious arguments. It's confounding and unsettling how the next morning they often wake up as though nothing has happened, joking together and discussing the day's plans, even as they set about their hair-of-the-dog hangover cures and begin the whole cycle again.

Honey runs back across to them. "I can't find Valentine, Lulu," she says, pulling on Lou's hand, her little voice breathless. "I need a clue."

Lou smiles at her. "He's in a hard place, for sure," she says. "Can you see anything hard on the beach?" She nods to the rocks that form a groin at the northern end.

Honey beams and runs over to the steep pile of weathered granite stone, scampering up there as adept as a mountain goat and then disappearing over the top.

"Not so far!" Lou calls. "You don't need to go—"

But the little girl has already gone.

Lou sighs, raising her eyebrows complicitly at Kai, who giggles as he sits on the blanket, only eleven months old but fully aware of his sister pushing the boundaries. She's hurrying over to the rocks when there's a high-pitched scream from the other side. Lou stiffens. This is exactly what she's dreaded. It would be a disaster to go back to the holiday house with Honey wailing from a fall, no matter that cuts and scrapes are part of childhood. It doesn't take much to turn Frannie's polite charm to cold fury. She casts a nervous glance back at Kai, who is still sitting on the blanket, and decides that if he sets off at a crawl she could get back to him before he reaches the water. So she turns and breaks into a run toward the sound, calling, "Honey? Are you okay? Did you fall?"

There's no answer.

She hesitates, envisioning telling Frannie and Kyle that one of their babies has been hurt on her watch. They would kill her. Literally. All that crushed, compressed rage would be released onto her. She wouldn't survive it.

She shudders and checks back again. Kai is still on the blanket, head turned toward her, watching, his expression solemn now, his back straight and alert in his little romper suit. She climbs the rocks, terrified of seeing Honey sprawled out and bleeding.

But when she gets to the top and looks down, it is much, much worse than that.

CHAPTER TWO
ROSE

Rose's eyes sting as she squints at her laptop. She hasn't turned the overhead light on—much too bright at this late hour—so she's stuck with the small desk lamp illuminating her notes. The room is dark and deadly quiet: Although the apartment is on the first floor of a busy street, there's little traffic at this time. The only other light is the mellow glow of the streetlamps outside, and the momentary headlights of cars passing by, their tires splashing through the runoff from an early-spring rainstorm.

She'd tried sleep a few hours ago, but there was too much on her mind. She should be thinking about the biggest project of her career: the looming deadline for a document she's been working on with a team of domestic violence experts, which will be raised in parliament to push for stronger legislation. However, she can't get her mind away from Bonnie.

She'd been rostered on at Safehaven earlier in the day when the young girl had walked in crying, her face and arms a mess of bruises. A dirty beige duffel bag was slung over one shoulder and a bald-headed baby with a thick flowery headband had been held awkwardly under Bonnie's other arm, the child's eyes wide with confusion as her mother jiggled her up and down. The whole team at Safehaven knew Bonnie, and everyone feared for her. The man she was with, Dean Salter, had put his previous partner in hospital, but he was out of prison and back to his old habits, escalating a little further each time. It was Bonnie's fourth time at the shelter, and each time she arrived with fury and conviction, determined to put that "arsehole" behind her and make a fresh start. But she would never press charges, and the longest she'd lasted away from him so far was four days.

Rose volunteered at the domestic violence center whenever she could, as well as being on the board of directors, but lately, with the other work pressures on her private consultancy practice, she'd only made it there once a fortnight. She'd been hoping to leave shortly after Bonnie arrived, but they had been short staffed, and Rose couldn't abandon the young woman without support. Once they had gone through the formalities and found a vacant room, Rose minded the baby so Bonnie could shower. Little Zara fell asleep on Rose's shoulder, and Rose had lost herself in the child's steady breathing, and the solid little body that fit so easily into her arms. Whenever Rose held a baby of this age, it was always an exquisitely beautiful and equally painful thing, as it brought back echoes of those other little bodies she'd once held close. She'd had to work hard not to run from the room, desperate to put this little one somewhere safe, and she'd been relieved to pass Zara gently back to Bonnie. It was clear Bonnie needed a friend, and they'd talked into the evening, while Zara woke up, fed, played for a bit, and then fell asleep again.

Rose let Bonnie decompress, even though she knew everything about Dean already. Not just because Bonnie's story was written in the patina of bruises across the girl's body, but because there were so many depressing similarities between Dean and other men who liked to beat up their wives and girlfriends. After fourteen years in the police—eight of them as a hostage expert—and another eight years working with domestic violence victims while gaining her PhD and writing a bestselling book, Rose knew these characters inside out. What she didn't know was how to dispel the malignant influence they held over their partners. Still, she desperately wanted to make sure that, this time, Bonnie wouldn't go back. She'd left vowing to check in on them first thing in the morning, aware that now she'd need to spend the night catching up on her other work.

In the dark, silent room, Rose presses her fingertips into her eyes, trying to rub the tiredness away, then shivers. She gets up and grabs an old sweater from the armchair—one that David left behind—and shrugs it on. It still smells of him—cigarettes and Paco Rabanne. She misses him at times like these, but although they'd kept one another company for a few years, it had become obvious they weren't ever going to be a long-term thing. Both of them were too married to their work, so they'd mutually agreed to call it quits. David moved back into his flat in Wimbledon, and now they met up for the occasional friendly dinner with benefits.

As she's thinking of him, before she can sit down again, her phone screen lights up on the desk beside her. David often works very late too, and sometimes they end up texting, so she picks up her device expecting to see his name, smiling at the idea that they are in each other's thoughts at the same time. Instead, there's a missed call, and a text message that makes her heart skip a beat.

Rose. It's Henry. Are you awake?

She stares at the text, outraged that Henry would have the audacity to message her in the middle of the night.

Louisa, she thinks.

Her stomach lurches.

Can it wait until morning? she types back, although she's already anticipating the response.

No. You need to call me now.

She considers this for a moment, takes a long, steadying breath, and dials the number.

Henry doesn't even say hello. Just, "Lou is missing."

Even though she'd anticipated something serious, the news still hits her like a body blow. Rose sits down heavily in the armchair, trying to focus as Henry continues to talk.

"She's been in Australia for a while, nannying for wealthy families, but she went AWOL this morning, and so did the two little kids that were with her. The girl is only three—the baby's not even a year old. There's a massive search going on. It's a fucking nightmare."

There's so much to take in that Rose can't summon a response.

"Rose? Are you there?"

A thousand questions are racing through her mind, but the one that comes out is practical. "Where exactly is she? Australia's a big place."

"Southwest coast. Place called Kardanup. I'm not exactly sure where it is myself."

"And how long has she been gone?"

"Almost twenty-four hours, I think. Shit, Rose, I don't even know that for sure. They're seven hours ahead of us, so it was early this morning their time. She took the kids to the beach and that was the last anyone saw of them."

A whole day. Rose tightens her grip on the phone. She's trying to reassure herself that this is all going to be nothing, but that's a long time to disappear, particularly with two young kids. And although Henry had initially sounded in control, she can hear the waver in his voice now. It heightens her nerves. Henry rarely gets emotional, at least not in her experience. But perhaps he's changed.

"Rose? Say something."

"I heard you. You need to give me a bit more context, Henry. I haven't spoken to either of you for, what, six years?"

"Our daughter is missing," he repeats.

Not since he'd left Rose, back when Louisa was tiny, has he ever said "our daughter" to her. He must be in shock.

"It's all over the bloody news," he continues. "I can't believe it. Rachel's just had twins, and it's been awful. It was a very hard birth and one of the boys is still in the hospital." He sighs. "Now this. I don't know what I'm going to do. It's a fucking disaster."

Rose says nothing. She's dismayed that, even in this moment, he can still feel sorrier for himself than anyone else. Typical Henry.

He'd taken Louisa and left Rose for another woman eight weeks after Tristan died, while she was still recovering from her injuries, along with her grief and depression. Rose had initially been in hospital for three days while they treated her for shock and operated on her nose, and although the bone injuries had healed, she still bore a silver scar on her right cheek from Joseph's knife, which had caught her as he'd grabbed his son. The police had captured him not far from his home and a few months later there had been a huge trial, by which time Dax had been sent to be raised by his maternal grandparents. But Joseph hadn't gone down quietly. Instead he'd blamed the police for causing problems between him and Natalie, insisting that she'd been killed accidentally when she fell over as she'd tried to take his son from him. Joseph was adamant that the police and social services had got into Natalie's head, convincing her that she and Dax were in danger. He'd shouted in court that he hadn't meant to hurt her, and he would never hurt his kid. Because if he'd really wanted to, the boy would be dead as well, wouldn't he?

The trial had been high profile, and other men began to rally to Joseph's cause. There had been protests outside court, small groups of men holding slogans like *Respect for fathers* and *Kids need their dads*. They were husbands who'd lost their families because of their own aggressive, menacing behavior, who now saw themselves as victims of a system that no longer allowed a man to be the king of his own tiny domestic realm. As Rose arrived to testify, she'd been surrounded and spat on; once the on-duty officers had bundled her inside, there had been a brawl and numerous arrests.

Rose was initially swallowed by the devastation of it all. With Henry gone, her parents had moved in for two months to take care of her, but once they left, she began to struggle with alcohol dependence and PTSD. She'd tried to take Henry to court to gain joint custody of Louisa, but by the time a date was set, Louisa was calling Henry's new wife, Evelyn, "Mum" and the family had moved to Scotland. Henry had warned her that, if she fought him, his lawyers would go after her as an alcoholic, unfit mother, which would not only deny her access to her daughter but also ensure she lost her job. Crushed and beaten, Rose had decided she couldn't take the stress of what seemed like an unwinnable situation. She'd backed off.

To begin with, she'd taken the train to Edinburgh every month, but Louisa clung to Evelyn whenever they met and seemed frightened of Rose. It was as though she could tune into Rose's intense, hidden emotions but didn't know what to do with them. And that rejection, along with the travel, slowly ground Rose down. She'd considered moving to Edinburgh, but she wasn't sure it would help, and she wouldn't have the support of her parents and sisters there. So she'd sent letters and birthday cards that went unanswered. Eventually she discovered that Henry and Evelyn had told everyone Rose was a recovering alcoholic, not to be trusted. She'd almost had another breakdown, and it had taken a long stretch of counseling before she finally decided that, to preserve her own sanity, she would need to set some boundaries of her own. So she put all her energy into her career. A few years later, she heard that Joseph had died in prison from problems due to hepatitis. But the destruction he'd left behind would never be undone.

"Rose, can you bloody well say something?"

Henry's peremptory tone draws her back to the present. "I'm sorry to hear all this, Henry, but what can I do? Thanks to you, I've not been part of Lou's life. You know she won't want me involved—she hates me. What about your mum?"

"Mum can't go—she's not been well lately. Come on, Rose, Lou's still your daughter. You owe her this."

Did he really just say that? Yes, she remembers that tone. The petulance of a man used to getting his own way. However, she made a vow to herself years ago that she would always keep calm around Henry, and never let him know how much he could rile her.

"You've always wanted to be involved," he persists. "Well, now you need to step up. I've got two-week-old premature twin boys to look after—one was in the NICU a week ago. Rachel's beside herself and still recovering from her C-section; there's no way I can leave her. I've done all the hard work over the years; you can't imagine how difficult it's been. It's about bloody time you—"

He stops himself. Or at least Rose imagines he does, because she's already hung up.

How. Fucking. Dare. He.

So much for her nerves of steel. She's shaking with rage as she wraps her arms around herself, recalling all the times in those early days that she'd cried and begged to see her daughter while standing on Henry's doorstep, as Evelyn huddled upstairs with Lou in her arms. The way Henry had sneered at her. "She only needs one mother, and she's got a sober one right here. Go drown your sorrows, Rose. You'll scare her if she sees you unraveling." She'd spent years struggling to cope with his behavior before a psychologist pointed out that it was just another form of abuse. But by the time she understood, it was too late to fight.

He calls back as she's about to head upstairs, and she taps angrily at the phone. "Talk to me nicely, Henry," she warns him, sitting back down. She wants to stand her ground, remind him that she might have commitments too—but everything is overlaid with the vision of Lou in distress somewhere, lost and afraid.

"Okay, okay, I'm sorry," Henry says in a breathless voice. *Is he upset?* She's never heard an apology from him before, and she's never seen him break down either.

Rose is trying hard to shutter her imagination, but terrible images maraud through all the chinks she can't close quickly enough: Lou alone, hurt, or worse. She shakes her head, trying to clear the panic. She can't go down any of those roads right now. She switches him to speaker so she can start searching the online news on her phone. Lou's photo flashes up on Rose's screen, and her breath catches. There is her daughter, cradling two extremely cute little children. It's been so long since Rose has seen her girl, and she's changed so much. And yet . . .

"I'm looking at the news now. Christ, Henry, I haven't seen a photo of her in a while. She's beautiful."

"I know," he says quietly.

Rose stares at the photo, her gaze lingering on each detail: Lou's elfin features, the small constellation of freckles on her nose, the soft rosebud smile, lips closed so you can't see the small chip on one of her front teeth. Then she sighs and scrolls further into the story, past the screaming headline: *Fisher Grandchildren Missing Alongside Nanny.* She scans the first few lines and pauses. "Hang on—it looks like they're suggesting she's *taken* the children?"

The silence is so thick she can almost hear Henry bristle. "Of course she hasn't taken them. For god's sake, Rose."

"I know that," Rose snaps back—even though a small part of her protests. *How do I know? When I hardly know her at all.*

She shrugs off her questions, trying to focus on what's best for Louisa. "Shouldn't you be asking Evelyn to go? Isn't she Lou's mother in all the ways that matter? Weren't those your very words?"

He snorts. "Evelyn won't fucking go, Rose. She hates us both. Lou made her life miserable as a teen, and I wasn't any better. And Evelyn was so needy and spiteful. Lou called her a wicked stepmother, for god's sake. They've got no connection anymore."

Rose sits down heavily. "But I thought . . ."

"Rose, there's no time to explain, but you don't know anything about what our life is like. Lou has been, well, pretty difficult."

"Henry, she really won't want me there. I could make things worse for her, if she's in trouble. I sent so many letters. I tried, but she didn't want to know."

"Rose," he begs. "She needs you. You have to—"

"No, Henry, stop. Can we please talk rationally about what is best for Lou here," Rose says sharply. "Why are you so sure that it should be me?"

"We hid your fucking letters, okay?" he shouts down the phone.

She freezes. "What?"

"Evelyn ripped up the first few. She always felt threatened by the idea you would come in one day and just take Louisa away. She couldn't bear it. We told Louisa all sorts of things about you, but we could sense she wasn't sure what to believe—and she still wanted to know you. So Evelyn tore up the first few, and once we'd started we had to keep going. When Evelyn left, I continued."

"But . . . but it wasn't just the letters," Rose says, reeling from the implications of this revelation. "When I did see her, she wouldn't speak to me. Remember that awful meeting at the Italian restaurant when she was thirteen? She just stared at her plate and gave me one-word answers?

And when I came to her sixteenth birthday party she yelled at me and demanded I leave—she called me a bitch, Henry! Said she never wanted to see me again. I'm the last person she'll want now."

"She was scared and angry and a bit wild by then," he says with a sigh. "She thought you didn't love her, and she hated all mother figures. Wouldn't have a bar of Rachel. That's why I sent her to spend time with Charlie in Australia. I thought it was my only option, and it seemed to be working, but now it's all gone to shit again."

The mention of Henry's younger brother stirs up old, uncomfortable memories for Rose, which she pushes away. "If Charlie's there, and he has a good relationship with her, would he be better?" But even as she asks that, she's clicked away from the news headlines and is beginning to google flights.

"Come *on*, Rose," Henry urges, his desperation clear. "We're her parents. It'll look awful if neither of us go. And Charlie has his own responsibilities. Besides, he'll give me hell if I ask him to step in for me. He's as sanctimonious as ever. Listen, Rose, I realize what I'm asking, but you're the only one that can do this. She needs you now."

Rose stares at the phone. What a manipulative prick he is. The deceit is terrible—all those letters, all that effort to connect with Louisa gone to waste. All the things Louisa never even knew. And Rose hadn't realized, so she'd stopped trying. The guilt is crushing. Of course she shouldn't have underestimated how far Henry would go to drive a rift between them. She'd occasionally had suspicions that her letters might have gone astray, so why hadn't she broached this before?

She knows why. She'd grown too weary of the fight. She'd done what she could to stay in Louisa's life, but in the end it had become too painful, too exhausting. How could she have given up on her daughter and left her with this nightmare of a father?

"I need time to think," Rose snaps, scanning the British Airways website, wondering if it might be better just to turn up at Heathrow. "I'll call you when I've made a decision."

She hangs up and sags against the armchair, eyes closed, mind whirring. She knows that the first hours in missing person searches are always critical. If days turn to weeks then it will become more likely that months and years might pass without Louisa and the kids ever being recovered. There are whole databases online of all those missing people who were never found. Simply gone—forever. She puts a hand to her throat, trying to breathe through the fear. If there's any chance she can help, she'll need to move fast.

She steels herself and gets to her feet, then hesitates. *Am I doing the right thing?* She weighs up her options. The uncertainties and heartaches of involvement against the regret and guilt of a daughter lost or found while she kept her distance.

Of course she's going. Not only is she Lou's mother, but she has lots to offer from her years in the Met. She's good at examining evidence, finding things others might miss. And there's no way she'll risk the suppurating wound of a cold case she might have prevented, or interminable months and years spent longing for answers that never arrive.

Lost in thought, she presses her thumb against the edges of her phone case until it comes away from the slim device. A small photo falls out from the place where she's hidden it so she can always keep it close. She stares at her own face in the portrait, as yet unmarked by tragedy. But the younger Rose isn't looking at the camera. Instead, her attention is locked on the tiny girl in her arms, who gazes back at her mother with those trusting dark eyes.

CHAPTER THREE
BLACKWOOD

When Malcolm Blackwood wakes up, he's grateful his wife is already downstairs. It means he can grab his phone without censure, and check on those missing kids and their nanny. He's hardly been able to think of anything else since he received a text last night from his colleague Angie that had made his skin prickle: *You'll never guess who those kids belong to. Kyle bloody Fisher.*

Blackwood doesn't read the social pages, but even he knew Kyle was the playboy son of multimillionaire Jock Fisher, the property tycoon.

Jeez, Angie, they're gonna need everyone they've got for this, he'd typed back.

She'd called moments later. "Nah, I know what you're doing. You stay put, make the most of your leave. Jesus, you're back on Monday. If this lot are still missing then I'm sure you'll be asked to get straight onto it."

"At least tell me the circumstances."

"It's a doozy," she replied in her familiar good-humored drawl. "Kyle Fisher called triple zero about ten thirty this morning. They think the kids and the nanny had already been gone for about two hours by then. The family have been staying in one of the family holiday homes in

Kardanup with some friends of theirs—Victor and Bridget Santos and their two older kids—and it sounds like they'd all had a big night. Kyle insisted the police went to the house double-quick, so a local drove round, but from Fisher's original tone, which has been described by the emergency operator as "demanding prick," everyone assumed it would be some kind of misunderstanding. They're in a gated community with a private beach—only about ten houses altogether, all McMansions by the sounds of it. How the hell the three have managed to disappear from that spot is anyone's guess. But the trail's already cold."

All through dinner last night Blackwood hadn't registered a word of his wife Margie's conversation, busy running through the possibilities, itching to pick up his phone and find out who they'd put in charge. Of course, there could be a simple explanation for the disappearance, but he's worked on missing persons cases for over thirty years, and he knows better. It's no surprise to wake up and see they're still gone.

But he really shouldn't be thinking about this today.

He takes a few minutes to come to, then makes his way downstairs in his pajamas, in search of his wife and a coffee. The fresh light of the warm autumn day streams through the windows, bouncing off the walls and illuminating the polished floorboards and well-kept furnishings of their cozy home.

Margie sits at the kitchen table, a matching satin robe over her long shift. She's reading a novel, but glances up, smiling, as he comes in.

"You found them then," he says, nodding toward a huge bouquet of flowers—three deep pink banksias artfully placed between leucadendrons and everlasting daisies. All the native plants he knows she loves.

"They were hard to miss," she replies, a quiet kind of happiness in her voice. "Thank you."

He leans over and she tilts her face up to him. "Happy anniversary," he says, kissing her. He thinks of adding, "my darling" or "my dear," but this new romantic version of himself is still a work in progress, and he falters at the last moment. Instead, he asks, "Coffee?"

"I've got some left," she replies, nodding to her mug, "but the pot's still warm."

Blackwood pours himself a drink, cautiously thinking through his next steps. He has a surprise lunch planned at her favorite city restaurant, Wildflower, and he's unsure when to reveal this to best effect. He should have put it on a card and hidden it in the flowers. *Damn.* This is so bloody hard. One minute he's awkward and perspiring, the next he's gloomy and irritated. He's worse than a lovestruck teenager, but he's promised he'll put his best foot forward, and he surely gets top marks for effort. He thinks—prays—that Margie can see how hard he's trying, but she's something of an unknown quantity nowadays. Thirty-eight smooth-sailing years, and then she'd walked out. Said she couldn't stay when he was obviously married to his job. That if she couldn't have a close relationship in the last decades of her life, she'd rather be alone.

He'd had no idea that Margie was so devastatingly unhappy. What a fool he was, walking around all smug and pleased with himself, proud of his family and their well-kept home on an elevated block in Ocean Reef, one of Perth's well-kept beachside suburbs. And he'd provided it all through his hard work as one of the leading detectives in the state for the last thirty years. His two bravery medals bookended his career. As a young constable he'd been first on the scene of a light aircraft crash and had pulled the pilot out of the smoking wreckage. Then, a few years ago, he'd been one of three officers to enter a burning building during a domestic incident, rescuing a woman and her child. That decision had cost him a stint in hospital with burns to his arms and torso, but it had added a bar to his Cross for Bravery medal and earned him the Australian Police Medal in the same year.

But that all feels like a long time ago now. And when it comes to awards for good husbands, he's been found wanting.

He takes the coffee across to their large, empty kitchen table, which had once been a flurry of activity, first with the chaos of high chairs and spattered food, and then with the detritus of teenagers—the clothes and books and half-eaten packets of crap lying around. He sits down beside Margie, and she lays her book on the polished surface, putting her hand over his. "I mean it, Mal. Thank you. I love them." She beams at the blooms, and his heart opens at the sight of her smile, just like it always has.

He knows he needs to trust her, or this will end badly. He's done his best to drive a stake through the heart of the old Mal, the one who'd been enraged at being left behind. Who couldn't talk to his wife for a couple of months, while he stalked around his empty house like a tormented, trapped animal. Who'd ranted when the boys sympathized with their mother and tried to bring him around. He'd charged into work every morning like a bull into a bullfight, roaring and raging whenever someone did something to make him see red. Until, on a lonely day off, he'd driven out of the city and stomped up the zigzag route at Gooseberry Hill, his heart pounding so fast that he wasn't sure he'd make it back down. He'd taken his time at the top, considering the view of the distant city spread out before him, an oasis of tiny skyscrapers in a swath of bushland. It had always been one of his favorite spots, but he realized he hadn't been there for nearly thirty years, when his kids had had such little legs they'd gone on his back in turns. Now they were doing the same with kids of their own.

The vista remained steadfast, but his perspective shifted. He marched back down, ruing the blind man he had become, the one who prioritized work and nights out with his colleagues above the needs of his wife and family. Now he could see it all, and Margie could come back.

Except it turned out Margie wasn't interested. Margie was having a mighty fine time on her own.

It had taken him almost another year of proving himself to her, while she remained polite but aloof at family gatherings. They attended the kids' barbecues and grandkids' birthday parties separately, making shy, stilted conversation when they needed to. But he'd known her eyes were on him when he rolled around on the grass with the grandkids, let them spray him with the hose, cuddled them when they got sleepy, or sat in rumpus rooms watching endless cartoons with them sprawled or fidgeting on his lap. His own kids had been bemused but overjoyed, commenting on the change in him, suggesting that perhaps the single life suited him, which had made him growl back at his youngest lad, and then, astonishingly for them both, burst into tears. It was this that got the boys onside in the plot to win Margie back, and he both hated their pity and was heartened by their support.

It took him another few months to pluck up the courage to ask Margie out to dinner, but although the evening had started awkwardly, with neither of them knowing quite where to take the conversation, as the wine flowed, the space between them grew warmer, until they'd fallen out of the restaurant laughing. "Come home," he'd said, his voice riven with emotion, and she'd taken a step back, held his gaze, and replied, "Not yet." She kissed him on the cheek before climbing into a taxi, and at first he'd felt the sting of rejection, but then he replayed her words. It wasn't "No"; it was "Not yet." Which meant there was hope. He went to bed that night happier than he'd been in a long time.

They dated for another few weeks before she moved back in. Life had settled down, until his yearly medical revealed a blockage in an artery close to his heart. Within a week he was in hospital, and the long recuperation period left Margie playing nursemaid for months. It had been excruciating at such a tender stage in their reunion, when he'd wanted to be so much more for her. Now he's pretty much recovered, and today is his last chance to romance her before he goes back to work.

At the kitchen table Margie is no longer holding his hand but tapping it to draw his attention. He's been so lost in his thoughts he hasn't even noticed the house phone is ringing.

They exchange a look. This particular phone hardly ever rings; they only keep it for work emergencies. He doesn't answer it, instead hurrying to his office to collect his mobile. There have been eight missed calls in the last hour.

He moves silently back into the kitchen and shows the phone to Margie. She sees the desperation in his eyes and squeezes his arm.

"Looks like you'll have to call in," she says, keeping her voice neutral.

"It's Bob Drake. It must be important," he replies carefully, knowing exactly why Drake is calling. The assistant commissioner of police doesn't get on the phone personally unless it's something big. Blackwood is being ripped in half, caught between a pang of remorse as he sees Margie's expression drop and a burst of adrenaline at the thought of taking over the case and finding the nanny and those kids. His mind is already running through protocols and procedures.

"Of course they want you," Margie says. "We all know you're the best. And those children have been missing for a day already." As his mobile begins to ring again, she leans over and slides the button to answer for him. Then she quietly picks up her mug and takes it over to the bench.

"Where are you? Are you home?" Drake says without preamble. "I was hoping you could come back a few days early. We need you."

"What for?" he asks, feigning innocence.

Drake snorts. "Come on, Mal, I'm sure you've been keeping an eye on it. Those kids and their nanny have been gone overnight now."

Blackwood ignores him. "Any news from the searches?"

"Not much, but they've found a few spots of blood on the rocks close to where they would have disappeared. Haven't told the family yet as we don't want it going public, but it doesn't bode well, does it? Look, this thing is going to explode today, and Webster can't handle it. I need you down there ASAP. It's probably the case of the decade, possibly bigger. I know you're only a few months from retirement, but don't you want to go out with a bang?"

Blackwood says nothing, and Drake takes that as agreement.

"It's a gated community called Kardanup on the south coast. You can get there by early afternoon if you leave in the next hour or two. I've spoken to Angie already. She'll brief you—call her when you're in the car."

As soon as Drake hangs up, Blackwood turns around to explain this to Margie, to name-drop Kyle and Jock Fisher so she understands just what they're up against.

But Margie has already gone.

CHAPTER FOUR
ROSE

"Rose!" On the other end of the call, Veronica's voice is full of alarm. "I just saw your text. What the hell is going on?"

Rose checks her phone—3:30 a.m.—as she walks through the airport concourse. Despite the hour, Heathrow never sleeps, and she's in the midst of a steady stream of weary travelers, many dragging large suitcases behind them or hunched under their hefty rucksacks. They weave around her, pausing to check signs and overhead monitors before moving on. There's little seating room anywhere as bodies are sprawled across each row of chairs, many with headphones on and faces turned toward the backrests, trying to block out their surroundings and snatch some sleep.

"I'm sorry, Vee, did I wake you? I should have waited until morning."

"Rose, you know I hardly sleep. So please, explain."

Rose stops at a vacant metal chair at the end of a row, putting her bag down beside her. She'd hurriedly packed her large hand-luggage bag, glad she'd learned to keep her wardrobe and toiletries to a minimum so she can travel light. She reads everything on her iPad, although this time she's pushed the draft government report into her bag too.

She explains as quickly as she can. "Henry called and begged me to help. Take a look at the news online, it's huge."

There's a protracted silence. Rose can only imagine her older sister's horrified expression. Veronica has often been livid at Henry's callousness over the years, and more than once has offered to use her legal expertise to take him on in court. She's unlikely to respond well to the mention of him.

"I realize this is completely out of the blue," Rose continues, "but I need your support, okay? Don't make me second-guess myself, because I've made up my mind."

There's a choked splutter on the other end of the line. "I'm sorry, Rose, but how is this suddenly your responsibility? I don't want to be cruel, but has Lou wanted to talk to you much in the past two decades? And haven't you got the biggest, most important report of your life to complete in the next few weeks? Why isn't Henry going? Oh, please tell me you're not going together. You won't survive the plane ride if you have to listen to his bullshit."

"Henry is otherwise engaged with his new wife and their premature twins."

"What?" Veronica squeals. "Jeeesus. You mean he's turned his back on his old kid now he's got some new ones? I realize he does that with his wives, but I thought even he might have some decency when it comes to his children."

"Guess what else he decided to spring on me? Remember all those letters I sent to Lou? She didn't get them. Henry and Evelyn ripped them up. Now I wish I'd found a way to ask her about them, but when she was younger they wouldn't even let me speak to her—and by the time I could, she was already so angry. I never even got the chance."

"WHAT the—? I'm . . . Oh, Rose, those absolute bastards. That's despicable, even for them. Hang on, let me grab my laptop." There's a pause and a series of crackles and thumps in the background, and then, "Okay, I'm looking at the news. Shit. Hang on, let me just scroll . . . Oh my god, Rose. This is huge." She blows out a long breath. "Seriously, can we just slow down for a second and think through your choices."

"There are only two from where I'm sitting. I either stay here and watch from afar, or I go. There's no time to think. You know I stepped back because I thought Louisa didn't want a relationship with me. But Henry and Evelyn deceived both of us. Whatever's happened in the past, I can't turn my back on my daughter when she needs me most."

"But Rose, this isn't an opportunity to make amends. It's a nightmare. She's not waiting for you. You'll go over there and be shoved into the center of whatever is going on. I realize those letters . . ." Veronica's voice cracks. "Oh god, those letters, Rose. How despicably, heartbreakingly cruel. But you need to think of yourself too. And you might have to face the fact that something has happened to Lou before you've even had a chance to reconnect. Are you prepared for that?"

"Not at all," Rose replies calmly. "But I know myself well enough to recognize that I can't endure sitting here and doing nothing. I have to go."

There's a pause, and when Veronica speaks again, her voice is steadier. "Okay, will you just wait for me while I see what I can get out of? You can't go on your own. I'll cancel every— Shit, tomorrow I've got a prelim hearing I can't delegate."

"Vee," Rose cuts in, "I love you for thinking like this, but you know how fast these situations move. Anyway, I'm forty-six years old, I think I can manage."

"I bloody well know that. The point is, you shouldn't have to."

"Well, don't you dare suggest that to Lydia or Jess, will you?" she insists, imagining their younger sisters' reactions. "The last thing I need is Lydia fretting or Jess trudging after me resentfully. And don't bother Mum and Dad either; they've got enough going on since Dad's diagnosis and I don't want to ruin their trip." The family were still reeling from discovering Peter Campbell had Parkinson's, and their mother had dealt with it by focusing on his bucket list, meaning they were currently in a motor home touring the Scottish highlands.

"I'm not stupid. Of course you need *me*," Veronica says, and Rose smiles. They've always been the closest pair, thanks to the big age gap between them and their younger two siblings. For a while it had been two happy pairs, but then something had happened a few years ago between Lydia and Jess that they'd never revealed, and they no longer spoke to one another. Lydia had married and settled down near their parents, while

Jess moved overseas to pursue her dreams as a wildlife photographer. In contrast, Veronica lives within an hour of Rose in North London, and has always been her rock. For the last six years they've worked together as volunteers and taken turns as board members of Safehaven.

"However, there is something you can do for me," Rose says, as a young man with a wispy beard and Harry Potter glasses sits down beside her, rummaging through his backpack and pulling out a bottle of Coke. She cringes as he swigs most of it in one go before belching loudly, wiping his mouth with his hand. She turns away from him. "Bonnie is back at Safehaven. I feel terrible about leaving, right when there's a chance of supporting her to finally make the break."

"Oh, Rose," Veronica sighs. "That's a tough one. But of course I'll check in on her."

"I really don't know how many more chances she's got." Rose shudders. "Dean's surveillance of her is terrifying—he wants to know what she's doing every second of the day. And his violent behavior is escalating. She needs to get right away to have any hope of being free of him."

"I know it's hard," Veronica says, and Rose can hear the weariness in her voice, the toll of working with such vulnerable women, "but right now you have to focus on Lou. I'll check in with the team first thing and keep you posted."

"Thanks," Rose says. "I only hope I'm not already too late to help Lou. I'm looking at a lot of hours on a plane, and this is the kind of situation that might be over by the time I even get there." She takes a deep breath. "I hope she's safe, Vee. This is all so messed up."

"I'm looking at her photo now," Veronica says, then adds softly, "Jeez, she's the spit of you. Poor Henry, he did his best to eradicate you, but even he can't control genetics. It must have driven him mad over the years."

"Yeah, probably." Rose closes her eyes. "Please tell me you understand why I'm going. That I'm not insane rushing off like this."

"Of course I understand." There's a catch in Veronica's voice. "You're her mother. You've always been her mother. No matter that no one *allowed* you to be her mother—not Henry, or Evelyn, or the courts, or even Lou for that matter—although she's been gaslit by the sounds of it. None of that changes the facts."

As Veronica talks, Rose's phone starts buzzing. "Vee, there's another call. I need to go."

"Okay, call me when you can. Love you."

Rose switches calls, and a deep female voice with an Aussie drawl asks, "Am I speaking to Rose Campbell?"

"Yes."

"This is Detective Sergeant Angie Lennard. We've just spoken to your ex-husband and he said you'll be coming to Perth."

Rose braces herself, preparing for bad news. "Have there been any developments? I'm at the airport now. The Dreamliner leaves in a couple of hours."

"There's nothing so far, I'm sorry. We'll be waiting at the airport for you. Can you text me your flight details on this number? And please take care of yourself on the long journey. Don't let your mind race with wild theories."

"Don't worry, I worked in the Met for a long time. I know what you're saying."

"You did?" DS Lennard sounds surprised. "All right then, so you'll have some insight into the protocols we'll be following." Rose doesn't miss the wariness that's crept into the other woman's tone. She knows it well: In high-intensity cases, the investigating officers are often suspicious of other so-called experts coming in thinking they know better. In an urgent situation like this, having a clear line of command is critical.

"Did Henry tell you it's an unusual relationship? That I've been estranged from Louisa for most of her life?"

"He mentioned it. We'll be sensitive to that while you're here; we're just glad you're coming. I'll book a hotel for you, and I'll call you back if there's any more news before you board your flight."

Rose is grateful for Angie's no-nonsense tone. It's what she needs: steady, practical, and unemotional.

As they ring off, the man beside her collects his bag and moves away. Rose relaxes and resettles herself, putting her bag beside her on the vacant seat. She rechecks her phone and sees she has a text waiting, from a number she doesn't recognize.

Rose, it's Charlie. Henry passed on your number, he says you're coming over. I have a cabin you can use if you need a place to stay. I also fly helicopters for a living so I was part of the search and rescue effort yesterday. There are hundreds of people out looking for them. Don't worry, Lou's a strong girl. And she loves those kids. She'll be okay.

Rose stares at the message, apprehensive about meeting Charlie again. They'd not seen each other since that one excruciating moment at Henry's mother's house over twenty years ago, and she rather hopes he's forgotten about it, even though it's imprinted on her memory. Charlie had always been good to her—and he'd always seen right through his older half brother, much to Henry's chagrin. She'd heard he'd got married, and so he probably has kids of his own. It'll be fascinating to see what he's like twenty years on, and at least he can provide her with more insight into the kind of woman Lou has become.

She spends a few minutes drafting a response, then ends up sending a simple *Thank you* with her flight details. She closes her eyes and dozes for a while before her phone alerts her that it's time to move. Once at her gate, she settles into a seat and trawls the internet, studying some of the images and news articles she'd saved from the last couple of hours. Her daughter's face is on many of them. *Lou.* Rose brushes her thumb across Lou's delicate features. She wishes she knew more of the mind and soul of this girl whose smile is so similar to her own.

She begins saving all the information she can find in case there are any problems with Wi-Fi on the plane. Then she logs on to social media and searches for Lou. There's nothing on TikTok, but "Louisa Thornton" comes up on Instagram as @loulouluvsyou and Rose skims through the photos. It's mostly landscape shots of beaches and close-ups of flowers and food, interspersed with happy groups of friends, drinking and lying on the beach together. Lou is a stranger with Rose's features, surrounded by more strangers, living a life Rose knows nothing about. It looks happy enough from the outside, but of course you can never know a person from what you see online.

She goes back to the beginning and browses more slowly this time, scrutinizing each photograph and reading all the comments. There's not much to see on most of them—just benign phrases like "beautiful pic," "love this," or heart emojis. The posts featuring people are only slightly more interesting: "what a great day," or "looking gorgeous as usual," or "love you babes." She reaches one taken from a distance, its focus on the ocean view over Lou's shoulder as she sits hugging her knees, staring at the sunset. The caption reads, "Hoping for better days tomorrow." Curious, Rose casts her eye down the responses, then stops in her tracks.

Has your stalker finally gone away?

It's from someone called @stellarstels.

In response, Lou had said, "Not sure. Hope so," with a worried emoji.

Has your stalker finally gone away?

Rose shudders. She keeps on scrolling through posts and responses, hoping to find something more, but by the time her flight is called she's gone back almost a year and found nothing else of note.

She returns to the sunset post as she waits in the queue to board, screenshotting it and sending it to Henry. *Any idea what this means?*

Three dots appear. She waits.

No. Lou didn't mention it.

Rose begins to reply, then stops. It was posted only a few months ago. If Lou wasn't on good terms with Henry, would she even have told him? Besides, "stalker" could mean all sorts of things; it doesn't always indicate a predator. It could be a joke. Or someone harmless, who had feelings about Lou that weren't reciprocated.

However, in the circumstances, the brief exchange has her rattled.

She messages Henry again with her email address. *Flight leaves in forty-five minutes. If I'm going to help our daughter, I need to know about her. Tell me the important things, good and bad. Don't let me go out there unprepared. It's the least you can do.*

She half expects some kind of curt response, but he replies imme-diately. *I'll email you now.*

She prays he keeps his word, otherwise she'll be walking into this whole situation blind. But whatever has happened, Rose is sure of one thing: This time she's going to show up for her daughter, and she won't let anyone turn her away.

CHAPTER FIVE
BLACKWOOD

Blackwood pushes the speed limit to the max on the three-hour journey south, his thoughts flitting between the case and his wife. Margie had been quiet when he left. He'd had to spill the beans about their restaurant booking and ask her to call and postpone it, and while she'd been polite and understanding, he'd sensed her frustration. It galled him to leave her that way.

Perhaps he shouldn't have taken Bob Drake's call. He could have feigned being out of signal at a remote fishing spot. Once upon a time Drake wouldn't have been fooled, knowing how much Blackwood was married to his job, but after all of Blackwood's recent health and marital issues he might have got away with it.

Well, too late now. He just has to hope Drake will let him run things without interfering. He's known the assistant commissioner of police for his entire career—they started out together as constables—but Drake has always been more ambitious, and capable of the kind of smooth-talking networking that allows a man to rise rapidly through the ranks. Blackwood, however, has always thrived in the thick of investigations, but he's had enough hassle from Drake over the years to know that their agendas don't always match. Blackwood only ever wants to solve cases, whereas Drake usually has all sorts of important people to keep happy. Which probably includes the Fisher family, Blackwood realizes with a groan, since they own so much of the state.

As Blackwood drives, a feeling of impending doom begins to tail him. He tries to outspeed the notion, but it proves difficult to shake, particularly when Angie calls.

"Run me through everything that happened yesterday," he insists.

"Sure thing. Carl Webster organized the initial response . . ."

Blackwood inwardly groans at the mention of Webster's name. The man is working hard and vying with Angie for the promotion that will become available when Blackwood leaves, but unlike Angie, who is shrewd albeit with an edge of cynicism at times, Webster's an automaton. Always goes by the book without considering the case or the people involved. And he's keen to report anyone who doesn't.

Angie is still talking. "We've done a preliminary search of the house and grounds, and the SES are covering the wider area. We've got a couple of helicopters searching from the air. We've contacted hospitals, requested phone records, and some of the team have been door knocking and checking CCTV." She pauses. "The media presence is growing by the hour. Oh, and when the family searched the beach, they found one of the kids' teddies. Apparently Honey never goes anywhere without it."

"Nothing else was recovered? No phone or belongings?"

"No, and Louisa would at least have had a bag with her for nappies and stuff for the baby. Get this, though: No one knows what any of them were wearing. Louisa always dresses the kids and the parents can't figure out which outfits are missing. So that's made things a bit harder. We've got police officers working with them, and a heap of photographs, trying to suss it out by a process of elimination."

Blackwood pulls a face of frustration. This doesn't bode well. "You've ruled out them all going into the water somehow?"

"Yeah, we dismissed drowning pretty fast as the ocean is super shallow and the bay is sheltered and calm. They'd have had to wade out intentionally. Not impossible, but very unlikely. There's nothing to suggest the nanny would do that. And we've had another development this morning. There's a car parked a bit further south in a beach car park, not too far away from the track that leads to Kardanup. It was a popular spot yesterday and we thought we'd spoken to everyone, but this car remained there overnight. It's a rental, and the hire company said it was on loan to a Mr. Fabien Dubois from Sydney. We're chasing more details about him now."

"Okay, good."

"I should also warn you that yesterday they had a doctor at the house as Frannie Fisher was in quite a bit of distress and had to be sedated. So be prepared, eh. Webster was his usual wooden self, which didn't help. I don't think he'll cope well with the emotions or the celebrity aspect of this job."

"Thanks, Angie. I don't suppose he's going to be happy to see me either," Blackwood says.

"Possibly not," Angie replies. They both know Webster is envious of Blackwood's credentials and likes to cause a ruckus on occasion, just to make an impression. "But I'm bloody glad you're back," she adds. "I need someone with my sense of humor around here."

Once they've hung up, Blackwood finds the Rolling Stones on Spotify and blasts out songs from *Sticky Fingers* and *Let It Bleed*, trying to take his mind off things. Despite his efforts, he hasn't subdued his foreboding by the time he pulls up at the entrance to the Kardanup gated community and shows his credentials to the young officer stationed there. He then gets lost between the diverging driveways and it takes him at least three attempts before he finds the correct turning onto the sweeping road that ends at the Fishers' holiday home.

The officer waiting in the doorway looks anxious. Blackwood braces himself as he climbs out of the car, ignoring the aches in his back and his knees that have been triggered by the nonstop journey and his infuriating, aging body. "They're all waiting for you, sir," the police officer says, his chubby cheeks flushing and his words slightly gabbled. Blackwood is used to the way some of the younger ranks struggle to talk to him, but it's tiring after all these years to shape his lips into unnecessary bonhomie, so he just nods curtly.

Before he can ask any more, Webster appears in the doorway, a shiny gray suit over his stocky frame, collar open. He wears his hair slicked back to hide his bald spot, and has narrow eyes and a demeanor that always reminds Blackwood of Ray Winstone in *Sexy Beast*. He can be a cocky little shit, though he looks solemn and subdued now, likely out of his depth here.

"Sir, we've got the parents and their friends inside—all very upset, as you'd imagine. Kyle was shouting and raging for much of yesterday; we've had trouble keeping him calm. Another nanny just arrived, and she'll take the Santoses' kids out for the day, which is good as they sat in front of the television all yesterday looking petrified. The SES are searching the dams to the south, then they'll start covering more of the bush to the north." He grimaces in a way that suggests he doesn't think they'll find anything good. "Are you ready to meet the family?"

Blackwood nods. They're about to head into the house when there's a noise overhead. "What the hell is that?" Blackwood yells, instinctively ducking, looking skyward.

"There's a news van at the gate," Webster confirms. "And a chopper doing flybys."

Blackwood taps the young officer on the shoulder. "Get someone on the phone to sort those pricks out," he growls. "I want search and rescue only in this airspace."

The officer nods quickly, pulling out his radio as Blackwood follows Webster inside.

He hears the occupants before he sees them, a series of somber voices rising and falling in agitation, and when Blackwood rounds the corner, he almost stops in surprise. He's in a goddamn airport hangar for Christ's sake. Three sides of the capacious living area have floor-to-ceiling windows, and the view of the southwest coastline spreads out before him while on either side of the house there's dense bushland. The white and silver surfaces inside the house gleam as though they've all been recently polished, and the glossy jarrah floorboards reflect the furniture. Two giant flower arrangements of lilies and greenery adorn each side of the mantel above a wide fireplace to his right-hand side. Nothing is out of place.

In front of him, two couples stand in a line by the windows, stiff bodied as they gaze out toward the ocean, like they're facing a firing squad hidden beyond the glass. One of the women is wearing what looks to be silk pajamas, and the man beside her sports a polo shirt and dark-navy jeans. The other two are dressed mostly in white. As they turn to greet Blackwood and Webster, the men look tense, the women grief stricken.

The scope of the impending search hits him, a gigantic punch to the gut, but he hardly has time to take in anything else before one of the men marches toward him, shirt unbuttoned and askew, a pair of what look like white jogging bottoms that should be on the legs of someone much younger clinging to his thick, muscular thighs. "Blackwood, finally. Thank god you're here. I'm Kyle Fisher," he says, and they shake hands.

Kyle is heavily tanned, his face just beginning to fold into the wrinkles that have ravaged his father, Jock. He has thick and suspiciously jet-black hair for a man his age, and his eyes are a piercing cool blue. "I heard you're the best there is and we're gonna need you, man. No one can tell us what the fuck is happening. I hope you know how you're gonna find my kids, like, today, because I'm not stupid—I realize that every minute counts in this scenario and we're already a day behind." He glares at Webster, who takes up a position by the door and stares at a spot beyond the family group.

"It's good to meet you, Kyle," Blackwood says. "And Mrs. Fisher." Blackwood goes straight over to the taller woman, his hand outstretched. He knows which one is Francesca Fisher from photographs, although he's trying to recall the other woman's name. "I'm Detective Senior Sergeant Mal Blackwood. I'm now in charge of the team on the ground here, and I can assure you we're doing everything to find your children and Louisa as quickly as possible. I hope you've managed to rest a little."

Frannie gives Blackwood a limp handshake, then turns and lays her head on her friend's shoulder, sobbing quietly, a raggedy blue teddy clutched tightly in her arms.

"I'm Bridget," the other woman tells Blackwood while she wraps Francesca in an embrace. Bridget's dark, oiled hair is swept back off her face into a ponytail that reveals a riot of tight curls. She's painfully thin in her white tank top and jeans, and her skin is deeply tanned. Her dark eyes are circled with a thick ring of eyeliner. "Why don't we go and sit down, Fran." She leads her friend across to the large white sofa.

"Good idea," Blackwood says amicably, absorbing just how much white is in the room. He's not sure how they manage to keep everything so pristine with a bunch of young children in the house.

From a corridor by the kitchen, a young woman appears with two terrified-looking children holding bags and jackets.

"Bridget, we're leaving now. I'll take them over to Yallingup; there's quite a bit to keep them busy there."

"Thank you." Bridget goes over and kisses the children, who scurry off behind their nanny. Then she comes to sit by Frannie, both of them watching Blackwood expectantly, as though he's about to provide them with all the answers. Blackwood understands they're still in shock, but he also knows this might be the beginning of a very long road, and his heart sinks at the highly charged atmosphere.

Kyle stomps to the sofa and sits, elbows on knees and his fingers interlinked as though in prayer. He leans forward, waiting. Blackwood holds a hand out to the other man left standing, who takes it and says, "Victor Santos. Of Santos Engineering. Friend of Kyle's. Call me Vic. Bridget and I will stay to do whatever we can to help." Vic glances worriedly across to the women. He's dressed in jeans and sandals, his dark arms covered in thick black hair. As he subconsciously rubs his forehead, his gelled quiff stays resolute, so shiny and thick that Blackwood instinctively compares it to his own thin crop, wondering how some middle-aged blokes get so lucky while others like himself are left rubbing lotion into their widening bald patch.

Vic sits down with the others, and Blackwood lowers himself onto one of the sumptuous sofas opposite them, hoping his stiffness doesn't show too much, and that he'll be able to get out of this damn cushion trap when he needs to. He knows from experience that it doesn't pay to show any kind of weakness in front of men like Fisher. It's all weighed and measured and retained to use against you as necessary.

But it's much easier to ask questions now Kyle isn't towering menacingly over him.

"Tell me everything you know about what happened with Louisa and the kids yesterday," he begins.

Kyle stares at him for a moment, then raises his hands in disbelief. "We've gone over this multiple times. For fuck's sake, they haven't even told you what's happening?"

Blackwood holds steady. "I know the brief. But I want to hear it again from you."

Kyle exhales. "Well, I got up to find Frannie stressed out of her mind because she couldn't find Lou or the kids, and Lou couldn't be contacted by phone either. So we drove down to the beach, which takes all of thirty seconds, planning to drag them back and remind Lou not to piss us about and stick to the schedule, but instead there was no sign of any of them, just Honey's fucking teddy on the sand." He nods at Frannie, who's clutching the teddy tight to her chest. "The police wanted to take it, but Frannie fought like a tigress to keep it. She won't let it go."

Blackwood stifles his annoyance. That teddy should have been checked in as evidence, but he doesn't want to get off on the wrong foot. He'll have to see if someone can sweet-talk Frannie round. He shifts in his seat to look at Webster, hoping the man catches his frustration, then turns back to the family.

"I'm sorry we had to pause the search while it was dark," he says, "but we're still hopeful for an outcome today. We don't believe Louisa could have wandered far with a babe in arms and a toddler."

"What if they all went into the ocean?" Frannie wails. "What if Honey ran in first, and then Lou went to save her, but she was holding Kai, and they all got swept away."

Blackwood leans forward. "I don't think that's the case, Mrs. Fisher. I've been told the water in the bay is very calm, and I gather it's like that all the time. There are no rips and currents to carry people away. I'm sorry that we don't know what's happened yet, but people don't disappear in calm water; we would have found them by now."

"There are sharks out there," Frannie insists.

"For god's sake, listen to the man," Kyle roars suddenly. Everyone stares at him as he glares at his wife. "We can't lose our shit here, you understand? Our kids are out there somewhere and we can't go to pieces if we're going to help find them."

Frannie lets out a wail, jumps up, and rushes out of the room.

"I'll go," Bridget says, hurrying after her.

"Jesus *Christ*," Kyle bellows as he tips his head back to stare at the ceiling. Then he looks at Blackwood and says, "I apologize for my wife."

"Her children are missing," Blackwood replies. "Her distress is understandable. No need to apologize for anything."

"*Our* children are missing," Kyle corrects him. "And she's going to have to think of someone other than herself for a change. She can hardly be bothered with them while they're here, and now she's acting like mother of the fucking year."

Blackwood makes a mental note of the words, and the tension between the couple. People react in different ways to a crisis, and he can give some credence to the initial shock coming between them—but this seems like more than that.

Blackwood twists in his seat to glance at Webster again, feeling his hip object with a twang. "Where did we get the photo of Louisa and the kids—the one that's circulating online?"

"I provided it to the first officer on the scene," Vic interrupts, swiping on his phone, then thrusting it toward Blackwood, who takes it and studies the image in front of him. There are four children in the photo, along with Louisa. She's slim and pale with delicate features, her light-brown hair layered around her face but falling past her shoulders. She's wearing a floaty, bright-orange top that makes her look like a hippie, and she's holding the baby in her arms, who beams at the camera, two little teeth showing and a small trail of dribble on one side of his mouth. The smaller girl is standing on the wall that the rest of them are sitting on, and has flung her arms around Louisa's shoulders, her chin resting on the top of Louisa's head. Her grin is wide, her face creased into happy little folds. The two older children lean in on either side, grinning. All five are wearing white-and-yellow flower crowns.

"That was taken a couple of days ago," Vic says. "My kids are the older pair; Honey and Kai are the younger ones. They all love Lou. Our families meet up quite often, and usually our nanny is with us too, but she had to stay home until yesterday as she's been unwell. Lou played with all four of them for hours every day. I don't know where she gets the energy from."

Blackwood stares at the photo with a lump in his throat. *These kids—Louisa, too—are so bloody young.* He pictures his own grandkids with a pang. *Damn*, he thinks. The three of them are out there somewhere, relying on him to lead the charge to find them. He'd driven the whole way trying to keep his guard up, knowing as soon as he let the situation in he'd have no choice: A mixed sense of justice, responsibility, and compassion would enslave him to the case until the very end. But it's too late now: One look at those faces and he's crossed the bloody Rubicon.

He comes back to the room, aware of everyone watching him. He studies the photo again. The kids are all over this girl; there's no distance or reserve at all. She looks gentle and kind. What the hell could have happened?

He realizes the men are waiting expectantly. He gathers his thoughts and focuses on Kyle. "Do you know the name Fabien Dubois?"

Kyle frowns. "No, should I?"

"Not necessarily. There's an abandoned rental car parked further south, registered to that name. We're just following all leads."

Kyle shakes his head and shrugs. "I'll ask around."

"Can you tell me all the ways Louisa would usually be able to get in touch with you?"

Kyle looks surprised at the question. "We text most often. Occasionally call."

"Does she have your email? Social media?"

"Of course, but she's not going to email me from the fucking beach, is she? Or post a selfie from wherever she's gone."

Blackwood ignores the fury coming from Kyle. "We don't deal in probabilities; we check out every avenue, however unlikely. I want to cover all bases today. And we can get someone to help monitor everything."

Kyle picks up his phone and dials a number, then holds it to his ear. "Sherri, the police want you to go through all my emails and social media accounts and check them right now, in case Lou sent something there," he says, and hangs up without adding anything more.

"So when you found the teddy on the beach," Blackwood continues, "what did you do next?"

"We walked up and down looking for them, calling their names," Fisher replies, casting a glance at Vic, who nods in agreement. "The place was completely deserted. It's a very small patch of beach, rocks either side and then bush beyond that at both the northern and southern ends."

Vic leans forward. "To the south there's a dirt track after the bush path that leads to the road about a kilometer down, so I ran along there to check for them. I called all the way too, but there was nothing."

Blackwood turns to Webster. "I presume the beach is cordoned off now?" he asks, annoyed at the thought of more evidence being trampled or destroyed.

"Of course," Webster says through gritted teeth. "As soon as we got here."

"So," Kyle says, "what's the next plan?"

Blackwood sits up straight. "We're checking all points of communication and pulling phone records. The SES are out again today, we've got search helicopters too, and we'll cover the area with every man available and use all the technological assistance at our disposal. I'd like to take more statements from you all, and for you to have a think about anything out of the ordinary that might have happened, particularly over the past few days." He hesitates. "And we need to search this property more thoroughly too."

"No fucking way," Kyle explodes. "You've already been through once, and I don't want you turning this place upside down while Frannie's so upset. Surely you only need Lou's room? Why are you treating all of us like we've done something wrong?" He looks to Vic for backup, but Vic only shrugs and then drops his head to study his hands.

Blackwood pats the air in what he hopes is a pacifying gesture. "Please, try to stay calm. This is standard procedure, and you can remain present while it happens. The officers are all very careful and discreet. We'll start with Louisa's room and spread out from there. This is a very important part of the search, and you need to let us look for any scrap of information that might help find your kids fast, okay? The bush isn't a good place to be overnight. They will all be hungry and thirsty by now."

Kyle looks furious, throwing himself back in his seat, but he doesn't say any more.

"The most likely scenario is that your nanny has taken the kids on an impromptu bushwalk and become lost. It happens. And there's plenty of people trying to find them."

"If only that were the case," Kyle mutters.

Blackwood's instincts prickle. "What do you mean?"

"Do you really think she's going to leave Honey's teddy on the beach and go for a fucking bushwalk? Honey would never leave Valentine behind. And I doubt Lou's going to get lost in the bush carrying one kid, when the other can hardly go fifty meters without complaining. No fucking way. Honey hates walking far, and she screeches like a banshee when she gets fed up. I think Lou has either run off with them, or it's something worse. You need to look into this Dubois bloke ASAP."

"We're doing that right now. Do you have any other theories that might help us?" Blackwood prods, glancing at both men.

Vic shakes his head, the fingers of his right hand tapping against his knee.

"I don't have a fucking clue," Kyle says. But he's obviously considering the worst. Blackwood sees the fear in his eyes, and decides to run with it.

"You don't know of anyone with a grievance against you, who might be looking to scare you?"

"No." Kyle stares at Blackwood. "But we're aware that plenty of people resent us and would like to get their hands on our money. As a family we've had a few legal battles, and one or two people trying to blackmail us in the past. But there's nothing going on right now as far as I know. I can double-check, though."

"Let's stick to what we're sure of for now," Blackwood says quickly.

"I'm sorry I had to ask, but at present we've found nothing to suggest that's what's happened." He thinks of the drops of blood on the rocks, undergoing testing. He's still hoping they can put this case to bed before the family need to know about that.

"Have the team asked you for DNA swabs?" he continues. "It can help to speed things up if we find any evidence."

"Yeah, they did it yesterday," Kyle replies, pushing his hands in his pockets and closing his eyes. Blackwood can sense how hard he's working to hold himself together.

"Right then." Blackwood hefts himself up from the sofa, his back and knees protesting with a few spikes of pain. "If you think of anything that could be relevant, we've got liaison officers here to assist you." He stares intently at both men, one after the other. "Please remember we'd rather hear a theory, however unlikely, than have you keep it to yourself." He walks over to the huge panoramic windows and gazes out over the ocean. "You can't see the beach from here then?"

"No, the houses are built on a hill, set back from a small cliff face. There's a steep path down to the beach from the end of the road."

Blackwood turns back to the room. "Okay, I'm going to head down there shortly, and check in with the team. I'll be back in a couple of hours with an update. Rest assured we're doing everything possible to find them fast."

Kyle doesn't respond, but his gaze shifts to the long, empty windows. Blackwood's heart goes out to the man. He can only imagine Kyle's turmoil at the thought his children are out there somewhere, and there's nothing he can do.

CHAPTER SIX
ROSE

Only hours ago, Rose had been contemplating her bed, and now she's somewhere over Europe, shell shocked and wide awake. The plane is uncomfortable and claustrophobic, with the drinks cart coming past regularly and people around her sipping wine that she can smell whenever she shifts in her seat. The older couple next to her seem as disinterested in conversation as she is, and since greeting her they have been glued to their iPads.

Has your stalker finally gone away?

The phrase circles her brain, menacing and unshakable. Did Louisa really have a stalker? As soon as she'd taken her seat on the plane, she'd immediately sent a private message to @stellarstels, hoping she's the kind of girl that can't stay off Instagram for more than five minutes. But there hadn't been a reply before takeoff, so she won't be able to find out more until she lands. She's concerned that her message might look like spam, because Rose hasn't used her account for a few years and it's been set to private for a long time. She'd texted DS Angie Lennard as well, telling her about the discovery, asking her to check Louisa's account and investigate the comment, but Angie's reply had felt dismissive: *Will get someone to take a look, thanks.* Rose would like to press her, but she doesn't want to come across as pushy before she's even arrived. She's stuck in this metal box for another half a day, with little to do but bite her nails and wish the time away.

At least the flight is a good opportunity to work on her emotions, because she needs to have them fully under control by the time she gets to Australia. There's a long email from Henry in her inbox, but she's still working up the courage to read it. She's sure there will be some gibe in there about her failure as a mother, and she doesn't want to let him back under her skin. It would be so much easier to treat this whole trip like it's a case she's been assigned to. She's become an expert at wrapping up her feelings and setting them aside to get the job done. You can't spend years in the police force, and working with victims of domestic violence, if you're unable to do that. Hope and prayers are not enough. Determination, strategy, and persistence are the attributes needed for results.

And yet—she can't stop looking at the news article she's saved: the one with the picture of Lou alongside those tiny missing children. Each time she scans their faces her heart twists—and her sympathies turn to Frannie Fisher, the young children's mother, who'll be enduring the same torture. The little girl, Honey, looks adorable, her pudgy arms tight around Lou's neck. But Rose can hardly look at the baby without enduring flashbacks to other babies, who were taken right out of her arms, no matter how desperately she wanted to protect them.

She remembers Zara, warm and sturdy as she sat on Rose's hip just a few hours ago. Rose prays that this time Bonnie will find the strength to stay at the shelter, even though it will be an uphill battle. Although domestic violence is often in news headlines, it can be very difficult to make people understand how complex and long term these situations are. By the time a victim has been degraded, undermined, and attacked for years, they have lost all sense of control: They exist from one terrified moment to the next, sometimes for years, and re-claiming their lives is a messy, protracted process. That ugly question,

"Why doesn't she leave?" can only be answered by walking in the shoes of these women.

Rose has dedicated her life to helping those like Bonnie. Within four years of returning to police work, after she'd recovered from her trauma, she'd been asked to join the specialist hostage-negotiation team—one of the youngest officers ever to do so. While there she'd discovered that over 50 percent of the callouts were related to domestic violence, which always surprised people when she told them. People imagine hostage situations are like a blockbuster movie, but most victims are held against their will in much more mundane circumstances. This is all the more terrifying because it can drag on indefinitely—and your captor is often the person who claims to love you most in the world.

Eventually Rose had grown tired of handling the same situations, year after year. She'd left the force determined to enact more systemic change, studying for her doctorate by working on the gaps in legislation that allowed women to keep falling through the cracks and straight back into these situations. She'd used her findings to write her bestselling book, *Behind Closed Doors*, aiming to reach a wider audience and expose some of the myths around domestic violence and coercive control. It was controversial in its detailed consideration of the male side of the violence—even though she had explained time and time again that it was not sympathy for the aggressors that drew her there, but her determination to stop the perpetrators early. And she also wanted people to know that abused women were not weak and helpless: They often went to great lengths to try to keep themselves and others safe. She'd explained in detail how the system could be rigged against those who complained, forcing them back to abusive partners to protect their kids from being alone and at risk, or to mitigate financial hardship as a single parent. She'd been immensely proud of her work.

However, the book had unforeseen consequences. On her promotional tour she hadn't discussed Joseph Burns, even though it was her encounter with him—witnessing an abuser become a murderer, and a friend and colleague dying at her feet—that remained pivotal to the direction of her career. However, she'd dedicated the book to Tristan, and all those who had given their lives trying to protect themselves or their loved ones. A few months after *Behind Closed Doors* was published, a journalist had made the connection to Burns in a detailed article that was syndicated around the world. Fortunately, this was after most of her in-person events were over, because the questions and emails became relentless.

And then the trolling began.

She'd had hundreds of anonymous messages, detailing how she might be kidnapped, degraded, abused, tortured, and killed. She'd reported each one, but most were untraceable. Eventually, she and Veronica had screenshotted them all, then she'd closed down her online profiles. Veronica reassured her that it was often only a few people using multiple accounts to cause trouble, not a baying mob out to get her, but it had left her unable to sleep properly for months. She wondered who these people were, whether they masqueraded as decent family men and women. And every time someone goaded her, it brought back haunting visions of Joseph, and his dead-eyed, grotesque expression as he raised the knife.

It had left her with the unshakable feeling that there were thousands of Josephs out there.

She puts her head in her hands for a moment, trying to breathe through the onset of panic, and when she looks up the elderly woman next to her is watching with concern.

"Are you okay?"

"Fine, thank you," she says, smiling in what she hopes is a reassuring way. The woman doesn't look convinced, but she turns back to her screen.

Rose works on grounding herself, feeling her feet firm against the thinly carpeted floor of the aircraft, aware of the steady vibration of the aluminum beneath. Her only protection against these attacks is the strength of the psychological wall she's built between herself and the murderous faces that crowd her nightmares. Over the years, she's become more and more determined that she will not let them win. Nevertheless, the stalker comment on Lou's Instagram has penetrated her defenses. She can only pray that there's a more innocent explanation for Lou and the children's disappearance—and that they haven't somehow encountered a monster in the form of a man.

CHAPTER SEVEN
STELLA

Stella knows people are calling her phone, but she's put it on silent while she watches the children. She sits on the dry, scratchy grass by the swings, looking around the small park with its run-down play equipment and trying to calm herself, arms hugging her knees. She wishes she knew someone who might tell her what to do. The screams from the melee of primary-aged children playing tag have begun to aggravate the dull thump behind her eyelids, and she's fighting the urge to lie down and sleep.

She doesn't want to talk to anyone. Unless she hears from Lou soon, how can she go back and face people? At some stage she'll either have to lie, or lose her job.

She flicks through her messages again, even though she knows there's nothing new. Rereads the ones she's already sent.

Message me back as soon as you see this.

Where the hell are you?

She types quickly.

I really hope you're okay, Lou. If you are, please get in touch. I don't know what to say to everyone. You have to come back!

CHAPTER EIGHT
BLACKWOOD

CHAPTER SEVEN
STELLA

As the sun sinks toward the horizon, Blackwood stands on the back veranda of their makeshift situation HQ, waiting for an update from the team and taking deep breaths of briny air. The swath of ocean is a distant steely blue beyond the drop-off at the edge of the long garden, and the immaculately manicured hedges and central fountain sit in stark contrast to the encroaching bushland on either side, the ragged, tangled branches of eucalyptus trees looming over the smaller, carefully spaced melaleucas.

His mind runs over search efforts and survival statistics, despondent at the thought of Lou and the two kids spending another night in the bush. As he heads back inside he's racking his brain, trying to think if he's missed anything that could provide a breakthrough. But they've covered everything, so far as he can see.

The local sergeant had proved a terrific asset and had managed to gain access to this home near the Fishers' place, to use as their temporary base. It's another stonking great mansion, painted a lurid lime green on the outside, and it's incongruously grand for the tasks they'll be performing. Blackwood had balked when told it was a holiday home for another über-rich family, who were hardly ever here. *What a bloody waste,* he thought, although he was grateful they'd immediately offered it for use. Right now it's proving vital as it means there's somewhere private to talk, away from the growing hysteria of the Fishers' house on the hill.

He's already had word from Bob Drake that Kyle's father, the legendary Jock Fisher, has fired up today and is demanding answers as to why the search is taking so long. "I can hold him off for another few hours," Drake had said earlier, "but he wants a call from you tonight with an update. I think he's been caught out like the rest of us, expecting a quick resolution, and only now is the scale of it sinking in."

Blackwood is still adjusting to this too. He thinks of the media scrum at the gate, growing all the time, while inside this room there's a bustle of men and women hard at work: SES trailing their dirty boots in and out with futile search reports; police officers being given practical instructions to help set up spotlights; and a few junior detectives busy on the phones. A handful of officers had been tasked to conduct a thorough search of the Fishers' house; it had taken all afternoon, and been unpleasant by all accounts—with Kyle barking objections at whatever they touched, and Frannie unable to stop crying. They'd taken Louisa's iPad and a number of items from her room—mostly notepads—to study further. It helped that she'd packed light for the holiday, and most of her stuff was still folded in her travel bag, which Blackwood found interesting: Why not unpack when you were there for a week? However, Louisa's toothbrush had been present in her private bathroom, a possible indication that she didn't intend to flee. They'd also found a diary, with hardly anything in it except a series of tiny hearts in the top corner of each of the blank pages for the last week.

When the officers moved into the rest of the house the most interesting items they'd turned up were the variety of sex toys in Kyle and Frannie's room, which they had carefully worked around in one of the drawers, none of them keen to get too close. Blackwood had been informed by a slightly pink-faced officer that they'd found vibrators, dildos, and nipple clamps as Webster smirked in the background. The Fishers had brought a decent amount of luggage with them, but it was still a lot quicker to search a holiday home than a fully lived-in abode, and for that Blackwood was grateful. They'd warned Kyle and Frannie that if there was any cause for another search they'd need immediate access, but Blackwood had asked for a warrant request anyway, just in case Kyle got less helpful as time went on.

His visit to the beach had been unsatisfying. The thirty-meter strip of sand was too soft to have retained proper footprints, and the tide had been coming in when Louisa and the kids disappeared, so any marks closer to the shore had been quickly washed away. There was a small cordon around the spot where the teddy had been found, and another next to the rocks where they'd spotted a few droplets of blood. Both had looked worryingly insignificant, underlining to Blackwood just how much they were clutching at straws. They're still waiting for the analysis of the blood sample they managed to lift from the rocks. If there is a match with Frannie or Kyle, they'll know it was one of the kids, otherwise they'll need to wait for Louisa's mother to arrive and take a sample from her.

No one else has been seen at the shoreline since Louisa and the kids disappeared. The police vans on the road that leads down to the small private beach may be putting people off, but most of the door knockers are reporting closed-up, empty houses. One of the officers mentioned a reasonably fresh dog turd down by the rocks on the northern side, so there must have been someone walking their furry friend in the last couple of days, but they haven't been located.

And that's everything they have: an abandoned car, a few drops of blood, a teddy, and a turd. Blackwood puts his head in his hands, wishing, as he does fairly regularly, that he were still a smoker.

He flicks through his phone messages to find a text from Margie, telling him what a lovely lunch she'd had with her girlfriends at Wildflower. When he'd let her in on his anniversary plan before he left, she'd said she would call and rearrange the date for them, but instead she's gone ahead without him. He knows he shouldn't mind—*It seemed a shame to waste the booking*, she'd written—but even so, it bothers him. She hadn't asked about the case at all, and after he'd read her text he'd had to turn his back to the team while he recovered his composure. Already, it feels like his wife lives in another, faraway world. And that's not a good sign when they're still trying to get back on track.

"Sir."

He glances up to see Angie hovering, her face flushed, her breathing elevated. She looks as tidy as usual in her dark suit, her hair pressed back into a tight bun. He's always grateful for her practical, no-nonsense presence: She's a straight talker who doesn't hold back from an opinion or suffer fools, and they share the same dark sense of humor. Some of the other officers find her a bit too abrupt and outspoken, but they've worked together for ten years and feel like family to each other now. He was delighted when she was recognized with one of the inaugural Aboriginal officers' service medals a few years ago, because if he could clone Angie he would. It would guarantee that everything would get done thoroughly and with maximum efficiency.

"I have some key updates on Fabien Dubois," she says as they head back out to the veranda so they can talk privately. "He was dating Louisa until she left Sydney six months ago. He's a radio producer in Sydney, and we've spoken to his work colleagues, who've confirmed he's on leave. No family here, all back in France. No one seems to know much about what he had planned with his time off, and his housemate is away too. We've followed up and that fella's gone to Bali on a surfing holiday, so there's no connection to the case."

"Shit. Okay, this is something. You think Louisa and Fabien ran off together?"

Angie purses her lips, hand on hip. "I don't know. I keep trying to let that idea run, but I get stuck. Something isn't right. Why leave the car?"

"Well, if they took it we could trace them more easily."

"Yeah, but to get anywhere else they'd have to do a long walk with those kids. On the security cameras there are no other vehicles leaving the estate."

"Unless someone else picked them up?" Blackwood suggests.

"Maybe." Angie doesn't look convinced.

"Let's ask the Fishers some more questions. Earlier I put Fabien's name to Kyle, but he didn't know it."

"I've checked social media," Angie adds. "Lou and Fabien are still friends on Insta, though neither of them have posted anything about each other lately. But on Fabien's page there are some pictures of him surfing not far from here in Yallingup, only a few days ago."

"It's too much of a coincidence," Blackwood says, calculating the distance between Yallingup and Kardanup, which isn't far at all. They lock eyes, and Blackwood knows Angie's thoughts are running as furiously as his own. "We need to find out more about Louisa's mindset. What could possibly make her run?"

"I'm working on it. And I also had a text from Louisa's mother, Rose," Angie continues. "She's obviously trawled through Insta and one of Louisa's friends mentions a stalker. But it's a few months ago, and I can't tell if it's a joke. Here." She flicks the screen on her phone and holds it out to Blackwood.

Blackwood reads the short caption. "Hmm. I'm way more interested in Fabien and Louisa right now—that car is our primary lead—but we can bear this in mind as we interview people. When does the mother arrive?"

"First thing tomorrow. I thought I'd drive back tonight, have a shift break and sleep in my own bed, give my kids a kiss before I come back down with her in the morning. I'd like to stay close to her—she's got an interesting background, and she can tell us more about Louisa."

"Sounds like a good idea." Blackwood trusts Angie's instincts more than anyone else on the force. "Although you know the situation, don't you? She and Louisa hardly know one another."

"She's still her mother," Angie says vehemently. "We don't know much about the estrangement yet. Let's not judge too quickly."

"I wasn't planning to," Blackwood says, seeing he's annoyed her.

"Unless she's a psycho of course," Angie adds with a grin, lightening the mood. "Also, we've gone round the hospitals again and nothing's happening there. Officers are still door knocking this area, with zip to report as yet. Mobile phone provider says that Louisa's most recent usage was yesterday morning—that's the final ping off a local tower. Nothing after that, not here or anywhere else. We're getting a call log for her. We've also unlocked her iPad. She likes reading fantasy novels and has crap taste in soppy Netflix films, but she's not on there much. No social media usage in the last four months—which coincides with when she began working for the Fishers, so we checked in with them about that. Apparently it was part of her contract not to post online while she works for them, so that explains her withdrawal." Angie takes another breath, ready to continue, when there's a noise behind them.

Beyond the windows Blackwood sees Webster spot him and come rapidly toward them, holding a mobile phone. He pokes his head around the door. "Louisa's father's on the phone. He wants an update."

"Right then." Blackwood raises his eyebrows. "Remind me what he's been told so far."

"Not much," Angie says. "The Fishers didn't have a number for him, but he wasn't hard to find. Name's Henry Thornton; he's a funds manager in Edinburgh. Pretty wealthy himself, though nothing compared to this lot. Didn't seem overly concerned earlier on, but I think his nerves are fraying now."

Blackwood holds his hand out for the mobile, removes the mute function, and puts it on speaker. "Mr. Thornton, sorry to keep you waiting. My name is DSS Blackwood; I'm in charge of the search at the moment." He places the phone on the high table next to a well-stocked outdoor fridge, but remains standing, not daring to attempt to heave himself onto one of the barstools. "Here with me is DS Angie Lennard. She'll be heading off to collect Rose from the airport later, and it's her job to keep you both updated."

"And there's still no sign of Lou at all?" The man's voice is deep and gruff.

"I'm afraid not. Would you be able to answer some questions? We've contacted the Scottish police force and you'll be getting a call from some local officers too. They can come and see you in person, as I realize this isn't an easy discussion to have on the phone. But since time is of the essence I hope you don't mind helping us out."

There's a long pause. A sigh. "No, go ahead."

Blackwood is surprised at the lack of enthusiasm. He tries to read the tone but stops. He'll let the local officers suss out the man's character a bit more. Concrete information is more important right now. "When was the last time you spoke to Louisa?"

Another pause. "I'm not entirely sure. A few months ago. Around Christmas."

Blackwood straightens, and Angie echoes the posture change, each of them becoming more alert, listening intently.

"That's quite a long time ago, isn't it?"

A longer silence follows, before Henry replies, "Louisa and I haven't been on the best of terms."

"I see. And what was your last conversation like?"

"She was staying with my brother, Charlie, for a few days. He lives over there now. It was . . . *stilted* might be the right word. A short call. She wasn't keen on making conversation."

"Was she upset about anything?"

"No. What exactly are you suggesting?"

"It's not my job to jump to conclusions," Blackwood says patiently. "But I have to explore every possible scenario. When people go missing we often ask how they were feeling in the time prior. Just in case it has a bearing on the case."

To his surprise, Henry lets out a short bark of laughter. "Louisa is not going to have had some kind of episode, I can guarantee you that. She's a fighter. Stands up for herself without hesitation. And she'd never want to do anything to upset the kids, either. She's always adored children. Spent most of her teenage years babysitting."

"What about a boyfriend?"

"Not that I know of."

Blackwood catches Angie's eye. Louisa was obviously keeping Henry out of the loop.

In the background of Henry's end of the call, Blackwood hears a woman say, "Find out if she left a note."

"What was that?" Blackwood asks, although he heard the comment clearly.

When Henry speaks it's obviously not to Blackwood. "It's not relevant. They don't think she's run away."

"Excuse me," Blackwood interjects politely. "Does she have a history of running away?"

"She had a reputation for it at one of her boarding schools," Henry says curtly. "But that was a long time ago. A bit inappropriate to discuss it now. I'd rather you were finding my daughter than thinking she's done some kind of runner with two young kids. I can guarantee you that isn't what's happened."

"I agree," Blackwood says in his most conciliatory tone, keen to keep the man onside. "While there's no harm in considering all angles, there's also no indication Louisa planned to leave. We're treating this as a missing persons case, but the search is in an awkward spot with lots of dense bushland. I'm hoping for a quick result, but sometimes that isn't the case. You need to start thinking about your plans if she doesn't turn up soon. You might want to look into flights."

This time the silence goes on for long enough that Blackwood asks, "Mr. Thornton? Are you still there?"

"I've spoken to your sergeant already." Henry sounds incensed. "I've had to ask Rose to come in my place. It's not ideal, but my newborn twins are only just home from hospital, one of them is struggling to feed, and my wife is recovering from a C-section. Besides, by the time I get there, Louisa will probably be back home with the kids."

"Mr. Thornton," Blackwood says, astounded by the man's flippancy in regard to his older child, "I'm advising you that your daughter has been missing with two very young children for over thirty hours, and we have no solid leads at present. It gets very cold in the bush at this time of year, and we have serious concerns for their welfare. Please consider your options."

There's the sound of a voice rising in panic in the background of the call, and Henry says, "I need to go. You'll have to make do with Rose. Although, be warned: She'll think she knows more than you do. She's quite the expert on everything these days." And then the line goes dead.

Blackwood stares at the phone, trying to process the father's reaction. Henry obviously hates his ex. But is it just new fatherhood making him so reluctant to fully confront the facts of Louisa's disappearance, or something more? Four months is a long time not to speak to your kid.

He's about to mention this to Angie when he notices she's distracted. He follows her gaze and realizes there's a crowd building inside, gathering around the tables set up in the main living area. They both head quickly back into the room, absorbing the immediate tension in the air. Blackwood straightens, trying to read the expression on Simon Faulkner's face as the SES commander hurries over to them. He doesn't look too grim, but he isn't happy either.

Blackwood breathes an inward sigh of relief. He's all too familiar with the shock and grief on searchers' faces when they find bodies, and this isn't it. But clearly something serious has happened.

"We've found a small boat about four kilometers to the north," Faulkner says breathlessly. "Right next to a bush track. Forensics are heading there now."

"What was in it?" Blackwood asks immediately, catching Angie's eye and then wishing he hadn't as he sees her fear echoing his own.

"A fuel container," Faulkner replies. "And a substantial amount of blood."

CHAPTER NINE
ROSE

Rose is unable to read even a paragraph of work without losing her way. Instead, the words become a blur as she dozes in and out of fretful sleep, the steady, lulling drone of the plane's engines overlaid by the squeals of restless children and the clank and clatter of the refreshment carts.

She keeps trying to push away visions of Lou hurt or worse, but her nightmares encircle her, pouncing as soon as she shuts her eyes. The air on the plane feels icy cold. Rose shivers, her throat dry.

Eventually, she gives up, shuffles herself upright, and opens her emails, searching for Henry's unread response, hoping it will help her refocus on how she might help. She can't afford to be paralyzed by her fears.

Rose,

It's hard to condense Lou into a few paragraphs, but let me try. She was a happy child, but a troubled teen. For high school I enrolled her in a fantastic boarding school, but she hated it and kept trying to run away. She'd turn up at my mother's house, and Mum would let her stay a couple of nights and then send her home, and from there we'd persuade her to go back to school. We were constantly getting calls from the headmistress about her attitude and behavior—she was a bit of a nightmare to be honest. As far as I can gather, she never set out to bully people, but she would defend vulnerable kids who were getting picked on. She was almost expelled after getting into a fight with another girl—they only let her off because she was the one that ended up with a broken nose.

I suppose I'm not surprised she's become a nanny as kids have always loved her, although I had different aspirations for her—she's brilliant at maths when she puts her mind to it. But she wouldn't listen to me, and she was always determined to make her own money whenever she could, rather than let me help her out. As a teen she was in demand as a babysitter most nights, earning quite a bit by working for well-off families. I was glad she was keeping busy somewhere else because there was a terrible atmosphere in the house as Evelyn and I grew apart.

Evelyn wasn't the best for either of us. I probably married her too quickly, because I needed her support with Lou, and Evelyn was desperate to be a mother. But as Lou grew more independent, Evelyn became increasingly clingy and highly strung. Both Lou and I hated her mood swings. Rachel came into my life when Lou was fifteen. I knew Evelyn would make life hell when she found out and so I waited for a couple of years, but it got to a point where we couldn't deny our feelings. Evelyn went crazy when she found out. To get back at me, she told Lou that we'd lied to her for years, and that we'd kept her from you, even though you'd always wanted to be part of her life. Lou was horrified because she'd felt such a lot of antipathy toward you, and she'd said those nasty things to you on her sixteenth. She went wild, drinking a lot, ignoring me, making life really hard for Rachel when she moved in. The partying got worse after she turned eighteen, and she ended up in hospital having her stomach pumped. I was very troubled and disappointed about the direction she was going in. You, of all people, know how hard it is once you're addicted—I didn't want her to end up like that.

Mum spoke to Charlie, and he offered her a place to stay, so for her nineteenth birthday I decided to pay for her to go to Australia. I knew Charlie lived in the middle of nowhere, so I hoped Lou would find it harder to get herself into trouble there. Charlie seemed to work some magic on her, and I was pleased that I'd made a very good decision. A year later she was on the nanny course in Sydney, and she's been employed ever since. She still doesn't want to talk to me much, even though I paid all her tuition fees for the nanny training too. I'd always hoped she'd become a bit more understanding and grateful as she got older. She hardly bothers with Rachel at all, never says more than two words to her on the phone, which seems a bit unfair. Particularly now the boys are here. I'm sure she'll love her little brothers.

Rose feels sick. She rereads the sentence about the alcohol poisoning. He'd written *I didn't want her to end up like that*, but Rose can read between the lines. What he wanted to say was *I didn't want her to end up like YOU*. Henry had never understood the terrifying flashbacks that had started whenever she held her daughter; the echo of that other baby she'd held close as she watched her friend die. The baby that, if she closed her eyes, she could still feel being ripped from her arms. Nor could Henry stop the agony she endured each time she thought of Tristan's three boys, left to grow up without their dad. Henry couldn't get his head around the notion of PTSD. He'd been expecting a wife who carried the burden of the childcare load, not one who could barely get out of bed. So he'd quickly found another woman to step into Rose's place.

She couldn't deny that in those early days there had been some relief as well as devastation. Her daughter was in safer, steadier hands than she could provide, and that was what mattered. After all, a good mother protects her child at all costs, even from herself. But now she wonders what Louisa had experienced growing up with Henry for a father. How she had handled his insensitivity and instinct for self-protection. She's grateful that Lou had discovered the truth, because it must have been terrible to think Rose didn't want to know her. Perhaps Lou will even give her another chance now. She prays they'll get the opportunity to find out.

Rose puts her iPad down and closes her eyes again, considering all she's learned. The one bright spot in all of this is that Lou is a fighter. Because wherever she is now, a strong and stubborn will might make all the difference in keeping her and those babies alive.

CHAPTER TEN
BLACKWOOD

Blackwood steps inside the police cordon and stares at the boat, now lit up under spotlights in the midst of pitch-black bushland. It's a small silver tinny with bashed-up sides, and he's not sure they even needed to section it off with tape: they've had to drive five kilometers down unsealed, heavily corrugated road to get to this spot, and he's very much regretting the greasy sausage-and-egg burger he'd scoffed for dinner a couple of hours ago.

The night makes everyone work quietly, soft voices punctuating the occasional shush of the ocean and rustlings in the leaves. The moon is bright enough for Blackwood to see that the beach here is hardly a beach at all, just a break in the scrubby bush that leads out to a small strip of sand. The boat lies tipped to one side on the shoreline, and two of the forensic team are already in full white coveralls, working on different areas of the vessel. He recognizes Kelsie Hughes, who comes across as soon as she sees him.

"Quite a lot of blood here," she tells him. "Some of it pooled in the bottom of the boat and a lot of smearing on one side. A few footprints too. Pattern could be consistent with a knife injury. Not a gunshot wound. It's fresh, so it fits the timeline. Some evidence of blood outside the boat here too." She indicates staining in the sand. "No sign of a body. Coast guard will be searching the area again at first light."

"Anything else?"

"Not at present. We'll see if we can get fingerprints and collect fibers. I gather you've got a relative coming who can provide a blood sample for the girl?"

"The mother. Angie's gone back up to Perth to collect her. The flight lands at six."

"Good. I'll let you get on then." Kelsie nods at the police officers waiting behind them, accompanied by two SES searchers in uniform.

Blackwood walks across to the SES team, and Faulkner nods at the boat. "You're thinking this relates to your case?"

Blackwood nods. "I reckon so. Kelsie says the timing works."

Faulkner gestures to the bushland. "Then we can concentrate on this area in the morning."

Blackwood sighs. "We're going to have to do a full search, but I still don't think we're going to find them here." He indicates the Land Rover that had brought him, parked some way back down the track with the interior lights on. "Any vehicle evidence would help, though."

"We did a quick sweep before the light disappeared. Showed forensics what we found, so they could take photos and imprints of tire tracks for you," Faulkner says. He points to the lit-up strip of indents of at least three sets of wheels that stop just before the tiny patch of beach.

"Thanks." Blackwood steps carefully on the grass so he doesn't disturb anything. "Now, unless you need me, I'm going to get DC White over there to take me back to base." He indicates the young man waiting in the Land Rover.

Faulkner nods. "All good. I'll talk to you in the morning."

Once in the car, White drives a little fast for Blackwood's liking, but he's also keen to get moving so he lets it go. He waits impatiently until they're back on sealed road, as there's intermittent signal and little point trying to call anyone while he's bouncing around the vehicle. He begins running scenarios in his head, while columns of ghostly gum trees leer at them from either side of the track. He's trying to figure out some way forward among all that blood and mess on the boat.

As soon as the signal comes back, his phone begins buzzing with missed calls from Bob Drake. He quickly phones his superior.

"You're gonna have to call Jock Fisher immediately," Drake says without preamble. "I've been trying to keep him at bay, but I can't hold him off any longer."

"Wouldn't it be better in the morning when we're all fresh?"

"No!" Drake snaps, his voice rising. "He's threatening to head down there on a chopper. It'll bring an absolute media frenzy if he does, but perhaps that's what he's hoping for. It puts pressure on all of us to work harder and faster if the world is watching. Aside from the online scoops, there's already a giant headline in London's *Metro*. And there's extra interest because Louisa is British and her father is some kind of high-flying funds manager in Edinburgh. There are all sorts of quotes from Louisa's friends online, and chatter around the mother being estranged. And the mother wrote a bestselling book a few years ago, so she's a minor celebrity too."

"You've got to be joking," Blackwood replies in dismay. Press attention is to be expected, but he's only ever worked on a couple of cases where the media went bonkers, and it was awful. Now, that all seems low key compared to the potential storm brewing here.

"Nothing we can do except try to stay one step ahead." Drake sounds exhausted. "The remote location might do us a favor, but I'll make sure you get someone from the media office pronto so you've got a dedicated liaison officer. I don't want this to put you off focusing on the police work. But listen, Jock is a force to be reckoned with. I told him we weren't doing an appeal as yet, and he's threatening to hold his own press conference early tomorrow. You need to talk him round."

"If you can't do it, I'm not sure I'm going to be any more successful," Blackwood replies, trying to control the frustration that he fears is evident in his tone. Drake always seems to think Blackwood has good people skills, but Blackwood's not so sure.

"Just give it a go. I'll text you the number now." Drake hangs up before Blackwood can raise any more objections.

The number pings up moments later, and Blackwood makes the call immediately. Too much time to think only means tying himself in knots. Better dealt with and done, rather than wasting time worrying.

"Is that Malcolm Blackwood?" says a gruff male voice on the other end.

"Yes, am I speaking to Mr. Fisher?"

"Call me Jock, please." The man is more affable than Blackwood had been expecting. After Kyle's initial aggression he'd anticipated being yelled at. "Tell me everything that's been going on," Jock says. "I'm desperately worried about my grandchildren. And the poor nanny of course."

"Right." Blackwood sits forward and takes Jock systematically through the search parameters, without revealing what they've actually found.

"So what about foul play?" Jock asks. "Do you think they could have been kidnapped? We're obviously aware that these things can happen to well-off families like ours." He seems calm despite his directness.

Blackwood thinks of the boat, and the blood on the rocks. All the things he wants to withhold as long as possible so the family doesn't panic. "We can't rule that out," he says cautiously, aware that well off is a laughable understatement. The man probably owns half the land in the state, and who knows what his influence can buy.

"But what's your best guess? You think the nanny's run off with my grandkids for some reason, or is it more sinister?"

"They're both lines of inquiry," Blackwood concedes.

"Well, I told Drake I'd give you until midnight to make some progress," Jock says. "But tomorrow I have to make a statement. Obviously I can get the word out fast. The press conference will be huge, and I have to do all I can to help find my grandbabies."

"I understand that, Mr. Fisher—"

"Please, Malcolm, do call me Jock," Fisher says.

Blackwood senses the words are spoken through slightly gritted teeth. He thinks of Bob Drake's obsequious tone when he talks about Jock, and has a shudder of misgiving. However powerful this man is, it'll be a disaster if he tries to control the investigation. "The problem is, Jock, that as soon as we open up to the public we'll get swamped with false leads. It can really hamper the search, so I want to make sure you understand the need for careful consideration before we take action."

"Listen, I think you're forgetting I have resources here. I can employ people to go through the callers, sift 'em out and give the genuine leads to you. You need my help, mate. I'm not asking, I'm telling you."

Blackwood bristles but quickly shuts down his temper. He doesn't want to point out that it's unlikely Jock's team would be of much help without proper training. He's learned not to negotiate late at night, whether it's with his wife or his kids, or on a criminal investigation. No one responds well when they're short on sleep. "I appreciate your offer. And your patience. Can I give you an update tomorrow morning, and we can take it from there?"

"Let's make it eight o'clock. I want to fly down first thing if there's no progress." Jock pauses for a moment. "And I hope my son is being helpful?"

It's a strange thing to say in the circumstances, and Blackwood debates whether to push for more information. But he decides to keep on the path of least resistance for the time being. "He's been holding up well today in the circumstances. His wife is extremely distressed."

"She's probably regretting not spending much time with her kids," Jock says matter-of-factly. "She's not a very good mother."

"I see." Blackwood can't resist following the bait. "Could you enlighten me further on that?"

"Sure." Jock laughs. "She enjoys her kids when they're clean and presentable, but she doesn't want to deal with two dependent human beings. My wife, Trisha, god rest her soul, had four, and she was hands on from sunup till bedtime. Still managed to accompany me to most things too. I thought I might marry again after she died, but I never found another like her. I don't think they make 'em like that anymore. We built the business from nothing, then our kids came along with silver spoons in their mouths, so we had to really push hard to give them that work ethic. But by the time you get to number four, you're tired, things are slipping through. So Kyle's a bit of a slacker, he likes the easy life, and he met his perfect match when he married Frannie. I love him to bits, love all my kids, but I wouldn't put him in charge of anything, if you know what I mean."

Blackwood doesn't know how to respond in the face of such forthrightness, but Jock counters the silence. "I'm a direct man, Malcolm. I call a spade a spade. Even with my kids. That way we all know where we stand. You'll get used to it."

"Not a problem. Matter of fact, I appreciate it," Blackwood interjects. He gets the feeling that Jock uses diversion tactics like this to run the conversation. He's going to have to be on alert with the man, but despite his frustration there's also a grudging respect creeping in.

"Great. I'll say good night now, and wait for that briefing in the morning then." He hangs up before Blackwood can reply.

Five minutes later, Blackwood's Land Rover reaches the media scrum outside the gates to the Kardanup estate. He waits, staring grimly ahead while they're driven through, as journalists shout questions in vain toward the car. He makes a decision, and calls Webster, wishing that Angie were still here instead.

"I'd like your backup," he says when the man answers. "I'm going to talk to the Fishers again before they go to bed. Can you set it up, and meet me outside."

"No problem," Webster replies, and by the time Blackwood reaches the Fisher residence, Webster is climbing out of an unmarked police car, buttoning up his suit jacket, his shoulders back and his jaw set. A policeman lets them inside and they find the four adults sitting in the lounge, the women chatting, the men on their phones. They all fall silent as Blackwood and Webster march in, and Blackwood immediately registers the fear on Kyle's and Frannie's faces.

"We'd like to have a word with Frannie and Kyle in private," Blackwood begins.

Vic and Bridget jump up immediately. Bridget squeezes Frannie's shoulder as she leaves, and Frannie pats her friend's hand in return.

Blackwood takes a seat opposite them while Webster remains standing.

"Please tell us they're okay," Kyle says quietly.

"There's no news yet," Blackwood replies.

Both Kyle and Frannie sag against the sofa. Frannie bites her lip and stares at the ground.

"Christ, man, when you asked to speak to us alone I thought you'd found them and something terrible had happened," Kyle says, his voice low and accusing.

"No, I'm sorry. But I've just spoken to your father," Blackwood replies, looking at Kyle. "He plans to come down in the morning and hold a press conference, try to get the media and the public behind us."

Kyle grimaces. "And you think that's a good idea?"

Blackwood shrugs. "I don't like it, but the media are already here, speculating. I was hoping it would all be over by now, but if this drags on then we could use all the help we can get. There are always leaks in cases like these, and we need to keep control."

Frannie leans forward, as though sensing some deeper meaning in his words. "Have you found anything at all?"

Blackwood braces himself. "We've found a small boat—a tinny, late this afternoon," he tells them. "A little further up the coast. With some bloodstains inside it. I've just come back from looking at it. And we've also sampled some droplets of blood on the rocks at the end of the beach."

Frannie gasps, then begins to moan. "No, no."

Kyle looks horror struck. He drops his head into his hands, making no move to comfort his wife, who is beginning to hyperventilate.

"Frannie," Blackwood says quickly, "don't let your thoughts get away from you. I realize this is awful, but there's no indication yet that it's the children's blood."

Kyle looks up, his hands steepled in prayer. He presses them against his mouth for a moment. "Tell us more about the boat."

"It was pulled up on the shoreline in thick bushland at the end of a rough four-wheel-drive track a few kilometers north of here. We'll use the DNA samples that we took from you both to check against what we've found. We can rush the tests through and we should have preliminary results by morning. However, I want to stress that until we get the results, we don't know whether these discoveries are even connected with the children's disappearance. This is what happens in these cases: We find and collect all sorts of evidence and follow all leads, but that doesn't mean everything we come across is relevant. It could just as easily be someone who cut themselves while out fishing or when filleting a catch. We're checking hospitals too, in case someone showed up bleeding. So please don't let your minds go toward dark places until we have the facts."

Frannie begins to sob quietly. Kyle glances at her, then wrinkles his nose as if pained by her uncontrolled emotion. Blackwood's heart goes out to her. He notices a tissue box on one of the small tables and passes it across.

"Thank you," she sniffs.

"No problem. I won't have much more to tell you about the boat itself until we've done tests, but the SES will be focusing their search around that spot tomorrow."

"Tomorrow!" Frannie squeals. "We can't be without our babies for another night. I won't survive it."

"Mrs. Fisher, I promise you we're chasing up every lead. While we can't search on land overnight, there's a lot we can do to keep the investigation going. Even though there's only so much we can achieve in the dark, we don't stop working. We'll be dedicated to this twenty-four seven until we've found your children and Louisa."

"What else have you uncovered?" Kyle asks curtly, cutting into Blackwood's speech.

Blackwood prepares himself, knowing he's about to open a can of worms.

"Do you remember I asked you about Fabien Dubois? We think he's in a relationship with Louisa, and we've discussed whether they may have been meeting on the beach without your knowledge? Were either of you aware that Louisa has a boyfriend?"

Kyle says "No," while Frannie says "Yes" at the same time. Kyle glares at his wife.

"I knew about them when we first hired Lou," Frannie clarifies, without looking at her husband. "I saw her social media accounts and we had a chat about him. Fabien's a radio producer in Sydney and he works for Robbie Reynolds. You know who he is, don't you?"

Blackwood nods. "Biggest DJ in the country. Likes to stir up controversy. Interviews everyone from singers to politicians and wears his shirts half undone to show off his hairy chest. That's him, right?"

Frannie smiles briefly, but then seems to remember the nightmare she's in and her face falls again. "That's him. His act is all swagger. He's a nice guy. It was Robbie and his wife, Bella, who recommended Lou to us in the first place. We'd just lost our nanny and Robbie's mother-in-law was coming to live in and help them, so they didn't need Lou anymore, but Bella said she'd been brilliant. However, I explained to Lou that we always ask our personal employees to put their relationships on pause while they're with us. This is not a nine-to-five job, they become part of the family, and we pay them handsomely for that. She readily agreed, so I didn't think we needed to discuss it any further."

"Fabien has been on leave for the past six days," Blackwood tells them. "He arrived in WA five days ago, and there's an abandoned car a kilometer south from here that he hired in Perth. At present we can't locate Fabien either."

Frannie's mouth drops open, while Kyle jumps up, exploding with rage. "That BITCH! You think they took them, don't you? They got together and did a runner with our kids. What the *fuck*," he yells, loud enough for the whole house to hear. "How the hell has he been getting in here anyway?"

"We're not sure, but the beach isn't gated, and there's a path from the road on the southern side," Blackwood points out mildly as Kyle towers above him, noting how intimidating Kyle can be to those around him when he loses his temper. "There are ways in if you're determined. I realize this is extremely concerning, but if they wanted to run off together, why didn't they just use the car? And why would they take the children with them—if Louisa wanted to leave, she wasn't a prisoner here, was she? She could have just quit and gone with Fabien. No, it's all very odd, and the whole sequence of events is still to be determined."

Kyle remains standing, eyeballing Blackwood as though he'd like to punch him. Webster moves a few steps closer to them, and Blackwood is grateful for the support. Webster might be wooden and difficult at times, but he goes by the book when it comes to threats to fellow officers.

"Until we know what's actually happened it's dangerous to jump to conclusions," Blackwood continues, getting up slowly. "But of course we're considering this angle. However, I've got to stress that it looks very out of character for both of them, and I really don't see what they'd have to gain. And we don't yet know if the boat is connected, as that would also alter the entire scenario."

"I don't believe they would do this to us either. Although Lou adores our kids," Frannie says through her tears. "She's very protective of them. And I suppose it's quite romantic, isn't it?" she adds, looking at the floor as she speaks. "Him flying across the country to meet her in secret. Loving her enough to do that." Her face lifts so she can meet Kyle's eyes; her jaw tightens, and something passes between them.

"Yes, it's all terrific, until they decided to kidnap our children." Kyle glares at her. "Perhaps she thought she'd be a better mother," he adds, raising his eyebrows at Frannie.

"Perhaps she's right," Frannie shoots back, her head high although her expression has darkened and her bottom lip is trembling. "Perhaps if I felt less fucking trapped and depressed every day then I'd be taking better care of them."

For a moment, they are all lost for words. Blackwood would be grateful for the silence except it makes him realize how hard his head has started to pound.

"I'll call Robbie now," Kyle says, "and find out what I can about Fabien."

"Please, let me do that," Blackwood adds quickly. "If you can give me his number it will save us time, as I'll need to contact him anyway."

Kyle gives Blackwood a dark look, pulls his phone from his pocket, and scrolls for a moment. "Here." He passes the device over.

Blackwood hands it swiftly to Webster. "Take down that number for me, will you."

There's a second's pause while Webster moves away, when everyone else is frozen. Blackwood studies the couple before him. Frannie is obviously terrified, while Kyle stands rigid, as though he's wound so tight he might snap at any moment. This isn't good.

"Remember," Blackwood says to them, as gently as he can, "the kids need you both to stay strong and support one another."

Kyle stiffens even more. "Is that all?" he snaps back. At Blackwood's nod, he turns and storms away, disappearing down a corridor.

Frannie gives Blackwood a desperate glance before she follows.

Once they're gone, Blackwood grabs his phone and texts Angie. *Kyle and Frannie are at each other's throats. Not much love in this marriage. Maybe more is at play here. Louisa could have seen or heard something she shouldn't have. What if she felt she needed to take the children to protect them? Let's watch both parents carefully, just in case.*

Then he sits back, trying not to get caught in thoughts of those babies lost somewhere with Louisa, cowering in the darkness, hungry and afraid, their lives in his hands.

CHAPTER ELEVEN
ROSE

As the plane descends, and the first threads of daylight creep over the horizon, Rose studies Perth's skyline: a modest cluster of skyscrapers beside a glistening river that dissects the landscape, widening and narrowing as it winds into the distance. The city is the centerpiece of what looks like a long, low, coastal suburban sprawl, patched with small areas of untamed bushland. It's very different to the densely populated areas and cleared green fields she'd flown over in the cold morning light on her way out of Heathrow, and she balks at the thought of Lou down there somewhere, lost. Finding her suddenly feels like a futile, impossible task.

As the wheels touch down with a heavy thump, she's overwhelmed by the unfamiliarity of the place, not to mention the daughter she's come here for. When she thinks of Australia she only knows the eastern states' landmarks, like the Sydney Harbour Bridge and the Opera House, or the Great Barrier Reef, but she's on the opposite side of this enormous landmass with little knowledge of Western Australia. She recalls seeing news clips of flooding somewhere in the country a few years ago, when hundreds of spiders and snakes crawled up onto fence posts to find higher ground. She shudders. She really hopes Lou isn't trapped in that kind of environment.

She'd suspected she would be greeted by the police after landing, but she hadn't anticipated the announcement of her name on the plane's intercom, or that she would be escorted off first, with rows of exhausted passengers glaring at her. She's led down the air bridge by an air hostess to find two officers waiting for her at the double doors leading into the concourse: a tall, rather spotty young man in uniform, who looks like he should still be at school, standing beside a middle-aged woman, short and stocky, wearing a dark suit, her hands clasped in front of her. "Rose?" The woman immediately steps forward to shake her hand, her expression solemn and her grip firm and brisk. "I'm DS Lennard. You can call me Angie. This is Sergeant Paul Brightwell. We're here to get you through customs and then we'll take you straight down to Kardanup, okay?"

Rose nods, and Angie points down the corridor. "This way." They set off at pace, and Rose hurries to keep up with them, trying to listen to Angie, who is talking rapidly. "First of all, with your permission, we'll do a DNA swab and blood test here in the airport. We have a room set up, and we need samples to compare with some evidence we've found."

"What evidence?" Rose asks quickly.

Angie stops and turns so they are facing one another. Rose can see the woman sizing her up, trying to gauge Rose's emotional capacity.

"I can handle it, trust me," she says, perhaps more forcefully than she intended, as one of Angie's eyebrows jumps a little, then resettles.

"Okay. So far we've found some bloodstains on rocks at the beach and more in a boat a few kilometers north of the spot where the three of them disappeared." Angie's eyes remain steady on Rose.

Oh god. Rose gulps hard. Her mind flashes through some of the other bloodstained crime scenes she's seen over the years. *This is not the same,* she assures herself. She breathes deeply and nods at Angie. "Okay. Let's get the tests done."

"Good," Angie says approvingly, beginning to walk again. "And we have a helicopter lined up to take us to Kardanup, which will save us getting stuck in the morning traffic. It was Louisa's uncle's idea. He was part of the search yesterday, and he flew up last night so he could collect us this morning. We've booked a hotel room for you not too far from the Kardanup estate. You must be tired."

Rose waves away Angie's comment. "I'm fine. Please tell me, what else have you discovered?"

Angie shows Rose into a small side room as airport staff watch on curiously. Sergeant Brightwell follows them in and closes the door. Angie continues. "Well, we think your girl might have a fella, name's Fabien Dubois, and he's missing too. We're working on a theory that they've been meeting up on the beach in the early mornings this past week, without Louisa's employers' knowledge or approval. His rental car has been abandoned in a car park not too far from where Louisa and the kids went missing." She stares unflinchingly at Rose. "You know anything about him?"

"No," Rose says, taken aback by the woman's intensity. "I saw there was a young guy on some of her Instagram pictures, but I don't know any more than that." *Oh, Lou*, she thinks, *I hope you haven't done anything crazy.* She's been hoping that Lou is innocently lost in the bush with the kids, and it's just a matter of locating them, but if Lou's boyfriend is also missing it radically alters the situation. Her mind returns to the blood in the abandoned boat, and a shiver runs through her.

She mulls over what Angie just said, and frowns. "Does she really need her employers' approval to see her boyfriend?"

"The Fishers run a tight ship, I guess," Angie replies, in a tone that indicates she's also uneasy about this. "It sounds extreme, but then I suppose we don't know what it's like to belong to a multimillionaire family in the public eye."

"What else do you know about Fabien?"

"He met Louisa in Sydney eighteen months ago, and they were dating for almost a year before Louisa moved here just before Christmas. He's a radio producer for Robbie Reynolds—the DJ. I've been talking to the police here in the airport, and we can see from records and CCTV that he arrived in Perth five days ago and hired the car, but now there's no sign of him." Angie raises her eyebrows, and Rose again feels the weight of the woman's judgment about what Lou and Fabien might have done. She'd hoped the police would be allies, but if they think Lou has kidnapped the children she's going to have to ready herself for much more hostility. Angie nods at her fellow officer. "Let's get these swabs done; then we can get moving."

As the police officers sort out the swabs, Rose pulls her phone from her bag. She's not going to let them accuse Lou of being a child snatcher without knowing they've considered all the other leads. "Did you get a chance to investigate that Instagram post I sent you?" she asks.

Angie looks irritated. "We follow all leads," she says.

Rose is tapping onto the app as she listens to Angie, her heart jumping as she sees that @stellarstels is online and has sent a reply. She skims it quickly.

Hi Rose, yes, I'm a friend of Lou's. The stalker comment is a few months old. Lou thought some guy was watching her and the kids at the park in Perth when she started working for the Fishers. It freaked her out, but she said he disappeared after a few days and she never spoke about him again after that. I'd really like to talk to you. Let me know when you arrive. Best wishes, Stella

Rose types back quickly. *I'm here now. With police. Please can you talk to them and pass this information on?*

She gets notified that Stella has seen the message, but there's no immediate reply. She debates pushing this as a topic for discussion, but Angie is ready with the swabs, and Rose suspects this might only antagonize the woman further. She decides she'll bide her time, submitting to the tests and watching while they package everything up.

Angie hands the parcels to Brightwell. "There are officers waiting out front to take these," she tells him. "We'll meet you outside."

Brightwell races away, and Rose jumps up, ready to go.

"Can you describe your bags to me?" Angie asks. "We can try to get them off first."

"I don't have any. It's all in here." Rose holds up her rucksack.

"Really?" For a moment, Angie's guard falls, and she looks impressed.

"I'm good at traveling light."

"Well, that'll save us some time." Angie nods, and Rose senses approval.

At the immigration desk they are waved to the front of the line, and the Border Force officer regards Rose for a long moment before stamping her passport. Five minutes later they are walking out of the airport toward the car park.

The outside temperature is comfortable, with a gentle breeze, and the fresh air is welcome after the long hours on the plane. The golden glow of the early sunlight bounces off the surfaces around them. The warmth at this early hour takes Rose by surprise, and it's much better than the chilly, damp spring weather she's left behind.

Brightwell is waiting to direct them to an unmarked police vehicle, for which Rose is grateful. She could do without faces peering in at her, wondering what she's done.

Once they're inside, Angie turns around to speak to her from the front seat. "It's only a few minutes to the helicopter pad. Please let us know if there's anything you need."

"Thank you," Rose replies. She thinks about Charlie waiting for them just moments away, which sets off a flurry of nerves. To distract herself, she pulls out her phone, finding there are over twenty messages from different people. Vee must have been busy sharing the news. Her younger sisters have both sent their love and support, and there's a worried message from her mum and dad telling her to look after herself and keep them updated. She texts Vee to say she's arrived safely and ask her to let the rest of the family know, also checking if there's any news on Bonnie. Next, she fires off two words to Henry: *I've landed.* She sends one more message on Instagram to Stella. *I'm heading south to the area Lou disappeared. How can we talk asap?*

She can see Stella is online, and tries to restrain herself from prompting a response, but Stella's reply pops up moments later.

I'm south too, close to Kardanup.

Rose types hastily. *I'll let you know as soon as I arrive. But if you have anything that will help locate Louisa please call the police now. Anything at all. Every minute counts.*

After she's pressed send, she turns her attention to her surroundings. They pass streets full of industrial lots, and then head down a wide divided highway lined with an assortment of fast-food restaurants and shabby terraced units with outdated signage. She can see the city in the distance, the small group of skyscrapers glistening in tones of orange, yellow, and silver in the early-morning light. As they turn off to the helicopter landing strip, Rose flicks her phone camera around so she can study her appearance, taking in her lank ponytail and the gray bags under her eyes. Not how she would have chosen to meet Charlie again, but there's not a lot she can do about it.

When they pull up to the small hangar she sees him straightaway, leaning against the wall, watching the car arrive. He still looks as fit as he did in his army days, wearing a navy sweater and jeans. His body is stockier than it used to be, though, and his forehead is creased with lines. He's also more tanned than she remembers and his dark wavy hair is flecked with gray. But despite all that, it's still the same Charlie she once knew.

Angie and Rose get out as he approaches the car, but then Angie turns back to lean into the vehicle, passing on instructions to Brightwell, who is obviously staying behind. For a moment, Rose and Charlie are alone.

"Hello, Rose," he says, leaning down to give her a polite peck on the cheek, his lips cool against her skin. "It's really good to see you, but I'm so sorry about the circumstances."

"It's good to see you too, Charlie," she says. "Thanks for coming to get us this morning." She glances at the helicopter. "This is all a bit . . ." She looks around, trying to find the words. "Surreal," she says with a helpless shrug, having to swallow a rising tide of emotion. She hadn't realized how grateful she would be to see a familiar face.

"Of course." He briefly touches her arm, then they both turn to watch Angie as she hurries across. Charlie holds out a hand. "Good to meet you. I'm Charlie, Lou's uncle."

"DS Angie Lennard," she says, as they shake. "How long will it take us to get down there?"

"About an hour." He gestures to the helicopter. "It's all ready for us. One of you can sit up front beside me, and the other can take one of the back seats."

"I'll take the back," Angie says, allowing Charlie to help her climb on board. Rose waits, watching as he hands Angie a headset, before he turns to Rose.

"Can I take your bag?" He nods at the rucksack. "Is that all you brought?"

She shrugs. "Yep, there wasn't time to pack much, and I prefer traveling light."

He grabs it and straps it into the seat next to Angie. Then he comes back for Rose. "Here." He holds out a hand to assist her into the cockpit.

She takes it, and his warm fingers grip hers tightly as he helps her aboard. He gives her a brief, encouraging smile, and a memory comes back, unbidden.

What the hell do you see in him, Rose?

It was the one night they'd let their guard down, back when she'd been dating Henry and she'd witnessed a family row. She'd found Charlie on the back porch, fuming, and she was angry too—mortified by the condescending way Henry had spoken to his younger brother, accusing him of jealousy because Henry had so much that he wanted: money, a good job, and even his girl.

If only it hadn't been true. But even though Rose and Charlie hardly saw one another, because Charlie's military postings meant he was away for long spells, Henry could see there was a connection between them. Charlie was a man of few words, but there had been times when they'd sat around the dinner table, with Henry and his mother making fun of someone or something, and Charlie's eyes had met Rose's in shared understanding.

That evening, sitting on the back step together, Charlie's head had moved toward hers, and she'd let their lips almost meet before she'd spoken.

"I'm pregnant, Charlie."

She had never forgotten the shock, anger, and grief that had flashed across his face.

He'd stood up and gone inside without a word. A week later he was back on deployment. And they had never spoken again. Until today.

She watches him now as he climbs up into the pilot seat, passes her a headset, puts his own on, and begins flicking switches. The cockpit is tiny, forcing an immediate intimacy that's disconcerting after so many years. He senses her eyes on him and glances toward her, flashing her a brief, polite smile.

His voice comes through the headset. "Are you ready?"

She looks at him and nods, and moments later the helicopter begins to rise. She watches the ground disappear as they bank to the south, and soon the cars are matchboxes moving along threads of gray road, and the trees become blurry dots of green.

They don't talk much on the journey, aware of the noise and the interruptions from the radio, as well as Angie listening in. Rose is tired and a little nauseous. Her attention lingers on the scenery, an endless rolling blanket of outback vegetation, broken by farms and the occasional township. Occasionally her focus wanders to Charlie's calm demeanor at the controls. She listens to him chat to various air traffic controllers along the way.

"The search is going on over there," he says at one point, gesturing toward the southwest coastline. "I'll go out again later too."

She nods, despondent at the dense bushland that stretches on for miles. She's unable to imagine how they might find Louisa in all that.

When they finally land, Charlie helps them both out of the helicopter.

"Thanks, Charlie," Angie says. "Saved us a heap of time. Although there should be a squad car here." She looks around. "Let me just make a call and check they're on the way."

She puts her phone to her ear and moves away from them.

"What's your plan for today then?" Rose asks Charlie.

"I'll head back out while there's plenty of daylight," he says. "I can't sit down here doing nothing when I might be useful in the air. But I'll come and find you again later this afternoon if you let me know where you'll be."

Rose nods. "DS Lennard said they've organized a hotel for me. I'll let you know which one." There's another pause, before Rose adds, "Henry mentioned that Lou stayed with you when she first got here?"

"Yeah."

"What's she like now?"

Charlie glances at Rose, his expression a mix of worry and heartache.

"She's great, Rose. Really great. In fact, she reminds me of you when you were that age."

His glance rests on her for a moment, unreadable, before he looks away toward Angie, who's talking animatedly on the phone.

Rose tries to refocus. "Angie said that last night they found a boat, a few kilometers north of the beach where Louisa was last seen, with a significant amount of blood in it. I had to give them a DNA sample at the airport. I'm not sure how many people know about that."

Charlie closes his eyes for a moment, breathing heavily, then looks at the ground, scuffing his feet against the tarmac. "That's terrible," he says quietly. "I hadn't heard about it, although I'm yet to check in with the search HQ this morning."

"And she also said that Lou's boyfriend was holidaying nearby, and he hasn't been seen for a few days either. His name is Fabien Dubois. Do you know him?"

"Fabien?" Charlie frowns. "He came over for a visit just before she started this job. Nice fella; although I was under the impression they might have broken up as she hadn't mentioned him lately. I didn't want to ask in case I upset her—and I didn't feel it was any of my business either. But . . . all right . . . really? Fabien's been nearby, and now he's gone missing too? I'm . . . Well, I don't know what to think about that."

"Me neither."

Charlie shakes his head. "I can't believe she would run off with the kids—although I almost wish I did believe it. It would make me less concerned for her safety. But no." He hesitates, and she can see him thinking things through. "Unless there's more we don't know—and she felt she had to protect them somehow."

He pauses, and Rose can't help but let the brief silence amplify her own worries. There's so much they just don't know.

Charlie registers her expression. "I don't think we should get carried away with that idea when there are other possibilities that make a lot more sense. I was never keen on her working for the Fishers. You don't have to go far to hear things. Kyle, her boss, is the party boy of the family. Bleeds money, but his dad must keep patching him up again as he's always rebounding with some kind of new enterprise. The Fishers are firmly stuck in the last century—their bottom line is always more important than native title rights or environmental protection—and they've funded some awful projects in the last few years. Lots of people hate them. I warned Lou about them, but she felt she could handle it—and I appreciated the fact it was an opportunity to earn well and be part of a lifestyle we can only imagine. That's pretty tempting if you're only twenty-two."

Rose thinks of herself at twenty-two: unexpectedly pregnant and a year away from life-changing trauma. She takes a deep breath. "Thanks for the warning. God knows what I'm walking into today. I'll keep you updated."

"Please do."

Angie is coming toward them, gesturing at the squad car pulling into the car park. "Are you ready, Rose?"

Rose nods and follows Angie, aware that Charlie hasn't moved, his eyes still on her as she gets into the vehicle. She gives him a wave, which he returns, before the car moves away.

From the front passenger seat, Angie turns to her. "I have to be straight with you. We're not just dealing with Lou and the missing children; we've got Jock Fisher and this connection to a famous DJ through Fabien. It doesn't get much more juicy for the public, I'm afraid. Media interest is already substantial, and it will only get worse from here. Missing kids are always a drawcard for them—if the littlies come from the right socioeconomic background, of course. They don't give a shit about state housing or Aboriginal kids going missing, but that's another story. Jock Fisher's likely to come down here today, and he'll bring a media storm with him, so you need to be prepared for a lot of questions and press intrusion into your life. We would ask that you don't speak to any journalists without consulting us as it may jeopardize the investigation, and in certain circumstances it could get you into legal trouble too. If there's something you'd like to say to them, please run it past us first, and we can discuss whether it benefits you, Louisa, or the children."

"I have absolutely no plans to speak to the media," Rose replies firmly.

"That's good." Angie gives Rose a quick nod of approval. "I've done a little bit of research, so I know you're not a typical civilian. I also know this is not a normal parenting situation for you, and we appreciate the fact that you've come to support Louisa and the investigation in these circumstances. I'd like to build an open dialogue between us, where you can ask me any questions you want, and vice versa. Does that sound doable to you?"

"It sounds good," Rose replies. "So my first question is, Can we talk more about the stuff from Lou's Instagram? The stalker I mentioned?"

Despite her words, Angie appears taken aback at Rose's directness, and her expression shifts from agreeable to wary. "Of course. I saw the comment, and referred it to DSS Blackwood, who's in charge of the case," she says. "But his primary focus right now is Louisa's boyfriend, Fabien. I'm sure you appreciate that this is a much stronger lead than a social media comment from a few months ago."

Rose's shoulders tighten, as she can see they won't be prioritizing this. "I understand that," she says, "but I think we still need to find Stella, in case she knows something significant. I've been exchanging messages with her, but she's not volunteering much information. If you haven't got the resources, I'm happy to talk to her first," she adds, knowing how much her words are likely to rile Angie, but nevertheless determined to get the woman to pay attention.

As expected, Angie looks annoyed. "Show me again what you found," she says.

Rose connects to Instagram and hands over her phone.

Angie scans the message, then clicks to Stella's profile as Rose watches. She flicks through Stella's photos, then stops, moving through the pictures in reverse, taking her time. Rose can sense the shift in her attention.

"What is it?"

Angie holds the phone so Rose can see it. "These. They look very much like the beach where Lou and the kids disappeared, which means Stella must have been there too." She turns away so Rose can't see her expression as she silently scans the images on the phone.

Rose waits.

Eventually, Angie turns to hand the phone back to Rose. "Perhaps we do need to speak to this girl," she says, without meeting Rose's gaze, "although she's obviously not keen to talk to us. Keep messaging her and encourage her to get in touch with the police directly, and we'll work on it at our end, too. Let's try to draw her out as fast as we can."

CHAPTER TWELVE
BLACKWOOD

Blackwood makes a beeline for the coffee pods in his room; he'll need to have at least two before he's ready to call Jock Fisher. He hadn't made it to the hotel until after midnight, then he'd slept, fully clothed, in fits and starts on top of the covers, waking as the first threads of daylight stole over the horizon. He's glad he took the time to pack an overnight bag with extra shirts, jocks, and socks, and he always keeps a spare suit in the car. In the early days he'd been caught out, and it wasn't much fun leading an investigation while morphing into an unshaven, stinking caveman.

He'd been incensed last night to discover Margie had gone line dancing with a friend called Harry. On the phone, when he'd not been able to restrain himself from asking who the fuck Harry was, Margie had replied, "Oh good god, Mal. He's a *friend*. Seriously, after everything we've been through, I would think you'd trust me. Or do I have to hide it whenever I talk to a man now? And can I just remind you that my life doesn't have to stop when you go to work." While he was still searching for an appropriate response, she'd wished him a curt good night and hung up.

He texts her an apology before he calls the overnight sergeant for updates. There are no major developments, so he takes his drink and phone onto the balcony, giving himself a moment to breathe as he gazes at the glistening aquamarine water of the large hotel pool, having a sudden desire to jump in and refresh. He's never been averse to an early-morning swim—at home it's only a short walk to the beach—but in the last decade he's rarely had the time. He can hear Margie tut-tutting about his priorities as clearly as if she were standing behind him. He's debating whether he should call her, or if she'll be annoyed if he wakes her up. Before their separation he probably wouldn't have made any effort to get in touch, too focused on his work, and now he's fretting about whether a text is enough. But wouldn't it be dangerous to fall back into the same habits? Doesn't he need to keep proving that he's a different man?

He makes the call, but it goes straight through to voicemail so he leaves a message. "Margie, it's Mal. I just wanted to, erm, see how you're doing and to apologize for getting testy last night. I know it's yet another example of the job coming between us, and I'm glad it won't be happening for much longer. I'll rebook Wildflower for us as soon as I can, and I hope you had a nice time with your friends. It's good the booking didn't go to waste. And of course you should go out with your friends while I'm not there. I, ah, well . . ." It's on the tip of his tongue to say *I love you* but he's never been good with this kind of thing, and even though he looks around and there's no one there, he can't quite bring himself to do it. "I'll call again soon, all right," he says, and hangs up. Honestly, if she doesn't know how he feels after all the work he put in to get her to come home, then there's no hope. Nevertheless, he finds himself going online and ordering her a huge box of Coal River Farm handmade chocolates, her favorites, just to make sure she knows he's thinking of her.

As soon as he's finished, Angie calls.

"We've just stopped at the servo," she tells him, "and I've found a quiet spot for a second while Rose uses the bathroom. Any news?"

"Nothing. I'm just summoning up the energy to call Jock Fisher."

"Wow, hanging out with the movers and shakers now," Angie says. "Is this the first time you've spoken to him?"

"We had a brief chat last night."

"What's he like?"

"Interesting. A force. But not necessarily in a bad way. I hope he'll be helpful if we can keep him onside."

Angie snorts. "Yeah, good luck to all of us in that."

"I got the impression he's not Kyle's biggest fan. Or Frannie's for that matter."

"Wouldn't surprise me," Angie says. "From everything we've uncovered so far, I'm not keen on them either. Francesca is Kyle's third wife, and Kai and Honey are his second set of kids. He's fifty-one, and his first marriage was to an actress from America, but that sounded a bit impulsive, as it only lasted a few months. His second wife was an Australian model called Ebony Fielding, and he was married to her for twelve years. She lives in Sydney with their two teenage boys, but she's been unwell lately, having chemo, so we haven't had a chance to talk to her. From what I can gather the kids don't want anything to do with Kyle; the split was acrimonious and Ebony took a hefty chunk of money in the settlement."

"All right then," Blackwood says as Angie pauses for breath. "It sounds like drama follows Kyle around, and he's not averse to creating it either."

"Yeah, and when Kyle and Francesca got married four years ago he had another massive white wedding—he obviously enjoys throwing a party if he's still going all out for wife number three. As far as I can tell, he mostly lives off the family estate, although he's always trying to make some business scheme or other work. But none of them seem to last very long."

Blackwood sighs, watching enviously as an early-morning swimmer puts his towel on a sun bed and then dives into the hotel pool. "Yeah, he might be tricky. But I think his father will be even harder to manage. Jock told me last night that he intends to hold a press conference today. I really don't like the idea, but he's a difficult man to deter."

"Shit. Well, I've just checked Rose into the hotel," Angie tells him. "I've suggested she rest for a bit, while there's no news. I have a hunch we shouldn't let the Fishers get their hands on her too quickly, especially while she's jet lagged. I thought you could deal with Jock first and then we can talk more to Rose. I should warn you—she has plenty of her own ideas and theories too. The team have been filling me in on her background: Before she wrote her book, she was a police officer for years in the Met in London—even worked in a special hostage team and did some training at Quantico, then left the force to focus on domestic violence victims."

"You've got to be kidding." Blackwood balks at the description of Rose, not keen on the thought of another relative of this missing trio dogging their heels and interfering.

"Sorry but no—she's running her own little investigation on the side already. She showed me the Insta page of the girl who suggested Lou might have a stalker. I wasn't too interested at first, but there are a few pictures on there that I'm sure are the Kardanup estate's private beach. So I'm working on accessing this girl's details, but I'm also getting Rose to help draw her out."

"All right, thanks. Can you brief me any more on the other leads?"

"Of course. We've found the CCTV of Fabien arriving at the airport five days ago. I've watched him walk through customs clutching a bloody great surfboard in a bag. Not really the gear you bring if you're gonna do some child snatching, is it? He rented the car at Hertz, then took off."

"Good work," Blackwood says. "I still haven't made it to see the car yet."

"I snuck a look on my way out of town. Nothing much worth noting—no belongings visible—but forensics are still going to comb through it. More importantly, we need to find out where Fabien was staying. We haven't located him at any hotels or hostels so far. And," Angie adds after a quick breath, "the phone records are in too. I've got officers working the data. Louisa and Fabien mainly seem to call and text each other—we can't get any of the contents of messages because they both use Snapchat, which is a pain in the arse since the company doesn't keep data. And neither of their phones have pinged off any towers since the morning they went missing. If they left of their own accord, they definitely don't want to be found, although Fabien will be easy to identify as he's got a tattoo going up the right side of his neck. Silhouettes of birds in flight. Pretty distinctive. How did you go with the tinny?"

"It's not looking good," Blackwood admits, glad that at least with Angie he can be honest and direct. "Blood all across the seat and down one side. It's in a remote area, at the end of an unsealed four-wheel-drive track that leads only to a small patch of water, so I doubt anyone would use the spot much."

"What's your hunch?"

"I don't know, but it puts some gaping holes in the theory that Lou and Fabien have run off together with the kids. You?"

"That story's still not sitting right with me. It's the obvious conclusion, but Louisa doesn't strike me as a daft kid willing to throw her life away. And Fabien's very much liked at the radio station; everyone says he loves his job. This is out of character for both of them. From what I gather, he comes from a well-respected family in Toulouse, and he's never been in any trouble before. He's worked here for six years, and loves his life. All a bit strange. I still can't believe he's a producer for Robbie Reynolds."

"Yes, it's all adding to the bin-fire feeling I've got about this." Blackwood pauses, frowns. "We're tackling an emergency situation that involves a hostage-expert mum turned bestselling author, along with multimillionaires, radio producers, DJs, and investment bankers," Blackwood says, his mouth dry. "I'm not sure I'm the right person for all this."

"Bullshit," Angie replies straightaway. "You're the best person by a mile. You don't take any crap and you don't give a toss about money or status or personal publicity. You just want to solve the bloody case and get the kids back safely so you can go home to your wife. Don't let Webster or those other show ponies in Perth get a look-in or we'll never get these kids home."

"Angie!" he growls. "Enough now."

Angie just laughs. "Chin up," she says. "Tell me more about Kyle and Frannie—you said they're at each other's throats?"

"There's a shitload of tension between them, way more than just the stress of current events."

"Well, there's plenty about them available online. They love showing their faces at parties and corporate events—or the races. They *adore* the races. Anything where they can dress up. Kyle's got two older brothers and an older sister who seem far more involved in the Fisher business. They're all board members. Toby's the COO, Ethan's the CFO, and Bronte's the head of communication and international relations. From the outside, Kyle looks like the misfit."

"Interesting," Blackwood says, downing the last of his coffee. "But who knows if it's relevant. We should always keep our options open. Kyle and Frannie and the Santos couple all have alibis that support one another, and there's a lot of things that seem to exclude foul play, including some security cam footage. However, I keep thinking about the spot Lou and the kids disappeared from—how remote it is. If it's a kidnapping, it's got to be targeted, hasn't it? In which case, there must be a reason. But whoever's taken them hasn't made any contact, so we're completely in the dark. What do you think?"

"The whole scenario has got me stumped. We'll follow all protocols, but I don't think we'll find them in the bush or the water. Louisa seems such a nice girl on the surface—from the photos we've seen and all we've heard it looks like she adores the kids—but could she love them a bit too much? Could something have made her want to run? Either because she's mentally unstable, or she witnessed some kind of abuse?"

"Uh-huh—I hear you. Keep everyone working on her background. And run some more checks on the Fishers' history too. It's best to cover all bases. Now, let's discuss what I want to happen today. The SES checking all the terrain again. The choppers continuing air search. The coast guard covering the water. The juniors door knocking to double-check those houses are empty. And I want all that organized quickly so we can focus on finding out as much as possible, as fast as possible, about Louisa Thornton and Kyle and Francesca Fisher. Perhaps include the house guests too, Vic and Bridget Santos. Formal details. What's online. Relationships. Family and friends. Gossip. I want it all. Okay? And the same for Fabien Dubois too, until we catch up with him."

"Consider me briefed," Angie says. "I'll see you at base."

"I'm coming there as soon as I've called Jock," he replies.

"Oh god, good luck with that," Angie sympathizes, before they ring off.

Blackwood takes the dregs of his coffee inside, rinses the empty cup in the sink, then picks up his mobile and takes a few long, slow breaths before dialing.

It's answered immediately. "What's happening then, Blackwood?" Jock demands.

"No news overnight, sir," he replies. "I'm about to head back to our temporary HQ at Kardanup."

"Right, well, I've decided to cancel the press conference in Perth this morning."

Blackwood breathes a sigh of relief.

"We're on the plane right now, landing in about fifteen minutes. We'll do a press conference on-site instead at around ten, so all the family can be there. From what my son tells me, most of the press are down there already anyway."

Blackwood's jaw clenches. "I really think we need to discuss the potential impact of this on the search," he replies briskly. "We want to ensure—"

"Already discussed it last night, didn't we?" Jock interrupts. "I'll see you soon. Oh, and Blackwood? I'd suggest you get rid of that grubby little friend of Kyle's, Vic Santos, as soon as possible. He'll be leaking things to the press before you know it."

Before Blackwood can respond, Jock has ended the call.

Blackwood makes a mental note to look harder at Vic Santos as he quickly dials Bob Drake, hoping his senior officer might try to reason with Jock. But Drake is unmoved.

"I'm sorry, but Jock is someone we need on our side at the moment. If he starts criticizing the job we're doing then we'll get pressure coming at us hard, right from the top. Let him do his press conference. We'll deal with the cranks—I've got extra staff coming in to take calls. I insisted we need people who are trained, and he's accepted that at least."

"Okay, that's something. So I just let him run?"

"Yes. He's going to appeal to any witnesses to come forward. It'll be far quicker than going door to door at this stage. He might even get us a lead. Just look after him, won't you?" Drake insists before ringing off.

Blackwood gathers his things and heads down to reception a few minutes behind schedule. Webster is already there and makes a point of checking his watch, and Blackwood just restrains himself from sniping back at the cheeky bastard. They don't say much on the twenty-minute drive to the small coastal townsite, but as they round one of the quiet countryside lanes, Blackwood sucks in a sharp breath. "Good god, what the hell is all this?"

"I think the word is out that Jock Fisher is on his way," Webster murmurs.

For about five hundred meters, the narrow lane leading to the gate is taken up with news vehicles and cars. There are at least a dozen big vans, a few with people sitting on the steps of open side doors, tinkering with equipment. The slouched, fatigued poses of the waiting journalists are immediately reenergized as the car reaches the throng, and people peer curiously through the tinted windows. Blackwood is known to enough of them that excitement sparks as soon as the first journalist recognizes him, and it runs through the group, igniting them into action one by one until they explode into a barrage of questions aimed at his tightly closed window.

"Detective, what's the latest?"

"What do you think's happened to the kids and their nanny?"

"What are you doing to find them all?"

"How are Kyle and Francesca Fisher holding up?"

There are at least half a dozen police officers ordering the journalists to keep away from the vehicles, their efforts making a marginal difference in the scrum. A few people ignore the instructions entirely, banging on the windows and peering in as they shout more questions. As they approach the sliding gate to the estate, it judders open like there's all the time in the world, while Blackwood and Webster are forced to wait, looking fixedly ahead.

Out of the corner of his eye, Blackwood can see that there are a few members of the public watching on too. When the car begins to move, he turns to stare at them with a frown. Why are they just standing there? Haven't they got anything better to do? Are any of them loitering to check out the chaos they've caused? It wouldn't be the first time a creep came to a crime scene to admire his work.

He nudges Webster. "That group over there." He points to the huddle of people in hoodies and jeans. "They're not press. Get someone to find out who they are."

"Probably just nosy neighbors," Webster says flippantly, staring at them as the car begins to move again. Blackwood doesn't respond, and Webster catches his eye. "On it, boss," he adds, his words clipped and his tone a note lower than a moment ago.

CHAPTER THIRTEEN
ROSE

The hotel is a large resort, much grander than Rose had been expecting, with a sweeping entranceway and long rows of two-story apartment-style rooms set between tall, swaying palm trees. There's a tropical feel to the place, which would have been fun and relaxing under different circumstances, but instead every detail adds to Rose's extreme disorientation. The autumn temperatures in the southwest of Australia are still warm enough to need air-conditioning indoors, and she's already been bitten a couple of times by mosquitoes.

Once she's checked in and alone, Rose paces back and forth inside the characterless room she's been allocated, trying to collect herself and focus on next steps. She has no independent means of transport, no family support, and no guidance as to what to do while she's here. Angie had told her that the team would be dealing with the Fishers' press conference for the next few hours, and they would come back for her later. Rose doesn't want to sleep in case she's needed, but after the snatched rest of the last thirty-six hours she can hardly keep her eyes open.

She checks her phone to find another message from Vee, telling her to take care of herself. She sends an update in reply, texts Charlie with the hotel address, then messages Stella. *I've arrived. I'm in a hotel*

called Seascape between Kardanup and Busselton—I think I'm quite near
the Kardanup estate. Are you anywhere near me? If so, let's talk in person.
I'm happy to pay for your taxi if it helps.

A message alert comes seconds later. *I'm close by. Thanks for the offer*
but I can drive. I'll be there soon.

Rose's heart pounds just reading the words, recalling the word *stalker*,
dreading what Stella might have to say. She tries to reassure herself that
it's too soon to panic. Until she knows what this is about, it's best not
to jump ahead.

While she waits for Stella, she scans Fabien Dubois's social media.
His Facebook is private, but his Instagram isn't. There are plenty of
pictures of him enjoying himself with celebrities at the radio station,
or hanging out at bars with his friends on weekends. He looks like a
handsome, successful guy in his twenties, making the most of city life,
although there are enough photos of the beach to convey how much
he loves the ocean. He has an interesting tattoo climbing up the side of
his neck, visible in a few of the photos: At first Rose thinks it's a constellation of stars, but then she realizes it's the silhouetted outlines of a
flock of birds in flight.

As she scrolls back through his posts, she begins to find a few photos
of him with Lou: Not too many, and nothing particularly romantic, but
they appear together with different groups of friends, at cafés in the day-
time, or on evenings out. There's also a shot of a beach at sunset with
two silhouetted figures kissing. Rose is pretty certain this is Fabien and
Lou, because the same photo is on Lou's feed too.

She's searching for anything that makes her uncomfortable, but
Fabien looks like a thoroughly likable guy. Bit of a poser, maybe, but
who isn't these days.

She's done the easy part first, but now she takes a steadying breath
before clicking on Lou's profile again. Her daughter hasn't posted anything in the last few months, and before that she hadn't been prolific.
Lou's photos are simple shots of daily life: walking with a pram, close-ups
of flowers, wide shots of beaches, the occasional selfie. Lou doesn't do
the standard social media poses; she just smiles for the camera. She

appears happy but pensive; there's something of a lost soul in her eyes. Or is Rose just imagining it? Is she still looking for ways to feel guilty about all the things she hasn't been able to provide for her child? From what she knows of Lou's teenage years, she'd expected to see anger and resentment in her daughter's expression, but something appears to have changed in the girl who had once called Rose a *neglectful bitch* before slamming the phone down. Perhaps she's softened. But then everyone's online profile always sells you some version of a lie. Rose has lost count of the times she'd checked the online activities of women she knew were being abused, only to find photos of them hugging and kissing their abuser, playing happy families for their unsuspecting audience. The terrible irony is that such efforts to cover up their shame and sorrow, often because of the kids, makes it so much harder for people to believe these women when they finally seek help.

"Where are you, Lou?" she whispers to one of the more recent shots of her daughter sitting on a beach, smiling at whoever had been behind the camera as the sun dipped below the horizon.

Rose sits heavily on the bed, leans back, and closes her eyes for a moment. She's beginning to drift off to sleep, the phone still in her hand, when its loud ping wakes her.

I'm downstairs. Which room are you in?

I'll come to reception, she replies, not wanting to be ambushed in her hotel room without checking out Stella first. She gets up, patting her cheeks a few times, and splashes her face with cold water, trying to bring herself round. Then she hurries down to reception, to find the desk staff have disappeared and the place is empty—except for a small, slim girl with curly blond hair, who is waiting in the lobby, hugging herself as though she's freezing, her expression miserable. There are two young children with her: a girl of about seven with shiny long dark hair, waiting anxiously at Stella's side, and a younger, skinny boy in a polo shirt and shorts who is busily investigating the pamphlets advertising local attractions.

"Rose?" Stella says, coming forward. "It's nice to meet you." She lowers her voice. "I had to bring them." She nods at the kids. "I'm sorry, I'm hoping there's a play area in the hotel grounds."

Rose empathizes with the girl's obvious discomfort. "Of course. And who do we have here?" She smiles at the kids, who are now both eyeing her curiously.

"This is Bianca and Luis," Stella says, patting them on their heads in turn as she introduces them.

"Good to meet you both. I think there's a little park area next to the pool. Shall we go and look?"

She leads them through to the back of the resort, and outside into a large garden area with rows of frangipanis, some still bearing flowers. Much to her relief, at the far side of the pool there is a large, timber-based play area. The kids run across as soon as they see it, with Stella calling them back to grab their hats. Rose and Stella watch them for a moment before sitting at an empty picnic table nearby.

Stella stares at Rose. "Wow, you really look like Lou," she says, a clear Irish lilt to her voice.

"Yep." Rose smiles. "Except for the wrinkles." She's trying to soften the atmosphere, but Stella's expression doesn't budge. "It's okay, I promise," she says, hoping to reassure the girl. "Please just tell me what's going on. You'll feel better when you do."

Stella waits a moment, her eyes fixed on Rose, assessing. "Before we chat," she begins, "please, please promise me that you won't tell my bosses I've spoken to you. If I lose my job I'll probably have to leave when my visa runs out, and I love it here."

Rose smiles sympathetically at Stella, hoping it will take the sting out of her words. "It's really hard to make those kinds of assurances if you have information that might find three missing people," she says. "But we can chat through whatever the police need to hear and see how we can minimize any damage. Is that okay?"

Stella nods, one of her thumbs picking and pushing at her chipped nail polish, her eyes darting to the children as they squeal on the slide. "I guess it'll have to be." She doesn't move for a moment, and Rose can see she is wrestling with how much she wants to say. Then she appears to fortify herself, taking a deep breath as she looks up. "I work for some friends of the Fishers', so I get to hang out with Lou quite a lot. The

Fishers and my bosses, Vic and Bridget Santos, often come down here on holiday together. I was meant to be here this week too, but I've had a vomiting bug and stayed home until yesterday." She pauses, takes a long breath. "Thing is, I've been worried about Lou lately. She hasn't seemed as bubbly as when she first started, and I hear things about the Fishers—sometimes through other nannies, and at times because my bosses aren't very discreet. The Fishers go through a lot of nannies. Frannie Fisher is a pain in the arse, she can be really rude and childish, and Kyle Fisher is known for asking his employees to do inappropriate things for a bit of extra money."

Rose feels nauseous. "What kind of things?" she asks, imagining the worst.

Stella picks up on her tone. "Oh no, not that. Well, at least, that's not what I've heard. More like picking up his drugs for him, and taking packages to people. I was concerned for Lou before she even started the job, and I liked her as soon as we met. We hang out together whenever the Santoses and the Fishers meet up, and that's quite often—every couple of weeks at least. And sometimes we arrange to meet and walk the kids to the park. That's where my stalker comment came from. Lou noticed some guy watching her, not long after she first began looking after the kids. She got freaked out because she saw him a few times, and from then on she always asked if we could go together. I even spotted him once—she pointed him out to me. But then, after a few days, he disappeared. When a few more weeks went by she began to relax. She never mentioned him again."

"Do you remember what he looked like?"

"Yeah, tall, skinny, dark curly hair. Quite young. Casual clothes."

"Would you recognize him in a photo?"

Stella pulls a face. "I'm not sure."

"Other than that, was Lou feeling okay about working for the Fishers?"

Stella pauses, and Rose thinks she's hesitating over her answer. Then she realizes another family has approached. They wait until the adults are far enough away before Stella continues. "She seemed to be having a good time at first. She said that Frannie and Kyle were both nice to her, and I know she enjoyed the luxury. You get your own suite of rooms when you work for them—walk-in wardrobe, big bathroom, even a little lounge. But a few weeks ago she went really quiet, and seemed even more troubled. Now I feel terrible, because if I'd been here this might never have happened." Stella pauses, gulps, quickly wipes her eyes. "I can't imagine what's going on, and I'm really scared for them all."

"Do you think she could have run away with the kids?"

Stella considers the question momentarily, before she shakes her head. "I doubt it." She's about to say something more, but appears to think better of it, closing her mouth. A pink flush begins to spread across her cheeks.

"You don't sound sure," Rose persists. "It's okay, you can tell me. Whatever's happened, I'm here to help her, not to judge."

Stella glances nervously toward her two charges, who are still racing around the playground. "She didn't talk about taking them—but she's been getting more and more upset about how the kids were being cared for. She would say things like she wished she could make things different for them. She hated the thought of them growing up with such selfish parents." Stella's flush deepens, and in the silence Rose realizes Lou had obviously told Stella something of her own experiences as a child. Her throat constricts as she wonders what exactly Stella has heard about Rose.

Stella leans forward, her expression earnest now. "I still can't believe she would actually take them, though. She loves those little kids. They're hard work but they're gorgeous. Thinking this stuff is one thing, but she wouldn't do anything to frighten them or put them in danger."

"The police mentioned that she might have been meeting up with her boyfriend in secret on the beach. Do you know anything about that?"

Stella's cheeks go a deeper red and she studies the roughened wood of the picnic bench. "She asked me not to tell anyone, and I didn't see the harm in it." She looks up defiantly. "Lou and Fabien shouldn't have had to meet up in secret. Honestly, Frannie and Kyle are so controlling."

"So, what about if she finally had enough and decided to run away while she had Fabien's help?"

Stella thinks this through. "It's possible, but if that's the case, something would have pushed her to it. But then"—Stella's eyes widen—"things were definitely getting worse."

"What makes you say that?" Rose asks, aware of her police negotiation training kicking in. She wants to draw Stella out by ensuring her tone remains gentle and nonthreatening, keeping her body language open. Nevertheless, she's having to work hard to keep her fears at bay.

Stella rubs nervously at her neck. "Right before they traveled down here from Perth, she said I was right. Kyle had asked her to do something inappropriate and it was making her uneasy. He suspected Frannie of having an affair and wanted Lou to be his spy. Lou said that at first she didn't believe him, but then she realized it might be true. A few days ago, she sent me this. I didn't connect the dots before—but maybe it's relevant . . ."

Stella produces her phone, taps the screen for a moment, and hands it over to Rose. It's a photo of a couple kissing in a garden, the focus slightly blurred as though it's been taken through an upstairs window looking down. The side profiles of the man and woman are easily visible as they gaze into each other's eyes.

Rose frowns at Stella. "Should I know who these people are?"

Stella points to the woman. "That's Frannie Fisher. And the man is my boss, Vic Santos."

CHAPTER FOURTEEN
EBONY

DECEMBER 31, 2019

Ebony wishes she'd had the guts to say no to this hideous party. It's a typical Fisher affair—all show and no substance—but the boys had wanted to come and see their dad, although she suspects they're really here for the food and entertainment. The twenty-odd kids in the pool are raucous, but it's the adults who are insufferable. Every time she wanders through Kyle's waterfront house, she hears people having inane conversations about which celebrities are flying in for the next charity fundraiser, the insane profit margins in the resources and property industries, and the spectacular achievements of their privately educated children.

The house is set back from the Swan River on a hill in Peppermint Grove, with a stunning view across the water toward the city. There's enough space for a tennis court adjacent to the pool at the back of the house, and Kyle has hired two lifeguards so the kids can have a sunset swim while the parents drink. Kyle is entertaining everyone on the large veranda, sitting on a chaise longue in front of an enormous trellis resplendent with cream and pink roses, his arm around his new girlfriend, Frannie. He'd raised his eyebrows at Ebony when he saw her, but hasn't made any attempt to chat. She knows he's only tolerating her and Asher's presence because of the boys, as he's still bitter that she'd instigated their divorce. Kyle likes to pretend he's a modern man, happy to deal with a blended family, but there are enough snide comments and aggravating behaviors when it's just the two of them for Ebony to know full well how much he resents her for taking her life back.

Asher has already disappeared: He'd told her he was going to walk down to the marina by Freshwater Bay to get some fresh air, his code for escaping the pretentiousness. Their new nanny, Marisol, has taken their toddler, Teddy, out for a walk along the river too before dinnertime, along with the other nannies, to avoid the little ones getting injured by the energetic older children who are practicing dive-bombing into the pool. If she plays this right, Ebony might actually have some rare time to herself.

She does a quick scout around to see who's here, and who she wants to avoid. Kyle's siblings are gathered in a corner, deep in conversation with their father. The oldest, Toby, is a head taller than the others, his jaw tight and his expression serious. Ebony has rarely seen him smile and he always walks with a slight stoop, as though there's an unseen heavy load upon his shoulders. He looks around, as though bored, while his younger brother Ethan hammers home a point. Ethan's hands don't stop moving: thrown up in the air, then a finger stabbing toward Toby's chest. Jock is animated too—leaning close to his kids, his hands patting the air as though trying to calm everything down. Ebony's glad she doesn't have to listen to them anymore—there's always some crisis at the helm of the Fisher empire, and the siblings rarely agree on the solution.

Jock's only daughter, Bronte, stands patiently beside them, in a bright-orange caftan, floor length and embroidered with gold. She's sipping wine as she listens, but glances around as though she can sense Ebony's eyes upon her. Ebony gives her a sympathetic smile, and Bronte responds in kind, raising her eyebrows as if to acknowledge "These men never stop talking!" before she turns back to the conversation. Ebony can't imagine what it would have been like to grow up with three condescending brothers and a father like Jock. The Fisher patriarch hadn't been too keen on Ebony either, because she'd never indulged his two-faced spiel. He might pretend to care about his family, but the man is a hawk, constantly looking for the weak spots in people so that he can exploit them.

She checks that her older boys are behaving in the pool, then trails into the lounge area and puts her feet up on the sofa, keeping herself busy answering emails on her phone, wishing the time away. The walls are dotted with professional photos of Kyle and Frannie dancing or hamming it up for the camera. Ebony used to feature in a similar set of prints, but she finds it hard to imagine what she ever saw in Kyle now. In her twenties she'd been seduced by the glamour that his family wealth provided: access to the best tables at private clubs, the grandest box at every gig or event in Perth, the designers begging her to wear their clothes to the next function. Her own family were concerned about her, since she came from a far simpler background: a two-story house on the northern suburbs coastline, modest by Fisher standards but still roomy and grand. Her father had held a senior position at the Roads Authority for over thirty years, and her mother was a teacher. She had two older sisters who had married in their twenties and settled into their quiet lives by the beach near their parents, but young Ebony had wanted more. She enjoyed being seen in high society, appearing in magazines, flying all over the world for modeling gigs and photo shoots, but her life had shifted when she had the boys, because she also wanted to be a hands-on mum, and she'd struggled to leave them to fulfill her husband's demands. Kyle acted like nothing had changed: He wanted her on his arm at every party, and if she wasn't up to it then he went anyway. He was often photographed enjoying drinks with friends and fans, while she gradually faded from the limelight, the modeling work drying up when she couldn't commit to the long hours and travel. She'd contented herself by chasing her boys around in their early years; she told herself it was enough, and for a while it was. But then they got older and went to school, and she'd felt adrift as she reached her thirties, as though she was heading downstream on a raft with no paddle, watching everyone else busy and contented on the riverbanks but with no idea how to get there and join them.

Her sisters had stepped in, and after many long conversations together they'd come up with the answer. Ebony opened her first fashion boutique on a popular shopping strip in Fremantle nine years ago. It was small but incredibly chic—she had years of experience in how to make clothes look amazing on people. She called it Bisoux, a nod to her mother's French background and the French couture she loved— and it was easy to lure in Australia's easygoing customers with the idea of an exotic European brand. She had a second shop in Sydney within two years, a third in Melbourne a year after that, and between the boys and the shops she could have forgotten she had a husband, had he not become keenly interested in her profits and procured some of them for his own investments, which never seemed to go anywhere.

She can't believe that she didn't leave him until the boys were in secondary school. She still asks herself what made her stay, and the answers are always uncomfortable. It had felt too hard to prioritize herself—there were always other people's feelings to consider. The boys liked spending time with their dad—he loved to play footie with them and whisk them away for adventure-sports weekends when he wasn't attending a club opening or party. But he also had a bad temper. If things weren't going his way he could be snappy and aggressive—to the point where she was often uncomfortable and occasionally scared. She knew that to leave him and take his children might well push him permanently into this territory whenever she dealt with him. She hadn't been sure she could cope with that.

But then she'd met Asher, with his aventurine eyes and his steady smile. He was an executive at the Perth Arena, responsible for hosting huge international acts and ensuring every tiny detail was taken care of. He tackled each day with an easygoing charm that made Kyle look like a petulant child. Ebony had been asked to bring a selection of outfits for an international fashion event, and he'd been the one who helped her when a van full of her clothes went missing. His calmness in dealing with the situation had made her think about him day and night. When she realized Kyle was sleeping around, she finally took her wedding ring off. She'd waited a few months and then asked Asher out to dinner. She'd been wined and dined all her life but had never been the one providing the experience, and Asher was man enough to let her take charge. It was clear he enjoyed every second of it. Kyle was too wrapped up in himself and his partying lifestyle to raise much objection to her decision to leave, and so Ebony and Asher were living together before her divorce was finalized. Her boys loved him too—he brought a much-needed steadiness to their lives. When they'd had baby Teddy together, her family felt complete.

At the thought of little Teddy, Ebony decides to check upstairs. The nannies must be back by now since it's almost dark. Sure enough, she finds them in the large playroom on the second floor, a group of five young women taking care of at least a dozen preschoolers. It's pandemonium, and she watches by the doorway for a while before approaching Marisol.

"Let me take Teddy to see his brothers," she says. "You should have a break. There's so much food downstairs. Go and help yourself." The girl looks pale today, she thinks. Not her normal bubbly, pink-cheeked self. "Are you okay?"

"I'm fine." Marisol waves away her concern. "Just a bit tired."

"Teddy is exhausting, that's why," Ebony replies, trying to make Marisol feel better. "I'll meet you here in an hour so you can take him back to our place and put him to bed. Come on, little man," she says, noting the other nannies looking on enviously as she relieves Marisol of her duties. Teddy throws his chubby little arms around Ebony's neck and she revels in his hug, all too aware of how soon this time will be over. It's hard to get any affection out of her two lanky teenagers now.

She follows Marisol downstairs and finds Asher, who takes Teddy into the garden to play soccer with his siblings. She spends a while chatting to some wives of Kyle's business associates, whom she hasn't seen for a few years. When there's a short scream, no one pays much attention because the kids have been yelling all day. But it's followed by more shouting and a bloodcurdling wail from the floors above. The mums with young children rush for the stairs, Ebony among them, racing up to the second-floor nursery.

Once there, Ebony sees the commotion is not inside the nursery room but by the windows. The nannies are looking down to the ground below. The murmurs and shouts are increasing. People are reaching for their phones, taking it in turns to look and then guiding others away.

Ebony edges closer, still unsure what's going on, only aware of the distressing sobs around her. When she peers down, she has to grab at the low wall to keep herself upright. Because Asher is leaning over Marisol, who is sprawled on the ground, staring upward, her eyes open and looking straight at Ebony, as though pleading wordlessly for help.

CHAPTER FIFTEEN
BLACKWOOD

Blackwood is back in the lurid green mansion near the Fishers' place, having another coffee with Angie while they run through the latest intel from the team, when an officer knocks on the door to the small front lounge they've appropriated as their office.

"Jock Fisher has arrived. Caused chaos at the gates just now."

Blackwood looks at Angie, taking a deep breath as he stands. "Right then. Sounds like it's time to join the circus."

Short on time, they find an officer to drive them back to the Fishers' house. When they get there, Kyle is sitting on the front doorstep, his hair unbrushed and his skin sallow, a mug grasped between his hands.

He greets them without enthusiasm.

"How are you holding up, Kyle?" Blackwood asks, his tone gentle and sympathetic.

Kyle looks up as though surprised at the question. "Not great. But thanks for asking."

"I hear your dad's arrived."

"Yup." Kyle's posture stiffens, and Blackwood makes a note of it. "He's inside. Chomping at the bit to get on with the press conference."

"I'd best go and say hello then." Blackwood exchanges a brief glance with Angie.

Kyle follows them inside. "These are my brothers, Toby and Ethan," he says as soon as they reach the kitchen. "And my sister, Bronte."

Blackwood shakes hands with them all, then steps back. It's easy to see the four of them are siblings: They all share the same ice-blue eyes. Toby and Ethan are wearing smart suits and ties, in contrast to their disheveled brother. They both stand to attention with their arms crossed, clearly sizing Blackwood up. Toby is tall and commanding, his face already heavily lined, while Ethan is shorter and chubby, sporting a full beard. Bronte is tall and robust looking; her blond hair, verging on white, is swept up in a French pleat. She wears a bright-pink pant-suit and a lot of makeup, and as she offers her hand, Blackwood notices her immaculate manicure: a swirly pink-and-purple design that appears to be inlaid with tiny gemstones. Her grip is the strongest of the three.

Kyle is the only one who looks stressed, Blackwood realizes. Bronte is calm, and the brothers seem irritated and aloof. He would expect such close family members to be caught up in the high emotion of the situation, but perhaps they're concerned about how much this investigation will mess with the Fisher brand.

Beyond them, the lounge is packed with people. Blackwood searches the crowd, dismayed at the size of the entourage, wondering who the hell all these folk are. Then he hears a familiar voice. Jock Fisher strides toward him, wearing a light suit with a sky-blue shirt open at the collar to reveal deeply tanned turkey-neck jowls. The man's face is an unnatural orange brown, riven with wrinkles, but his eyes are the same blue as his shirt and they regard Blackwood curiously. There's an element of bemusement in Jock's countenance, but perhaps that's because of the concertinaed laughter lines around his eyes.

"Sorry about the crowd," Jock says, gesturing at the others. "I know it might seem a bit much, but I've brought everyone who might be useful. I also stopped at the gates and told the journos I'd go back and speak to them in fifteen minutes, so let's do that first, eh. We'll take the boys and Bronte with us. And Andrew. Andrew!" he calls, and a tall young man with dark hair and ghostly white skin turns and comes quickly to his side. "This is my PA," Jock says. "If you can't find me, Andrew knows everything. I'll introduce you to the rest of them later. Right, I want to get the press over and done with." He turns to Andrew. "Can you drive me and Blackwood up there now? And get someone to bring Bronte and the boys."

"Dad, I don't think—" Kyle interjects.

"Don't worry, I didn't mean you," Jock replies, his eyes not leaving Blackwood. "You should keep a low profile, obviously. The press will have a field day if they see you like this."

"You want me with you?" Blackwood asks, aware of Angie's eyebrows steadily climbing over the course of the conversation.

"Of course, you're leading the investigation, aren't you? Let's go! You wanna bring your sidekick too?" He holds a hand out for Angie to shake.

Blackwood looks apologetically at Angie. "This is Detective Sergeant Angie Lennard. She's my second-in-command and the best we've got. We'll walk up and meet you there."

"Don't be daft. Plenty of room in the Range Rover."

Damn, Blackwood thinks as he follows everyone out. He'd been hoping to speak with Angie first, to figure out what he would say if he had to talk to the press. *Damn. Damn. Damn.* He thinks longingly of his quiet kitchen and Margie's soft smile. He'd love to make a bolt for it, but he's never been one to shirk a duty, even though it's seen him get into hot water at home.

The drive up to the top of the hill is so quick that no one has much time to say anything. They all get out of the car before they reach the closed gates, where there's a huge throng of press waiting. As Jock approaches them they begin to call out, and he gestures with his hands that they need to calm down. When they quieten and the gates have opened, all Jock's children except for Kyle line up on either side of him, and he begins to speak.

"Right then, please give me the courtesy of listening, because I don't plan on repeating myself today."

One segment of the crowd erupts as half a dozen people dressed in jeans and beanies begin to chant. "Hey, Fisher, what goes around comes around! Hey, Fisher, what goes around comes around!"

Blackwood marches over to two of his uniformed officers. "Get those idiots out of here, *now*."

The cameras swing in his direction and then follow the officers as they bundle a few individuals roughly away. Blackwood can make out some of the words amid the cacophony. Phrases like "Get the fuck off me" and "Fuck you, Fisher!"

He turns to Jock, aghast, but Jock's face is impassive as he watches the interruption being dealt with, as though it's an event as benign as waiting for traffic lights to change. Once the protesters are secured inside a police van, the cameras drift back to the family, and Jock shrugs and shakes his head.

"Right, where was I?" he says. "Look, I can't be long. I've got family down here who need support. Now, as you know, my two little grandchildren have gone missing with their nanny, Louise."

Blackwood winces at the mispronunciation of Louisa's name, but lets it fly. He can't imagine what Jock would do if Blackwood interrupted to correct him, but it's best they don't play that out in front of the country's media. Jock continues to talk in a loud, booming voice, as reporters adjust and withdraw their microphones a little.

"We have no idea what's happened so far, but we've got the best team in the country on the job. I'm providing the police with all the assistance I can, and we're determined to bring them home *today*," Jock growls. Blackwood can only watch and admire his commanding presence. He's not the only one by the looks of it: The journalists are hanging on every syllable.

"So I'm asking you to spread the word because someone out there might have seen something or know something that will help us get this sorted quickly. I'm prepared to offer a two-million-dollar reward for any information that leads to their safe return. I hope you all heard that: We've got two million dollars up for grabs here. The police will provide the hotline number. And now I'll let Inspector Blackwood have a word."

Jock immediately walks to the side and stands with his arms crossed in front of him, waiting.

Blackwood is still reeling from the hefty reward being offered, and his unexpected promotion, as he steps forward, the sweat beginning to bead his brow. A throng of microphones are shoved at his face.

"My name is Detective Senior Sergeant Blackwood," he begins. "As you can imagine, this is a very distressing time for the Fisher family, and we're grateful to Jock Fisher for stepping in so quickly to offer his support. I want to assure you all that we're doing everything we can to locate Louisa Thornton, and Honey and Kai Fisher, but we need everyone's help. Please, stay alert, look at the photos of the three of them, and pass on any information you think might be relevant, no matter how small. We have teams waiting for your call."

Angie discreetly steps to his side and presses a piece of paper into his hand. He glances down to see a phone number scrawled on the back of a receipt. This is why he adores working with Angie. He gives the press the number and then finishes with a simple thank-you.

As they walk back to the car, Jock claps Blackwood on the back as though they're old-time chums. The press can only see that stance, but as Jock pulls him in close he says, "Might've been a good idea for you to mention the two mill again, but I'm sure most people will register it the first time they hear it."

"I can't legally talk about rewards without clearance from my superiors," Blackwood replies immediately. "Have you spoken to Bob Drake about this?"

Jock's expression tightens. Blackwood takes that as a no, but realizes he's getting the man offside when he's had distinct orders from Drake to appease Jock.

"But we really appreciate the reward; it could make a big difference," he blusters, even though inside he's cringing at the thought of all the extra crank callers Jock has just galvanized into action, and all the fruitless leads they'll be following while people rub their hands expectantly in case their luck comes in. Jock obviously believes he knows a lot more than he actually does about how to run a police investigation.

"Can I ask you about the people who began chanting at the beginning? Do you know who they are?"

Jock laughs. "They're my regular shit stirrers. Greenies and hippies mostly. Got their knickers in a twist about some of our development projects, refuse to understand that we follow all the protocols when we chase new sites for housing or resources. They always want to protect some rare little warbler finch or a rock with enduring historical significance. They come with the territory unfortunately, turn up everywhere. I once sent them a load of pizza when they were sitting outside one of our product launches—it was hilarious watching them wrestle with the moral struggle of whether or not to eat it. Course, they all did in the end."

"But you don't think they're involved in this?"

Jock pauses, staring at Blackwood, obviously assessing the question. "They've been around a long time," he says eventually. "I'm not sure why they'd do something like this now. And why Kyle's kids? He's the least involved in the family business. I guess we can't rule it out, but they'd be crazy to try it. They rely on supporters for their cause, and who's going to have sympathy with them after they've kidnapped a young woman and two young kids? No. I can give you a list of our adversaries, but I'm afraid it's quite extensive. You don't get to the top of your field without pissing a few people off."

"It would still be good to look through that list," Blackwood says evenly.

"I'll get my team on it," Fisher replies magnanimously.

They head back to the Fisher residence, where they find most of the family gathered on the large sofas, watching the TV. Frannie and Bridget are noticeably absent. "That was good, thanks, Dad," Kyle says, and Jock nods in reply, but Blackwood is aware of the tension between father and son as they meet one another's gaze. He tries to read it, but the moment slips away as other people begin to discuss the reward, and what to do next. Blackwood takes the chance to excuse himself, and heads back outside with Angie.

He texts Drake—*Were you aware of the reward before Jock announced it to everyone?*—and then he and Angie head down the hill in silence. He doesn't need to explain anything; he knows Angie will understand his discomfort.

Halfway down, she says, "Well, there's nothing quite like the helping hand of the rich and powerful," in such a way that Blackwood briefly cracks a smile.

His phone pings. Drake's answer is succinct. *No.*

Blackwood can picture the grimace on his superior's face. Neither of them like surprises, or the feeling of losing control, but it appears that Jock Fisher is going to be a handful.

CHAPTER SIXTEEN
ROSE

Rose is curled up on the white cotton sheets in her hotel room. She's still digesting Stella's visit, along with the headlines that Jock Fisher has offered a $2 million reward for information, when she receives a text from Angie.

Press conf over. Coming back for you now.

Rose has watched the press conference twice already, but replays it a few more times while she waits. Her spirits sag at the disruption from a small group of protesters. It doesn't bode well if the Fisher family have enemies prepared to turn up and cause a ruckus even at this moment. Jock's no-nonsense speech is followed by DSS Blackwood looking distinctly uneasy as he addresses the press. It's discomfiting to think that these are the people she'll need to work with to bring her daughter home.

She wonders how the Fishers' riches will affect the investigation, because the $2 million reward, offered by Jock as though it were petty cash, isn't reassuring her as much as it should. So many people can only see reward money as a lure, not realizing that it can also be a disastrous distraction. Rewards attract the wrong kind of people, and the media and the public can be hypnotized by money, swiftly encouraged to look in the wrong direction.

She fights off her anxiety and lets the adrenaline take hold instead, along with a surge of determination. All of her training, all of her experiences up to this moment, will be channeled into resolving this situation. The outcome of the next few days and weeks will determine the future course of Rose's life, as well as Lou's. Which means that, for now, she won't be trusting anyone fully, except herself.

She's sitting on the bed ready to go when the call comes from reception. She heads down to meet Angie, who leads her straight to another unmarked vehicle, with a uniformed driver waiting inside. This time Angie slides into the back alongside Rose.

"I already had a visit from Stella," Rose says as soon as the car is moving. "She's the nanny for Vic and Bridget Santos—I gather they've been staying with the Fishers."

"Jeez, you're a fast worker," Angie says, in a way that makes Rose think she doesn't entirely approve. "I hope you encouraged her to talk to us."

"Of course, but she's scared of her bosses. Do you know much about the Santoses?"

Angie gives Rose a strange look. "We're working on it," she replies. "They were staying with Kyle and Frannie, but they've moved their family somewhere else in town now the entire Fisher clan are here—they wanted to give everyone a bit more space. What did Stella tell you?"

"Lou thought she was being followed in the park a few months ago." As Rose talks, she counts the facts on her fingers. "The Fishers are mean and controlling. And Vic Santos and Frannie Fisher are having an affair. Stella is terrified of losing her job for telling us this, so please protect her as much as you can."

Angie lets out a long sigh and gazes out of the passenger window for a second. "Looks like we have some more interviews to do today. It's going to be chaos from here on, especially with two million bucks in the mix. I can't promise to protect Stella, but I'll do my best to help her out." She phones ahead to fill Blackwood in on everything Rose has discovered, while Rose sits there listening, not able to glean much from the one-sided conversation.

WHEN SHE WAS GONE   119

They reach Kardanup estate within twenty minutes, causing a rush of interest as the journalists struggle to see who's inside the car. Once they're through the gates, the quiet roads of the private estate are a relief. They drive for another minute before pulling up beside a house painted a lurid shade of lime green, with three stories and a triple garage. Rose gets out of the car and Angie comes to stand beside her. "This is our temporary operations HQ," she says. "And I have to say it's the fanciest one I've ever worked in. The Fishers' house is a bit further up the road, and even bigger than this one. Also, the family have asked to meet you," she adds, with such a distinct look of sympathy that Rose feels instantly uneasy, "but let's get you up to speed first. Come inside, and I'll introduce you to DSS Blackwood, the detective in charge."

They walk through an entranceway into the giant open-plan living area, where at least a dozen officers are busy on laptops or around maps laid out on makeshift desks. A few more are gathered in the kitchen, drinking from large disposable cups. Many of them take a moment to eye Rose with interest as Angie leads the way, tapping a bulky man in a tight-fitting suit on the arm. "Is Blackwood in the front room?"

"Yep."

Angie shows Rose into another hallway and stops at a glass-paneled door, knocking before opening it.

"I have Rose Campbell with me," she says as she enters.

A tall man with a receding hairline swings round, his mobile phone held to his ear, his other hand fiddling with the buttons on his dark suit jacket. "Got to go," he says quickly, and pushes the phone back into his pocket.

He holds out a hand. "Rose. It's good to finally meet you. How are you feeling after the flight?"

Rose takes stock of the man in front of her. He has an imposing presence but there's nothing overtly condescending or dismissive about him, which is a relief. She's all too familiar with those undesirable hallmarks in some of the older men on the force back home.

She relaxes as she takes his hand and they shake. "I'm a bit woolly headed from the flight, but okay."

"All right then," he says. "Please, take a seat." He gestures to an arm-chair. "This is much more glamorous than the usual surroundings we work in, but we're grateful to the owners as it means we can stay on-site for the time being." He sits down opposite her on a dining room chair that's obviously been brought in. "Angie has filled me in on your background, and since time is of the essence, I hope you don't mind if we jump straight in with a few questions."

"Not at all," Rose replies, sitting forward. "I've come to assist how-ever I can."

"Okay, well, we've spoken to Henry a couple of times about Louisa, and he's enlightened us a bit. But what can *you* tell us about your daugh-ter that might help here?"

Rose opens her mouth. Closes it again. Stares at them. She should have known they would ask this, but she isn't prepared for the flood of pain as she struggles to come up with any useful information. She bites her lip, determined to push away the rising emotion, reminding herself she's not here to make friends.

"I'm sure you've been informed that Louisa and I have been estranged for most of her life. Henry will be able to fill you in much more than I can. I'm not sure what else you're hoping I'll tell you."

In the effort to stay composed, her words come out curt and abrupt, far more so than she intended. Angie looks startled, and Blackwood shifts in his seat.

"My apologies," he says, his tone more clipped than before. "Why don't we start again. Would you like anything to drink?"

"No, thank you. But I'd like your assurances that you'll look into the stalker that Stella mentioned—as well as the possible consequences of Vic Santos and Frannie Fisher's affair. Because from what I've heard, it's very unlikely that Lou and Fabien have simply run away, and I don't think examining my daughter's background is going to give you any kind of a breakthrough."

"Rest assured we are covering *all* angles on this," Blackwood says, his expression darkening.

"And I'd really like to see the beach where Lou and the kids were last seen," Rose persists, ignoring the thunderous looks on the police officers' faces.

Blackwood stands and buttons up his suit jacket. "That we can do."

Rose doesn't miss the tightening of his jaw, or the eyebrow raise he directs toward Angie before he leads them out. *Good*, she thinks. The sooner they know she isn't a pushover here to do their bidding, the better. She's happy to stir up as much trouble as she needs to if it gets Lou back fast.

CHAPTER SEVENTEEN
BLACKWOOD

As Blackwood leads Rose and Angie onto the beach, he's struggling to regain his composure. He'd expected an emotionally wrecked mother, not an acerbic, composed woman who appears to mistrust him. Rose is acting more like a senior colleague in competition for his job than the mother of a missing girl. Perhaps that's what long-term estrangement does, but if so it's jarring. Could Rose's streak of steel have been passed on to the daughter? He's stared at the girl's photo many times over the last forty-eight hours, and the two women are undeniably similar. Is there a crucial element of empathy missing in their genes, something that might make a young woman think it's okay to abscond with two children? He knows it's too hasty a judgment, but the lack of a substantial lead is beginning to get to him. He wants to crack the case, not get immersed in managing a cast of difficult people. He needs a breakthrough today.

Or perhaps he doesn't. Perhaps he should hand this case to Angie and Webster and go back to his wife. But he knows he won't. Once he's called in to an investigation, it's a matter of principle to see it through. He's here for Louisa and the kids, and it's for them he won't quit. Margie told him once, a long time ago, that the fact he cares so much is what makes him a damn good detective. He wonders if she still feels the same way, and wishes he could have got hold of her earlier, to apologize directly for being jealous and possessive.

"The beach is much smaller than I thought it would be," Rose says, as they stand at the end of the path that leads onto the sand. Blackwood watches her taking everything in: the landscape, the police tape, the different exit and entry points, the height of the rocks. Decides he'll hang back and let her take the lead in the conversation.

"You didn't find any good evidence here?" she asks them.

"Only Honey's teddy and a few drops of blood on the rocks."

"When do you get the lab samples back?"

"We're expecting them any minute," he says, once again caught off guard by Rose's directness. Angie catches his eye and raises her eyebrows in bemusement. Dealing with Rose is as disconcerting as trying to keep a handle on Jock Fisher, but at least there's no sense of power play behind her words. Blackwood suspects she just wants to cut the crap and get to the facts. Nevertheless, he's glad they're away from the situation room so she can't start quizzing everyone and snooping around.

Rose folds her arms. "What are your theories? Do you think she took the kids for some reason? Or are you leaning more toward an abduction or foul play?"

Blackwood looks over her head at Angie, his eyes widening briefly. "They are both possibilities," he admits. "We've got so little to go on in terms of evidence or witnesses." He hesitates, then adds, "As you know, it appears that Louisa's boyfriend Fabien Dubois is missing as well, so we have two distinct scenarios. Either Fabien and Lou have taken the kids and gone somewhere, or all four of them have been taken against their will in broad daylight with no one noticing. I'm struggling with the fact that the first scenario makes much more sense, but they have no obvious motivation. The second scenario is so audacious it's almost unbelievable."

Rose stares toward the water as she contemplates his words. "If it's the latter, you'd have to be pretty determined, desperate, or evil to attempt something like this, don't you think? There must be a compelling reason behind it." There's a protracted silence, then she asks, "Can I walk around on the beach?"

"As long as you stay away from the cordons," Blackwood replies.

Rose immediately marches across the sand to the waterline. "She's quite something, isn't she," Angie murmurs, moving closer to him.

"Yep, she really is."

"She's pressing my buttons a bit, but I think I like her. You?"

"Haven't decided yet."

Angie laughs. "You just don't appreciate her getting the better of you." She elbows him gently in jest. "Go on, admit it."

He cracks a smile. "You're determined to make me out as a sexist old bigot, Angie."

She laughs, but doesn't push it further. His mind is working hard as Rose scans the shoreline and turns toward the rocks. He glances back at the steep hill behind them. Unfortunately, the beach really is private and well hidden from the houses on the estate. Only the top floors and portions of the roofs are visible. He turns to inspect the small groin that stretches out into the ocean, and the thick bushland at either end of the small strip of sand. "We should find out if there's any kind of surveillance through there. Sometimes the environment agencies have wildlife cameras. You never know, we might get lucky."

"Good idea," Angie agrees. After a moment, she follows Rose, but Blackwood stays back. He wants a quiet moment alone to look around, to consider if there's anything he's missed.

As he's waiting for them to return, his phone rings. It's Webster, and Blackwood turns his back to the beach as he picks up the call.

"Blood lifted from the rocks and the boat isn't a match for Louisa or the kids," the sergeant says without preamble.

"Righto," Blackwood says, keeping his voice neutral. It's a welcome development, but he wants to keep the information to himself for a moment, while he considers what it means.

However, when he turns around, he sees Rose hurrying over, with Angie trying to keep up. "Was that the blood results?" she demands.

For a moment he just stares at her, while Angie looks down at her shoes.

She's the mother, he reminds himself. *She has a right to know.* Even if he wishes he had time to get his head around it first. "It wasn't a match for Louisa," he reveals reluctantly.

A look of pure relief washes across Rose's face. It's gone in a flash, but it's the first time he's witnessed the extent of her fear.

"So," he continues, "we can't confirm whether she was in the boat. We're waiting for the other results to come back too—we've already tested the Fishers, but Fabien's will take a bit longer as we're having to liaise with police in France. We've got fibers and prints as well—it just takes a little time, as you would know. We're checking the local hospitals to see if someone came in with an injury after a boating accident, but there's nothing so far."

Rose frowns. "Have you located Louisa's passport?"

Unsure, Blackwood turns to Angie, who says, "No. We've checked here, and officers in Perth have searched the Fishers' home. There's nothing."

Rose thinks for a moment. "Have you asked Charlie about it? She stayed with him for a while. Perhaps she left some of her stuff there."

"No, I don't think we did," Angie says.

"I'll give him a call."

"I'd rather you didn't. We can take care of it," Angie insists, through slightly gritted teeth.

"It's okay—I need to talk to him anyway."

Blackwood watches as Angie lays a gentle but firm hand on Rose's arm. "Let us do our job, okay?"

Rose turns away for a moment, obviously calming herself down.

Blackwood rubs the back of his neck, where an alarming throb is beginning to hammer at the base of his skull. He walks forward as though surveying the beach, leaning close to Angie so only she can hear him. "We need to go talk to the Fishers," he murmurs as quietly as he can. "Help me get her out of here."

Angie doesn't blink but steps closer to Rose. "I'll get an officer to take you back to the hotel."

Rose looks surprised.

"We need to talk to the Fishers again, and then we can give you a proper update," Blackwood adds.

Rose nods. "Angie said they'd like to meet me. I'd like to meet them too."

The insinuation is clear: She should go with them. Blackwood does his best to hide his grimace. He can think of nothing worse than allowing Jock and Rose to be in the same room before he absolutely has to. From what he's seen so far, Rose probably assumes she can sit in on interviews and interrogate people. "We'll let you know when the time is right," he says, indicating that they should start moving. "There's a lot going on for them, as you'd imagine—and they might be hostile toward you if they think Louisa has taken the children."

Rose doesn't reply, but turns to survey the beach again for a moment. "Thanks for showing me this place. It's difficult to imagine what might have happened." She turns to follow Blackwood and Angie, glancing up at the rocky hillside. "I can see it's pretty private, but you're sure that no one saw anything?"

"Everyone in the community has been interviewed," Angie calls over her shoulder as she leads the way. "Some more than once. I can promise you that we're on top of this."

Rose smiles politely, but Blackwood isn't sure if she believes them. They all take the short walk uphill from the beach, with Blackwood aware he's breathing a bit harder than the others. As they reach the row of squad cars outside their temporary HQ, Rose turns back to them. "I assure you I'm not trying to push the investigation in any particular direction, because I understand that Louisa's motives have to be considered. I also realize, from what I've learned so far, that the Fishers are a powerful local family. But I hope you'll take me seriously, because after the photo I saw earlier it looks like that family also have things to hide. From what Stella told me, the nannies are not always treated very well, and there's been some inappropriate behavior from Kyle in the past."

Blackwood is caught entirely on the back foot again. "I . . . I'll always appreciate any information you provide, Mrs. Thornton. We're intending to debrief Stella ourselves, and we'll make sure all those questions are asked."

"Thank you. And it's Dr. Campbell."

"Sorry, yes, of course, Dr. Campbell." He hopes his grimace isn't obvious. "As I say," he continues, straightening, "the entire team are busy assessing all the angles."

An officer shows Rose into a car, and Blackwood and Angie watch the vehicle drive away.

"Jesus Christ." Blackwood blows out a long breath. "She's almost as tricky as Jock Fisher."

"Looks like she'll keep us on our toes," Angie agrees.

Blackwood groans. "It might be better to keep her at arm's length as much as possible. We haven't got time to take care of all these relatives' demands: We need to plan the next few hours, fast." They make their way hastily through the green house, heading toward the private front room. Once the door is shut, he continues. "Tell me what else has been going on. Can you sum up the media stuff for me so I don't waste time scrolling? What's in there so far?"

"Well, obviously there's the shock that the kids and Lou are missing, and the usual morbid fascination about the circumstances," Angie replies. "Then there's the extra layer of it being Jock Fisher's grandchildren. Despite all Kyle and Francesca's PR appearances it seems that most of the articles are more interested in Jock. Everyone loves watching rich people go through a crisis, don't they? Social media's a bit more interesting: The news outlets haven't really picked up on it yet, but there's some talk about how wild Louisa was in the past, between people who knew her in her schooldays. It's like they see this as a natural evolution of 'the Lou show.'"

"Show me those," Blackwood insists.

Angie scrolls through her phone, then passes it over. "I screenshotted everything I saw, so just swipe through."

Most of the saved shots are from Instagram. A post with a screengrab of a headline has the caption, "OMG I know this girl." And a number of people are tagged. There's a conversation in the comments:

Why doesn't this even surprise me?

Looks like Lou has gone next level.

No way!!! I guess if this was going to happen to anyone, it was gonna be Lou.

They don't think Lou's taken these kids, do they? Hope she's not got herself lost in the bush.

Doesn't say, does it. I know Lou was feral at times but she was hardly a kid-snatcher.

She was a complete headcase, is all I remember. Surprised she never got expelled, I can't believe how much she got away with.

Can you tell us more? I didn't go to school with her.

I only remember a few things: pranks on teachers, disrupting class, running away, and always had to give her opinion on every topic in the universe. Can't imagine her working as a nanny.

Are you kidding? She loved kids. She had umpteen babysitting jobs. Kids loved her too, she was so much fun.

Let's hope she's looking after these two kiddos, wherever they are.

Blackwood has seen enough, and passes the phone back.

Angie takes it. "The girl who posted that normally gets about five likes on each of her posts and she's got over a thousand on this one," she says. "So it might not have gone mainstream yet, but people are noticing. Although there's nothing about Fabien, so that's something. But I don't suppose it'll be long before our shock-jock buddy puts his own exclusive out there."

As she finishes speaking there's a knock on the door. It opens and Webster peers in, his face shiny and mottled.

"We're getting tons of calls after Jock's press conference," he says. "And I have a few tidbits here you should know about. We've had two or three calls from disgruntled former nannies, and Robbie Reynolds wants to speak to you as well. Also, one of the officers spoke to a local who walks his dog on the beach—he claims he saw Lou and Fabien together there this week."

"All right, thanks," Blackwood says to Webster, in a tone that makes it clear he's dismissed.

"Do you want me to run any of those leads for you?" Webster persists.

"Angie and I will discuss them and then I'll let you know," Blackwood replies.

Webster disappears so rapidly that the door slams behind him.

"It's gonna get out of control fast," Blackwood tells Angie. "So, let's figure out our priorities."

"Vic and Frannie and this stalker question," Angie says immediately. "Because we can't do much more on the Fabien–Louisa abduction angle at present, and we already have everyone out looking for them."

"What's your hunch? You think Kyle knows about Frannie's affair? How could that lead to this scenario?"

Angie shrugs. "I dunno. Why would the consequences fall on Louisa and the kids? Surely it's more likely Frannie would be the one missing—buried in a shallow grave somewhere?" She pauses, thinking. "How about I talk to Vic and Bridget, and see if I can locate Stella too and debrief her properly? I'll make it subtle, like I'm interviewing everyone."

"Good. But get Vic to the nearest police station ASAP. I want to talk to him while he's well out of his comfort zone." Blackwood purses his lips. "If we don't get a solid lead soon, I hardly dare think about the media intensity coming our way." He rubs the back of his neck and closes his eyes for a moment, trying to gather strength.

"We just gotta keep breathing," Angie says, "and working hard. You never know, you keep up this amount of media attention and you might be on *I'm a Celebrity* next year."

"Fuck off, Angie," he replies with a smile.

CHAPTER EIGHTEEN
ROSE

Once back at the hotel, Rose mentally replays her visit to Kardanup. It was clear the detectives had wanted to get rid of her, and she understands things from their perspective, but it's hard to feel shut out, and frustrating when she knows she can help.

She messages Charlie to see how the search is going, taking the opportunity to ask about Louisa's passport.

Nothing to report yet, he replies. *And I haven't seen the passport. But she did leave some things with me. I can check when I go home.*

Rose is struck by the sudden impulse to be with someone else who knows Louisa, rather than stuck on her own in this featureless room with its expensive Wi-Fi service. *Can I take you up on the offer to stay?* she writes back. *Hanging around the hotel is driving me mad already.* She hesitates for a few seconds, then presses send.

His reply comes back almost immediately. *No problem. I can be there by four thirty, and we'll drive straight home and check out Lou's stuff.*

Rose messages Angie to let her know that she'll be staying with Charlie, and contacts Veronica, filling her in and asking for the latest update on Bonnie. Then she sits down on the bed, going over her conversation with Stella again. She hadn't realized how much these rich, entitled families sought to control every aspect of their nannies' lives, but it's clear the girls are regularly taken advantage of and disturbingly dependent on their employers, especially since they're all trying to stay in work for long enough to get a permanent visa. It makes her uneasy about meeting the Fishers, not to mention that she'll have to interact with Frannie, the traumatized mother of two missing kids, while also knowing the woman has been having an affair.

She can feel herself getting drowsy, so she sets her mobile's alarm for two hours' time, falling asleep almost instantly. She wakes to the insistent trill of the phone, and sits up to check her messages, praying for good news, but there's nothing. Despondent, her head full of fuzz, she gets up and stretches out the stiffness in her back. She hunts down the coffee pods and a mug, then boils the kettle with water out of the bathroom sink. She puts it all together to find it tastes revolting, and decides she'll have to find something drinkable elsewhere.

Charlie is due to collect her in less than an hour. She has a quick shower, changes her clothes, and is packed in seconds. Downstairs, she grabs a pastry from the café and sits down with her second attempt at coffee.

She's only been seated a few moments when a man she doesn't recognize strolls over. "Excuse me, are you Rose Campbell?"

"Yes," she answers hesitantly.

"Great," the man says, taking a seat opposite her. "My name's Rick Malone; I'm an author and journalist. I work for a local newspaper here, *The West*. I'm very sorry about your daughter."

Rose's mouth drops open as she stares at him. How does he have the nerve to approach her so boldly?

He waits for her to speak, smiling pleasantly and watching her mouth open and close. She suspects it's a game; he's hoping to get a reaction. She won't be giving him one.

"Thank you," she says. "Right now I'm waiting for a friend, so I'd appreciate some space."

"I understand," he replies, making no effort to move. "But I'd like to talk to you more about your daughter and the Fishers."

Rose clenches her fists beneath the table, making an effort to remain calm. "This isn't the time. Please, leave me alone."

"Wait a second. I—"

"Is this man bothering you?"

The new voice is deep and deadly serious. Rose sees Charlie hurrying across the room to stand beside her, glaring at Malone. He turns to Rose. "Why don't you grab your food and bag, and you can eat in the car. I'll get you another coffee on the road."

Rose gets up and reaches for her belongings.

"No, wait." Malone jumps up. "There are a few things you need to know."

"Mate, this is really inappropriate." Charlie steps forward to stand between the man and Rose.

The journalist closes his eyes and shakes his head, obviously irritated. "Can you just assume for one second that I'm on your side, *mate*." He grabs a napkin from the table as he speaks, and produces a pen from his inside pocket. "I wrote a book on the Fisher family," he tells them as he begins to scribble on the napkin. "Spent years researching it. You should be aware that they're very good at cover-ups and manipulating the narrative of whoever gets in their way. Jock protects his kids at all costs, so you be careful, okay?"

Rose stills, trying to absorb what the man is saying.

Charlie senses her indecision and shakes his head. "It's not a good idea to talk to journalists right now, Rose." He folds his arms and glowers at Malone.

Although Charlie's words remind Rose of the promise she'd made to Angie a few short hours ago, she hesitates, desperate for any information that might help. Malone leans past Charlie and offers her the napkin. "My number—if you want to talk," he says. "I'd be happy to tell you more about the Fishers. There's a lot you should know."

Rose takes the napkin and stares at it, trying to process what she's just heard. When she looks up again, Malone is already walking away.

"Let's go," Charlie says urgently. They leave the café, and Rose begins heading for the front doors beyond reception, but Charlie gestures toward another exit. "I've seen a few more of those vultures out there," he tells her. "So I parked in the staff car park. Come on, before that arsehole decides to follow us. I'm glad you're staying with me if they're going to pester you like that."

Rose follows silently. She doesn't want to disagree with Charlie, and set them off on the wrong footing, but Malone's words are replaying on a loop in her mind. She knows from experience that the wealthy often escape police interrogation. What if the police aren't looking at the Fishers hard enough?

She pushes the napkin deep into her jacket pocket. She needs to find out more, and fast; she'll have to go hard in pursuit of whatever angles are being overlooked.

They find Charlie's car, an old Land Rover, and both of them are quiet as they leave the car park, turning onto the main road. Rose is lost for words at the surrealness of the moment, and Charlie doesn't appear to know what to say either. She remembers that about him: his long silences, along with the feeling he was always assessing the situation, and seeing too many things for exactly what they were, however hard she tried to hide them.

"Your timing back there could not have been better," she says eventually.

"Yeah. I don't know how people like that live with themselves. We should tell the police about him—and what he said."

Rose grimaces. "I know the police are focused on finding Fabien, but I've been here for less than a day and I've already had two people approach me stealthily about the Fishers. The detectives look guarded whenever their names come up, and they don't want me to meet the family yet. Is something else at play here? How worried should we be?"

Charlie takes a moment before he answers. "The Fishers feel a bit like the West Aussie mafia to me," he says. "Fingers in every pie in the state. Lots of nepotism. Rumors abounding, but nothing ever able to be proved. And friends in high places, including the police."

"So you don't think the investigating officers will look at them properly?"

"I don't know. But I can tell you I had a migraine the day Lou went to work for them. I didn't ever imagine her leaving them with glowing references; I thought I'd be picking up the pieces at some stage. They're notoriously hard to work for—it was like delivering a lamb to the lion's den. But I kept telling myself she'd already survived Robbie Reynolds, and I wondered if I was being too much of an overprotective uncle. So I decided I needed to let her make her own choices. And now, here we are."

Rose's fingers brush against the folded-up napkin in her pocket. She's aching to call Malone immediately, even though she knows it would be playing with fire and will put the police completely offside. She needs to keep working through all the options. "I realize we've spoken about this already, but do you think there's any possibility that Lou ran away with those kids?"

"I really doubt it," Charlie replies. "And I guarantee she wouldn't ever do anything to hurt them. The only reason she'd run would be to try to protect them from something."

"I want to trust that the police will work all the angles," Rose says, watching the scenery intently, seeing nothing except thickets of trees, empty fields, and dense bushland, "but I'm finding it hard, as I know how much pressure and influence people like the Fishers have. And I've got to be careful how much I make a nuisance of myself. I'm sure DSS Blackwood was glad to see the back of me this morning. On these kinds of investigations, you get harangued from all sides, and I realize the pressure is immense, but I haven't got time to feel sorry for him. These scenarios come with a ticking clock. The more time we lose, the less likely we are to find them alive."

"Shit, Rose, I can't even . . ." Charlie stops, but Rose can see he's agitated.

"I'm sorry," she says quickly. "I know that sounds cold. It's the legacy of my years on the force: problems first, emotions later. I've had to be this way, otherwise I'm no good to the people who need me."

"You don't work for the police anymore, is that right?"

"No, I don't, although I went back for a long time after Tristan died." Subconsciously, Rose touches the scar on her cheek, not realizing until she catches Charlie watching her with concern. She lets her hand drop. "I did some great things—trained in America, then worked with a specialist hostage team for a while. But we often came across domestic violence victims in horrendous circumstances, who had been abused for years. After a decade of picking up the pieces, I went back to uni, to study criminal psychology and see if I could make a difference in another way. I wanted to study how we might intervene earlier, before these situations become so dangerous. I got my doctorate, wrote my book, and I've been working as a private consultant ever since. I lecture and advise on policy, but I'm also on the board of directors at Safehaven, a network of women's refuges, and I volunteer there too."

"Wow—I had no idea." Charlie sounds impressed.

"I just hope some of my skills can help us out now," Rose says. "Have you got good Wi-Fi at home?"

"Good enough, why?"

"Once we've found Lou's things, we need to do some digging of our own."

They lapse into silence again. Charlie turns the radio on low, while Rose gets lost in her thoughts, watching the endless green-and-brown vista of bush and spindly gum trees. Now and again they pass places where the tree trunks are black and the leaves are a vibrant orange. This must be from bushfires, she realizes, fascinated at the patchy verdant shoots of life along some of the branches of trees that appear dead at first glance.

A few songs go by before the news is announced, and neither of them are quick enough to turn it off before the presenter begins reading the headlines. "*Jock Fisher's grandchildren are still missing with their nanny after vanishing from a private beach estate in Kardanup.*"

"Sorry," Charlie says, quickly reaching to change the station, but Rose puts a hand on his.

"Don't," she tells him. "It's okay."

"*The search for Honey and Kai Fisher and their nanny, Louisa Thornton, has entered its third day. There appear to be no new developments, despite Jock Fisher offering a* two-million-dollar *reward for information. Members of the public have flooded the area today, intent on helping with the search and possibly claiming the reward.*"

The third day already, Rose thinks desperately. Time is pressing in on all sides. Charlie has gone quiet too, and she's not sure how to break the silence again.

"Are you driving miles out of your way?" she asks eventually. "I don't even know where you live."

"It's about half an hour from where they went missing. A little spot called Karoa, not even a town really, just a collection of houses with a lot of bushland surrounding us. It's just north of Margaret River, which is a famous wine region here."

"And you're doing search and rescue full time?"

"I also do joyrides for tourists, taking off from the local helicopter strip. I job share with a friend, Tony—he's been out looking for Lou too."

"It sounds like a great way to earn a living."

"I love it," Charlie agrees. "I've been flying since my army days. Pri's mum stays with us a few nights a week, helping me out with Trixie. Her name is Nin." He smiles. "That woman gives me so much shit about literally everything I do. Constant nag, but she's been brilliant. She's driven down today, and she'll take Trix back to her place for a few nights while all this is going on."

"So Trixie's your daughter? Do you have any other kids?"

"No," he says, taking a sharp bend a bit too fast. "Just Trix. And she's not biologically mine; she and Pri came as a package deal."

Rose nods, sensing something strange and guarded in his tone. "Well, it will be nice to meet them both while I'm here," she says, hoping to get him to relax a bit more.

Charlie looks at her sharply and the car veers toward the curb before he rights it. "I think you might be a bit behind the times. Pri died four years ago."

Rose's entire body goes cold. "Oh god, Charlie, I'm so sorry." She looks across at him and sees a muscle twitching in his jaw. His eyes stay fixed on the road. She turns to stare out of the window, dismayed at the casual error, and spends the next lengthy period of awkward silence cursing Henry for not thinking to pass this information on.

CHAPTER NINETEEN
BLACKWOOD

"Thanks for your patience, Vic," Blackwood says as he enters the small interview room at the Dunsborough police station. As he sits down, with Angie beside him, he registers Vic's lackluster appearance. The man looks like he wants to throw up, and a few strands have come away from his slicked-back hair to persistently taunt his left eye.

Angie explains that they'll be recording the session, and Vic shrugs.

"I'm not sure what you think I might know," he says. "But I can tell you I don't have the first clue about how Lou and the kids went missing."

Blackwood doesn't immediately respond, happy to let the man sweat. Perhaps Vic doesn't see the fact he's been shagging Frannie as significant. Well, they're about to find out.

"Some evidence has come to light that you've been having an affair with Frannie Fisher. We'd like to talk to you more about that."

Vic sits back heavily in his chair, obviously shell shocked. "What evidence?"

"We've seen a photograph of the two of you," Blackwood tells him, deliberately leaving Stella out of it. No need to get the girl in trouble unless he has to.

"Can I see it?"

Blackwood produces the image on his phone and moves it around so Vic can look. Vic sends his gaze to the ceiling and lets out a long, slow breath, closing his eyes for a moment, then turns his attention back to Blackwood and Angie, who both watch him, waiting.

"It's not entirely what it looks like," he says. "There's a private agreement between the four of us. Sometimes, in the past, we've swapped partners while we've been down here. It's no one else's business; it's just a way to spice things up a bit."

"Is everyone happy about that arrangement?" Angie asks.

"Of course." Vic looks disgusted. "No one is forced into it."

"Not exactly what I meant," Angie persists. "But you're sure your wife loves having sex with Kyle, while knowing you and Frannie are getting it on?"

Vic has the grace to look shamefaced. "We don't do it as much as we used to," he replies. "Everyone has to be in the mood, and there's been a lot of tension lately between Frannie and Kyle. It hasn't felt like a good idea to add to that. But I guess Frannie and I have grown closer because of the previous arrangement, and she's leaned on me lately, while she's been having trouble with Kyle."

Angie's eyebrows lift. "You think they're on the rocks?"

Vic shrugs. "They've always fought a lot, but lately they've both seemed very bitter about everything."

Angie leans forward. "Are you planning on leaving your wife for Frannie?"

"What?" Vic looks horrified. "No!"

"So where exactly do you see your little dalliance going then?" Blackwood asks.

"Nowhere," Vic cries, clearly affronted. "I just comfort her sometimes, that's all. Kyle can be cruel when he wants to put her down."

"And Frannie will say the same thing, will she, when we talk to her later?" Blackwood persists. "That this thing between you two isn't really anything?"

"Well, I hope so." Vic looks uncertain. Then he asks, "Will you be talking to Kyle too?"

"We may have to at some point."

Vic's expression is somewhere between insulted and furious. "I'm trying to figure out why this is a line of inquiry. Do you think we've stowed Lou and the kids somewhere until we can run away and join them?"

"Actually, that thought never crossed my mind until now," Blackwood says, once again letting the moment hang. When Vic goes to speak, Blackwood continues, cutting him off, "But Louisa took that photograph. And there's every likelihood she was planning to show Kyle. Or she may have done so already, before she disappeared."

Vic's mouth drops open as he stares at Blackwood and then Angie.

"What else does Louisa know about you that she shouldn't?" Blackwood presses. "And how far would you go to stop this photo being exposed?"

Vic leans back in his chair, his face darkening, then lets out a sudden bark of laughter. "I came down here quickly and of my own accord because I thought you wanted my help in finding the kids. But if you're implying what I think you are, then I'm not continuing this conversation without my lawyer."

Blackwood knows he's pushing the man close to the edge, but this is not the moment to blink first. "Then let me offer you the opportunity to make a call."

Vic appears momentarily incredulous, then lets out another snort of laughter and leans forward. "If you're turning your attention to other people, you need to look elsewhere. Start with Kyle's creditors. I've been bailing him out for a while whenever he gets too nervous to ask his dad. Jock Fisher is an arsehole. I've known Kyle since we were teenagers and Jock loves it when Kyle messes up and has to go begging. That's why Jock can't stand me, because I put a stop to that, and I give his son somewhere else to turn."

"Does Kyle owe you money too?"

Vic shakes his head with another humorless chuckle. "Why do I feel like everything I say is self-incriminating? Yes, he owes me a bit, but he works off his debts too—we're friends, and we come to our own arrangements. I don't loan him anything I'm not prepared to lose. And

Frannie's just lonely. Kyle's been treating her like crap lately. He enjoys having sex with her when he's drunk—loud enough so we can all hear it—but otherwise he doesn't want to know. He was yelling at her the night before all this happened. I'd had enough of him to be honest. And that's all you're getting from me." He leans back. "So now I'd like to go, please, or I will make that call."

Blackwood pushes himself to his feet. "I think that's everything we need for the moment, but you won't be going anywhere, will you, Vic? You're staying close by in case we need to talk to you again?"

"We're staying here to support our friends." Vic glares at Blackwood.

"Then have a good day and we'll speak to you soon." Blackwood turns to go, and Angie follows him out.

As they head to the car park, Blackwood looks across to Angie. "What do you think?"

"I think some of those arrangements are only going to lead to trouble. If Kyle's indebted to Vic, how much hold does Vic have over him? Can Kyle complain when Vic sleeps with his wife?"

"Hmm. I don't know what to make of it. Right now this whole affair seems more of a grubby sideshow, and I can't afford to get distracted by a loose lead. Ask someone to visit Vic and take a formal statement from both him and Bridget. We should keep Vic on his toes, even though he and Bridget have given each other alibis for the time the kids went missing." Blackwood pauses at the waiting police vehicle. "We really need a breakthrough, and this doesn't feel like it."

"Let's talk to Kyle and Frannie again," Angie says. "Put them on the spot a bit more. Oh, and I've got Robbie Reynolds's number for you too."

Blackwood nods. "I'll call him in the car."

CHAPTER TWENTY

ROSE

Rose and Charlie have hardly spoken since her faux pas about his wife. He'd been so taciturn that she'd almost asked him to turn around and take her back to the hotel, but the lure of more information about Lou, as well as the potential of Charlie's free Wi-Fi connection, kept her quiet.

Eventually, Charlie turns the car onto an unsealed track and climbs out to open a gate. Once through, they bounce down a rutted driveway, which leads them across an open field, then through a forest of spindly trees. A few minutes later they arrive at a two-story straw-bale house with tall windows and a long wooden veranda the entire length of its southern side. It sits on the crest of a hill with an incredible view into the valley beyond. Bushland surrounds them on the other three sides.

"Oh wow," Rose says. "What an amazing place to live."

"Yeah, it's a beauty," he replies. "Wasn't intended for just me and Trixie, though."

Rose's heart contracts at the sadness radiating from him, and although she wants to offer some words of comfort, she comes up short.

He lets them in through a set of redwood double doors with stained-glass inlays featuring pretty patterns of red and white roses.

"Looks like Nin and Trix have left already," Charlie says, looking around and switching on the lights.

They're in a large, open-plan room with a kitchen in one corner and two sagging gray sofas facing an unlit fireplace. On the other side, a dining table covered in books and paperwork is positioned next to a floor-to-ceiling window with views across the fields beyond.

"Sorry about the chaos," Charlie says, surveying the cluttered surfaces and scattered stems of what looks like hay along the wood-paneled floors. "I'd usually tidy up a bit more for visitors. Trix is good at making a mess while she's feeding all her animals—she's got quite a sanctuary going out the back and in the shed, always rescuing some little creature. Right, I think Lou left a bag in the spare room," he adds. "I'll go get it."

He disappears for a moment, and Rose has a chance to absorb her surroundings. The disarray lends a cozy but neglected feel to the place, and there are photos of Pri on the wall and tacked to the fridge. She walks closer to one, studying the short woman dressed in bridal white with her arms around Charlie and Trixie. She has a round face and a huge smile, and her eyes dance with joy. She looks like someone Rose would have enjoyed meeting.

Rose quickly turns away as Charlie returns with a zipped-up reusable shopping bag with neon pictures of fruit all over it. He gestures to the dining table. "Let's take a look."

As soon as they're sitting down, he opens the bag and pulls out a small wooden jewelry box with elephants carved into each panel. He sets it on the dining table. This is followed by a few novels, a couple of hardback notepads, two winter scarves, a cap with *Australia* emblazoned on the front, and a Rip Curl sweater.

Rose pulls the small wooden box toward her, unclipping the clasp and opening it. It's filled with jewelry, little mountains of colorful beads on delicate silver strings. And nestled on top of it all is Louisa's passport.

She holds it up. "Bingo. We need to let the police know. It reinforces the theory that she didn't plan to abduct the children."

Charlie picks up his phone, but Rose says, "Wait." She tentatively opens one of the notepads, sees handwriting inside, and closes it again. "It's last year's diary."

"You think the police will want that too?"

"Perhaps we should take a look first, while we've got the opportunity."

He pulls a face. "It feels like such an invasion of privacy. But okay, I get it."

She pushes the smaller notepad toward Charlie. "You look through that one. I'll check this."

The diary in her hands is an A5 hardback with clouds on the front, and *Follow your dreams* written in tiny gold letters. Inside, it has pre-printed sections, each week on a double-page spread. Lou had used it mostly to note appointments of one sort or another, but on occasion she'd also added brief comments about her experiences. One dated six months ago read: *5 pm cocktails, The Rocks* in black ink, but then there was a blue scrawl next to it: *Walked with Fabien to Circular Quay* along with two little hearts. Against another entry, next to a restaurant date with friends in Darling Harbour, she had scribbled: *Never go back. Rip off!!*

Rose is trying her hardest to retain her sense of professional expertise, but as she studies the small, neat cursive, she is captivated by the echo of Lou's presence. *I'm reading my daughter's handwriting. Her fingers moved over this paper.* She has to steady herself before speaking. "I can't see anything particularly enlightening," she says as she skims through the pages. "What's in that one?"

Charlie is flicking through the smaller, plain black journal. "It's a record of her photography," he answers, sounding intrigued. "She's noted details of shots including apertures and shutter lengths, times, weather conditions, quality of light." He looks up, his surprise obvious. "I watched her taking photos, but I didn't realize she was so interested in the technical side of it." He stares back down at the notepad. "She did this for a couple of months, but it's all from last year too."

Rose thinks immediately of her sister Jess, whose photography obsession had started in a similar way. She'd love to watch the two of them compare notes . . . but there's no time to get lost in daydreams. She refocuses, scanning everything on the table and thinking hard. "She's probably got her current journals with her. What about the camera? Did she leave that here?"

Charlie shrugs. "Not that I know of. She has a good camera too—a Canon 5D from memory. One of the big SLRs."

Rose makes a mental note to talk to Angie about that. As she looks at the diary again, she notices a few small pieces of paper folded into the back of it. She pulls out the first slip and opens it, to find herself staring at a picture of her own face, next to her book cover. It's a printed article about her book.

She's frozen with surprise, trying to imagine what was running through Lou's mind when she printed this out, cut it down to size, and slipped it into the diary.

When she finally looks up, Charlie is watching her, as though sizing her up. "What is it?" she asks.

"I'm . . . protective," he admits. "It's taken a long time to get Lou to relax. Until she came here, no one in the family had tried to understand who she was; they just kept forcing their ideals on her. I wasn't sure whether you'd be any different."

Rose opens her mouth to object, but he cuts across her thoughts, arms folded in a challenge. "You were with Henry to begin with, after all."

"Yes," Rose says, pulling a face and looking again at the article. "Although I can't for the life of me remember why that was. I hated him for a long time for what he did to me, but I slowly realized he's just weak and fearful, and uses evasion as a coping mechanism. I can't help but feel sorry for his new wife. The poor woman has three needy babies to contend with, but at least two of them will grow up, eventually." She meets Charlie's eyes after she's said this, wondering if she's gone too far, but he laughs.

She smiles back cautiously. "You still don't get on with him then? Nothing's changed over the years?"

Charlie snorts. "Stuff changed all right. He got worse. So possessive over our mum. So righteous about you. Pretending he was father of the year while Lou slowly went off the rails and he shagged around behind Evelyn's back—mind you, I don't have much sympathy for her either; she was awful. My saving grace was moving here, so far away that I didn't have to think about it. They never met Pri, never even spoke to her. I doubt that they even know Trixie's name."

"I'm sorry, Charlie," she says, inwardly cursing Henry for causing so many people such pain. "Pri looks like a beautiful soul."

Charlie glances toward the photos on the wall. "She really was. She was fun and kind. Pri was always thinking of others, even when she was sick." His expression softens, but then he turns away, back to Lou's belongings. "Anyway, let's get on with this, shall we?"

Rose begins to check the other papers slipped into the back of the diary. Most are innocuous—cutouts or printouts of beaches and adventure tours along the WA coast, presumably things Lou wanted to do in future. However, one of them is handwritten.

I've given this to Stella to pass on to you. It's a tradition we've created for those who work for the Fishers. Be careful. You don't have to do everything they ask. And get Stella to tell you about Marisol.

"Check this out," Rose says, passing it over to Charlie and waiting while he reads it before asking, "Do you know anything about Marisol?"

Charlie pulls a face and shrugs. "Don't recall ever hearing the name before."

"It's pretty unusual," Rose says. "Let me text Stella now and ask about it." She fires off a quick message, then goes through the diary again, trying to find anything that might be relevant. There are social meetups at restaurants and bars, a record of the last day Lou worked for Robbie with a sad emoji drawn next to it, and a note of the January date when she would begin working with the Fishers. Nothing else sticks out.

Charlie studies the ceiling for a moment, blows out a long breath, and then looks at Rose. "When she comes back, she'll be so happy to find you here," he says. "For so long, Henry trained her to think you didn't care." Rose can clearly see the distress in his face. "God, he even had me believing it."

"Well, your brother is a master manipulator."

They stare at each other for an extended moment: assessing, understanding. Then she says, "I should call Angie, let her know about all this."

He nods. "I'll just go and check which animals Trix left behind, as there might be a few that need feeding."

Once he's gone, Rose picks up her phone, then hesitates. Before she makes the call, she flips through each page of Lou's diary, taking photos of everything written there. That way, she still has a record if the police want to take these as evidence.

She dials Angie's number and waits, but it goes through to voicemail.

"We've found Lou's passport," Rose tells Angie's message bank. "And a few other notebooks, including last year's diary. There's a name in there, Marisol, mentioned in connection to the Fishers. Along with a handwritten note from an unknown person warning her about working for the Fisher family. And there are lots of photography records, but no sign of her camera. Have you found that among her belongings? Please call me when you can."

She ends the call and dials again immediately, hoping she'll get Angie this time, but it's still voicemail. She wonders if the investigating officers have already had enough of her; perhaps they're determined to keep her locked out of whatever they find, unless it suits their own purposes. She thinks about calling the investigation room and talking to someone else, but knows her intel will be even more likely to get buried if she does that.

Charlie comes inside again and heads for the kitchen. "Can I make you a drink?" he calls.

"I'd love a coffee, please," she replies, sitting back in her chair and staring across the valley that stretches away beyond the window, as the last of the light surrenders itself to dusk. Charlie doesn't speak, and she lets the silence wash over her for a while, hoping it might clear her thoughts. But the napkin with Rick Malone's hastily scribbled number is burning a hole in her pocket.

"You know, I told Angie I wouldn't talk to the media, but I'm seriously thinking about calling that journalist," she announces.

"What?" Charlie looks concerned. "Perhaps you should think that through a bit more. Once you let those kinds of people in, they're hard to shake off."

"But there isn't time to sit here deliberating." Rose throws her hands in the air in frustration. "These investigations so often become weeks of unbearable waiting. Lou's already been missing for three days: If there's something we need to know, we haven't got time to waste. And I'm happy to take some heat for that if it brings her home."

"At least drink your coffee first," Charlie says, coming across and setting a mug down in front of her. He goes back to the kitchen and collects his own drink, bringing it to the table, sitting down, and opening his laptop. "I'll see what Google will tell me about Kyle's nannies."

"Okay then." She pauses, looking between the phone and her iPad. "While we wait for an update, I'll check out Rick Malone's book. If we don't hear anything in the next few hours, I'm going to have to find out what he knows."

She goes to Google and does a search for Rick Malone, and the book immediately comes up: *The Fisher Empire: How One Man Built a Fortune and a Legacy*. She downloads it to the tablet and begins to flick through, scanning for anything useful. Instead she finds a lot of information about Jock's early life, how he'd been born into poverty and built his fortune from scratch thanks to his engineering prowess and his aptitude for dealmaking.

"Jock Fisher appears to be an Aussie Richard Branson," she tells Charlie, thinking of the wizened man at the helm of the press conference, offering two million as though it were small change. "I wonder what he's been like as a dad, though."

"From what I can find, Kyle seems to be the only one who doesn't work for the company," Charlie says. "Not sure what he does do actually. When you google his name you generally get pictures of him at high-society events or watching the races."

"Perhaps you don't need to work if your dad has enough money to fund your extravagant lifestyle," Rose suggests.

"Maybe." Charlie gets up and collects the mugs, putting them on the countertop. "Not very fulfilling, though, is it? Being a kept man. You'd have to pay me big money to do half the vacuous things he seems to like doing."

"Have you found anything more about his nannies?"

"No, but I suppose it's probably not something we're going to locate in the public domain, is it? Which is typical: You can find so much crap online, but the one thing we really need to know isn't here."

They both continue searching, scanning through endless articles for oblique mentions of the Fishers' employees. "I've found a potted biography," Rose says, "appended to a review of Malone's book. Looks like Kyle's divorce from his second wife, Ebony, was stressful. Hefty payout. Wonder if that was about more than the public ever got to know. Listen to this." She begins to read.

"Jock Fisher has dedicated his life to transforming the Australian landscape and culture, building everything from high-rises to marinas to five-star luxury hotels. He's also pledged his empire to the next generation, once joking that he hoped to have enough children to 'fill the boardroom and make decisions a lot easier.' His four children—three sons and a daughter—were raised with this ethos, and three of them willingly stepped into the jobs that Jock had waiting for them once they finished tertiary education. Jock's eldest son, Toby, is the most prominent member of the Fisher team, working as chief operating officer, taking over the running of the company during the first years of the new millennium. Jock's second son, Ethan, works in the financial side of the business, while his daughter, Bronte, is the public face of the Fisher family. Bronte is best known for her infamous appearance on Question Time *alongside Bob Brown, where she staunchly defended land development in the old-growth forests of Western Australia, proving outspoken and quick witted and drawing admiration from the Liberal Party, who have since courted her as a parliamentary candidate."*

"I didn't realize the kids were such a big deal," Charlie says.

Rose holds up a hand. "Wait, there's more.

"Jock's youngest son, Kyle, has pursued a different path in life and is known as a party man. He threw his energy into building a nightclub empire as soon

as he finished university, and began organizing raves on the beach that were attended by thousands. However, when his company collapsed in the early 2000s, engulfed in a scandal around money laundering, Kyle was lucky to escape prosecution. It was rumored that Jock stepped in to pay off his son's debts. In 2015, Kyle got involved in promoting stunt shows for the kamikaze motorbike group the Daredevil Riders. That only lasted a year before a motorbike went flying into the crowd, killing the rider and seriously injuring three bystanders. Since then, Kyle has withdrawn to a quieter life with his family, and his public appearances generally revolve around the horse racing calendar."

"So it sounds like Kyle is drawn to danger, and Jock has had mixed results trying to rein him in." Charlie stands up and stretches. "Do you want another drink?"

"No, it's okay." Rose is lost in contemplation for a while. Eventually, she says, "Do you think Kyle has been tempted into some sort of dodgy enterprise again? From the kinds of businesses he's in, he probably knows quite a few underworld figures. Perhaps he hasn't been able to pay up, so they've taken Lou and the kids as hostages. But if so, where's the ransom demand? And what about Fabien? Unless," she continues, "Fabien wasn't meant to be on the beach when they turned up. So the plan has gone wrong?" She raises her eyebrows and waits, wanting Charlie's thoughts. When he doesn't speak, she continues, "We need to make sure the police are asking all these questions."

Charlie sits back down, holding Rose's gaze as they each think through options. "Why don't you call Angie again and ask her?"

"I can tell she's unsure of me already," Rose confesses. "I have to tread a fine line here. They're going to stonewall me completely if I get too pushy, and I don't want to be out of the loop." Frustration ignites a sudden fire in her belly, and she sits up straighter. "Actually, I don't care what they think of me. I'm used to having to fight to be heard, and perhaps it's better that I kick up a fuss and demand to be listened to. Life is a lot easier when you stop trying to avoid offending everybody, and I've not come here to be liked."

She touches Malone's number in her pocket again. She knows that if she calls him she'll lose any trust the police have in her. Nevertheless, it's getting more tempting by the minute.

CHAPTER TWENTY-ONE
BLACKWOOD

"Fabien's a stand-up guy," Robbie Reynolds insists in his deep, polished radio voice. "He's been with me for five years. Funny. Talented. Hardworking. We're all really worried about him, but I can tell you one thing: He ain't run off with Kyle Fisher's kids."

"What makes you so sure?" Blackwood asks. He's sitting outside the Fishers' house having this chat, while Angie has gone inside to see how the land lies, hoping to keep everyone calm. He doesn't envy her the task.

Robbie sounds as animated as he must do on the radio. "It's fucking nuts, that's why! The guy was embarrassed when he got a parking ticket. You think he's gonna take on the Fisher family? I've never even heard him talk about wanting kids! And I'll tell you the same thing about Lou. We shouldn't have let her go. She was a lovely girl, quiet, kind enough to laugh at my jokes. Our baby never cried when he was with her—not like now, with my witch-in-law living with us. Do you think I'd have let Lou near my kid if I thought for one second she had dodgy intentions? I tell ya, you're barking up the wrong tree if you think those two are kidnappers. I fixed them up in the first place, for Christ's sake. It's like pegging Snoopy and Woodstock for gang violence."

Blackwood keeps his eyes closed as he listens to Robbie. He's surrounded by fast thinkers and smooth talkers, and it's taking all he has to keep up.

Robbie doesn't pause for air. "People here are saying he went over to WA for a surf, and perhaps, if he was lucky, a quick shag on the beach with his woman. Six months is a long time to be apart. And those two were clearly in love. Couldn't keep their hands off each other."

Blackwood's phone buzzes. Angie is trying to reach him.

Need you inside, her text reads. *Frannie's struggling. And Rose won't leave me alone. Messaging every few minutes with new theories and people for us to talk to. I haven't replied yet.*

"I'm sorry, I have to go," he interjects when Robbie finally takes a breath.

"Hang on a sec, I haven't finished. We were Lou's first big job, and she was thrilled. It's not easy to get a break in the celeb child-minding world, and she'd hardly been out of nanny college when we hired her, but she came with the highest recommendations from the people there, and we just loved her and the way she took care of our son. She was a sweetheart. Saved my wife's sanity, I reckon, and helped us to enjoy Luca while he was a baby because he was always so calm around her. Now he's two and he's an absolute fucking nightmare, ego as big as the Harbour Bridge. Rules our house with a rod of iron." He chuckles proudly. "So let me think what else I can tell you about Fabien. He and his mate Azir have a large apartment in Rose Bay. It was a good bachelor pad before they both went soft and shacked up. Always a girl there now. But I've had a few fun nights there with them."

As Robbie talks, Angie's name comes up again on Blackwood's phone and he checks his watch to see it's gone five. The sun will set again soon, and they're no further ahead. "If you think of anything else, please call us," he tells Robbie, trying not to sound as desperate as he feels. "Thanks for your time, and look—go easy with the speculation on the radio, okay? It can create problems for us if the public gets too interested in these cases."

"Can't make any promises, mate, but I'll see what I can do," Robbie answers, before hanging up.

———

Inside, Blackwood is shocked by Frannie's appearance. Her hair is unbrushed, her eyes are sunken, and her cheeks are a mottled red. A patchy rash has crept along her chest and neck.

There's an obvious pattern now: the Fisher family gravitating to the heaters on the veranda, leaving Frannie and whoever is looking after her indoors. Frannie is flanked by Angie and another woman, who is introduced as her sister, Sadie. Frannie and Sadie eye Blackwood intently, assessing his posture, wary of news.

"Have you found anything?" Frannie asks, her eyes dark with fear.

"There's no sign of Lou and the children, but some new information has come to light. I need to speak to you in private."

Frannie pales. As she gets up, Blackwood's attention is drawn to Jock, seated on the outdoor chairs with his children. He's holding court about something, his offspring all focused on him, three faces open and engaged while Kyle's expression is closer to a scowl. Bronte wears a brightly colored caftan over her ample frame and has her feet up on the table, while all the blokes have half-full beers in their hands. It sets Blackwood on edge. Why the hell are they drinking today? And how reliable is their word going to be if they're all half cut? There seems little attempt by any of them to take care of Frannie, and it's starting to piss Blackwood off. No wonder she'd gone looking for love elsewhere.

Kyle spots Blackwood and jumps up, coming in but leaving the sliding door to the veranda open so the others can hear. "Good to see you, Blackwood. Is there any news?"

"We need to speak to Frannie alone," Blackwood replies.

"I don't think so," Kyle retorts, his face turning a deep red. "You're investigating the disappearance of our kids. You can bloody well talk to us together."

"Kyle," Angie interjects. "If you can't calm down we're going to have to take you to the local station whenever we need to brief you. Is that what you want?"

Kyle makes a visible effort to control his breathing and his fury.

"Frannie, do you feel safe talking to us here?" Blackwood asks openly. He wants Kyle to be well aware of their suspicions about his temper.

"What the—?" Kyle looks shocked, then his eyes go to Frannie. She doesn't meet his gaze.

"I'm not sure," she murmurs.

"Then let's go," Angie says, bundling her through to the den.

Once inside the small room, Angie sits beside Frannie, while Blackwood stands in front of her. If ever there were a time to play good cop, bad cop, it's now.

"Some evidence has come to light that you might be romantically involved with Vic Santos," Blackwood begins, deliberately avoiding preamble to gauge Frannie's reaction when caught off guard.

Frannie's gaze shoots up to meet his. Her fear is palpable. "What on earth does that have to do with my babies going missing?"

Blackwood watches her carefully. "Right now, we don't know. We're not looking to get you into any kind of trouble here, but we need you to tell us the truth. We've seen a photograph of you and Vic, taken when you were in the garden. It looks intimate. We believe Louisa may have taken it. We've already spoken to Vic."

"Do you know where Louisa's camera is?" Angie adds. "It didn't turn up in the house search. We have reason to believe that Kyle asked her to take these pictures, to spy on you. Did you have any idea that this was going on?"

Blackwood is anticipating a no, but instead Frannie nods reluctantly.

"He's been getting more and more jealous," she says. "He suggested the couple swap in the first place, but he didn't like it when Vic and I got closer. I suspected he might have enlisted Lou's help to keep tabs on me, because I know he keeps a close eye on me whenever Vic's around."

"The couple swap?" Blackwood queries, despite already knowing what's coming.

Frannie looks from Angie to Blackwood. "We're all consenting adults. We've known Vic and Bridget for quite a few years and we have a good time together, so about a year ago, Kyle suggested that when we come to Kardanup we could swap partners for the night. Everyone thought it was a great joke to start with, but then we tried it, and it became a thing we did, until there was an incident with one of the kids walking in at the wrong time—and we all agreed it was best to stop." She looks up at them briefly, then quickly down at her hands again. "But Vic and I had formed a connection. He loves Bridget, but it's been hard for both of us to go back to the way things were. I love Kyle too, but he's become more and more controlling. His temper is scary sometimes. The night before the kids disappeared, he was screaming at me, saying that he'd kill me if he found out I was sleeping around. I thought it was just the drink talking—but now . . ." She trails off, then asks, "Can I see the photo?"

Angie scrolls through her phone and produces the picture.

Frannie claps a hand over her mouth. "Oh my god, we look completely in love." She stares at them in desperation, her eyes pleading for understanding. "I had no idea this was taken. Shit. If Kyle has seen this it's a fucking disaster."

"Why on earth do you continue coming away together with the Santoses if it's so awkward now?" Angie asks.

"Vic's been helping Kyle financially, with some investments, so Kyle needs to keep him sweet. I only know that because Vic told me. Otherwise Kyle would have to beg his dad for money again, and I think he'd rather shoot himself than do that." Frannie's face has gone red, the mottling across her chest deepening.

"Frannie, this is important." Angie leans forward, maintaining eye contact. "Finding Lou's camera might shed light on her recent movements—and locate your babies. If you have any idea where those items might be, please let us know immediately."

"I . . . I don't," Frannie says, her hands fretting in her lap. "You searched the entire place, didn't you?"

"Yes," Angie says. "But it may have been moved. Please keep thinking about this, Frannie. It's important."

She nods. "Okay."

"Vic also mentioned that he heard you and Kyle arguing the night before Lou and the kids disappeared," Blackwood adds. "Can you remember exactly what Kyle said to you?"

Frannie avoids meeting his gaze. "He was furious with me, seemingly out of nowhere. He said I was a lazy whore. That I didn't respect him. He said he'd given me everything, and I didn't deserve any of it. He was shouting so loudly—he probably wanted Vic to hear. Perhaps he was warning him off."

When she stops talking, Blackwood lets the silence hang for a moment. "Frannie, has Kyle ever been violent with you?"

"No!" Frannie frowns.

"Have you ever felt scared around him?"

There's a long hesitation this time, before she says, softly, "Once or twice. He can be intense, and very controlling. His last wife, Ebony, left him quite unexpectedly, and he gets scared it might happen again—and that he might lose the kids. Which is ironic, really, as his fear causes the behavior that drives everyone away. When he forgets about all that, he's good fun. I think he tries too hard sometimes, but he wants to make up for being a shit dad the first time around. I do love him, you know."

Her tone is feeble, and Blackwood isn't convinced. He thinks of Honey's blue bear, which Frannie would hardly let go of to begin with. He'd thought that had been about the kids, but now he's starting to understand how much she might need comfort and protection.

"How do you think Louisa felt, being asked to spy on you? Could she have panicked at what was happening, sensed Kyle might be out of control, and tried to run off with the kids to protect them? Could Fabien have been helping her, if she was scared something was brewing here that might put her and the children in danger? If she heard the way he was talking to you that night?"

Frannie looks between them both, stunned. "I . . . I don't know.

Kyle can be aggressive and angry but it's all talk—he's never touched me. I can't imagine him . . ." She trails off. "You really think he's got something to do with the kids and Lou going missing?"

"Do you?" Blackwood asks.

Her blotched face reddens further. "I have a hard time reconciling it. But the night before they disappeared, while Lou and the children were in the next room, he said I didn't deserve my kids," she confesses. "He said I would get my comeuppance one day for neglecting them." She looks from Angie to Blackwood, her eyes wide. "He said I didn't deserve to be a mother anymore."

––––––––––

As soon as they step out of the house, Blackwood says, "Let's walk back to base. I need some fresh air."

"Good idea," Angie agrees. "And just FYI: Rose's message also asked about the camera, and she said they've found Louisa's passport at Charlie's house."

"So if Louisa is the instigator of this sudden disappearance, it suggests it was impromptu. I was interested back there in Frannie's comment about Kyle's ex-wife. Has anyone spoken to her yet?"

"No, remember, she's not well at the moment so she's hard to contact, but I'll get onto it." Angie stretches her arms above her head, twists herself from left to right a few times as they walk, then shrugs. "I'll put together a complete list of all the nannies that have worked for Kyle, and we'll have someone chat to the previous Mrs. Fisher as a priority." She starts texting, fingers tapping rapidly on her phone.

"Thanks, Angie," Blackwood says, his phone beginning to buzz. He sees Jock's name on the screen and his throat tightens as he picks up the call.

"Hello, Jock," he says as pleasantly as he can.

"I'm calling to let you know that Kyle is planning to have a chat with Stacey Sewell tomorrow," Jock announces.

Blackwood's hand tightens around the phone. He has no idea who Jock is talking about, but instinct tells him this isn't good.

"One moment," he says, then leans over to Angie. "Who's Stacey Sewell?"

Her eyes widen. "Young reporter on *Sixty Minutes*," she replies. "Oh no, they haven't—"

Blackwood has already gone back to the call. "That's not a good idea, Jock," he says wearily, doubtful he can persuade the Fisher family to sit on their hands for much longer. "We need to work as a team here."

"And I'm telling you we've gotta do something," Jock growls, just as Blackwood had suspected he would. "Come on. You can't expect us to wait around indefinitely. It's the end of day three, and as far as I can see, you lot haven't found squat. I'm not blaming you for that. If the nanny has taken them she might have planned the whole thing out, and if someone else has them it could be a professional. But the only thing in our favor is that we can continue to stoke the media fire, get attention, have everyone looking out for these kids, or watching for people who might be behaving oddly. Surely you can see that?"

"I'll need to talk to Bob Drake again," Blackwood says, "before I can agree to anything."

Jock's voice goes down a few notches. "You do that. But Stacey Sewell is already on her way to Perth." As soon as he stops speaking, the line goes dead.

Blackwood and Angie finish the short journey in silence. Once inside the green house, they head to the quiet front room. Blackwood lays his phone on the table and walks across to the window, alarmed at how quickly the sun has crept stealthily toward the horizon on yet another fruitless day. He rubs at his sore neck, trying to ease the tension. He can feel Angie's eyes on him.

"You okay there? What can I do to help?"

"Go check in with the team. I'll call Drake."

When Angie has gone, Blackwood reluctantly dials his superior.

"Let me guess, this is about Stacey Sewell," Drake says as soon as he answers the call.

"You've already talked to Jock then."

"I want you to work the case, not spend time trying to control the Fishers. In a way, Jock's right—it does keep attention on this, even if it complicates the job and the crowd control."

Upon hearing Drake's practical approach, Blackwood feels calmer. "Okay then."

"Also," Drake adds, in a tone that upends Blackwood's two seconds of relief, "I'm getting heat from the premier's office. They're wanting to keep tabs on this one. So make sure you explore every angle, dot the i's and cross the t's. I don't want us looking like idiots."

Blackwood pulls at his collar, loosening its chokehold. "Right."

The door bangs open, and Angie rushes in, her eyes wide. "Is that still Drake?" she asks. "Put him on speaker."

Heart racing, Blackwood does as she asks.

"We've just had a call to say there's a body on a strip of beach about nine k's north, just south of the Dunsborough township," she tells them both breathlessly. "Some kids found it on a fishing trip. Emergency services are heading there now. They're saying there's a tattoo on the neck. From the description, it could be Louisa's boyfriend, Fabien Dubois."

Blackwood gets a sharp spasm in his chest. It's the break they've been hoping for, but in the worst possible way. He grabs his jacket and yells at all the faces peering in through the door. "Come on, then, let's go!"

———

They keep the sirens on all the way to Dunsborough. Constable White drives, with Blackwood in the passenger seat and Angie in the back. No one says a word, but Blackwood's focus darts between the horizon and his watch. They only have about an hour before the light goes. Every minute counts.

They race through the Dunsborough township and pull up in a foreshore car park that's already crowded with vehicles, including four police cars and an ambulance, as well as a gaggle of onlookers. Blackwood is ushered over to an unmarked four-wheel drive, and they've barely got the doors shut before they're careening onto the sandy beach and heading south again.

In the distance, they can see a spotlight has been rigged up over the body and strips of police tape have been attached to poles hammered into the sand, forming a makeshift barrier. The body is a few meters from the shoreline, and around it there's an expanse of flat sand and low scrubby bushes behind the dunes. The vulnerability and loneliness of this final resting place hits Blackwood hard.

Three skinny young men with bad haircuts sit on the hood of a battered Hilux, all in board shorts and surf T-shirts, shoulders hunched as they watch the proceedings. There's no one else here except for the police. At least by the time the media get word it will be too dark for the news helicopters, and Blackwood is grateful for that.

He strides over to the cordon and is once again greeted by Kelsie Hughes. "You're lucky I was still down here," she says. "I was about to drive home. We're doing all the evidence collection as fast as we can, then we'll get him to the morgue."

Blackwood tries to keep a check on his emotions as he surveys the dead man's young, lifeless face. He's seen plenty of corpses, but there's still a small section of his heart that he's deliberately kept unhardened. He's known of coppers who can watch video evidence of car crashes resulting in multiple fatalities while eating hot dogs and cracking jokes. It's a recognized fact in the force that when you reach that point it's time to move on to a different posting. Blackwood has witnessed plenty of good police officers burn out and break down.

"I reckon he's been in the water for a day or so, judging by the bloating," Kelsie says. "And he was there long enough for something to take a chunk out of him." She nods at a deep bite mark on the left forearm. "You're incredibly lucky that he washed up," she adds. "If he'd drifted further out it wouldn't have taken long for him to get divided up between the sharks, and there's every chance the current could have carried him in a different direction. But the cause of death is pretty clear."

The dead man is wearing a light-blue T-shirt, and a deep wound is visible between his right shoulder and armpit.

"Looks like the brachial artery was severed," Kelsie confirms. "He would have bled out quite quickly."

Blackwood turns and looks over his shoulder at Angie, who stands slightly behind him, staring at the body. "How far north are we from where the boat was found?"

"Only a few k's," Angie replies.

"You think this might be one of the people you're looking for?" Kelsie asks, her eyes moving back to the corpse.

Blackwood surveys the inked images visible beneath the left ear: a series of silhouetted small birds caught in flight along the side of that ghostly white neck. "I'm afraid it is," he says, imagining Fabien's tormented parents, about to receive news that will destroy them. Then, as he often does at these times, he thinks of his own children, and that he'll call or message them tonight, to make sure they're okay. It's a ritual he has to do after one of these incidents, before he can have any hope of sleeping.

Kelsie shakes her head. "I'm so sorry. What a waste."

"Yep. We'll leave you to get on in a second." Blackwood looks around. "Beware of journalists and photo leaks, okay?"

"Already on that. We'll keep him covered as much as possible and I've got plenty of eyes on watch. I'll get him moved as soon as we've finished, and I'll text you when we've left the beach."

"Thanks."

"We've got his wallet too," she says. "Bagged up over there." She indicates the police vehicle, where another couple of officers are busy on phones and laptops.

"Good. We can ID him from that as well. Angie, can you check the wallet for me now? We need to photograph the contents ASAP."

"On it."

Blackwood turns and walks over to the men sitting on the Hilux. Close up, he can see how young the three of them are, with wispy mustaches, gold chains, and badly cut mullets.

"DSS Blackwood," he says, producing his badge for them. "I gather you three found the body?"

"Yeah, we were going to head down there for a bit," one of the lads says, pointing further along the beach. "Do a bit of sunset fishing, then have a few tinnies."

"So you stopped your vehicle, looked at the body, and then called the police?"

"Yeah," they all mumble, hands hidden between their knees, heads down.

"Was there anyone else around?"

"Nah."

"Did you do anything else before or after that, or did you just sit and wait for the police?"

"Just waited for you guys," the smallest of the three responds. They seem to have mutually decided he'll be the spokesperson.

"All right then," Blackwood says. "Now, can I just have a look at all your phones?"

Instantly, their heads snap up.

"What d'ya need to do that for? We only found him," the smallest boy says indignantly.

"You're now witnesses in a murder investigation," Blackwood explains. "And refusing to cooperate with the police is an arrestable offense. So we can either take you all down to the station and do proper interviews—which usually take hours—or we can sort it out here, get your details, and you'll be free to head home. Which would you prefer?"

The boys make their disgruntlement clear as they each pull their phones out of their pockets. Angie appears to have heard his speech and comes across to help. Blackwood passes two of the phones to her, and holds the third one up.

"Whose is this?"

"Mine," the shorter boy mumbles.

"Can you put your passcode in, please," Blackwood asks. This isn't strictly by the book, and he's grateful for Angie's silence. She knows exactly what he's doing.

"Then open your photo app for me, will you," Blackwood adds politely.

The boy opens his photo album. Blackwood points to the five photos of the body. "I'm going to get DS Lennard here to take copies of those, and"—he looks at the other two boys—"we'll need any on your phones too. Now, did you send these photos to anyone?" he asks.

"No," they all mumble.

"And do you know that if you share these photos it may be an arrestable offense?"

"We're not sickos," the smallest pipes up indignantly. "We just wanted proof, I guess. You know there's a rich fella offering two million for information on that missing girl. This might be connected."

Blackwood grimaces, inwardly cursing Jock. "If those pictures get into the wrong hands you'll be in a lot of trouble. So, while DS Lennard sorts out the photos, can I get some ID from all of you, and then we'll let you go back to the car park. The officers there are expecting you. They'll talk you through making your statements."

Once they've finished, Angie stands beside him as they watch the Hilux drive slowly down the beach. "Oh, the young-uns of today," she says. "Gives you so much optimism, doesn't it? I bet that's about a quarter of the speed they were doing racing down here. But," she adds, turning back to look briefly behind her toward the screen that shields Fabien's body, "thank god they found him. This changes everything, don't you reckon?"

"It sure does." Blackwood's mind is spinning, recalibrating the new possibilities that have just come into play. "We're on a murder investigation now. *Damn*." He rubs a hand over his mouth, taking a breath before continuing. "Even after seeing that boat, when it wasn't Louisa's blood, I still hoped the two of them had run away to play happy families somewhere. But Louisa's not going to turn around and suddenly stab her boyfriend, is she? No, she and the kids have been taken, and violently too, for god knows what reason." He checks his watch. "And we're almost at the end of day three without any leads. I think we need to push ahead with that press conference after all, first thing tomorrow."

Angie nods. "I'll get the wheels in motion."

She moves off, leaving Blackwood standing alone in the growing dark, aware of his smartly polished shoes slowly sinking into the sand. As his theories shift and spin, he stares at the red taillights of the Hilux until they're a distant blur.

CHAPTER TWENTY-TWO
LOUISA

THREE DAYS EARLIER

"You need to follow our instructions exactly," the man says as Lou comes into view. At the sight of Honey wriggling in his arms and the fear on the little girl's face, Lou almost overbalances on the uneven rocks. She grabs one of the cool, sharp stones to steady herself.

"Are you listening to me?" the man snaps when she doesn't respond. He's middle aged, with sunken eyes in his round face, and a receding hairline. A small tinny has been pulled onto the sand a few paces behind him. He's sweating profusely as he glares at Lou, his navy polo shirt clinging to his chest and riding the contours of his loose skin, his doughy stomach hanging over his trousers. Nevertheless, his arms are thick and strong as he holds Honey tight in his grasp. Honey squeals and gives little moans of distress as she pants and squirms, trying to get away.

Lou's mouth begins to open in response.

"If you scream I'll take this kid right now, and you'll never see her again."

Lou looks back at the beach to Kai, and sees to her horror that another man, younger and muscular, with a shaved head and a sleeve of tattoos, is leaning over the baby, scooping him up with Lou's bag and blanket.

She starts to tremble. "Please don't hurt them."

"Just do what we ask and you'll all be fine."

"The family I work for have a lot of money," she tries desperately. "I'm sure they'll give you whatever you want if you just let us go."

"We know," he snaps. "That's why we've come. Get down here now."

She scrambles down the other side of the rocks onto the narrow strip of beach between the groin and the bush. The other man has almost caught up with them. His face is pinched, his skin drawn too tight over his skull, his front teeth chipped and uneven. He holds Kai with one hand as he comes closer, swiftly negotiating the uneven rocks, his arm across Kai's middle so that the baby's legs flap with each movement. Kai looks surprised more than afraid, but his eyes remain fixed on Louisa, seeking reassurance. To her horror, she sees a knife in the man's other hand.

"We're going to take these two for a little day trip," the older man says, "while you deliver a note to your boss. If he does what we ask, the kids will be home by dinnertime."

"No, no, no," Lou begs. "I can't go back without them. He'll kill me. And what if he doesn't do what you want?"

"That's his call, isn't it. Do you really think he's going to say no?"

Honey is watching Lou, seeming to sense her rising panic. She holds her arms out. "Lulu," she screeches. Her feet flap and kick against the man holding her.

"Take this," the man insists, pushing an envelope toward Lou. But before Lou has time to grab it there's a scrabbling sound behind them.

"HEY! What the fuck are you doing?"

Their heads whip around in unison. Fabien is coming quickly over the rocks, slipping and sliding in his haste to get to them, his expression contorted in fury.

The younger man holding Kai is about to climb into the boat, but he stops and glares at Fabien. "We're just taking the kids for a ride, mate," he says.

"No, you're not," Fabien hisses, his French accent more pronounced than usual as he spits each word in rage. "Let them all go. Now."

Fabien wades into the water and tries to grab one side of the boat, to pull it further onto the sand.

"Take him," the younger man shouts, shoving Kai at Louisa, who instinctively grabs the baby. Once the young man's hands are free he wades across and punches Fabien hard in the chest, twice. Fabien steps back, shock etched onto his face as he stares into the other man's eyes. Then he looks down, at the crimson stain coming through his T-shirt, beginning to spread across his shoulder.

Lou screams.

"Shut UP," the younger man yells, roughly pulling Fabien's body into the boat, so that he collapses, half on a seat, half on the floor. "Get in the boat. NOW! You too, Dad."

Lou watches the older man wade unsteadily into the water, passing Honey across to his son before climbing in himself.

"LULU!" Honey screeches in panic, her arms held out desperately, imploring Lou to grab her.

"Get in NOW," the younger man snarls at Lou, "or are we taking this little girl alone?"

"But the note," the older man says, staring at Fabien, who is trying to pull himself up, hands gripping the edge of the boat.

The younger man kicks Fabien hard, and he curls into a ball. "Not the plan anymore," he says, jumping out of the boat and grabbing Lou's arm. "She's seen too much now."

Lou can hear nothing but the hammering of her heart in her ears. She's pushed toward the boat, walking unsteadily into the water, clutching Kai. The younger man snatches the baby off her and waits while she climbs in. He passes Kai back and jumps in with one swift movement. His father is already yanking the engine cord, and it complies with a roar.

The boat judders to life and turns away from the beach, tipping to one side as it guns through the water. Next to Lou, Honey is rigid with shock, her eyes on Fabien. "Look down at the ocean," Lou whispers to her. "Cover your ears, and watch for fish." She pulls Honey's hands up and pushes them against her ears. The little girl obeys.

"Reid, what the FUCK did you just do?" the older man shouts.

"Just keep moving," Reid hisses.

Kai begins to cry.

"But what will we do with her now?" The older man nods at Lou. He's almost as shocked as she is.

"We'll figure it out," the younger man says. "But we can't go back." His tone is dark and menacing, compounding all of Lou's worst fears.

She sinks to her knees in the middle of the boat, with Kai clamped awkwardly against her hip, stroking Fabien's hair. He makes no effort to move, and she can hear a long, drawn-out wheezing each time he breathes. She leans over to kiss the side of his face, pushing her mouth close to his ear, noticing that his eyes are fixed on some indeterminate point beyond them both.

"Stay with me, Fab, please. Stay with me. I'm here," she pleads.

His eyes flicker briefly to her, then away. His fingers brush lightly against her arm, as though searching for something to hold on to.

But she fears it's already too late.

CHAPTER TWENTY-THREE
ROSE

Rose knows she should rest, but each time her eyes close, all the fears and questions work away at her composure, whittling her worries into sharper stabs of panic that slice through any hope of sleep. She's endured some agonizing waits before, but never one like this, and it's accompanied by a growing sense of doom.

There's some small comfort in the homeliness of her surroundings, as she sits with her feet up on the double bed in Charlie's "shack," which isn't a shack at all, but a granny flat with a large double room, kitchenette, and en suite. He'd explained that he'd built it for Nin from an old shipping container, a venture he'd started before Pri died, and which had kept him sane afterward. It certainly feels like a passion project, every detail of the wood-paneled floors and beveled windows as perfect as if it had been done by a master builder.

She's still skimming through Rick Malone's book on her iPad, trying to understand the Fisher family before her inevitable meeting with them. It's clearly an authorized biography, with photos provided by Jock and those close to him, which means that Jock will have been able to control and edit out any of the more salacious details of his family and empire. She's curious as to why Malone is skulking about in hotels trying to meet her, when he must have had access to the Fishers' inner sanctum at one time.

She remembers the note in Lou's diary, stops reading, and checks if Stella has replied, but there's been no response. She decides to push a bit more and sends another message. *Do you know any of Kyle's previous nannies?* she writes to Stella. *If so, do you think they would talk to me? I found a message in Lou's diary from one of them: a warning about the Fishers. I think you may have passed it on to Lou?*

She checks the clock: It's only nine, but the jet lag is finally catching up with her, and she's dizzy with exhaustion. She's tried Angie's mobile a couple more times, but there's been no answer, and therefore no updates. She's reluctant to settle, particularly if she falls into a deep sleep: It means letting go of so many crucial hours while Lou remains lost out there somewhere with those precious babies. Every time she thinks about it she gets a fiery blast of pain in her chest.

She gets up and makes herself a hot drink in the little kitchenette, knowing caffeine is a bad idea, but hoping the coffee will stave off the inevitable crash for a little longer. She listens for sounds from the main house, but the walls and doors must be too thick. Instead, the silence is so complete that it feels charged with an unsettling energy. At home in the city there is light and noise all the time, but here there is only space, to be filled with questions and fears. She gets back into bed and pulls the covers tighter.

She must drift off, still wearing her jeans and hoodie, because she startles awake to a loud banging on her door. "Rose," Charlie calls. "I need to talk to you."

She jumps up immediately, sensing the urgency in his tone.

"Have they found them?" she asks as she opens the door. But instantly she knows it's not good news. Charlie's eyes are wide with fear.

"Fabien's body was discovered on the beach in Dunsborough a couple of hours ago." His voice is a broken, ragged whisper.

The shock is so great that Rose doubles over as though someone has punched her hard in the stomach.

"And Lou?" she manages to ask.

"No sign of her."

"I need to sit down," she says, stumbling back over to the bed, beginning to shake. A wave of heat overwhelms her and she pulls her hoodie off, clutching it to her chest, her knuckles white.

Charlie sits beside her. "We can't panic," he says. "We can't panic." He's talking to himself as much as to her.

Rose grabs her phone and sees she's missed a couple of calls. "It's automatically set to silent overnight," she says. "I forgot to cancel it."

"Of course," Charlie replies. "You must be shattered. I'd crashed out on the sofa, didn't even realize I'd drifted off until my mobile rang." He rubs his face, his eyelids swollen and his hair unkempt. "I feel so guilty, because for the last few days I've had this horrible doubt nagging in the back of my mind that they took the kids for some reason. I've been imagining trying to support Lou through all the hostility when they're discovered, but I also thought she'd have a really good reason, because there's no fucking way she would intentionally cause those kids any harm." He leans over and puts his face in his hands, his palms covering his eyes. "Now my mind is going crazy trying to cling onto some hope, and all I can picture is a psychopath attacking them. Fabien was stabbed, Rose. It sounds like he was left in the water and bled to death."

Rose's mind races wildly between every possible scenario she can think of, including Lou having had some kind of psychotic break. No, that can't be true. "What else did they say?" she pleads, desperate for more information. "Who did you talk to?"

"It was Angie. She said to hang tight, not to contact anyone overnight as they're still informing people, and she'll be here for us at first light. She said she'll call us later because they're thinking of holding an emergency press conference first thing in the morning and they want us involved. They've already told Fabien's parents, but they haven't spoken to the Fishers yet. God, his poor family. They'll never recover."

Rose pats Charlie's leg to comfort him. She makes the gesture instinctively, then realizes it might be overstepping, but he puts his hand on top of hers and squeezes it gently. "Rose, you're shaking."

"I know," she says, gritting her teeth, struggling to catch her breath. But the air has turned to water and she is drowning in it. She closes her eyes, but instead of darkness there's a man lurching at her with a knife, the flash of an hourglass tattoo—but no, he's not coming for her this time, it's Lou and the children in front of him, he's going for them and there's nothing she can do but watch until the blackness swallows her.

"ROSE!" She jumps, and opens her eyes to find Charlie in front of her, both hands on her arms now, gently shaking her. "Are you okay? Do I need to call someone?"

"I'll be fine," she murmurs. "It's a panic attack. Give me a minute."

He lets go but stays crouched in front of her for a moment, watching her face intently. As she recovers her breathing, she sees him exhale in relief.

"You gave me a scare for a moment," he says softly.

"Sorry."

"No, don't apologize. What happened?"

"A flashback. I haven't had one in a long while, but tonight it's all too much." She rubs her cheek at the spot where the silver scar runs along it, and watches his expression turn to understanding.

"Jeez, Rose, I'm so sorry. Shall I get you a whiskey? It's good for shock."

"I don't drink," she replies quickly.

He hesitates and rubs his forehead, recognizing his faux pas.

"It's okay," she says. "What else have you got?" Even as she asks, she's longing for a solid glass tumbler with a slug of brown liquid in the bottom, and the satisfying burn in her throat.

"I might have some chamomile tea," he says.

"Perfect."

They go through to the main house and she watches him hunt around in his kitchen cupboards, pulling out a box of tea bags and switching the kettle on. He seems lost in thought as he waits for the water to boil, and Rose is glad of the silence as she works on controlling her breathing. By the time he brings the drink across, she's almost stopped shaking.

He sits opposite her and neither of them speak for a while. Eventually, Rose says, "I've come across a lot of awful situations through my work; I've got so good at shutting down my emotions that I sometimes feel immune to trauma. And I know it can come across as cold." As she talks, she stares at her drink, not wanting to catch his eye. "But this . . . tonight . . . I'm struggling. I can hardly bear it."

"I admire what you do for a living," Charlie says gently. "I don't underestimate how traumatic it must be to work around people who are being abused. Particularly after what happened."

"There's just so much of it," she tells him, sipping her tea. "More than anyone imagines. And that's only the relationships that don't stay hidden. There will be so much more happening in silence. After I wrote my book, I had hundreds of threatening and abusive emails from men wanting to put me in my place. I've been called every name under the sun; I've had messages detailing graphic ways in which strangers would like to hurt me, rape me, kill me. I like to think I'm pretty strong nowadays . . . but it takes a toll."

Charlie's mouth drops open in shock. "That's horrendous. I can't imagine. You know, Pri suffered too—with Trixie's dad."

"Oh, Charlie, that's terrible." Rose instinctively takes his hand, squeezing it. His grip tightens around her fingers, and they stay that way for a moment, before pulling away at the same time. Rose doesn't know what to say next, and it seems that Charlie's also lost for words.

She hunts for something practical. "We should phone Henry," she says. "Or were the police going to do it?"

"No, I told Angie I'd contact him. But I need to prepare myself first. He's been texting me a lot today, and I've been staving him off. I know he cares about Lou, but he has a way of making everything about him. I can't deal with it well at the best of times. Tonight, if he's a selfish prick, he might tip me over the edge."

Rose makes a sympathetic face. "I still don't get how you and Henry come from the same family."

"Yeah, we were always going in different directions. I think Henry probably resented me from day one. An annoying little half brother he didn't want or need, taking away everyone's time and attention, when he was still getting over his father abandoning him and our mum. But I guess I'd better get this over with. It isn't going to get any easier, is it?"

Rose listens to the one-sided conversation as Charlie breaks the news. "There's nothing about Lou yet," he begins. "But we've had some terrible news. Her boyfriend, Fabien, has been found dead on a beach tonight. He was stabbed." There's a pause. "No, I don't think anyone's saying Lou did it, but obviously there was a violent altercation with someone. We've just got to pray that Lou and the kids are okay." Another pause. "I know you do," Charlie says, "but Rose has been doing a great job. You couldn't have a better person on the ground."

Rose's eyes widen, wondering what Henry will make of that. She hears Charlie promise that they'll stay in touch, then he ends the call.

"He's probably fuming now," she says. "I don't think Henry likes hearing people praise me. It ruins the image he's constructed of his pathetic ex."

"I know." Charlie gives her a satisfied smile. "That's why I said it. Underneath all his shit, he knows how formidable you are. That's why he's always been frightened of letting you back into his life. If Lou had had you to turn to when she was growing up, there's no way she would have stuck with Henry."

Rose has never considered Henry from this angle before: how scared he might have been of losing his daughter to her, or of not being the father Lou wanted. She can almost feel sorry for him when she thinks of it like this, and it's the same when she hears the distressing childhood stories of domestic violence abusers. But she realized long ago that these people only deserve her sympathy when they demonstrate full accountability for their actions. Otherwise, all her focus goes on helping the ones they're hurting. If Henry had been born poor, he could so easily have become Joseph: running at her with his fists instead of his injunctions, because he enjoyed control just as much as the other narcissists she'd encountered over the years. Which meant it was only circumstance and fortune that separated Rose from Natalie,

Joseph's wife, and once Rose understood that, she'd never forgotten it. She'd stopped seeing these traumatized women as victims, and understood them as women just like her, trapped in circumstances beyond their control. It had made it a lot easier to help, to show compassion, and to do good work.

She drums her fingers against her cup, glad to find she's no longer trembling. She remembers the promise she'd made to herself: to bury her emotions and treat this like a case that needs solving. She works furiously to push away the images running through her mind, of that beautiful young man in the photos she'd seen on Instagram. The life in his eyes. His arms around Lou. *No.* She can't afford to go there. "This changes everything," she says, jumping up, "and we can't just wait around. I know I'm not meant to speak to the press, but what if Rick Malone knows something crucial? The police are going to vet all the information they provide to us—they always keep the worst things away from the families until they're sure. But I need the truth. And if Lou's still out there somewhere then the clock is ticking on the chance to bring her home safely."

Charlie considers her words. "I'm out of my depth here," he admits eventually. "I'm normally one for urging caution and restraint, but in this case I'm going to back you, whatever you decide."

Rose immediately pulls Malone's number from her pocket—but hesitates, remembering Angie's warning. Is this a good move? Or is she panicking because of the news about Fabien—unable to think clearly—because talking to Malone will certainly infuriate the police. And what if Charlie's instincts are right and Malone wants an exclusive? How much is she willing to trade for information, and how will it reflect on Lou if her mother is seen as colluding with the press?

"I'll hold off until morning," she tells him, "while I absorb the news about Fabien. But I'm not ruling it out tomorrow."

"Good plan," Charlie agrees.

She needs to do something else to keep her racing thoughts at bay, so she phones Veronica, pacing in Charlie's kitchen as she explains what's happened.

"I don't know what to say," Vee says after she's finished. "Except I've canceled and rearranged everything now, and the boys are set up to stay at their dad's. Lydia will check in on them too. I'm heading to the airport in an hour."

Rose hasn't realized how much she's missed her sister until she hears those words, but they almost break her. "Thank you, Vee," she says, her voice thick with emotion. "I'll see you soon." They're about to hang up when she suddenly remembers. "Any news on Bonnie?"

"Last I heard, she was still at Safehaven," Vee says.

"Thank god," Rose replies, grateful for this small piece of good news.

"Veronica is coming to help," she tells Charlie after the call has ended. "She's my rock."

"I think I remember her," he says. "Tell her that she's welcome to stay here too. I can pick her up when she arrives." He hesitates. "You don't have a partner then? Or is that too personal a question? Sorry."

"No, it's fine." She thinks of David, who will be oblivious to all of this. It's comforting to think that there's still another world where people are carrying on as normal. Somewhere she might return to. "I'm not long out of a relationship, but it was a mutual decision to end things—we were keeping each other company, not really going anywhere." She looks around the room, wanting to keep their conversation away from Fabien's body on the beach—to quell the panic that threatens every time she thinks of it. "Do you like talking about Pri?" she asks. "I'd love to hear more about her. These photos"—she waves her arm at all the images in different frames—"they're all beautiful."

Charlie smiles, but there's sadness in his eyes. "She was *my* rock. I met her when I was flying helicopters for mining companies, and earning a shitload, but it wasn't a life. Pri was mates with one of my colleagues' wives, and she was the best thing that's ever happened to me. We decided to get some land and see what we could do for ourselves, living off the grid. It was amazing for the first few years, and then she got sick. But I promised her I'd keep it going. I spent so many years helping people dig things out of the earth; now I'm trying to put a small part of it back together again."

"And Trixie, how's she coping?"

Charlie grimaces. "I'm not entirely sure. Trix is a one-off. She's on the spectrum, has never been too fond of talking, but she's pretty much gone mute since her mother died. Poor kid was only eight. Pri was from Thailand originally; her first Aussie husband had a temper, and he ran off with someone else, so her folks weren't keen on her shacking up with another Westerner, but I won them round eventually. However, when Pri died, the family didn't want Trix living with me on her own out here, so they tried to take her, but she played hell until she got to come home. And when Pri's folks realized how much Trix and I loved one another, they came around. So it's been the two of us mucking along these last few years, with lots of help from Pri's family and our extended neighbors, and the kind people at the temple Pri used to go to." Charlie sighs. "I'm praying we can get Lou home safely before I need to tell Trix anything. They adore one another. It was watching them together that made me suggest the nannying work to Lou. I think Henry had the notion that she'd follow the family business and become a banker." He snorts. "He had no idea the kind of girl he was raising. She was so defeated and angry when she came here. Wouldn't come out of her room at first, and hated being stuck in the bush with us. But we just let her be, and slowly she began to bond with Trixie. Trix would show her things on the land, and they both loved looking after the animals. After a few months you could see Lou unwinding a little more each day, realizing there were no expectations on her, no humiliation around the corner if she didn't do as expected. And from that point, she blossomed."

"There's so much I never knew about her," Rose says sadly. "I should have thought more about how she might be struggling. She asked to see me a couple of times in her teens but then wouldn't talk—and we were always supervised by Evelyn or Henry. She was obviously very angry on the last few occasions we spoke to each other, and I couldn't get beyond that—I felt pretty helpless about it all."

"Perhaps it's just the life she needed to live." Charlie rubs a hand over his face as though trying to brush away his exhaustion. "Sometimes sadness and struggle is the making of people. I think we can spend way too much time trying to figure out how we might have changed the world, or other people's lives, if we'd done things differently. We all go through crap, but it's still up to us to decide how it defines us. Henry always felt hard done by because his dad left, but he never saw how much my dad—not to mention me and Mum—bent over backward to support him. So he's remained a selfish bastard for his entire life. But sometimes even the most traumatic experiences end up lifting people higher, help them achieve more and give back to others. Pri's family are Buddhists, they believe in karma, and for the most part I like their religion. It's made me rethink a lot of my place in the world." He takes a deep breath and releases the air in a long exhale. "But right now I'm not sure I believe in anything benevolent. Not till we get Lou home."

As they fall silent, Rose's phone buzzes. "It's Stella," she says, scanning the message.

The note was from Bree—the nanny who worked for Kyle and Frannie before Lou. I'll see if I can contact her. If you're up, can I come and see you again tonight? The atmosphere here is horrible, and the walls are way too thin. I can tell you about Marisol.

Rose looks up at Charlie. "She wants to drive over and talk to me in person. She thinks I'm still at the hotel. Shall I tell her to come? Or is it too late? She might not want to drive this far—maybe I should meet her somewhere else?"

"Nothing's too late in an emergency," Charlie replies. "And there's nowhere to meet halfway; it's all bush. Text her the address and see what she says."

Rose replies quickly, talking as she types. "If she doesn't want to come, I'll try to go to her. I want to know exactly what she told Louisa about Kyle's previous nannies, and who this Marisol is." Her phone buzzes again. "She says she'll be here in half an hour." Rose checks her watch. "It's half past nine, and I've still got a third of Malone's book to skim-read. At least it'll help with the wait."

Charlie runs his fingers through his hair. "Those police officers are going to be pissed at us if they find out we're interrogating witnesses late at night. I hope we're doing the right thing."

Rose shrugs. "Me too. But we can't sit around doing nothing, not after tonight. Surely they'll understand that?"

But even as she tries to rationalize her decisions, watching Charlie work to smother his unease with a reassuring smile, Rose knows she's playing with fire. She can only hope that her instincts are good enough to help push the case along, otherwise all her attempts to get information might be about to go horribly wrong.

CHAPTER TWENTY-FOUR
BLACKWOOD

Blackwood stands in the crowded situation room, at the center of chaos. All around him there's momentum: new search protocols, and a constant stream of analysis and updates about Fabien's body, which is now heading for the mortuary in Perth with a police escort. Preliminary feedback from forensics indicated that although Fabien had been fatally wounded by the stabbing, the brachial artery severed as Kelsie Hughes had suspected, he'd still been alive when he entered the water. There were no other remarkable wounds, only a few bruises that might not be connected, and the gash in his arm looked like a small shark bite. The entire taskforce agreed that it was highly unlikely Louisa was involved in the stabbing, and they therefore needed to work on the basis that she and the children had been abducted. There were two logical possibilities: Either Fabien had met her with someone else that morning, and had been involved in the snatch, or strangers had turned up on the beach, and Fabien had been in the way. Everyone agreed it was the second option that made sense.

Blackwood has just finished a late-night briefing with Drake and all the senior officers dialing in. They had unanimously supported the idea of the press conference. The consensus was that the situation was dire, and they wanted the media onside quickly. When he'd expressed his grave fears for Louisa and the children, particularly if the kidnappers' plan had gone awry, no one had disagreed.

Drake had asked him to call back for a private chat, and now Blackwood holds his phone to his right ear, aware of a dull throb behind his eyes.

"Our next moves are critical." Drake is almost shouting down the phone. "You need to keep on top of this by the minute, and placate the Fishers as much as possible. I've just had Jock ranting at me. He's got word of the body on the beach and he's furious, accusing us of being inept, of taking too long, of hiding things, and of not letting them speak to the public. Stacey Sewell is holed up in a Perth hotel setting up her cameras, and Kyle is begging to talk to her. I could hear him shouting and cursing in the background. We're going to completely lose control of them soon."

The ache in Blackwood's skull spreads down his neck and across his shoulders. He wishes he could have spoken to the family before they'd heard anything about the body, but he'd had to send support officers ahead. Too many people had witnessed the discovery for them to be able to keep it under wraps for long. "I'm going to talk to them next, in person, and I'll post some fresh liaison officers with the family tonight, and make sure they're the best we've got," Blackwood reassures his superior. Angie is the obvious candidate because she has the best people skills, but she's a detective, not a babysitter, and he objects to the idea of sidelining her and having to take Webster everywhere instead.

"Pull out all the stops to keep them calm," Drake insists. "Whatever you need."

As Drake hangs up, Blackwood hardly has time to take a breath before DC White rushes over. "I have Fabien's housemate on the line, do you want to talk to him?"

"Yes," he says immediately, holding a hand out for the phone.

"His name's Azir," White says, handing over the mobile, "and he's just come back from ten days surfing in Bali in the middle of nowhere. He's completely shell shocked. The phone is muted until you're ready. I can sit in with you if you like?"

Blackwood nods, and moves quickly to one of the smaller side rooms, closing the door after White has followed him in.

Blackwood unmutes the device and turns on the speaker. "Hello, Azir, I'm DSS Malcolm Blackwood and I have Detective Constable White with me too. We've put you on speakerphone. First of all, my condolences to you over the loss of your friend Fabien."

"Th-Thank you. I can't believe this. It's a bad dream. I came back this morning and saw the stories about Fab being missing and I had hundreds of messages when I switched on my phone. And now I hear this unbelievable news—that he's gone." Azir's voice cracks. "What is going on?"

"That's what we're trying to find out. When did you last have contact with Fabien?"

"Just before I left. He took me to the airport. He said he had decided to take a short break from work and was planning to try to see Lou. He was going to do some surfing, stay at a friend's house—I think they rent it out as an Airbnb."

Blackwood nods at White, who scribbles a note.

"And what was his mood like, before he left?"

"He wasn't happy. He was missing Lou and very worried about her. They really hit it off when she was in Sydney, but her new employers wouldn't let her talk to anyone. He thought they were spying on her, monitoring her phone. And when he asked around he heard rumors that other people working for them had had bad experiences. So he wanted to go to Lou and make sure she knew how he felt, and to persuade her not to work there for any longer than the six months of her contract."

Blackwood paces as he talks. "Do you know anything more specific about these rumors regarding the Fishers?"

"Not much. Something happened at a party a few years ago, a woman got hurt, but no one will give details. Fabien even wondered if people were being blackmailed or paid for their silence."

"Do you know the names of the friends he was staying with?"

"No, I'm sorry."

"And he didn't mention making any specific arrangements with Louisa?"

"I don't think so. I've been racking my brains, but we only had one conversation about it—and it was pretty last minute. I didn't pay too much attention; I was focused on my trip, you know how it is. I rushed off at the airport without even saying a proper goodbye." His voice cracks on the last word.

"I won't keep you on the phone, Azir. I realize this is incredibly stressful. Please don't hesitate to call us if you think of anything, okay? Even if it might sound far fetched. We'd much rather hear it than not know."

"All right."

"Thank you. And please make sure you have some good support around you tonight. Again, we're so sorry for your loss."

Once they've hung up, Blackwood checks his own phone and sees that while he was talking to Azir he's missed a message from Angie. He quickly calls her back. "Are you still with the Fishers? How's it going?"

"It's awful; they're beside themselves. When we confirmed the discovery of Fabien's body, Frannie screamed and collapsed into her sister's arms. So she's lying down and Kyle has stormed outside and disappeared into the garden. Although thank god, it seems to have sobered everyone up and stopped the flow of beers among the men. I've told them you'll be here shortly," she says. "They're on board with doing the press conference, and I've also spoken to Rose. She and Charlie will represent Louisa's family. Am I right in thinking it's going to be Jock and Kyle and Frannie fronting up for the Fishers?"

"I think so. I'll brief them when I come up to the house. I'd like them all to be involved, but we won't ask Frannie to talk."

"Good. I'm worried about her. She's going to be catatonic soon, but she'll get everyone's sympathy just by her presence. Although I'm concerned about Rose coming across as cold next to her."

"Then it's good we'll have Louisa's uncle up there as well—it will balance things out a bit."

"Jock appears to be pushing for them all to go back up to Perth tomorrow. Kyle looks half convinced, but Frannie is refusing to leave, which is understandable. She can't bear the idea of going home to an empty house without the kids."

"I'm surprised Kyle wants to go."

"I think Kyle will do whatever Jock tells him to at this stage." Blackwood silently wishes they could just get Jock out of the way, to stop him influencing everyone. "Any news on the ex-wife?"

"Still trying to reach her."

"And what about a venue for the press conference?"

"DC White has been in touch with the resort at Dunsborough—we can use their conference room."

"Good. I'm coming up to the house now," Blackwood says, his feet heavy as he makes for the door, his body protesting at another sortie with the Fishers.

"Ready when you are," Angie replies.

Blackwood hangs up and heads through the situation room and outside. It's a beautiful clear night as he takes the now-familiar ten-minute walk up the hill and down the private laneway to the Fishers' residence. He looks up at the smoky pall of the Milky Way, finding the emu in the dark space amid the swirls of light, and thinks of Margie wrapped up and sitting outside as she likes to do on these cooler autumn nights, beneath the fairy lights that twinkle along the eaves of their veranda like rows of tiny fallen stars. He'd had a text from her earlier, and looks at it again now, while he's alone. *Thanks for the chocolates, you didn't need to, but I appreciate the gesture. Everything is fine here. Get those kids home, and I'll see you soon.*

Margie has always understood that his desire to set things right is an integral part of who he is. He pictures her staring up at the same sky, as though he might force a connection between them through sheer will. He misses his wife. It feels like she exists in another life, parallel to this one.

He types back *I miss you*, and hits send before he can second-guess himself. As he repockets the device, he shakes his head. What is happening to him? When did he become such a soppy old fool?

As he approaches the Fishers' door, he braces himself. He sure as hell doesn't envy any of the Fishers their privileged lives or their complicated relationships, or even their swanky house and wads of cash. All he has ever needed is waiting for him in his well-kept little cottage in Ocean Reef. He only hopes that Margie is confident in their rekindled spark, and his absence isn't allowing her doubts and fears to creep back in. The Fishers aren't worth that—but the same can't be said for those two little kiddies and a young girl who's hardly had a chance at life.

Inside the house, the atmosphere is thick with fear and panic. No one is sitting down anymore. Jock and his two oldest sons are on the veranda, in the midst of a heated discussion, while Bronte stalks around the kitchen, checking the contents of cupboards. Angie hovers by the countertop.

Blackwood marches over to the sliding door that leads to the veranda. "Is Kyle still out there?" he asks, gesturing at the garden.

"Yep," Toby says dismissively.

"Well, can you bloody well find him for me," Blackwood growls. "I haven't got time to waste while he goes for a midnight stroll." He turns back to Angie and Bronte. "And get Frannie down here right away too. We have things to discuss."

He's not as angry as he sounds, but he needs to assert control. Angie gives him a brief nod of admiration as the Fisher siblings hurry off on their various missions.

Jock, meanwhile, comes inside and glares at Blackwood. "So what's the plan now?" he asks. "I hope it's a good one."

Blackwood holds the man's gaze, determined not to be intimidated. "We're dealing with an incredibly unusual situation," he begins. "It's very rare for a madman to murder someone and then grab a woman and two children in broad daylight. So I'm wondering if it would have taken more than one person to carry out this particular snatch. And unless this person or persons are deranged, there's a reason behind this. With Fabien's death, it looks increasingly like he and Louisa have been caught up in this as innocent parties, so the spotlight has to fall on exactly what might make someone kidnap Fisher grandchildren. Let's discuss."

Kyle comes in ahead of his brothers, in time to catch the end of this speech. Frannie has also reached the bottom of the stairs, with Bronte trailing behind.

"I want all of you thinking through every possibility," Blackwood instructs them. "We need names, right now, of anyone who might wish you harm or have something to gain by doing this."

"I don't think you get it," Ethan says, his irritation obvious. "The Fisher brand is everywhere. How the hell are we meant to know about everyone with a grievance?"

Frannie rounds on him. "Can't you at least think about it for more than two seconds, and help them find my fucking children," she shouts, her pitch rising with every word.

"Calm down, Frannie," Toby snaps sourly, hands in his pockets.

"For fuck's sake, Toby, leave her alone," Kyle rages at his brother. "Not everyone is an emotionless moron."

Bronte lets out a sudden burst of laughter, then quickly covers her mouth with her hand.

"Shut up, all of you," Jock bellows, hands aloft. "Can everyone just sit the fuck down and stop bickering?"

"Louisa said someone was following her a few months ago," Angie reminds them, as the Fisher siblings make their way sullenly to the lounge chairs. "Perhaps she's been under surveillance for a while. Please, think."

"That wasn't anything," Frannie says in a small voice. "That was me."

Blackwood swings around. "What do you mean?"

"I always watch the nannies for a bit when they first start." Frannie shrugs. "I had someone tail her for a week to check she was doing her job properly. They're my babies," she adds fiercely, registering the surprised expressions around her. "Do you really think I'm going to leave their care to chance?"

"Fucking hell, Fran, how did you afford that?" Kyle looks thunderous.

"None of your business," she bites back.

He shakes his head. "You better not have borrowed more money from Vic."

They glower at each other. "Fuck you," Frannie yells at him. "You should be grateful I didn't get Louisa tailing *you* with a fucking camera. I'm sure she'd have captured plenty of your dirty little secrets."

Kyle's choked-off sigh is spiteful. "You're such a bitch," he goads her. "And a deceitful whore, as it turns out."

Frannie charges at him, nails ready to claw, and Kyle grabs her wrists to defend himself while everyone shouts and tries to separate them.

"For god's sake," Blackwood yells into the disarray. "I'll arrest you both for obstructing an investigation if you don't stop right now. Angie, take Frannie outside to cool off for a moment, will you?"

"Absolutely." Angie grabs Frannie's arm and pulls the woman with her. Frannie's rage has dissipated into a flood of tears, but Angie doesn't look impressed.

"Jesus, Kyle," Bronte says, sitting down with a bump on the sofa. "Why did you and Ebony get divorced again? Surely it wasn't as bad as this." She looks across to Frannie, still visible through the glass. Her tears are streaming now, and she wipes her nose with the back of her hand while Angie talks to her.

"Stay focused," Blackwood insists, prowling around the group as he talks. "I need names fast. What about that group of protesters outside the gate? You must know who's most riled up by your business and your fortune."

He doesn't miss the looks that are exchanged between them all. It only lasts a few seconds, but an agreement appears to have been reached. No one speaks.

"Please," he implores them, making sure he catches everyone's eye in turn. "Kyle's babies need everything you've got right now."

"Look." Jock takes a seat, elbows on knees and hands steepled as he leans forward. "Ethan's right—it's hard to give you a short list. We can only give you a very, very long list of all sorts of people who probably aren't relevant. Do you know how many complaints we get in a day? Do you know how often we're caught up in legal battles, and how many people that involves? There must be some other way of getting a better lead than us trying to figure out the one person out of the hundreds—no, thousands—of people that we've pissed off over the years who might still hold a grudge."

"I know what you're saying," Blackwood persists calmly, "but we have to start somewhere. Otherwise, with no contact from the kidnappers and no evidence leading us anywhere, Louisa and the kids have just vanished. So get a piece of paper, or open your phone, each of you, and get to work."

Blackwood leaves them to it for a moment and goes outside to Angie and Frannie. "You need to go and help them, Frannie," he says firmly. Frannie looks up, and he can see her debating whether to argue. Eventually she nods and pushes past him, heading inside.

"We'll see if they come up with anyone significant," Blackwood murmurs, surveying the Fishers through the glass as they confer with one another, while Frannie observes them from the kitchen in sulky silence. "Might as well keep them busy while we're stuck waiting for forensics on Fabien. But shit, Angie, I'm boxed into a corner here. The press conference in the morning had better come up with something or we're stuffed." As they watch the family, Bronte goes over to Frannie and puts a consoling hand on hers for a moment, before moving round to grab a bottle of water from the fridge.

"Yeah," Angie says. "And I've been thinking: If Kyle's got someone spying on Frannie, and Frannie's spying on Louisa, it starts to make you wonder who they've got spying on us."

Blackwood's gaze narrows as he studies the family group inside. The siblings are still busy talking, but he catches Jock's eye. They hold each other's stare for a long moment, before the older man looks away.

CHAPTER TWENTY-FIVE
ROSE

When Stella arrives, Rose waits impatiently while Charlie takes the young woman's jacket and offers her a drink. There's only one overhead bulb in the lounge and its yellow light doesn't reach far, leaving the corners of the room in shadow. Stella looks like she's already dressed for bed, in red pajama pants with white stars, and a loose-fitting red long-sleeved top. She accepts the offer of tea, and Rose invites her across to the sofa while Charlie goes to the kitchen.

"What's happening at your house?" Rose asks, sitting opposite Stella.

"Vic's in a foul temper. I think he was talking to the police this afternoon—and I'm pretty sure we know what that will have been about." She glances at Rose, her cheeks pink. "Particularly since the detectives questioned me too. They promised they would do everything to keep me out of it, and that they wouldn't mention who passed on the photo, but I was still terrified they might have gone back on their word. I kept waiting for Vic to march up the stairs and order me out, but instead he had a massive fight with Bridget."

Rose shifts forward in her seat. "Could you hear what it was about?"

"Not too much. At one point I heard her say, 'You always have to take things that bit too far, don't you?' And something about it being the last time she'd go through this. But she hasn't packed her bags, and they seem to have calmed down. They took the kids out for takeaway, so I got a break, and when they came back I kept myself busy putting the kids to bed. By the time I'd finished they had both disappeared upstairs."

"Do you think they know more than they're saying?"

"It's hard to tell. They've always been pretty above board. But Vic sometimes seems jealous of Kyle—and I guess Bridget might be jealous of Frannie now too. Although I can't see how any of that is relevant to this scenario." Stella accepts a mug of tea from Charlie, and Rose sees that her hands are shaking. Stella notices Rose watching her, and sets the mug down carefully. "I'm really frightened," she admits. "The news tonight said there's a body on the beach in Dunsborough. What if it's one of them?"

Charlie catches Rose's eye across the room and she acknowledges his unspoken question with a small shake of her head. It won't help Stella to hear what they know. Instead, she says, "If it helps, I'm frightened too. I think we're both having a very normal reaction in these circumstances."

Stella takes a steadying breath. "You're probably right. It's just, I would've been on that beach with Louisa if I'd been well enough. I keep wondering: Would that have saved her and the kids, or would I be missing too? I know so much private stuff about both families. The more people ask questions, the more it makes me anxious about why this has happened, and who's involved. Whether I'm next." She looks up. "Am I being silly?"

"Of course not, those feelings are completely understandable," Rose reassures her. "But this is a very unusual set of circumstances. I don't think whoever is behind this would risk more attention right now, with everyone on high alert. That said, if at any time you don't feel safe, you should remove yourself from the situation immediately, and don't be scared to call the police. Their job is to protect you."

Stella listens, but still looks unsure. She goes quiet, lost in thought, holding her mug close to her mouth with both hands as she takes regular sips of tea.

Rose waits, trying not to overwhelm the girl with questions, but itching to find out what more she knows. Stella's gaze wanders around the house, falling on the haphazard piles of books, fleecy bags, and scattered stems of hay, and Rose realizes she'll have to take the lead. "So," she says gently, "what can you tell us about Marisol?"

Stella shuffles forward on her chair. Charlie comes over and puts tea in front of Rose, then sits down holding another cup of his own.

"It was before my time," Stella begins, "but everyone knows about it. There's a network of nannies and au pairs, and we all tell each other stuff: warnings about different employers, tips on how to stay on our bosses' good side, or how to keep your energy up when you're expected to be at the family's beck and call all day. We try to look out for one another where we can, especially those of us with high-profile employers. There's lots of gossip too: which bosses have straying hands, who has a terrible temper, and stories about the nannies and au pairs who left their positions abruptly. That's how I heard about Marisol."

"She worked for the Fishers?" Rose asks.

"Not exactly," Stella replies. "She worked for Kyle's ex-wife, but she was mostly caring for a little boy from Ebony's second marriage—although I think she did school runs for Kyle's sons sometimes too. They were all living up in Perth, not too far from Kyle." Stella pauses, setting her mug down on the table. "I never met her, but I gather there was an accident at one of Kyle's house parties. I think he might have been with Frannie by then, but I'm not entirely sure. Anyway, everyone went to this thing, including Ebony and her second husband, her older boys, and the new baby. And Marisol. And while the party was in full swing, Marisol somehow fell off a third-floor balcony. She landed on the concrete, broke her neck and a heap of other bones, and fractured her skull too."

"Jeez," Charlie says, blowing out a breath. "That's horrible. Did she survive?"

"Yes, but she was paralyzed and severely brain damaged. She's been in a bad way ever since. I heard of this through Bree, the nanny who worked for Kyle before Lou. Bree had a few different positions with the family: She was working for Toby Fisher back when Marisol was around. Bree tried to stay in contact with Marisol's family afterward, though I'm not sure she'd still be in touch now. The incident was blamed on Marisol's mental health issues—the official line was that she jumped—but Bree never believed that. Marisol couldn't tell anyone what happened, and there was gossip that some people suspected she was pushed."

"But nothing ever came of it?"

"No, but there's a feeling among the nannies that the Fishers only bring you bad luck. Bree stayed longer than many of the others—said she liked the money—but even she'd had enough after working for Kyle and Frannie. There's always some sort of drama going on, and there have been some really nasty divorces over the years. Kyle and Ebony obviously didn't like each other after they split, but they tried to be civil for the kids. Kyle's brothers are rumored to be really controlling and we hardly ever see their wives at social events. According to the gossip, Toby is quiet in public but has a temper behind closed doors, and Ethan is full of himself and sleeps around." Stella pauses to take a long sip of her drink, before continuing, "Bronte had some bad luck too before she met Eddie—in her twenties she fell for an actor who used her name to get auditions in LA, married her in Vegas, then dumped her months later and spilled his guts on a reality TV show. Bree used to say the family were completely dysfunctional—get them in a room and they'd just argue and antagonize each other. Then in the papers they're smiling and acting like they're having the best time in the world together. It's all bullshit."

Charlie looks from one woman to the other. "So we have one nanny with a secondhand connection to the Fishers who had an accident several years ago. And another missing now. It's hardly a long list of suspicious events, is it? The link between them is tenuous at best."

"But why the note passed from Bree to Louisa?" Rose persists, her eyes on Stella. "Why do former nannies feel the need to warn current ones about the Fishers?"

"It's not just about accidents and stuff," Stella says. "It's the whole vibe. The Fishers really don't give a shit about their employees. They completely control these vulnerable girls going in to work for them, who are often from overseas and have no idea what they're getting themselves into."

Rose's chest constricts, knowing how perfectly Lou matches this criteria. "And what makes you say that," she asks, "about the Fishers not caring?"

"Plenty of things. For example, on the night Marisol was hurt, they called an ambulance, which took her away, but then the party just carried on until the police arrived an hour or so later. Bree said Kyle didn't even stay out the front of the house; he just came to see what was going on, then disappeared back inside. Ebony's husband, Asher, went in the ambulance with Marisol, and Ebony took the boys home. But the rest of them continued like nothing had happened. All the nannies were really upset, obviously, but they couldn't do much as they had little ones to look after. Bree said she'd heard that Ebony was so disgusted with Kyle she barely spoke to him after that, and the boys must have picked up on it as they don't want much to do with him either nowadays. They're both young adults now, and hopefully see him for what he is: a shallow, self-centered man."

Rose absorbs the words. "You don't think he has any redeeming features?"

"Well, ironically, the one thing I would say is that he adores messing around with his little kids. Perhaps he's trying to make a better go of fatherhood this time around." She shrugs. "The kids make him laugh—and they're probably closer to his mental age than most people he hangs out with." Stella raises an eyebrow. "I think that if he'd step up for anyone, it would be them."

Rose checks the time on her phone. "I really appreciate you coming, Stella, but it's very late; you should go and get some sleep."

"Are you comfortable driving back at this time?" Charlie asks. "You could sleep in my daughter's room—she's not here tonight—and head off when it's light?"

"That's kind of you," Stella says, getting up, "but I need to go back for the children. If they wake up in the night I'm the one who takes care of them. I've taken a risk coming here, but they're always out for the count for at least a few hours." She gets up and hands Charlie her empty mug.

"I would really like to speak to Bree, the Fishers' previous nanny," Rose says. "Can you put me in contact with her?"

"Sure—I messaged her earlier, but I'll remind her now." Stella pulls out her phone, and her fingers move at lightning speed as she sends a text. "There—done."

"Thank you."

At the door, Stella turns back to Rose. "You know," she says shyly, "Lou once told me she was sorry she hadn't had a chance to know you better. She confided in me a bit about what happened—her dad sounds like an arsehole. I think she'd be glad to know you're here now."

"Thank you," Rose replies, letting the words in just enough to console, but careful to withstand the emotions that threaten to cascade through her. She can't go there yet. "I appreciate that."

They see Stella out and into her car, and watch her drive away down the pitch-dark track, headlights fading into the gloom. Once she's gone, Charlie turns to Rose.

"So what do you reckon? Something or nothing?"

Rose shrugs. "I don't know. I'm very tired. I want to talk to Bree in the morning, but we have the press conference too." She looks at her phone again, just to check for anything new, but there's nothing. "It's nearly midnight," she says, glancing at Charlie in despair.

"Do you think," he suggests gently, "you could get a few hours of sleep? I know it's hard, but you'll be sharper if you can manage it."

"I'll try," she agrees. "Thanks for all of this, Charlie, you don't know how much I appreciate it."

"Anytime," he replies.

"Good night, then," she says softly, and takes herself to bed, where soon she's lost in fitful dreams, pursued by footsteps that hound her in the dark.

CHAPTER TWENTY-SIX
BLACKWOOD

The conference room at the Dunsborough hotel is well apportioned, sizable enough to fit over a hundred chairs, with parquet flooring and a view across the pool. It's mostly used for weddings, and a few cream and gold helium balloons from recent nuptials still nestle up against the rafters of the high ceiling. There's also an adjacent room with a bar and dining tables, sectioned off with sliding doors, which has been allocated for the families to allow them some privacy.

Blackwood has been here since eight o'clock, prepping and making sure he's happy with the setup. Now, half an hour before kickoff, he's waiting for everyone to arrive.

It's been a shitty morning so far. He'd been informed by a text from Angie that the photos of Fabien's body were already on the web—those little shits on the beach had obviously sent them somewhere before he checked their phones. He'd hurried to get up and ready, but before he'd even had a coffee, the local police had called and complained about the cars lining the verges of the tiny road into Kardanup, blocking access for SES vehicles and local traffic. People were coming from near and far now, lured by Jock's massive reward and the potential of a murder to spice up the search. It had turned the case into a real-life mystery adventure with a massive prize for the person who solved it. No one was mentioning the money, of course; they'd all convinced themselves they were heroes, gallantly lending a hand.

One of the journalists had managed to get inside the gates and all the way up to the Fisher house, taking photos through the windows and causing a stir. Blackwood was ready to string up whoever was responsible for the breach, until they realized the journo had taken advantage of a gap in the wall five hundred meters down the small country road. The police couldn't be everywhere, but there was now some junior constable bored out of his mind watching that spot, to ensure it didn't happen again. This event had also highlighted that there were other ways Fabien could have gone down to the beach, and the team would need to double-check everything. In Blackwood's experience it's often these little details, so easily missed, that prove vital.

He rubs his tired eyes. There are so many factors to this case it's beyond exhausting, and on top of it all, trying to keep the journalists at bay is like fighting off zombie attacks. They are relentless. If they pick up the scent of a story they'll do anything to find the source of it. And in about half an hour, he recalls with a grimace, checking his watch, he's going to dangle the facts and two terrified families in front of them all, like bait.

Angie had gone outside to wait for Rose and Charlie, to delay their arrival into the briefing room for as long as possible. Between the Fishers' growing unpredictability, and Rose's sniffer-dog senses, Blackwood isn't keen to allow them too much time together. He wants to avoid the conversation going south before they've done the formalities.

While he's waiting for everyone to arrive, he texts Margie with an update. He'd messaged her again late last night about Fabien, and she'd responded immediately. *That poor boy. My thoughts and prayers to his family.* But aside from her adding a small red heart to his message about missing her, there had been nothing else. Not *Miss you too* or *How are you?* or *This must be very hard on you* or even *Are you sleeping?*, which she used to ask regularly when his life was taken over by a big case. The lack of concern increased his agitation, reduced his quality of sleep, and is distracting him even now, which is aggravating when he's about to manage such a huge press conference, one that will be getting international interest as well as intense attention closer to home.

The body on the beach has been covered by all the media outlets this morning, and while the journalists have a sense of what's coming, most are thankfully waiting for official confirmation of identity lest they make fools of themselves. From what Blackwood has heard, Robbie Reynolds is using the timing of the press conference as a countdown to the moment of truth, anticipating his own grief, and telling listeners how broken he'll be if this is, as suspected, his good friend Fabien. Blackwood hasn't tuned in; he's happy to get updates from those willing to sit through the disingenuous emotional charade. The more the DJ insists on his close friendship with Fabien, the more Blackwood suspects the man hardly gave his producer the time of day outside of work.

Webster enters the room, his expression neutral. "They're arriving now, sir," he says. "Also, we've had a call from Bridget Santos, Vic's wife. Apparently, their nanny put the kids to bed last night, but she isn't at the house this morning. They're concerned as it's out of character for her."

Blackwood receives this news with another jolt of discomfort. "That's worrying. Get onto it right away, please. I have to stay focused here." There's no time to think about it any further. He can already hear voices coming closer as he stands and pulls on his suit jacket, ready to greet everyone.

As people begin to file in, it's apparent that the entire Fisher family have come as an entourage to the conference. Frannie has brought Valentine the blue bear, and she clings to it like it's a talisman. Kyle has three days' worth of stubble and messy hair and wears a T-shirt and jeans. Jock is as crisp as ever in a smart dark suit and open-necked white shirt, and he's wearing aviator shades even though they're indoors. His assistant, Andrew, finds a corner to lurk in, staying permanently on the phone, while Bronte and Toby head to another table by the long windows, talking quietly and casting concerned glances toward Kyle and Frannie. To Blackwood's surprise, Ethan marches over to him.

"After we've done this," Ethan says, without preamble, waving at the room, "how long before you actually get some results? We can't all stay here indefinitely, you know. I've got a business to run—multiple businesses actually—thousands of people depending on me."

Blackwood opens his mouth, ready to deliver a particularly acerbic response, then stops. This isn't the moment to lose his cool. "The press conference will start in a few minutes," he says, patting Ethan's arm. "Let's get through that first, then we can talk," he says, putting a hand on Ethan's back to turn him around and guide him toward his siblings. He's planning to stay well away from Ethan for the rest of the day.

It's clear from the rising cacophony that the conference space is filling up. Blackwood peers through the double doors and sees that every seat is already taken and people are beginning to stand at the sides. As well as local and national news reporters he can spot the BBC and CNN, along with Japanese, Korean, and French news channels. He's sweating again; his shirt is damp beneath his suit jacket. He continues to check his watch until there's ten minutes until kickoff. He and Angie agreed earlier that Rose and Charlie will come in at this point. Moments later, he sees them being shown through the doorway at the back of the bar, flanked by Angie and three uniformed officers. All heads turn.

Rose looks around, her expression solemn, largely unreadable. She sees Blackwood and her eyebrows lift in recognition, but before she can move much further Frannie accosts her, flinging her arms around Rose.

"I'm so sorry," she bawls. "We love Lou so much. I swear we don't believe she'd do anything to hurt the kids."

Rose accepts the embrace, and steps back, dry eyed. "Thank you. You must be Frannie. And is this Honey's teddy, the one that was found on the beach?" She squints at Valentine as though she wants to examine him thoroughly, perhaps even send him for forensic tests. Blackwood feels mean as soon as he has the thought, but he's uneasy at the obvious disparity between these two mothers—one so utterly broken while the other remains self-contained and assured. He hopes it's not going to be commented on in the media. The gossip would add more unneeded stress.

Kyle shakes Charlie's hand and they introduce themselves, both of them solemn and forgoing any small talk. Jock does the same, then they all sit down and turn to Blackwood expectantly.

"Five minutes," he says. "Let's go over the plan one last time. The only speakers with prepared statements will be myself, Jock, Kyle, and Charlie. In that order. Rose, Frannie, if I see you getting distressed or if the questions are too intrusive, we'll end the conference as quickly as possible. You do not have to say anything, okay?"

He half expects Rose to object, but she nods in agreement and casts a brief concerned glance at Frannie, who keeps her head bowed.

Blackwood beckons Angie over. "A word, please." They move into a corner. "Webster just informed me the Santos nanny is missing now too."

"What?" Angie hisses.

"She wasn't in their house this morning. Webster's leading the team looking for her. Stay alert—things are amping up, I can feel it."

They move away from each other without another word, and Blackwood is relieved to see the family haven't tuned into their tense conversation. There can't be any more distractions right now.

At exactly half past nine they file into the conference room one at a time and take seats at a long rectangular table with microphones in front of each of them. Blackwood begins straightaway.

"Thank you all for coming. We want to give you a brief update on the missing nanny, Louisa Thornton, and the children, Honey and Kai Fisher. To my left I have Louisa's uncle, Charlie, and mother, Rose, and then, to my right, Honey and Kai's parents, Frannie and Kyle, and their grandfather Jock. I realize some of these people are well known to you in other spheres of life, but I want to ask that you take the utmost care and respect in the way you talk to them today because this is an extremely distressing time for everyone involved." He pauses to glance around the room, making eye contact with as many of the journalists as he can, to reinforce his request before continuing.

"We're making a press release available now, confirming the key points I'll be running through with you. As you already know, last night we recovered a body on the beach just south of the Dunsborough township, which was found by three local boys. We can confirm to you that this is the body of Fabien Dubois, Louisa Thornton's boyfriend."

There's a sharp rise of gabbled noise in the room as the journalists react, and Blackwood holds his hands up to quieten them.

"There's still no sign of Louisa, Honey, or Kai. We remain extremely concerned for their welfare. Fabien is a Sydney resident, and although he may have been visiting Louisa, we do not know for certain why he was in the area, and we appeal to any member of the public with information to call us immediately. Likewise, we would ask you to take a good look at the photo behind us"—he indicates a large-scale cropped photo of Louisa, Honey, and Kai—"and let us know if you have seen any of these three people in the last few days, or if you know anything that might help us locate them. We have reason to believe they may have been abducted by persons known or unknown to them, and if so we urge those responsible to immediately return these three young, vulnerable individuals to their families." Frannie lets out a sob and Blackwood falters for a moment, distracted, then recovers. "Due to the sensitive nature of the ongoing investigation we cannot release any further details at this time. Jock Fisher will now make a brief statement."

Jock looks sternly around the room before he begins. "Thank you for coming. I would like to remind you that we are relying on every single one of you to make your journalistic skills count. We are talking about a three-year-old and an eleven-month-old here. I urge anyone who knows anything to get in touch, and to consider the reward on offer—which,

I repeat, is two million dollars shared between all those who can give us relevant, useful information. Thank you."

Kyle speaks next. "On behalf of Frannie and myself," he says in a strange monotone voice, his hand unsteady as he grips the paper, "we want to appeal to the person who has Louisa and our children to return them to us safely today. We love and miss them very much; our lives are in pieces while they're not here. We don't know why you've taken them, and we wish you no harm; we just want them home."

Blackwood nods at Charlie to indicate it's his turn, but Charlie hesitates, perhaps intimidated by the assembled crowd. Blackwood wonders if he's got stage fright—it would be understandable—but the pause goes on for so long that he's about to interrupt when Rose starts to talk instead.

Damn. Blackwood holds his breath. This is not in the plan.

"I speak for the whole of Louisa's family when I say we love her very much and want her safely returned to us," Rose begins. Blackwood stiffens; she sounds so formal, so strained. Then she glances at Charlie and something passes between them, and when she turns back to the press she is dewy eyed. "If you're out there, Lou, and by any chance you're watching this, we want you to know that you are more special to us than you could possibly imagine. We want to bring you back safely and wrap you in love. So if anyone can help us find all three of our children, we urge you to get in touch right away. Please." Her jaw clenches as she stammers out the final *please*, and Charlie rubs her back briefly. On the other side of Blackwood, Frannie sits, head down, with Valentine on her lap, and punctuates the silence with sobs.

"What kind of injuries did Fabien have?" a reporter calls out. "Or did he drown?"

Blackwood glares in the direction of the inconsiderate arsehole, unable to determine exactly who it is. "We will not be taking questions at this time," he finishes.

As the families get up, the journalists ignore Blackwood's instructions and begin to shout questions at them all. Blackwood keeps his eyes on Rose and Charlie as they walk back to the side room, trying to figure out how much of Rose's speech had been spur of the moment, or if they'd planned it all along. The whole purpose of Charlie talking was to keep the eyes *away* from the mothers. And no one was supposed to make a direct appeal to Louisa, because it made it look like the police still considered her a suspect, and while he couldn't entirely rule her out, he didn't want the media to take control of the narrative.

Although hadn't he lost control of this a while ago? He rubs at a tight spot in his chest. Dear god, between the Fishers, the media, and Louisa's family, the situation is impossible.

As soon as the door is shut behind them, Blackwood marches over to Rose, cornering her and Charlie. "Can I remind you that I'm running this investigation," he snaps. "I didn't appreciate the sudden change of plan in there."

"Yes, what happened? We went over your speech quite a few times this morning, Charlie," Angie adds. She always says everything with a smile on her face, but this time it's stretched just a little too wide. *She's as furious as I am*, Blackwood realizes gratefully.

"I'm sorry." Charlie looks surprised. "It didn't feel right for me to speak," he says simply.

"We didn't rehearse that," Rose adds defiantly. "It just happened." She glances across at the Fishers, who are all listening intently. "Could we talk in private for a minute?"

Jock visibly bristles. "That's not necessary, is it? We're all in this bloody nightmare together."

"Just for a moment," Rose persists, giving Jock an apologetic look and then turning back to Blackwood.

Blackwood points to the kitchen beyond the bar, and follows Angie, Rose, and Charlie. They traipse through the double doors and stand amid workbenches and hanging pots and pans.

"Whatever has happened," Rose begins, "we want Lou to feel it's safe to come back."

"You can't still think she took those kids?" Angie asks in astonishment, her eyes trained intently on Rose. "Have you considered what that would mean in regard to Fabien?"

"No," Rose says sharply. "I'm not saying that at all. I'm saying that a solid investigation covers every angle until we know anything for certain. I'm trying my hardest to keep my emotions out of this, and I don't think you fully appreciate how difficult it is. I was thinking it through as you were all talking, trying to imagine how it looked to everyone watching. Frannie wept for the cameras. That's what you needed: Her children are tiny; it's exactly what she should be doing. Kyle appealed to the potential kidnapper of those children, and Jock appealed to the public. But then I realized how indifferent I looked, and how bland Charlie's statement was. What was it again? *We ask that you all keep vigilant and if you see any sign of Louisa or the children, please call the police straightaway.*" Rose shrugs and shakes her head. "I was looking at that wording when Charlie had it laid out in front of him, and I was thinking, *Who is that appealing to?* It's so stilted, when nobody even knows who Charlie is in this whole scenario, anyway. And besides, who forms an emotional attachment to the uncles when they speak? Sorry, Charlie, but it's true."

Charlie raises his hands and shrugs as Rose continues, "And in the meantime, *no one* was appealing to Lou. And if Lou is hiding somewhere, frightened, having run away, and now is too scared to come back for some terrible reason—perhaps not because of what she's done but because of what she's seen—we want her to know that we're here for her. That *her* family are waiting for her. Because she may not understand that. She hasn't had any contact with me for six years. Her father is a selfish prick. So if Lou is watching, she needs to know she has people in her corner. Who else was going to say that in a way that resonated with the public? If Charlie had spoken, everyone would have been wondering why I'd stayed silent."

"We were trying to keep the attention away from you," Blackwood mutters, although as he's weighing her words, a grudging admiration is creeping in.

"I don't care," Rose says. "Let them gossip—how the hell are we ever going to stop them? All that matters is that we cover all bases and get our children home." She raises her chin determinedly at Angie and Blackwood, then adds, "And of course I don't think she killed Fabien."

Blackwood has no response. As she'd spoken, his fury at her impertinence had turned into astonishment at her awareness of all the angles and her fortitude in this situation. Angie's mouth has dropped open. She looks at Blackwood, apparently as stunned as he is.

"You're right," Blackwood says. "I don't think we've fully taken into account the unusual circumstances you've found yourself in, and we've underestimated your ability to compartmentalize, and therefore also undervalued your high level of professional insight and expertise. I apologize."

"There's no need." Rose waves him away. "I'm just trying to get you both to see our side of things. And to trust me a little more."

"We appreciate that." Blackwood hesitates, but decides to trust them. "And look, I should inform you that the Santoses' nanny may have gone missing this morning—actually, it's too early to tell, but she wasn't in the house. We're following up on this as priority."

He doesn't miss the anxious glance exchanged between Charlie and Rose, and he's suddenly on full alert. "What is it?"

"She came to see us late last night," Rose admits. "To talk about Lou—and to tell us more about some of the other nannies . . . and the incident with Marisol . . ."

All Blackwood's newfound empathy vanishes in the wake of this revelation. "And did she have any new information?" he asks through gritted teeth. "Anything it might be helpful for us to know?"

"No, but—"

"I really don't appreciate you interviewing witnesses on your own late at night," Blackwood snaps. "And we'll discuss that further very soon. However, right now, I need to debrief the Fishers, as they don't like waiting." He turns to Angie. "Tell Webster and the team to look at the route between Charlie's house and the place the Santoses are staying—and to go *fast*," he adds.

"We didn't see anything before we took the turnoff for Dunsborough," Charlie says, frowning.

"Doesn't mean anything until we've checked the route properly," Angie mutters, pulling out her phone and turning away.

Rose looks like she's about to speak again, but Blackwood jumps in. "I'll take the lead now, thank you, Rose. It would be better if you and Charlie could keep yourselves low key around the Fishers for the time being. The situation is becoming extremely volatile, and it won't help anyone—particularly Louisa and the children—if emotions get out of hand."

She nods. "Of course. We'll go for a drive while we wait to hear what you want us to do next."

"I'm not sure all the journos will have gone yet," Blackwood reminds them. "It might be better to stay inside somewhere."

"We parked in the private staff car park at the back—it's gated," Rose replies. "So I think we'll be okay."

It takes all Blackwood's strength to stay courteous. This woman just won't be contained, but since she's not doing anything illegal, they can't control her.

Angie turns back to them, sees his expression, and takes over. "Please be wary," she cautions. "We may need to keep a stronger police presence around you now. Since you're in the media spotlight, there could be renewed interest in you. In Kardanup we've had people scaling the walls and jumping onto the beach from boats in the last few days. I don't want you to get unwelcome visitors at your property or have people accosting you."

"We'll bear that in mind," Rose says. "And when you're ready, please let us know what we can do to help today."

Blackwood nods curtly. He waits while Angie accompanies them to the staff car park. When she returns, he says, "I want you on the Fishers. Keep a close eye on them. Try to pick up on anything suspect. I'll get another sergeant to cover the SES briefings and the searches from the green house. Let's go and talk to everyone."

They head back into the dining area that had earlier served as the preparatory room. To Blackwood's surprise, only Kyle is there.

"Where the hell is everyone?" he splutters.

"They're on their way back to the house," Kyle says. "I think Dad's making a point to you about not expecting him to wait around. And Frannie went off with her sister."

Blackwood is stunned. He's only been gone a few minutes and everyone has scattered. There's a tightness pulling at his rib cage. The situation is untenable.

"Get back to Kardanup as fast as you can," he hisses to Angie. "And tell me what's going on."

Kyle jumps up from his seat and comes closer. "Frannie isn't talking to me after last night," he grumbles. "I've tried to apologize, but she insists she wants to leave me when this is over." He puts his hands on his hips and stares at the floor for a moment, blows out a long breath, and then looks up again. "I waited here as I need to talk to you urgently. Could we go somewhere private? Right now."

CHAPTER TWENTY-SEVEN
LOUISA

Something is happening outside her room. Louisa can hear murmurs interspersed with raised voices and expletives. The sound of a woman shushing, trying to calm someone down.

She sits on the double bed, her arms around Honey, who is doing a jigsaw puzzle. Kai is asleep next to them.

For the past few days they've been trapped in this bedroom. It has an incongruous country-cottage vibe: a double bed with a flowery bedspread, two mismatched wooden chests of drawers, a tall mirror, and a rug on the floor made of ragged pieces of fabric. There's also a toilet and shower in a small adjacent room. It would feel deceptively normal, except the windows have been boarded up and nailed shut, leaving only the unnatural light of the overhead bulb. And there's a lock and bolt on the thick wooden door that leads to the rest of the house.

It's the older man from the boat who tends to them. The younger, shaven-headed guy who killed Fabien with a knife-punch hasn't been in here at all, much to Lou's relief. She dreads coming face-to-face with him again. The blank look in his eyes had terrified her, as he'd tipped Fabien over the side of the boat and sent her bag of belongings in afterward. There'd been no emotion or remorse, although the older man had obviously been struggling to contain himself, breathing heavily, groaning each time he looked at his son. The whole sequence has taken on a dreamlike aspect that she suspects is her brain trying to protect her from the reality that Fabien is dead. Her throat thickens each time she thinks of him charging toward them in a determined fury, spending what was probably his last few minutes on earth intent on rescuing her and the children.

And although she knows it would be a miracle, she can't help clinging to a small hope. Perhaps it looked worse than it was, and Fabien wasn't dead when he went into the water. Perhaps he was found, and is in hospital, recovering, telling the police what happened and helping them find her.

Perhaps.

She has no idea where she is now. They'd been bundled out of the boat, pushed into the back of a van with no windows, and driven to this place. Lou tried to get an idea of the length of the journey, but without a watch or phone, she could only estimate. And time had grown sludgy. It felt like they'd driven for hours, but maybe it wasn't as long as she'd thought.

Once at the house, they'd bound her wrists with cable ties. However, Honey had done her a favor, freaking out and screaming while trying to pull the plastic bindings loose so she could have a proper cuddle. The ties had come off, with a warning. *Try anything, and you'll regret it.* Despite the intimidation, she's spent every hour since they arrived going over the possibilities of escape. But she hasn't tried anything yet. She's too scared of what might happen if she does.

There seems to be an effort to take care of them. Food is sent in regularly. There's a small hand towel and a bar of soap in the bathroom. Once or twice she'd glimpsed an older woman with dark hair and sad eyes staring into the room, their gazes catching for milliseconds before the woman stepped out of view. Despite her inner distress, Lou has made an outward effort to remain compliant in order to appease them. Nevertheless, items are delivered silently, despite her thanks. She's asked the older man why they are here, what the plan is for them, but there's been no response. She hasn't left this room in three days now, and every moment is a struggle to keep her head together.

Sometimes the kids are with her, and sometimes they're taken elsewhere. When they cry they are brought back to Lou for comfort, but both seem to have adapted to their circumstances, although they look confused at times. Dirty nappies are collected, but the new ones delivered are cut-up strips of towel and safety pins that are way too small to do the job properly. They regularly fall off Kai's tiny frame.

Lou is still in the same clothes she'd been wearing three days ago. There had been an offer to clean them, but she'd refused. She's washed her body in the small bathroom and put the same clothes straight back on, the streaks of Fabien's blood across her white T-shirt turning hard and brown. The smell is getting worse, but she won't let her kidnappers coddle her. Beneath the fear that burns through her, there are moments of fury too, glowing embers that she keeps fanning with dark thoughts so she can put up a fight when she needs to.

The murmur of voices interrupts her thoughts. She gets up and goes to the door, pressing her ear against it and trying to make out what's being said. It sounds like the television is on, and she thinks she hears her name, but she can't discern the thread of the conversation. Only one sentence comes through clearly. An older male voice.

"That's it then. We're out of time." Both sentences are delivered with a finality that burrows into Louisa's bones.

"No," a woman's voice wails. "No, please, not that."

Lou moves away from the door and puts her arms tightly around Honey, who is still intently fitting pieces of her jigsaw puzzle together on a tray. There's a rush of blood to her head, and a pounding in her ears as her chest tightens.

She pats the side of her bra, checking the tiny metal nail file with its sharp tip is still safely concealed. It's the one weapon she's been able to find so far, and she wants to be prepared to fight back. But how can she ready herself, when she has no idea what they're about to do?

For now, she can only wait.

CHAPTER TWENTY-EIGHT
ROSE

As Rose and Charlie stride across the hotel car park, Rose is already checking her phone. "There's no word from Stella." She dials Stella's number and waits, but it goes through to voicemail. "No answer. I'll send her a text. Oh god, I hope nothing's happened to her."

"Let's not jump to any conclusions." Despite his words, Charlie looks scared.

"We should go and check the route she would have driven, see if we can find anything."

Charlie shakes his head. "I don't think that's a good idea. You heard Blackwood, he's already got people on it—he won't appreciate us jumping in. We should stay focused on Lou."

Rose looks up. "Yes, you're right, but I'll text Angie and ask her to let us know as soon as Stella is safe." She goes back to her phone to send the message. It's been on silent during the press conference, and she's had two missed calls from Henry and one from her mum. There's a whole bunch of unknown numbers listed too. "Henry's trying to contact me," she tells Charlie.

"I'll deal with him. And I'll remind him I'm here, so you don't have to talk to him."

"Thanks. How's he holding up?"

"Precariously," Charlie replies.

Once inside the Land Rover, Rose leans back in the seat and rests for a moment, eyes closed, steadying her breath. When she sits up and refocuses, Charlie is watching her with concern. "You all right?"

"Yes," she says, grateful he's here and she's not doing all this alone. She's starting to feel comfortable again around Charlie. Their straightforward way of communicating and their instinctive moments of understanding one another are making everything so much easier. They're working as a team without even discussing it.

Charlie begins to drive toward the gated exit to the car park, past groups of journalists talking intently and photographers packing equipment away, when Rose suddenly spots Rick Malone in a small group by the front steps that lead to reception. She'd noticed him earlier, standing on the left-hand side of the room, and he'd given her the briefest of nods as they locked eyes, before his gaze ran over the rest of the speakers at the front. She wondered if he and Jock would acknowledge each other, but Jock had made minimal eye contact with anyone else, except during his speech. When he began talking, Rose had tried to gauge Malone's reaction, but by then he'd moved position and she couldn't see him anymore.

"Stop!" Rose cries. As soon as Charlie pulls up, she's out of the car, running across the car park. She taps Malone on the shoulder, and he turns around, frowning at first, then obviously startled to see her. "Can we talk?" she asks. "Somewhere private," she adds breathlessly, sensing people around them coming to full alert, a few cameramen beginning to grab equipment. She curses her impulsivity, realizing her mistake.

"Please," she says quickly, "will you come in our car? It's just me and Charlie."

She's grateful when Malone nods. They run across to the Land Rover, leaping in and pulling the doors closed as the journalists move toward them in a swarm.

"What the hell are you doing, Rose?" Charlie snaps. "I really don't think this is a good—"

"Just drive!" she yells at him, her heart pounding and her head down as he slowly guides the car through the melee of people.

"It would have been a lot simpler if you'd just talked to me yesterday," Malone says accusingly. Beside her, Charlie shakes his head.

Rose turns around to see Malone better. He must be in his sixties, and he's thin but doesn't appear to be in great shape. He's still breathing hard from the short run. "I've been reading your book," she tells him.

"Then you'll know how well acquainted I am with the Fisher family," Malone says. "Which means I hope you'll trust whatever I tell you."

"Of course," Rose replies, as they turn out of the hotel grounds onto a long, straight country road, "but can I also ask that you keep whatever we discuss confidential. My daughter's life is at stake here, as well as those small children with her. They are not gossip fodder. Especially not today."

Malone considers her, his gaze sharp and shrewd. "You needn't worry," he assures her. "I'm not that kind of journalist. I want to help you, not make things worse. But you should understand what you're up against if you're trying to get to the truth. Jock Fisher sees only two types of people in life—players and pawns—and from his perspective the pawns are dispensable. He's paid off a lot of people over the years to protect himself and his children. Perhaps this time he's not going to be able to cover things up so easily if someone is really pissed at him, although it looks like he's already trying with that two million. It must be a tempting amount of money for whoever's got them."

Rose considers this, wondering how much to trust Malone. "Can I ask, if you've written an authorized biography, why are you in a car with us, and not back there"—she waves a hand at the hotel as it recedes into the distance—"with the Fisher family? Shouldn't you have access to them?"

"I'll be honest with you. Jock authorized the biography, but by the end we weren't on speaking terms. He had me pegged all wrong, you see." Malone has a strange intonation of speech, slow and deliberate, as though he's weighing up every word before he says it.

"He thought I wanted his grace and favor—he imagined I'd write a long-winded glorification of all his achievements. But I wanted to understand the guy, the good and the bad. I asked lots of questions—I spoke to people he'd done business with, people he'd fallen out with, distant relatives, basically anyone who would talk to me. And what I found out is that there are two sides of the Fisher story: One is a tale of success and hard-won victories, and the other is a story of bribery, corruption, and cover-ups. I ended up digging a bit too hard, and by the end he cut me off. He threatened me with all sorts of legal repercussions and once the book was published I never heard from him again."

"Why am I not surprised?" Charlie chimes in, turning onto a quiet little lane and slowing down. "I think you've got to be pretty cutthroat as a businessman to accumulate as much wealth as Jock has. But what do you think all that has to do with current events? It's Kyle's kids who've gone missing with Louisa. Isn't that one step removed from anyone with a grudge against Jock?"

Malone shakes his head. "This situation doesn't surprise me at all. Jock keeps his children close. Their lives are deeply interconnected. I'm of the opinion that Kyle has done something shady, and this time whoever he was working with has taken revenge. In the past he's had his hands in the pockets of gang members, nightclub owners, all sorts of businessmen, and he pretty much always leaves them high and dry. He trades on the Fisher name, and it was only a matter of time before someone came after him for it. I don't know why they took your girl as well—perhaps she was just in the way, or they needed her to look after the kids. But I can guarantee you she's an innocent caught up in the Fishers' nefarious lifestyle."

"Tell me everything you know about Kyle," Rose says, trying to ward off the despair she feels at his words and turn it into something more productive.

Malone is quiet for a moment, thinking this through. "There was a lot that didn't go into the book," he says, "for fear of legal problems. But I do know that Kyle didn't have the money to afford the settlement with his second wife, Ebony, so Jock bankrolled all that—he probably still pays her maintenance. And the properties Kyle lives in—they're all Fisher owned; none belong to him. The house in Kardanup is a company investment and a family getaway; Kyle just takes it in turns with his siblings to holiday there. I don't think he has much of his own at all; he's either working for his dad, or trying to build things that fall down one way or another. And the man doesn't seem capable of self-reflection, so he just keeps making the same mistakes over and over. It must be excruciating for Jock to watch, especially since his other children have all been assets to the Fisher empire. Kyle is the black sheep of the family, and everyone knows it."

As Rose listens, she almost feels sorry for Kyle. It must be incredibly challenging to live with the realization that your own family, and the wider world, considers you substandard. And it would be hard for him to escape such labels, especially if he didn't have the brains or strategic ability to find a way past them. In Rose's experience, once people have decided who you are, it's very difficult to get them to change their minds, even if their beliefs are bullshit.

"So why were you so keen to talk to Rose yesterday?" Charlie asks Malone. "Did you just want to pass on information, or are you hoping for an exclusive?"

Malone's glance falls on Charlie, then Rose in turn, as though deciding how much to say. "I'd always like a story," he admits, "but more importantly, if the Fishers are responsible for this situation, I want to see them exposed. Jock almost destroyed my life. I spent three years working on that book for him, and when he didn't like it, he refused to pay me my share. I've tried the court, but the contract was between Jock and the publishers, I was only employed by him, so his lawyers found holes in our agreement. Jock doesn't need the money, but he made sure I didn't get a bloody thing. I nearly lost everything from the stress—my house, my wife—and he didn't give a shit. It's incredible how much he gets away with. And I've seen Jock photographed with senior members of the police force and the government on so many occasions I've lost count. So I don't think the police will investigate Jock or Kyle closely enough—but if they do, they'll start to uncover all sorts of things." He pulls a piece of paper out of his shirt pocket. "I've made a list," he says. "I was hoping to give it to you yesterday. It's all the places the police might begin if they really want the truth. Keep that safe. And use it when you need it."

Rose opens the folded paper. It looks to be the names of companies. "None of this is in the public domain?"

"No. I compiled it from things I learned during my research and in the years afterward. I suspect you'll find all these companies are shell organizations for the Fishers' illicit dealings, but I have no proof, and I don't know how many of the family are involved."

"So you just want to see the Fishers go down?"

There's a twitch in Malone's cheek. "I'd like them to stop trampling over other people to keep themselves out of trouble. So many lives have been ruined by this family. Your girl is the latest in a long line of victims."

"I promise I'll keep this safe," Rose says, waving the piece of paper he's handed her. "But I might have another angle for you to consider. I'm interested in former nannies, particularly Kyle's. There are rumors about the way they're treated. I've heard some specifics of Kyle going beyond appropriate boundaries when asking them to do things—and he appears to cut them off from the rest of the world while they work for him. Do you know anything about that?"

Malone looks thoughtful. "Really?" He pauses, staring down at the floor. When his head comes up again, his face is solemn. "Do you mean he propositions them? Are you talking about sexual relationships?"

Rose frowns. "Actually, no. If Kyle is possessive of anyone, it's his wife. It's more that he coerces his young employees into being couriers in shady business deals, gets them to spy on people, that kind of thing."

Malone looks disappointed. "Oh. Well, no, I haven't heard anything about that, but it wouldn't surprise me at all. There are many, many instances of him being inappropriate and inept while trying to keep his businesses afloat. He's certainly not a gentleman. Is that the angle the police are working on too?"

"I'm not sure," Rose says. "I've spoken to them about it, but they play their cards close to their chest. I've also heard mention of someone called Marisol. Do you know the name?"

Malone frowns. "It doesn't ring a bell, but I can look into it, and let you know if I find anything."

"I'd appreciate that. She's a former nanny, worked for Kyle's ex-wife. There was an accident at a party at Kyle's house, when Marisol fell off a balcony. She was seriously injured."

"Ah, hang on a sec." Malone sounds intrigued. "I do remember something about this. A few years ago, yes? But I hadn't made a connection to the current situation."

"We're not sure if it's relevant," Rose concedes, "but the general consensus among former nannies is that Kyle and Frannie are difficult to work for—and sometimes overstep boundaries. There must be a reason for Lou and the kids to be targeted like this."

"Got it." Malone sounds much livelier than he did a few moments ago. "Well, I'll see what I can uncover and let you know." He turns to Charlie. "If you can go partway back toward the hotel, let me out on the roadside and I'll walk the rest. It'll save you getting into a scrum up there."

Charlie follows Malone's instructions. When he pulls up a short distance from the hotel, Malone opens the door, then pauses. "I'm praying for a good outcome," he says. "I really am." He holds Rose's gaze a little longer than necessary, and the look on his face is so sorrowful that it frightens her. And then he's out of the car and strolling down the narrow road, without looking back.

"So what did you think of all that?" Charlie asks Rose once they are alone.

"It all adds fuel to the fire," Rose says, "but the Fisher family are locked down, and not likely to come clean about anything unless we can prove it relates directly to the missing children. All this is only speculation without more evidence. I need to find something substantial, and fast."

"So where shall we go now?"

"Back to my hotel room, I guess. I want to stay close to Kardanup and the investigation today. We can make a plan from there."

"Got it." Charlie accelerates, heading for the next turning toward the coast.

Rose pulls out her phone and inhales sharply.

"What is it?" Charlie asks.

"I've had so many calls in the last hour." She stares incredulously at her phone. "All from unknown numbers." She turns to Charlie in confusion. "What's going on?" The question is rhetorical—she's already dialing her voicemail and listening to messages.

"Hi, Rose, my name is Alan Daly, I'm from *The New Zealand Herald*..."

"Hello, Rose, my name is Jane Walker, I'm from the *Chicago Times*..."

"Hi, Rose, my name is Don Jerome, I'm from the *Sunday Times* here in WA..."

She puts it on speaker. On and on it goes.

"What the hell?" Charlie's shock echoes Rose's surprise at the sheer number of messages. "I guess you should just keep deleting them."

"Yeah, but how are they getting my number?" She frowns at the phone screen, trying to figure it out, and then it hits her. Her consultancy: Her mobile number is listed on the website contact page, along with the office number.

"I think it's my work website," she says, going to her email, intending to message Lianne, her admin assistant. She wants to make sure the number is removed as soon as possible, but as she clicks on her emails she sees there's one from a senior colleague telling her they're all thinking of her at this difficult time, and asking her to hand over the latest version of the draft report so they can continue the work in her absence.

Rose's heart sinks, but she knows it's the right thing to do. She's spent five years working on it, but the report is too important to wait for her now.

"You okay there?" Charlie asks, sensing her despondence.

"I'm fine," Rose replies, biting back her emotions. She doesn't want to tell him about this right now. A work matter is so trivial compared to this nightmare, and he might not understand. But one person will. She texts Veronica. *The government doc just got taken off me. It's for the best, but it still really hurts.*

Veronica probably won't reply for another few hours—she'll be in the air by now—but just sharing the news eases the weight of it a little. And despite the pain and frustration, she recalls the image of Lou and those gorgeous little kids at the press conference, and imagines the alternative road she could have taken: staying in London, watching from half a world away as Charlie sat alone at the appeal, asking for the public's support, while she made herself a coffee and went back to reading her papers. That was never going to happen.

She moves back to her voicemail and continues deleting the journalists' messages. They are interspersed with the occasional friend or colleague expressing their concern and wanting to know if they can help. It would be touching if she weren't so tired.

The voices are all the same after a while: polite, professional, eager, to the point. "Well, I guess we know what I'm doing for the rest of today," she says, trying to lighten the moment.

Charlie gives her a sympathetic look.

Texts and alerts continue to pop up, showing little sign of abating. Rose's eyes begin to blur as she continues to delete them. She's almost given up scanning them when another unknown number appears on her list of text messages, but the first words catch her attention.

My name is Bree. Stella gave me your number. Can you call me asap?

"I just got a message from the nanny who worked for Kyle and Frannie before Lou," Rose tells Charlie hurriedly, as she dials the number.

"Hello—Rose?" a young female voice asks.

"Is that Bree?"

"Yes. I got Stella's message this morning. I'm so sorry about this situation—you must be out of your mind with worry."

"It's a very difficult time," Rose says, aware of Charlie listening intently. "Thanks for contacting me. You haven't spoken to Stella this morning, have you?"

"No, I just saw her message and called you."

Rose decides not to worry Bree yet. She hopes desperately that Stella is okay. "Have the police been in touch—about Lou and the kids going missing?"

"No, not yet."

Rose tries to quell her frustration. "Well, I'm Lou's mum, but I used to be a police officer, so I'm following up on some of the leads that the police can't prioritize. We're just trying to ascertain if any former nannies have previously had concerning incidents while working for the Fishers—anything that might have been scary, unnerving, or overstepped boundaries?"

There's a long pause. "There wasn't anything terrible," Bree says. "At least, nothing that happened to me. But the job is crazy intense and draining—it takes over your whole life. I was only there for nine months—I couldn't handle it for any longer. I managed two years with Toby and his wife, but Kyle and Frannie are something else. Both of them can be volatile and terribly insecure."

Rose feels deflated, although she isn't sure why. This is good news, isn't it? She doesn't want to learn anything awful about the Fishers if it would put Lou at greater risk of harm. Nevertheless, it contrasts with the narrative she's been building, and she's not willing to let it go.

"Why the hesitation before you answered?" she persists. "If you don't mind me asking."

"I . . . Well, there's been a lot of gossip over the last few days. There's a bit of a nanny grapevine, and people are bringing up old mysteries."

"Is this about Marisol?" Rose asks. "Stella told me about that. Or is it something else?"

"Mostly Marisol. Some other inappropriateness, like Kyle asking nannies to lie about where he was, that sort of thing."

"If there's a grapevine," Rose says, "can you pass on a message to everyone from me? Tell them that I really want to talk to anyone who has concerns, and it will be completely in confidence. I won't reveal their name to the police. We just want to find Lou." Rose pauses, trying to think how she might make her appeal more compelling.

"We're not interested in pursuing public accusations against the Fishers or getting people into trouble. We just want any information that might help."

"I'll send messages to everyone I know as soon as we hang up," Bree says.

"Before you go," Rose adds quickly, "tell me a bit more about your experience with the Fishers. Did you like working for them?"

"It was . . ." Bree pauses as though searching for the right word. "Tricky—at times," she finishes. "I worked for Frannie when Honey was a toddler and I was there when she had Kai. She struggled with newborns—she told me that she was almost too scared to hold them. She was really insecure about being a mum and constantly asking for advice—as though I knew it all," Bree says with a small laugh. "She didn't seem to realize that I was just winging it like she was."

Rose feels a stab of sympathy for Frannie, remembering how much it had frightened her to hold Lou, once upon a time. How terrifying it had been to know that this tiny helpless human depended on you, at every single moment, not to falter or fall. How everything in the house had suddenly seemed like a potential source of injury, and how she'd hit rock bottom when she realized that it was she herself who'd become the most dangerous thing for her child. If Frannie had experienced something similar, it was understandable that she would shy away from the children. Rose's mind flashes across the faces of some of the most vulnerable women she's encountered over the years. *If we dig deep enough*, she thinks, *we are all connected*.

"Poor Frannie," she says to Bree.

"Yeah, I felt sorry for her too. And now . . . I just can't imagine. She's always loved those kids—even if she isn't sure exactly how to be a good mum."

"Please, if you think anyone might have information, I'm desperate to talk to them," Rose says. "Every hour counts. We need to get Lou and the kids home fast."

"I'll do my best," Bree assures her. Then she hesitates, before adding, "You sound remarkably brave. If it were my mum, I think she'd have fallen apart days ago."

Rose is about to explain the estrangement, but stops. Why is she continuing to operate as though the unusual circumstances mean she's not supposed to have feelings?

"I'll fall apart after they're all home safely," she answers instead. And then she shudders at the fragility of her own statement, because the situation grows more perilous by the hour. Nevertheless, she can feel things turning, shifting, as though the truth is edging closer. For now, she's just got to keep going.

CHAPTER TWENTY-NINE
BLACKWOOD

The press have all gone. Hotel staff in black uniforms are busy moving tables and rearranging chairs, clattering back and forth between conference rooms, making it impossible for Blackwood to press Kyle for more information.

Kyle's phone buzzes, and he moves away from Blackwood to check it. Blackwood glances around and spots DC White. He motions for the constable to come over.

"We're getting a lot of leads already," White says, presuming he's after an update. "And we've found Fabien's friends, the ones with the Airbnb. They're in total shock, but helping us with details."

Blackwood cuts him off. "That's good. But right now, Kyle and I need a room for an urgent chat."

"Oh, okay, I'll sort it," White replies, hurrying away.

Kyle remains where he is, slumped and dejected as he leans against a wall, his fingers moving furiously across his phone screen. Blackwood wishes he could see who Kyle is texting.

White returns a few moments later. "We've got somewhere. Follow me."

"Kyle," Blackwood calls, and Kyle jumps and looks up, startled, as though he's momentarily forgotten where they are. Blackwood gestures that they should follow DC White. "Come with us, please."

As hotel staff look on curiously, they are shown through reception into what seems to be the manager's office, an oppressively small room with a desk and shelves strewn with paperwork.

"Stay with us, White," Blackwood insists when the constable turns to go. "I want you as witness."

As soon as the door is shut, Kyle whirls to face them. "Okay, I need to tell you a few things."

Blackwood holds up a hand. "Just stop right there and listen to me carefully. We're going to do a witness record of interview. You're not under caution or under arrest, and I'm not reading you your rights, so you're free to leave at any time. But I am going to record this conversation. Do you understand?"

"Yes, I guess," Kyle says warily.

"All right then." Blackwood moves around the desk and sits down, gesturing that Kyle should take the chair opposite him. As soon as Kyle is seated, Blackwood pulls out his phone, finds the right app, and presses the record button, before laying the device on the table. He quickly states practical details for official purposes, outlining the date, time, and location and the names of the three men present in the room, while praying that none of this puts Kyle off from revealing whatever it is he wants to say.

"So, Kyle," Blackwood begins, "you said you needed to tell us something?"

Kyle looks briefly at each of the men, then takes a deep breath. "Yes, I do. First of all, I have Lou's camera hidden in my car. I panicked, and I'm sorry. I didn't want Frannie to know I'd asked Lou to spy on her, and I wanted to check it before handing it over. I thought they'd all be home by now, but this is turning into a crazy nightmare."

The man's cool blue eyes are glistening, but Blackwood is too furious for empathy.

"You're telling me that when your kids first went missing, you had the presence of mind to hide evidence?" Blackwood hopes his expression and tone are fully conveying how livid he is right now.

"Come on, man, it wasn't like that. You can't blame me for wanting to protect my marriage. Things haven't been great lately, but I love my wife. And I adore my kids. I can't bear to think of anything . . ." Kyle stops, his voice trembling on the last few words.

Blackwood leans closer. "Look, from what I've seen, you and Frannie have a lot to do if you're going to make your marriage work. To begin with, when you have marital problems, you sit down and talk. You don't start spying on one another or cursing each other out." As he berates Kyle, Blackwood becomes aware that on his last phone conversation with Margie he'd practically accused her of cheating on him. He winces, then reminds himself to focus. "What if Louisa's camera contains information that might help us get your kids back?"

"But it doesn't," Kyle whines. "I checked it out myself. Most of the photos are of flowers or the kids. I think she probably used her phone to take the pictures she showed me."

"You're the detective now, are you? I'm sorry, but you don't get to be the one who determines what's relevant in this investigation. Concealing evidence is a crime, you know." Blackwood pauses to make sure the statement hits home, and is satisfied to see Kyle swallow hard. "So why come clean now?"

"Because shit has got real, and Frannie will never forgive me if she realizes I've lied while the kids' lives are on the line. When this is over, I'm going to do all I can to save my marriage, and I'm hoping you'll do me a favor and keep this on the q.t. And I'd rather you weren't wasting time looking for the camera anymore, as I need you searching for my kids."

Blackwood stares at Kyle, incredulous for a moment, before he has a flash of understanding. Kyle hasn't yet grasped the dreadful reality of the situation. He's so used to his father providing get-out clauses, or someone else setting his world to rights when things go wrong, that he cannot comprehend a scenario where his children are not returned. Well, Blackwood will not pander to him.

"For god's sake, Kyle, we are gravely concerned for your children's welfare," Blackwood roars. "And do you realize this makes it look like you've got something to hide? How do we know that you didn't delete evidence from the camera? It's pretty easy to wipe an SD card."

Kyle's mouth drops open. His eyes are wide. "My god, man. You can't really think I've done something to my own babies?"

"Why not? You've been hiding things around the house; you've been spying on your own wife; you've cut your nanny off from the world, and when we told you she might have secretly liaised with her boyfriend you were extremely angry about it. The boyfriend is dead, and I'm wondering what he saw that meant he had to be killed? And another nanny has disappeared this morning too—the Santoses' nanny, Stella—and it so happens that she knew about those photos Lou took. So can you tell me anything about *that*?"

As Blackwood had spoken, Kyle's face had slowly transformed, eyebrows furrowing, his jaw slack, but it's upon hearing about Stella that he rears back as though he's been sucker punched. Blackwood lets the silence magnify the moment. Then he persists, his tone low and menacing. "Kyle, do you know where your children are?" He waits. "Do you know where Louisa Thornton is?" He waits again, and there's another beat of silence. "Do you know where Stella Archer is?"

"You're fucking insane." Kyle's eyes are wide with shock. "I want a lawyer," he says. "And I want you off this investigation right now."

"That's not your call, Kyle," Blackwood replies, although he suspects that once the news of this particular conversation travels through Jock to Bob Drake, Blackwood might actually be given his marching orders. Well, if that's the outcome, so be it, because they can't keep going round in circles. "But okay, you contact your lawyer." Blackwood gets up, covering his frustration with a look of antipathy. "You can sort that out now, and I'm going to find a more formal interview location at one of the local police stations, where we'll go over this again. Stay here, and DC White will remain with you for the time being. If you need anything, let him know." He heads for the door.

"You can't just keep me here without arresting me," Kyle rages. "I haven't done anything wrong."

Blackwood turns and comes back, leaning across the desk with his palms flat on the table. "I'm not playing games, Kyle. I've supported you as a traumatized father, but now I think you're hiding things. So I promise you'll find me a worthy adversary. I'm retiring soon—I'm not after accolades, or pay rises. I just want to find your kids and Louisa, and get them back home safe and sound. So, if you really are innocent, I hope you'll appreciate knowing that I will not rest until this is over, and if anyone acts suspiciously I won't give them an inch of breathing room until I uncover the truth. Now, would you like to be formally arrested and cautioned, or are you going to stay here and assist us of your own accord?"

There's a moment of stalemate, neither man willing to move first. Then Kyle throws himself back on his seat with his arms folded and glares at Blackwood.

"Good," Blackwood says. "I need a moment. I'll be back soon."

Outside the interview room, Blackwood sags against the wall in the corridor that leads to reception, breathing heavily and wiping his brow. He's too old and cranky for this. He should have pursued Kyle and Frannie from the start. Jock has practically rolled him over and tickled his belly so he can dominate the direction of the investigation, and Blackwood's submitted to it like a faithful hound. He's let his sympathy for Kyle and Frannie, as the grief-stricken parents of missing children, cloud his investigative instincts. He's followed the standard search protocols, and he's tried to push the Fishers to cooperate, but it hasn't been enough.

Perhaps this whole debacle is showing him that he's doing the right thing by retiring. Maybe he hasn't got the stamina for this kind of challenge anymore.

He swallows hard, clenching his fists and admonishing himself. Enough of that crap. There's a reason Drake had called him: Blackwood's always been the best at managing catastrophes and difficult people as well as making quick, tough decisions. Nothing has changed. And even if it kills him, he's going to get these kids home safely.

He picks up his phone and dials Angie. "I want the Fishers kept in that house with you, debriefing us on every possible person with a grudge."

"I'm on it," she responds. "I'm almost there now."

DC White unexpectedly appears beside him, looking frightened. "Sir—" he begins.

Blackwood can't believe his eyes. "I told you to stay in there," he barks, infuriated at White's sudden ineptitude.

"Sir, you need to come back inside urgently," White insists. "He's freaking out."

Blackwood glares at White for a second, then follows him into the office again.

Kyle is rocking back and forth on his chair, his arms folded around himself, his eyes on his phone, which lies in front of him on the small laminate table. He makes a small, muffled sound, somewhere between shock and pain.

"What is it?" Blackwood asks, confused.

Kyle pushes his phone toward Blackwood. "My office just received this. Jesus *Christ*. Now do you believe me, you absolute arsehole," he yells at Blackwood.

Tentatively, Blackwood takes the phone. And when he sees what's on there, his entire body goes cold.

CHAPTER THIRTY
ROSE

Thirty minutes after their first conversation, Bree calls Rose back just as Charlie turns the car onto the hotel driveway. "I've got a contact for you," she says breathlessly. "She wants to meet you urgently. Her name is Carmela, and she says she's sure she can help you find your daughter. She worked for the Fishers too, but she's very scared of the family and the police. She'll only talk to you if you meet her alone."

"I'll do it," Rose replies immediately. "Just tell me where."

"There's a small café called the Blue Peacock on the outskirts of Margaret River. Where are you now?"

"Close to Dunsborough."

"I think it's less than an hour away from you. Carmela says she can be there in an hour too."

"Tell her I'm on my way," Rose replies. As soon as she hangs up, she turns to Charlie, who has slowed the car to a crawl, searching for a space in the hotel car park. "Turn the car around. That was Bree. I need to go to a café in Margaret River to meet a former employee of the Fishers'. Apparently this woman has information that might help us."

"Really?" Charlie sounds dubious. "Then why not just call the police?"

"They're all frightened," Rose replies. "It's the same here as every-where: Money equals power and cover-ups. I guarantee you that no matter how many shady deals the Fishers have done in the past, there will be people high up in the police force trying to pull out all the stops for them right now. You think that it's as easy to take down rich and powerful abusers as it is to prosecute small-town or middle-class of-fenders? No, it's never straightforward, because there's always a web of obsequious support."

"But don't you even want to clue the police into this?" Charlie is al-ready at the car park exit, looking both ways before turning right onto the main road.

"You saw what happened this morning." Rose's voice rises on each word. "The police don't even want me speaking up as Lou's mum, never mind investigating! I'm going to need hard evidence before I'll get any further with them. And maybe this new witness will provide that." She glances at Charlie. "You can't come with me either. She asked me to go alone and you have that ex-military vibe; you might scare her off."

"Gee, thanks," Charlie says, but he smiles so she knows he's not offended. "Can I just say that I don't like the thought of you going to meet people without any support."

Rose is searching for the café on her phone, but she looks up at his words. "You don't have to protect me, Charlie. I'm a trained police of-ficer—hell, I spent time at Quantico," she reminds him. "I might have been out of the force for a while, but I reckon I could take you down if I needed to." She folds her arms and stares at Charlie, aware she's talking herself up but wanting to be clear that she doesn't need mollycoddling.

"Is that right?" Charlie replies, a muscle twitching in his jaw. "Okay, point taken. And I don't plan on testing you. Let's just hope this woman has something useful to say."

They fall silent for a while, but Rose can sense Charlie is struggling with something, debating whether to speak. She doesn't push, and even-tually he takes a deep breath. "Actually, there's something else I've been wanting to say to you." He glances briefly at her while he drives, and she sees how anxious he looks. "I think you've been doing an amazing job since you got here, and I'm really sorry my brother has been such an utter arsehole. I hate what he did to you and to Lou. Twenty years ago, I decided, wrongly, that it was none of my business. So I did nothing, and I regret it. You were my family, and I could have stepped in and tried to help, but I didn't. It wasn't good enough, and I owe you an apology. I've already said the same thing to Lou."

Rose is stunned. "It was a long time ago," she says. "I've moved on."

"And yet here you are," he replies. "Willing to save Henry's arse and fight for Lou by coming at a moment's notice, despite how you've been treated for years. I know what Henry did, making it impossible for you to have a relationship with Lou. Evelyn was just as bad. Pri thought so too." He sighs. "Remember that printout you found in Lou's diary. She doesn't hate you, Rose. I suspect she wanted to reach out. She probably didn't know where to start after everything that's happened."

"She's not the only one," Rose answers quietly. She thumbs the edge of her phone case, until it releases enough for her to pull out the photograph of herself and baby Lou, taken all those years ago. She lifts it up so Charlie can see. "I didn't know how to reach her either. But I held on to her too, in the small ways I could."

Deep inside, she can feel the dam she's built to hold back her emotions beginning to crumble. Long-buried torment is seeping through the cracks, but she cannot succumb to it. Lou needs her to stay focused right now.

She puts the photo back inside her phone. "Thanks for being kind," she says. "Of course this is painful, but I haven't come all the way over here to get maudlin or watch from the sidelines. I won't stop until she's safe."

"I'm right with you on that," Charlie agrees, his tone soft and reassuring.

They fall silent for a while as the road becomes an endless blur of tarmac between towering eucalyptus trees. Eventually, they take the turning for Margaret River. Rose continues going through messages and voicemails, deleting all the irrelevant ones. As they approach the small township, Charlie says, "I'll drop you a short distance from the café, then go and grab a coffee somewhere while you chat."

They drive along the main street, which is mostly smart little boutiques and eateries. It's a sunny morning, busy with locals and tourists wandering in and out of the shops, some enjoying refreshments at café tables along the sidewalk. For everyone else, life is carrying on as normal, and the disappearance of a nanny and children at a holiday spot an hour away is the stuff of five-minute gossips over countertops. Meanwhile, Rose's and Charlie's entire lives are reduced to one purpose—to find Lou—because nothing else makes sense or matters until they do.

They both watch the Blue Peacock café getting closer on the car's GPS. "Looks like if you get out here and walk up to the top of the hill, it's about two hundred meters on your right," Charlie says, pulling the car over to the side of the road.

"Okay." She goes to open the door, but he stops her, giving her arm a gentle squeeze.

"I'm right here," he reminds her. "Don't forget it."

She smiles at him. "I won't."

Outside, the air is warmer than she'd expected, the autumn sun blazing down from a clear blue sky. She tilts her face up to it, letting it heat her skin, enjoying the lungfuls of fresh air. As she gets to the top of the hill she sees the café is a short walk away from the main strip. There's not much traffic around, and the place is quiet as she approaches. The café is painted a vivid turquoise, with an array of multicolored wind chimes jangling softly at the front and a few cast-iron seats with brightly colored cushions on them. No one is waiting outside, so she heads in, setting off a tinkling bell as she does so.

The place is decorated with pictures of peacocks, and arrangements of slender, glossy peacock feathers are displayed in tall vases around the room. There's an elderly couple having tea in one corner, and a mother bouncing a baby on her lap, sipping her drink while watching her preschooler coloring in. By the window is a woman on her own, with shoulder-length dark hair, wearing a neat purple dress, her thin face revealing the lines of middle age.

Could this be Carmela? Rose wonders, surprised. She'd expected a girl the same age as Stella and Lou. She approaches hesitantly as the woman watches her. "Carmela?"

The woman nods quickly, fingers fretting at the tablecloth hem, eyes darting around the room. It's obvious that Carmela is terrified.

Unnerved by the open distress in the other woman's demeanor, Rose sits down carefully, wary of spooking Carmela by doing or saying something wrong. She really needs to hear what this woman knows.

"I was hoping we could get takeaway drinks and go for a walk," Carmela begins, her voice soft and unsteady, her gaze flicking to the window and back again. "Can I get you a coffee or tea?"

"I'll have a coffee, but I can get it. Would you like one?" Rose asks, standing up, hoping to win favor through generosity.

"Okay, thank you," Carmela agrees, with a series of small, rapid nods.

Rose goes up to the counter, places the order, then sits back down while they wait. "I really appreciate you taking the time to talk to me," she says to Carmela.

Carmela's smile is strained, and as their eyes meet Rose tries not to react. That expression—she's seen it a thousand times before. It's the haunted, desperate look of a tormented woman.

"I'm so sorry about your daughter going missing," Carmela whispers, her voice trembling.

"Thank you," Rose replies, unsettled by the emotion in Carmela's tone. She looks around again at the other customers. No one is watching, and she doesn't want to draw their attention. She can't risk asking more until she and Carmela are outside.

The drinks seem to take forever to be delivered, but in reality it's probably only a few minutes before an older lady in a pinafore puts their takeaway cups down in front of them.

"Shall we walk?" Rose suggests, and Carmela does that repetitive little nod again.

They head outside. "There's a park over here," Carmela says. "With a bench."

They make their way across in silence, and sit down together. Carmela glances around, as though checking they're alone.

"I watched the press conference this morning," Carmela begins. "And I looked you up online. Your daughter is very lucky to have a mother like you."

If only she knew. Rose can't get into that right now. "So how do you know the Fishers?" she asks.

"I used to work for them, over twenty years ago now, as their house-keeper. Back when Jock's wife, Trisha, was still alive."

Rose absorbs this, unsure why Carmela and Bree are in touch. "So what can you tell me that might help?"

"Do you *promise* that you will hear me out?" Carmela asks, her voice wavering, wrung through with trepidation.

"Of course." Rose is trying to appear calm, but her fingers are clamped so tight around her cup that the coffee is burning her hand through the cardboard. The woman's fear is spreading fast, seeping into Rose's pores and settling under her skin.

When Carmela speaks again her voice is so quiet that Rose has to strain to hear her.

"I know where your daughter is," she whispers.

There's a beat, a moment where the world tilts and fails to resettle. The words hit like scalding water, sharpening Rose's senses, stinging so deep into every pore that it's agony to sit still and wait for more.

Carmela gulps. "My husband has taken her. And she's almost out of time. I need your help right now if we're to save her."

"Carmela," Rose begins. "You know I was in the police force, right? This isn't the way—"

"The police will *not* understand," Carmela insists, her voice sharper now, low and pleading. "If my husband or son get any hint of a rescue attempt, they will kill Louisa immediately. She's only alive now because I pointed out that we needed her to care for the children and keep them calm, but that will change today. They don't want to release her because she's seen too much. She saw what happened to Fabien—watched my son kill him—and my husband will do anything to protect his boy. They know their backs are against the wall since Fabien's body was found, and they're about to make their move in the next hour or two. If you don't help me right away, they will make sure Louisa is dead before the police arrive."

Everything stops. Rose can feel nothing, not the breeze in the trees, nor the sun on her face, only the abject, brutal reality of each word and the realization that her worst fears have come true. Lou is in immediate and grave danger.

"I am pleading with you for help, mother to mother," Carmela begs, "because I swear I didn't know about any of this until it was too late. Perhaps I *should* have known." Her eyes meet Rose's. "But I've been too distracted with my own child, trying to keep her alive. My daughter's life is already ruined, but yours doesn't have to be. I need your help because I cannot stop them alone."

"Why is your daughter's life ruined?" Rose asks, although she already suspects she might know the answer.

Carmela's tears brim and begin to spill. "My daughter, Marisol, had a terrible accident, and she'll never recover." And just as Rose is thinking, *Of course*, Carmela adds, "And Marisol is Jock Fisher's child."

CHAPTER THIRTY-ONE
CARMELA

DECEMBER 31, 1999

Carmela hasn't stopped all day. For weeks she's heard Trisha telling her friends that this New Year's Eve party is going to be the "celebration of the century," all of them tittering at the pun. There's been an endless succession of contractors traipsing through the house, from florists to stylists to caterers to the lady who will be playing the harp as guests arrive. They all leave their mark: smudged footprints on the polished white-tiled floors, detritus in the ornate, gilt-mirrored bathrooms, rings on every surface from countless mugs containing remnants of tea and coffee. And Carmela must deal with it all, scurrying around after them so that the house looks immaculate again by the time the next person arrives.

It's hard enough normally, especially when the housemaids are unreliable and often only last weeks. As housekeeper, Carmela must pick up all the slack, and she hasn't been herself lately, some kind of bone-crushing tiredness making it almost impossible to resist the temptation to sit down for ten minutes and close her eyes. She's had to resort to setting the timer on her watch to make sure she's not discovered snoozing on the job. Trisha has already caught her once, a shocked "Carmela!" ricocheting from her lips as Carmela jumped to attention, leaping off the couch. There had been nothing more said, but Carmela had watched Trisha's frown, and she'd known the moment was being mentally tucked away.

Carmela had been excited to be offered the job. The last family she'd worked for had moved overseas so the husband could take up a position at the UN, and they'd left her with glowing references. However, they'd been much friendlier than the Fishers and now, almost twelve months later, Carmela is lonely, with barely anyone to talk to during her long twelve-hour days. She knows they overwork her, but how can she complain when there is no HR, no agency support, just Trisha determining her workload each day and only Jock seeming to sense each time Carmela is close to breaking, stepping in with a few words of encouragement. And she needs the money. Her father died a few years ago, and her mother's medicine and daily care are costing the family a fortune. Her brother, Matteo, tries to do his bit too, but there's never enough. They lost the family restaurant a few years ago, unable to afford the burgeoning rents, and now Matteo is bricklaying every day in the sweltering Western Australian sun.

Carmela still isn't used to the opulence around her. Each month, workmen come to clean the chandeliers that adorn almost every room of the seven-bedroom, four-bathroom home, one of the grandest in Perth, overlooking the Swan River. And it's not the only Fisher house that needs to be taken care of. Carmela often travels with Jock and Trisha to their other homes in Western Australia—the farmhouse down near Bridgetown, the country estate in the Chittering Valley, and the house by the ocean at Kardanup. Everywhere she goes, she has two objectives: keep the place immaculate, and stay invisible as much as possible. When it's just Jock and Trisha this isn't too hard, but as soon as their grown-up children join in, the older Fisher boys bringing their own wives and babies, Carmela is run off her feet.

Kyle is her favorite of the Fisher children. His father and siblings might look down on him, but he's always got a smile for her; he asks about her day, and treats her as an equal rather than a servant. He'll make her cups of tea, and tease her about her Italian twang, which she's never quite lost despite having lived in Australia since she was ten. He'll tell her about life on the party scene, and which famous people he'd hung out with lately at the trendiest bars and clubs in town. It's a whole other world to Carmela, even though she's only a few months older than Kyle.

The other three Fisher siblings are much more serious, all polite and courteous, but they talk to her no more than they have to. The smart attire of the older boys is a stark contrast to Kyle's ripped jeans and surf T-shirts. Bronte is recently married to a hotshot lawyer called Eddie, bouncing back from being humiliated on TV by her former husband, who'd called her frigid and unstable. Carmela had seen Bronte emerge grim faced and furious from crisis talks with her father, but the woman had mastered her poker face and seemed determined to succeed no matter who tried to crush her.

Carmela has barely finished preparing the bedrooms when the family starts to arrive. Bronte is first, followed soon after by Ethan and Toby, with their spouses and nannies in tow. Carmela has set aside a large room upstairs as a playroom-slash-nursery, keeping the children as far away from the garden as she can. Ethan's two-year-old twin boys are constantly on the move, but Toby's daughter is still under a year old and not yet walking, which is something of a relief. Carmela can already picture the chaos when all three of the Fisher grandbabies can run through the entire house causing mischief. But it's hard to worry about that when the little ones are so sweet and cuddly, and she spends a few minutes cooing over them before she's called back to work by Trisha, who needs her to make sure there's enough ice in the kitchen and that everything is ready for the New Year's family breakfast. Trisha is always thinking three steps ahead, and it's a challenge to keep up.

The party is in full swing by the time Kyle arrives with his girl-friend, Ebony, a young, beautiful model who's already hit the catwalks in Paris. Trisha has told Carmela that if everything is done she can finish at nine and join the party, so she heads upstairs to her small room to change, but once there she finds she doesn't have the energy. She'll feel completely out of place downstairs anyway, in a cheap dress among the designer-clad throng, with no one to talk to as her friends will be busy waiting tables or serving the drinks. She thinks about visiting the nursery for company, but suspects the nannies might see her as an extra pair of hands. So she calls Matteo and her mother to wish them a happy New Year, then turns on her television and prepares to ring in the new millennium with Rove McManus and Tracy Grimshaw.

She's fallen asleep in her clothes when there's a small knock on her door, and a voice whispering, "Carmela."

The clock says 12.45 a.m. She struggles up and opens the door, trying to blink away her tiredness.

"I'm sorry, it was the first chance I had to get away." Jock strolls into the room in his tuxedo, his eyes crinkling into a smile as he sees her. He looks around. "Didn't Trisha invite you to come join the party?"

Carmela shrugs, but she's glad to see him. When he isn't distracted or upset by his business deals, he always seems pleased to see her, even if his intensity sometimes unnerves her. "I didn't fancy it. I've been working all day."

"You did the right thing. Everyone's completely wasted down there. It's a mess, although the dancing was fun." He moves closer, his hands encircling her waist. "Happy New Year, Carmela."

He kisses her hard on the mouth and she can taste champagne and cigars. She leans into him, her own desire sparking as his hands run over her body, under her top, squeezing her breasts.

"I want you," he murmurs.

Although her body responds to his touch and his obvious desire, she breaks away. "I don't think we should tonight."

He laughs. "Oh, we definitely should tonight. What better way to ring in the New Year?"

She steps back but holds his gaze. "I think I'm pregnant," she says.

His hands drop instantly to his sides as his shoulders slacken. He stares at her.

His expression sets her heart racing and she steps away, dreading what his next words might be. Over his shoulder, she thinks she glimpses a shadow at the open doorway, but before she can do anything, it disappears out of sight.

CHAPTER THIRTY-TWO
BLACKWOOD

Blackwood is in an unmarked police car, racing back to Kardanup. DC White is driving, while Kyle is sprawled on the back seat.

Blackwood is still deliberating, working on who to include in his circle of trust. If he gets this wrong, the consequences are unthinkable. The only call he's made so far has been to Angie. "You need to leave the Fishers right now and go and get everyone out of the green house. No exceptions. Tell them that in light of the press conference and Fabien's death we'll be having two bases of operations. They are to assemble at the Dunsborough police station and wait for our instructions there. And I need the best, most trustworthy IT expert we've got. Here or in the city, doesn't matter. Just get me a name."

There's a pause, and he knows she wants to ask what's happened. *Trust me*, he implores her, aware of Kyle and White listening in.

She reads the silence perfectly. "On it," she says, hanging up.

He's going over and over the ransom note. Kyle's assistant had promised to be discreet, but there's no doubt in Blackwood's mind that this won't stay under wraps, not when it was delivered to a regular office email address. It had been brief and exacting in its demands:

Tell Jock Fisher that his grandchildren will be returned for four million. Delivered as Bitcoin. Instructions to follow. Our first and final
offer, today only. We will not be negotiating. When this is done,
Jock Fisher must come to us alone to collect the children. We will
let you know the details when we have the money.

Each word felt like a knife tip held up to the throat of everyone
involved in the investigation, but the stab came with the accompanying picture of the children, sitting together, their chubby little
limbs on show and their pale faces forming identical expressions for
the camera: absolute confusion. Kyle had recognized their outfits, so
at last they knew for sure what the kids were wearing the day they'd
disappeared.

And then the kicker, the twist of that cruel blade, which seems to
have gone unnoticed by Kyle.

*Where the hell is Louisa? Why is she not mentioned? Why no photo of
her? No demand?*

Blackwood is well aware that if word gets out about any of this, the
police will be negotiating with kidnappers while a swarm of reporters
and sticky-beakers try to live stream their every move, and that is unthinkable. He's had a lucky break already, by being with Kyle when the
note came through. It doesn't bear thinking about the chaos that might
have ensued if the whole family had seen it right away. Blackwood also
knows he should be phoning Bob Drake, but for some reason that he
doesn't want to admit to himself, he's delaying that conversation until
he's had a chance to talk to Jock.

"I want to speak to my dad," Kyle announces, his mouth a thin, petulant line. He pulls a pair of aviators from his pocket, putting them on
to cover his red-rimmed eyes. He's slumped on the back seat in his de-
signer jeans, and Blackwood's heart goes out to him. Even though Kyle
is essentially a fragile fifty-one-year-old man-child, this is every decent
human being's worst nightmare—and Kyle was already in paranoid free
fall over Frannie's affair before this fresh horror began.

"We'll bring Jock out to the car when we get there," Blackwood replies. He wonders if it could be the first time Kyle has ever faced a traumatic situation without his dad being immediately able to solve it for him—although it might still be Jock who saves the day now there's a ransom demand. "You need to work with us, okay?"

"He won't do it, you know," Kyle mutters. "He won't collect the kids. He's not an errand boy. He'll think it's beneath him."

"Why don't we talk to him first?" Blackwood insists, hoping to god that Kyle is wrong and Jock will at least cooperate in discussions. In truth he's not keen to put a multimillionaire in the path of a violent kidnapper, but he's also not yet sure of the alternatives.

"Go as fast as you can," Blackwood tells DC White. He pulls his front visor down so he can use the mirror to keep an eye on Kyle in case he decides to covertly contact somebody, but Kyle just stares out of the window as though in a trance.

Blackwood's phone begins its two-tone call alert, and he sees it's Webster. He answers with a sinking feeling deep in his gut. "Any news on the Santoses' missing nanny?"

"Not yet," Webster replies. "Some local police are with the family now, building up a picture of where she might have gone. We're still searching the roads too, between Charlie Thornton's place and the Santoses' holiday rental."

"The minute you get any information, I want to hear it."

"Of course." Webster's voice is level, but a note of steeliness betrays his irritation at Blackwood telling him how to do his job. "What else is going on? I'm getting word that people are being pulled away from the incident room and reassigned to Dunsborough. Has something happened?"

"I'm just in the car with Kyle Fisher," Blackwood says pointedly. "I'll debrief you later."

Before Webster can ask more, Blackwood ends the call.

There are only a few media vans outside the Kardanup estate. Most of the journalists haven't returned since the press conference, and Blackwood is grateful for that. They get through the gates easily, and when they eventually pull up onto the drive at the Fishers' beach house, Blackwood gets out and strides briskly through the front door. Even from the entrance hall he can hear a cacophony of voices trying to talk over the top of each other. As the main living room comes into view, he sees Jock giving Andrew urgent instructions, while everyone hovers around them. Jock registers Blackwood's presence and looks up.

"Jeez, Blackwood, where have you and Kyle been?"

He's obviously furious as he glares over Blackwood's shoulder, expecting to see Kyle coming into the room. When this doesn't happen, Jock's eyes narrow and he straightens. "What the hell is going on?"

Kyle's siblings murmur among themselves, watching their father and the detective apprehensively.

"You'd better not be putting my son in the frame for any of this, Blackwood." Jock moves closer, and although Blackwood is the taller by at least six inches, he can feel the fiery menace of Jock's stare burning a hole in his composure. "I know what happens when you lot get desperate: you start trying to pin things on anybody in order to get a result."

"I'm not accusing Kyle of anything," Blackwood retorts, setting his jaw, as Jock's face relaxes a little. "Not yet," he adds, and Jock's chest puffs out again. "But the fact is, he hasn't been very cooperative, so I could arrest him right now for obstructing a police investigation. If you'd like me to play nicely, then I suggest you come with me so we can have a talk."

Jock's gaze lingers on Blackwood for a moment, which Blackwood presumes is an intimidation technique. It isn't working, but Blackwood waits it out until Jock swings round and nods to Andrew. "I'm heading out for a chat with the detective here. Hold the fort."

"Where's Frannie?" Blackwood asks, unable to see her among the throng.

"Her sister booked a room for them at the hotel we were in this morning," Bronte says. "So she can get some rest. She wasn't keen to come back here. Do you want me to come too, Dad?" she adds quickly. "I can get my bag."

"It's okay," Blackwood cuts in. "I only need your father for now."

Bronte looks disappointed, but Blackwood ignores her. He follows Jock toward the front door and out onto the driveway. Jock sees Kyle waiting in the back of the police vehicle and marches across.

"What the fuck is going on?" he snaps, climbing in beside his son.

Blackwood gets into the passenger seat just in time to hear Kyle say, "There's been a ransom note."

Blackwood cuts in quickly. "And we're not discussing it for the next few minutes while we lock down a secure space in the other house," he says, making sure his tone brooks no argument. "I'm the only one here with experience rescuing people held against their will, and every decision we make from this moment forward will determine the outcome. If you can't trust me, you don't have a hope of resolving this successfully."

His words stun them into a silence that grows along the short journey, until it feels as though the air inside the car is flammable, on the verge of explosion. When they arrive at the green house, Blackwood automatically loosens his tie as he climbs out of the vehicle.

There are people and cars moving away from the house, uniformed officers glancing curiously across as they arrive. Everyone knows something is going on, but the longer Blackwood can keep them in the dark about exactly what it is, the greater his chances are of preventing another crime scene and a media spectacle. He's been in policing long enough to remember when most operations could be done covertly. How he longs for those days right now.

Angie waits at the doorway and leads them through into one of the front rooms. DC White shuts the door and stands by it.

"How much?" Jock asks as soon as they're alone. He rocks back and forth on his heels, arms folded, lips pursed.

"Let me run you through this systematically," Blackwood replies, but Kyle interrupts.

"Four mill in Bitcoin. And *you* have to collect the kids. Alone. Here, see for yourself." He passes his phone across, then folds his arms belligerently and waits for his father to respond.

Jock looks at the screen for a moment, and then his head snaps up to stare at them all. His mouth opens and closes like a fish out of water, but nothing comes out. Blackwood glances to the heavens. He's not a religious man, but a quick prayer for strength never did anyone any harm. When he refocuses, Angie is watching him, eyes wide. He nods, to confirm the reality of the situation.

"Right, let's start again," Blackwood says, looking around the room. "First of all, it's vital that we work together. No one else is to hear about this until we've made a plan, and then we'll decide collectively who needs to know. This is essential if we're going to get the kids back unharmed. Okay?"

Jock and Kyle haven't broken eye contact. Something is passing between them.

"Okay?" Blackwood repeats.

Jock turns to him. "What does Bob Drake say about this?"

"I haven't spoken to him yet."

"You haven't spoken to your superior—the assistant commissioner— about this ransom note?" Jock asks incredulously. And Blackwood finally has to admit to himself why he hasn't: because he fears Drake will back whatever Jock wants to do, whereas Blackwood will do whatever it takes to get the kids home alive.

"We got the ransom note less than half an hour ago. It was delivered to an email address at Kyle's offices, and I haven't been able to have a secure conversation with Drake yet," Blackwood clarifies. "Because I prioritized talking to you," he adds pointedly.

They watch Jock study the demand and the accompanying picture again.

"I don't know what the current police procedures are about paying ransoms, but I'm happy to sort out the Bitcoin if it makes all this go away. I can get Andrew onto that. But I'm not going to collect the kids alone," he adds. "That's just asking for trouble."

Kyle shakes his head, his disgust clear. "You won't even do that for your own grandkids?" He turns to Blackwood. "What did I tell you?"

"You calling me a coward?" Jock replies with a laugh. "Take a look at yourself."

"Can we just not—" Blackwood begins, but Angie interrupts.

"I need a word," she demands, touching Blackwood's arm gently and indicating with her eyes that they should go outside.

Blackwood nods. "Stay right here," he instructs the Fisher men, then adds to DC White, "and you too—do *not* move."

He follows Angie into the corridor and shuts the door. As soon as it's closed, she rounds on him. "What are you doing?" she hisses in a low whisper, flinging her hands into the air. "Are you mad? You can't keep this scenario under wraps and let it play without involving anyone else. Are you planning to send Jock Fisher off on the quiet to collect his grandchildren from these kidnappers?"

"Wait a sec," Blackwood replies, moving closer so he can keep his voice low. "I know what you're saying, but listen to me. I'm not going to keep everyone in the dark forever; I just want this to unfold in a certain order. If we don't get Jock to agree before his family and his cronies get hold of him, it's unlikely that he'll do it. Did you see the note? Offer is for today only. They're not negotiating. This is their final play, and if we get it wrong those kids might be gone for good. It's taken these arseholes three bloody days to get in touch; they're not big on communication. Following the instructions—along with some careful thinking about police protection—is our best option."

Angie blows out a long breath, shaking her head. "I don't know. And where is Louisa in all this? Why do the kidnappers ignore her in their message? I don't like it at all."

"Me neither," Blackwood admits. "And it's telling that neither of those blokes in there have even noticed she's not mentioned."

Angie rubs her neck. "Well, it's your call. But you're so close to leaving with your head high, and you're going to stuff up your entire career, and probably your pension too, if you get sacked for this."

"That's a risk I'm happy to take, if we can get everyone safely home today," he assures her.

As they head back inside, Blackwood readies himself for the explosive atmosphere, but something has changed. Jock turns to them.

"We'll do the Bitcoin. And I'll do the pickup—but with you along for the ride"—he nods to Blackwood—"and armed officers. That's my final offer."

Blackwood has to remind himself to lift his jaw up off the floor.

He's sure he's getting an insight into a conversation between father and son that has played out many times before, where Jock treats the parenting process like a series of business predicaments to be solved with a financial fix. He wonders what Kyle might have agreed to in order to get his father's cooperation. Jock might as well be discussing a donation to charity, or a new business proposal, rather than the safe return of his precious grandbabies. There's no emotion coming from him, and no acknowledgment at all of Kyle's distress. No gesture of comfort. His wife must have done all that when their children were little. At least, Blackwood hopes she did.

"Understood," he says. "I'll talk to Drake now, and I suggest you ask Andrew to come here so we don't have to tell your entire entourage yet."

"I will. But it's a shame you didn't let me in on this earlier," Jock complains. "You should have called us from the hotel. We've been sitting up at the beach house twiddling our thumbs when we could have used the extra time on this." He gives Blackwood's arm a few taps with the palm of his hand. "Anyway, what's done is done. Let's get on with it."

It takes every ounce of Blackwood's willpower to silence his snarky comeback. He thinks of the greater cause and takes a long, measured breath.

"So what's next?" Kyle chimes in.

"We have experts tracing that number and analyzing the photo." Blackwood nods at Kyle's phone. "And so we wait."

CHAPTER THIRTY-THREE
ROSE

Rose watches Carmela's hands, which are gripped viselike around the steering wheel, taking corners too fast as they head away from town. Rose holds on to the sides of her seat each time they approach a bend. She's here because she's operating on instinct and intuition, aware she's putting herself at risk while breaking every single protocol of police work and hostage negotiation. But protocols do not tell you what to do when your own daughter is in peril. Protocols do not tell you how to react when a woman comes to you with a revelation so terrible that you feel it grind into your bones, leaving a dragging ache deep within your heart. Protocol does not highlight how agonizing each of these choices are, or the time frame in which you are forced to make them, especially when you're leaving a good man behind who will, at this very moment, be panicking, wondering where you've gone.

They've been traveling in silence for the past fifteen minutes along a series of small, quiet country roads. The car is an old Hyundai sedan, with dirt in the footwells and some of the switches missing from the center console. It's hot and stuffy inside and Rose is desperate to put the window down, but she doesn't want to increase the noise level in case she misses anything Carmela might have to say. Her phone has buzzed twice in her pocket already, and she knows it's Charlie, trying to find her, but she daren't look at it or reply in case it aggravates Carmela.

She's waiting for Carmela to stop trembling, resisting the urge to offer to drive. She recognizes all too well the acute level of Carmela's distress: the telltale signs of a woman who has been manipulated and controlled to the point where her life is in peril. Rose's heart breaks as she thinks of all the women she's met who seem barely able to function after enduring sustained campaigns of fear: the endless mind games, interrogations, stalking, and violence. For years she has walked down the street fully aware that she might be passing a woman who is essentially a hostage in her own life, hurrying somewhere under duress before scurrying home to appease the partner who claims to love her and yet seems to delight in making her afraid.

Dread makes Rose nauseous as she wonders about the psychopathic state of the men Carmela is driving them toward. "Carmela, you need to help me understand," she insists, using the steady voice she's been trained to stick to in delicate negotiations. *To succeed, you must persuade the kidnapper that you're on their side.* "Then I'll be better placed to help." She searches for a question that might feel safe to begin with, rather than forcing Carmela to discuss their current nightmare. "Start from the beginning. What happened when Jock found out you were pregnant?"

Carmela responds with another series of those strange, rapid nods, her eyes flitting quickly to Rose, then back to the road. "As soon as Jock knew I was having his child, I was dismissed without notice, with a lump sum payout—a bribe for my silence. I moved back home to care for my mother, who was seriously ill, and spent most of the money on medical and funeral expenses." She pauses to focus on overtaking a large truck that's slowing them down. "When Marisol was a couple of months old, I was evicted for not keeping up with the rent. I slept on my brother's couch for a while, with Marisol in a portacrib beside me, but my sister-in-law didn't like that, so they decided to find me a husband." Carmela is speaking in short, panting bursts, her voice rising with emotion, then falling again as she tries to keep herself in check. "Gerard was kind to us at first. He's a farmer, ten years older than me. He'd lost his wife a few years before and was struggling to raise his son." Carmela takes a long, shuddering breath. "Life wasn't too bad to begin with—although Reid was a handful even at seven years old, and only listened to his dad. But then we had the droughts, and the fires, and the constant struggle to sell livestock at profit. Gerard had to gradually partition and sell off his family land until hardly any farm was left. Each time it shattered him a little more, and slowly I lost the decent man I married. Soon we all lived on a knife edge, balancing our decisions around his mood."

"And you didn't try to seek any more financial help from Jock?"

Carmela sighs. "For a long time I never told anyone who Marisol's real father was. Gerard didn't want to talk about it to begin with. He was happy to be Marisol's dad, so I felt sorry for him when Marisol began pressing for details as a teenager. I could see he felt such a deep sense of rejection, but he became curious too." Carmela shudders, her fingers clamped on the wheel so tightly that her knuckles are white. "I gave in and told them the truth. And then our lives went completely off the rails."

She falls silent for a moment and Rose waits.

"Gerard was furious," Carmela continues. "He realized that he'd taken on a rich man's child and paid for her and raised her while slowly losing everything. He pestered me all the time about getting money, contacted lawyers, and we eventually made an official request to Jock to backdate childcare or be forced to take a paternity test. Gerard thought we could shame Jock by threatening to go public, but he never thought about what it might do to me. I was brought up Catholic, and I dreaded the thought of court battles and being known as the other woman, the home-wrecker." She pauses, casting a brief look at Rose, her eyes pleading for sympathy. "Then we received a message from the Fishers' lawyers saying we were trying to extort Jock, and if we continued they would take us to court and make sure we were portrayed in the worst possible light. At the same time, our property was vandalized. Some of our livestock were poisoned. My car tires were slashed while I was parked outside the supermarket. So we backed off." She shrugs.

Rose feels her phone buzz again. She glances at Carmela sharply, but Carmela's eyes are fixed on the road. Rose has been subtly working the device out of her pocket as Carmela talks, and now it's concealed in her hand, which she's keeping by the side of the seat next to the passenger door. She doesn't dare look at the screen. If she spooks Carmela now, she might lose Lou forever.

Carmela continues to talk. "I didn't care that Jock had won. But Gerard became consumed by bitterness, and Reid was growing increasingly frustrated and aimless. He began getting into more and more trouble with the police, taking casual laboring jobs that he could never hold down, and eventually he ended up in prison for assaulting someone he worked with. The atmosphere was so toxic that I encouraged Marisol to leave. As soon as she turned eighteen she traveled up to Perth and took a course in childcare. It's a small world up there. What I didn't realize was that she sought out nannying vacancies that would get her close to the Fishers, edging herself nearer to her half siblings and her father." Carmela's tone shifts to despair. "I knew nothing about that until the call from the hospital on New Year's Eve. Marisol was in intensive care, with four broken vertebrae and a fractured skull. They told us she was brain damaged and permanently paralyzed from the waist down. And then we discovered that the accident had happened at Kyle Fisher's house."

Rose's thoughts spin as she tries to fit all these pieces together. She recalls Charlie's fears when he'd dropped Lou off to begin working for the Fishers. What had he said again? *It was like delivering a lamb to the lion's den.* He'd been closer to the truth than he realized.

"Since then," Carmela's tremulous voice continues, bringing Rose back to the present, "we've been crippled by ongoing medical bills. Reid got out of prison with no plans for the future, and no prospect of inheriting a healthy farm. Gerard turned to alcohol to ease the pain, and I battled to keep us all alive and fed, caring for Marisol day and night."

Carmela pauses, and when she speaks again, her tone is a shade lower. "The first I knew of their dreadful plan was when they brought Louisa and the babies inside the house. Reid and Gerard were covered in blood. The girl was sobbing. The children appeared confused and frightened out of their wits." Carmela's voice cracks on almost every word now. "They thought they could extort money from Kyle as a way of getting to Jock—because Reid had heard about Kyle in prison, the nonchalant way he paid off creditors and underworld figures like bikies, who would do him favors to keep his clubs running at a profit. Everyone knew he was bankrolled by Jock, so it was a chance of getting Jock's money."

Rose frowns. "But how did they know where to find Lou and the kids?"

"Apparently, Frannie Fisher was constantly showing off their holiday home on social media, and that house is less than an hour away from our farmhouse. Reid and Gerard cased the area for weeks, or so they told me afterward, working it all out. And when the family showed up, they realized that Louisa was bringing the kids down to the beach early every day. They saw that her boyfriend always left around eight thirty, and they convinced themselves it would be easy: take the kids for a ride on the boat and send Louisa back with a note to pay a ransom. Once the funds arrived they'd leave the kids somewhere." Carmela lets out a wail. "But the plan went wrong and they murdered that poor boy."

She turns and grabs Rose's arm, nails digging into skin as the car swerves. Rose grabs the steering wheel in alarm, and Carmela's eyes flash back to the road, correcting their course. "I'm sorry, I'm sorry, but you must listen. Reid has no remorse. He's planning to kill your daughter. To silence her because she's the only witness to what happened. He wants to get Jock's money and run." Carmela shakes her head furiously. "Gerard is helping Reid escape. He cannot see how evil his son has become: He blames everybody else instead. Reid is his only flesh and blood, and he's always loved his child more than anyone else in the world."

She pauses for a moment, her eyes scanning the rearview mirror as though someone is following. Rose turns to look, but the road is empty.

"I've been pretending to be on their side," Carmela admits quietly. "They told me I was part of it now, whether I wanted to be or not. They said the little kids won't even remember what happened, and Kyle and Jock would hardly notice the dent in their finances. And they threatened me, saying if we went to prison I wouldn't see Marisol for years—and she would have to go into one of those awful care homes."

Rose is rapidly assessing her options. Had she made a mistake getting into the car? She doesn't think so. The clock is counting down too fast to consider alternatives, and she'd never forgive herself if Lou died because she'd hesitated at the crucial moment.

"Bree messaged a group of former Fisher nannies earlier today," Carmela explains, as though hearing Rose's thoughts. "I'm only on there because they like to check in and see how Marisol's going. Marisol can't speak or control her movements well, and she even has trouble swallowing. But her face lights up when I say the girls' names and pass on their news, and some of them have been incredibly kind and thoughtful by staying in touch. Anyway, Bree's message said you were reaching out to see if anyone could help; that you were desperate. After I looked you up and discovered all your credentials and your background as a police officer, I knew you might be my only hope. If I let the police come in all guns blazing, Reid will go mad and hurt people. But they won't be expecting you to come alone." Her voice softens. "I understand what it is to feel the pain of losing a daughter. Perhaps God will look more kindly on my sins if I help you now."

Rose can feel her panic beginning to rise to the surface. "How do you know Lou is still okay, if you've been out for an hour?" she asks. "Why did you even leave her?" She feels desperate, unable to quell the horrific idea that they might already be too late.

"She'll be all right for now—they need her to keep the children calm. I tipped away the formula powder without them realizing, then told them that we needed more supplies for the baby—I reminded them that once they sent their demands we wouldn't be able to get more food until this was over, and it would be a nightmare if we ended up with a screaming, hungry child. They didn't like it, but I promised I would be quick. Louisa will be okay until I get home. But then, I don't know."

This rescue attempt is so precariously balanced that Rose wants to vomit from the panic. "So what are we going to do when we get there? We can't just confront them; we'll be overpowered. How do we get to Lou and the kids?"

"I . . . I am not sure yet," Carmela says, her voice wavering as the car rattles along the empty road.

Rose thinks quickly, running through all the options. These men have passed the point of no return; they are beyond reasoning with. Which means Rose and Carmela's best chance is to take them by surprise.

And suddenly, she knows what they should do.

"I think I have an idea," she tells Carmela, watching the other woman's chin quivering. "But you have to follow my instructions." She inhales deeply, trying to steady herself. Exhales. "When we're ten minutes from your house, I want you to pull over."

"Why?" Carmela looks confused.

"Because I'm going to hide in the trunk."

CHAPTER THIRTY-FOUR
BLACKWOOD

"For god's sake, what the fuck is going on?" On the other end of the line, Drake is apoplectic. "And why haven't I been informed? Webster says you're keeping everyone out of the incident room, and the entire team's been sent to Dunsborough without explanation. You'd better have a bloody good reason for this."

Blackwood stifles a groan. He might have known Webster wouldn't let it lie. Now Drake will be on the warpath. Reluctantly, he runs Drake through the last couple of hours, and his plan to meet the hostage takers' demands.

"You can't be serious," Drake splutters. "Are you insane? I won't allow you to send Jock Fisher in to negotiate with violent kidnappers. And as for leaving me out of the loop, I'll want you in my office as soon as this is over."

"We're out of time and options," Blackwood replies calmly, even though his insides are roiling at the thought he might have just blown his entire career and his generous retirement package in one morning. "And he won't be going alone. I'll be in the vehicle to support him, and I've requested two snipers from the Perth tactical response unit; they're on the way by helicopter now and should be here within the hour. We'll have his back at all times, and we'll get him to draw them outside where we can deal with them."

"I want to speak to Jock right now," Drake demands, and Blackwood holds his phone out to Jock, who takes it and moves into one corner, where no one can hear the full conversation.

Jock's assistant, Andrew, is hunched over his laptop at the table. He'd appeared at the house ten minutes ago, and his colorless face had somehow turned even more ashen as the circumstances were explained to him. He's working on the crypto and has assured them it will be doable.

Kyle jumps up. "Their next demand has just come through," he says, showing his phone to Blackwood.

"Okay, we've got the Bitcoin trading details." Blackwood turns to Angie. "How's tech going on the email address?"

"Got our boy Calvin on it in Perth. He says they used a VPN, so they seem to know what they're doing. Calvin is looking to see if he can work around it, but it isn't easy, particularly with the time limit. He'll get back to us if it's possible."

Blackwood's and Angie's phones begin ringing at almost the same time. Blackwood sees his caller is Webster, but before he can berate the man for running to Drake behind his back, Webster cuts in. "We've found the Santoses' nanny. She's been in a car accident, run off the road at a remote spot, and she's broken her leg. She couldn't move far enough to reach her bag and call someone. We've got an ambulance there now."

"Thank god. Are the circumstances suspicious?"

"I don't think so. She said a kangaroo startled her. But get this: She was on her way back from Charlie Thornton's house late last night when it happened. Said she'd been talking to Charlie and Rose about Louisa and the kids. They were asking her about the Fishers' former nannies."

"I'm aware of that." Blackwood's jaw tightens. "And I really wish Rose Campbell would stop running her own bloody investigation."

"Would you like me to talk to her?" Webster replies.

Blackwood bristles. "Not right now. But thanks for the update."

"There isn't much more I can do here," Webster continues. "I'll make my way back to Kardanup."

Blackwood mentally runs through different scenarios to keep Webster at a distance without putting him completely offside. "Actually, please can you head to Dunsborough? I need someone there, ready to take charge on my instruction." He hopes the mention of leadership will be enough to placate Webster.

"Right," Webster replies, and hangs up. Blackwood's sure the man won't be happy once he discovers he's been left out of the key part of the rescue mission. He reminds himself that soon he won't have to care much about Webster, and waits for the usual twinge of the grief that comes when he thinks of his retirement. But for once it doesn't arrive, and instead he experiences a distinct sense of relief. He quickly smothers the feeling and refocuses, turning to Angie. "Let me speak to Rose Campbell. Stella wouldn't have been in this position if Rose hadn't wanted to run her own investigation. I'd like to have a word with her about interfering."

"Wait, that was Charlie on the phone just then," Angie replies, obviously flustered. "He says they went to meet a lead, another nanny, he thinks, called Carmela. Rose insisted on going to talk to her alone, at the woman's request. Anyway, he's lost her. He dropped her off in Margaret River ninety minutes ago, and now she's not answering her phone. Appears to have gone off the radar. Charlie's panicking."

"For fuck's sake," Blackwood hisses. "What is she doing? If she gets in the way and messes up this rescue mission, it'll be an absolute tragedy, and one she'll have to live with."

Angie shrugs. "If she's found out where her daughter is, of course she's gone to get her. I might well do the same in her shoes. And we haven't given her much confidence that we're listening to her, have we?"

"Possibly not," Blackwood concedes. "But now, if we don't know where she is or what she's planning on doing, we have to consider Rose as an unpredictable factor in this whole thing. So let's be prepared for that as well. See if we can track her phone. We're leaving as soon as the snipers arrive, yes? And you'll be in one of the follow-up vehicles?"

"That's right. We'll be tracking your phone and have you under surveillance, but we'll hang back unless we think you're in danger. Once you've retrieved everyone, we'll go in and round up these bastards."

"If they're still there."

"Yep. Otherwise we'll have the entire Western Australian force conducting a manhunt later on today."

Blackwood doesn't want to think about that, or the incredibly high stakes at play. He glances across at the other men in the room, who wait while Jock finishes on the phone.

"I think I'm ready," Andrew says once Jock has ended his call. "If you definitely want to do this?"

Jock nods. "Get it done."

Andrew presses a few more buttons and then says, "It's gone."

They all fall silent, as though expecting something to happen instantly. When it doesn't, Jock throws himself down onto one of the two comfy chairs in the room. "They'd better not be playing us," he growls.

Blackwood moves to sit opposite him. "While we wait, you should know that the Santoses' nanny has been found. She's been in an accident, run her vehicle off the road, but she should be okay."

Jock shrugs, only mildly interested.

"Also, Louisa's mum, Rose, has disappeared," Blackwood adds. "DS Lennard spoke to Charlie, Rose's former brother-in-law, just now. He says Rose went to talk to someone called Carmela. Does that name ring any bells?"

Jock stares at Blackwood as though he's just conjured the dead. "Carmela?" he croaks eventually.

"Who the fuck is Carmela?" Kyle asks.

"Oh no." Jock closes his eyes. "Oh no, oh no."

Blackwood is struggling to contain his surprise and stay professional. For the first time in this entire crisis, Jock appears to be terrified.

Kyle sees his father's reaction and frowns. "Dad?"

Jock puts his head in his hands.

"Dad!" Kyle yells.

Jock looks up, his eyes wild with panic. "Don't you remember? She was our housekeeper, what, over twenty years ago now. She . . . I think she had a child." He frowns. "But I thought we dealt with all that. Andrew?" he asks uncertainly.

Andrew comes across to his side. "I'm not sure what you're talking about," he says soothingly, crouching down in front of his boss. "But I can help you now. Who do I need to talk to?"

"The kids," Jock splutters, staring wide eyed around the room. "Get all my kids down here right now."

CHAPTER THIRTY-FIVE
TRISHA

Trisha has had to wait days for this moment, when she's finally alone with her husband. There's always someone hovering, be it the family, the household staff, or a member of Jock's entourage. Their home is never at rest: Things always need fixing, cleaning, polishing, enhancing. She used to love it when they were first married, but now it's just exhausting.

She sits at her dressing table in the large powder room between the bedroom and the bathroom, examining her face. She's had Botox to take away some of the lines, but she should have done more about the bags under her eyes and the loosening jowls around her neck. She'd planned to wipe off her makeup before bed, but she's not sure she's brave enough to have this conversation without some kind of mask.

She's wearing a long, navy satin nightdress with a matching robe and curlicues of flowers along the hems. Years ago she would have felt exquisite, but now the clothes are too good for her, unable to hide the small potbelly that had come with the menopause, or the sun damage on her chest and arms.

She has worked so very hard, all her life, to make herself acceptable. But clearly, she is no longer enough.

She walks through to the bedroom. Jock is already in the bed in his light-blue pajamas, reading glasses on, flicking through one of those endless company documents. His mind will be full of statistics and profit margins, and it isn't the best time to disturb him, but who knows when this moment will come again? She sits on the edge of the bed. It's less confrontational than standing, but still far enough away from him that she can run to the bathroom if she needs to, and lock herself in.

"I know Carmela's pregnant," she says.

Jock looks at her over the top of his glasses, frowning for a moment as though he's trying to catch up with the conversation. Then he sighs, puts his papers down, takes off his glasses, and rubs his eyes.

"I'm sorry."

The air in the room thickens. Trisha tries to gulp down her panicky breaths. She's always known that Jock has had affairs, but she'd never seen the point in fighting about it, confident that it was just sex: He'd never leave her. In their thirty-year marriage she'd enriched her life with the children, and made the choice to be an outwardly perfect wife and mother. Hell, there'd even been a couple of men for her along the way: an old schoolfriend, and the father of one of Ethan's mates. She's not been attracted to Jock for a long time, and it's fine if he doesn't want intimacy, but her entire identity is built around being his wife. She'd planned to always play along for the sake of peace and security, and to protect the family's reputation.

However, pregnancy is different. Pregnancy threatens their entire foundation, and her children's future. Pregnancy is public humiliation. She cannot let a pregnancy slide.

"What are you going to do?" she asks quietly.

Jock stares at the ceiling. "I've offered her money for an abortion, but she won't take it. Against her beliefs, apparently. So I'm paying her to go away." He grimaces. "I'll give her enough to make sure she stays quiet. I'll take care of whatever's needed." He catches Trisha's eye. "I've always been careful. I'm furious with myself, if that helps at all."

"I've put up with a lot," she says, trying to keep her voice even. "But this feels like too much."

Jock sits up straighter. "Do you want a divorce?"

"Of course not," she replies quickly. But as she meets his eyes she sees something she hadn't expected. Hope, quickly turning to disappointment.

He's ready to move on, she thinks. So what is he waiting for? Does he want her to jump first so that he doesn't have to blame himself? Or is it not worth the stress until he finds another woman—younger, buxom, and beautiful like Carmela, but with the right pedigree.

She gets up and moves over to her side of the bed, legs unsteady, keen to be done with the conversation.

"I trust you to do what's right," she says, pulling back the covers and climbing in next to him. "But please keep me informed if there's anything I need to know."

"Thank you, Trish." He turns to her. "As always I appreciate your understanding and discretion." He pats her hand. "You've been a terrific wife and mother," he adds softly, his eyes crinkling at the corners as he gives her a benevolent smile, before collecting his glasses and going back to his paperwork.

Was that a goodbye? After so many years, could it really be so easy, and so distant? So banal? Trisha's heart is in her throat as she turns her light out and pretends to sleep. After a few minutes, Jock gets up and leaves the room.

She knows he won't be back. She stares at the boutique furnishings, the heavy velvet drapes, the chandelier with its tiny crystal icicles poised above her. And she understands she has spent her best years coasting, a passenger in her own life, riding it out while others steered her course. There's no way of changing that, but the burn in her mouth and the fire in her chest is telling her a truth she doesn't want to hear. She's always reassured herself that she could fix whatever she needed to, but now it's clear just how much she's got terribly, terribly wrong.

CHAPTER THIRTY-SIX
ROSE

The trunk of Carmela's car is so stifling that Rose has to work hard to steady her panic, hoping she'll still be conscious by the time they reach their destination. The space smells strongly of petrol and is cluttered with small objects. So far she's found a few old towels, a couple of empty burlap bags, three shopping bags, two small boxes of light bulbs, and a canvas tool bag. It feels like at least half a dozen objects are poking and scraping at her skin as she lies curled into a fetal position, one hand gripping her mobile.

She keeps checking the phone's screen but the signal remains low and unpredictable. They must be too remote now for reliable mobile reception. She texts Charlie anyway, awkwardly typing with one finger, hoping the message will be sent as soon as the signal comes back. *Going for Lou. Track number or follow map. Be careful. They want to kill her.*

She screenshots her map, praying it helps Charlie figure out where she's going. She knows how dangerous her position is, but she couldn't think of any other option. From Carmela's descriptions she could envisage the years that have led to this insanity, as Marisol's family's narrowing possibilities became a huge, disastrous clusterfuck of decisions. They are too far into this catastrophe for there to be a reasonable way out.

Carmela had agreed with Rose's plan. "I'll find somewhere to pull over," she'd said. "There's a long driveway and a grassy area in front of the house where we park. I'll go inside, and if it's possible, I'll bring Lou back to you, and you can both run. But Reid is planning to take her somewhere else, so he may use the car. If he does, and I can't get Louisa away from him, at least you'll be with them, to notify the police so they can find you. Whatever happens, keep Reid unaware of you until the last possible moment—if he thinks the police are close then he'll kill your daughter straightaway. And you too."

"You're sure they're beyond reasoning with?" Rose asked, already knowing the answer.

"Yes. They've lost their minds. Gerard doesn't care what happens to him now. It's all about helping Reid escape, and getting revenge. Neither of them can see the humanity of the people in their way. They have no remorse for what they did to Louisa's boyfriend; in fact they're furious with him for causing this problem." As she spoke, Carmela pulled across to one side of the road. "Are you ready?"

Rose stalled for a few seconds, her mind whirring, searching for another way. But Carmela's eyes were desperate. "Please, Rose, we need to move fast. As soon as Jock pays the money, it's over, and Reid will take Louisa somewhere she won't be found. This is our only chance."

And so, with the voices of all her colleagues clamoring in her ears, screaming at her stupidity, Rose had climbed into the trunk and let Carmela close her in.

Now, stuck in her cramped position, she tries to collect her thoughts, while the car begins bouncing around with greater intensity, suggesting they're off the asphalt. She pictures Carmela driving steadfastly back into this nightmare, and wonders what's going through her mind. The woman has risked her life to get Rose's help, but Rose knows from experience that abused women can be unpredictable. Their entrenched fear can make them suddenly realign with their abusers in order to keep themselves or their loved ones safe. Women like Carmela are constantly dealing with agonizing choices—to run, hide, or fight—but these are all equally exhausting. What they really need is a *fix*, but the only way to do that is if they can hold their abuser accountable and escape their control. Pretty difficult if you're struggling with a sociopath, often the father of your children.

Rose checks her phone again. One bar of signal. Quickly, she flicks onto her maps app, watching the little blue dot moving slowly on a white background, praying for a stronger connection to give her some idea of where they are. It takes a few agonizing seconds, but then the maps image fills in, and Rose zooms out, screenshotting the surroundings a few times, dismayed at how little else there is close by. She messages Charlie the screenshots, then hesitates, not wanting to give in to helplessness but unsure of what else she can do.

When she'd got into Carmela's car, she'd known the situation was bleak, but now she's realizing just how insane and hopeless this feels. It's clear she needs all the backup she can get. She only hopes the police will pay attention. She sends the same map images to Angie, and is still typing when, without warning, the car judders to a stop. She quickly sends the message, then pushes her phone deep into her jeans pocket—not easy in the position she's in, but she needs both hands ready.

She waits. Hears the driver's door of the vehicle open.

She doesn't dare move.

The door closes with an abrupt bang that shakes the car and startles her. She can hear footsteps, but they're getting quieter. Walking away. Trudging across gravel, the clink of glass bottles becoming fainter.

No, no, no, no, no, no.

Rose pushes frantically at the lid of the trunk, mere inches from her face. It doesn't budge. How could she have been so stupid? Now she's trapped. Helpless in whatever they've planned next. Her breathing spirals out of control, and she forces herself to slow it down. She can't afford to hyperventilate and use up all the remaining oxygen. If she's unconscious, she won't be able to fight.

Her hand moves to her phone. To tell Charlie what's happened. To say sorry. And possibly goodbye.

And then there's a small click, a catch releasing, and the lid of the trunk pops up a couple of centimeters.

For a moment she's stunned, uncomprehending.

Then she realizes. A remote. Of course. Carmela had used a remote.

Everyone uses a remote.

In her panic, she'd forgotten.

She tries to recompose herself. Listens. Waits.

But there's only silence.

CHAPTER THIRTY-SEVEN
LOUISA

There's a commotion in the central area of the house, although Lou has no idea what it means. But she hears a gruff voice say, "They did it, they fucking did it," and she knows it's the younger, tattooed man, the one who stabbed Fabien. The joy and incredulity in his voice, the lightness of it, fill her with a momentary hatred that goes deeper than she'd ever known a feeling could go.

Their voices become murmurs that she can't make out even with her ear to the door, so she goes back to the bed and sits on it. The kids are glued to an old detective program on the television; it's totally inappropriate for them, but it's keeping them quiet so she doesn't care. They both smell of urine and stale food, despite her attempts to wash them. The three of them haven't brushed their teeth for days. The older man has been the one unlocking the door and sliding trays of food through on the floor. Usually it's either ready meals, overcooked pizza, or packets of crisps.

She hears a car door slam outside, footsteps coming into the house, then a loud booming voice. "Mum! It fucking worked!"

And then a pause.

"Be happy, Mum. I told you, it worked."

Another pause. Then, "Go get them then. It's time for me to leave."

To Lou's surprise and horror, the door bolts are suddenly pushed back, and the older man stands in front of her. "Come on," he says gruffly. "Bring the kids."

Trembling, Lou gathers up Honey and Kai, one on each hip, and reluctantly enters the lounge room. Three people stand in a semicircle, watching her. There's the woman she'd seen a glimpse of on the first day, and the two men who snatched them. The younger man, with his sleeves of tattoos and his terrifying gray eyes, has a flick-knife in his hand. Fabien flashes through Lou's mind. Her heart aches and her legs almost give way. But she steels herself, raising her chin. For as long as possible, she won't show them her fear.

The younger man pushes the blade back and forth, in and out, and stares at her with menace. She gets the message.

"We're going on a trip," he says. He turns to his mother. "You left the kid's food in the car, yeah?"

The woman nods rapidly, her eyes wide.

She looks almost as scared as me, Lou thinks.

The younger man scowls at Lou. "Give the girl to my mum."

Honey clings tighter to Lou and begins to whimper.

The older lady comes forward, arms outstretched, and says in a soft crooning voice that contrasts with her stricken expression, "It's okay, little one. Shall we go and find some lollies?"

Honey hesitates, then solemnly lets the woman take her. The woman won't meet Lou's eyes as she whisks Honey away toward the kitchen.

Lou watches them go, then notices another door is open to her left. Just beyond the doorframe, there's a young woman in a wheelchair, her head lolled to one side. She wears a loose-fitting T-shirt and jogging bottoms, and her long dark hair is unbrushed. She watches Lou without really appearing to see her. There's something familiar about those ice-cool blue eyes.

"Time to leave then," Reid says, grabbing a backpack. He turns to his father. "I wish I could be here to see Jock Fucker's face." Then he glares at Lou. "Come on then, we're going on a trip. You stay ahead of me so I can keep an eye on you."

Clutching Kai, unable to even see Honey, Lou has no choice but to go out of the front door and down the steps toward the old Hyundai sedan that sits on the gravel driveway in front of the house.

As they get closer, Reid says, "Give him to me," and holds his arms out for the baby. Not knowing what else to do, Lou passes him over. "Now get in." Reid points to the car. "Back seat."

Lou climbs in and Reid sets Kai down on the ground for a moment, pulling a couple of zip ties out of his pocket.

"Wrists," he demands, as Kai begins to grizzle.

She lets him bind her wrists and then her ankles.

"Sit back," he says. Then he picks up Kai and pushes him through the gap in Lou's arms. The little boy squirms, trying to twist himself free, but Reid pushes him roughly back in place, and this time Kai gets the message and stays still, his bottom lip stuck out slightly, an indignant frown on his face. "There, he's all tucked in," Reid says with a snigger, and then he closes the door, not bothering to put a seat belt on them.

He goes around to the driver's side and gets in. "Any trouble and you'll regret it," he warns as he starts the engine.

Lou doesn't say anything, just stares out of the window in despair as they circle away from the farmhouse, leaving Honey behind.

CHAPTER THIRTY-EIGHT
BLACKWOOD

Blackwood watches Jock, Kyle, and Andrew exchange glances as they wait for the snipers to arrive. The tension in the small dining room is unbearable.

Angie's phone chimes and she studies it for a moment. "Snipers are ten minutes away," she says, looking up. Her eyes move to Blackwood. "A quick word, DSS Blackwood?"

He doesn't like her expression. Angie rarely looks this scared. He follows her quickly into the corridor, closing the door behind him.

"It's from Rose," she says as soon as the door shuts, shoving her phone in front of his face.

He takes it. There's a series of photos and a brief message. *Come now I have found Lou.*

He frowns. "Shit, shit, shit. Do you trust her?"

"Yep." Angie's eyes are wide.

Blackwood feels momentarily unsteady. "I do too. So we need that location, to see if it matches where Jock and I are heading. Go find help, and don't walk," he urges Angie. "Run."

Angie sprints down the corridor.

Blackwood would prefer to stay put, waiting for Angie, but he doesn't want to leave Jock and Kyle alone to concoct anything. As he heads back into the small room, his thoughts are racing. Ten minutes ago he'd been furious with Rose. Now, he's terrified for her—for all of them. If she's found out where the kids are, she's on the verge of walking into a highly volatile scenario. He should have trusted her more, kept her close and onside. She's been one step ahead of him since she got here, but he's been worried about protecting his chain of command rather than listening to her.

"What's happening?" Kyle demands.

"Still waiting for the tac team," Blackwood reassures him. "Any minute now."

He's texting Angie as he talks. *As soon as you have her location, find out who's closest. Get them on the phone, standing by for instructions.*

He gets a reply straightaway. *On it. Charlie also heading to a helicopter. He got the same map—I can't stop him.*

Just keep in contact with him. He might be useful, Blackwood writes back.

He's pocketing his phone when there's a knock at the door and the Fisher siblings are shown in. As soon as Jock sees them, he jumps up and begins to yell.

"This is all about Carmela," he cries. "Fucking Carmela—and Marisol. I thought we'd made that go away."

The three older Fishers stand in silence, but Blackwood can see the ripple of alarm across their faces. Kyle is the only one who looks confused. "Who's Marisol?"

"Did Dad not tell you?" Bronte replies, her voice a scathing purr. "Marisol is Dad's love child."

"What?" Kyle's mouth drops open as he takes in the expressions of his family members one by one.

"I thought we'd sorted all this a long time ago," Jock roars, without a shred of remorse or self-consciousness. "Please tell me that we're taking care of them."

Ethan steps forward. "They were trying to extort us, Dad." The red patches on his cheeks deepen with each word. "They kept wanting more. We couldn't let them blackmail you."

Jock stalks closer to glare at his children in turn. "So what did you do instead?" he asks menacingly.

"We warned them off. We got people to make it difficult for them to pursue us for more money. It wasn't right."

"That woman ruined our mother's life," Toby adds, scowling at his father. "And besides, you never even took a paternity test."

Jock marches across to Toby until his face is inches away from his son's. "This wasn't your call," he says menacingly. "When I give you explicit instructions, I expect you to follow them."

Toby stands his ground but doesn't respond, his eyes locked on to Jock's intimidating stare. Blackwood suspects they've had altercations like this before, although probably not on the same scale. He's bracing himself in case he needs to jump in and separate them.

"So now I've been asked to go and collect Kyle's children from these bastards, as some kind of humiliating retribution, I'd guess," Jock splutters. "They'll probably film it live and upload it to social media. All because you lot didn't follow my instructions. Well, you're all fired. All of you. You've royally fucked your chances of inheritance. I'll make sure each one of you lives to regret this."

Still no reaction from the kids. Blackwood watches this play out with growing unease. He's not sure who'll explode first, but he can sense it building.

Then Kyle steps into the fray. "I don't know what exactly you fuckers have done," he growls. "Or why I'm the only one who doesn't know we have a bloody half sister. But right now, it's *my* kids' lives on the line, and if you don't all support me at this moment, *I'll* fucking kill you. And believe me, I know the right people to get the job done."

At this, Blackwood steps forward. "That's enough. No more now, any of you. I'm letting that one go because of the emotional state you're in, Kyle, but threatening to kill is an arrestable offense, and I presume you'll want to be here when your kids get back, not stuck in a holding cell."

"Fine." Kyle turns to Blackwood. "And I want Frannie here too. Does anyone know where she is?"

"She went to a hotel," Bronte says approvingly. "She's had enough of us at last."

"Actually, she's with the Santoses," Angie murmurs. "We've briefed her on some of this, but not everything."

Kyle throws his hands in the air. "Of course she is. Well, can you get her here, please? And can someone tell Bridget and Vic that we don't need them hanging around anymore." His phone buzzes in his hand and his attention snaps straight to it. He gulps. "The bastards have sent us an address," he mutters, shoving it at Blackwood.

Blackwood scans the message. *Money received. Come to Dovedale Farm, 204 Newthorn Road. Arrive by road. Jock to approach the house alone. You have one hour.*

He passes the phone to Angie. "Get that distributed to everyone who needs it. And tell me exactly where it is."

Angie puts the address into her phone. "About thirty-five minutes from here. Looks like a farmhouse in the middle of nowhere."

Blackwood chooses his next words carefully, not wanting to reveal Rose's situation to the Fishers. "Does it fit with the other location we're tracking?"

She nods. "It does."

There's a stab of pain in Blackwood's chest, thinking of Rose out there all alone, intent on saving her child. A brave move or a ludicrous one? They won't know until it's over.

"Initial assessment?"

"Not easy for backup to approach in secret."

There's another knock on the door, and White comes in. "The armed police are here now. We're ready to go."

Jock grabs his jacket and glowers at his children. "You'd better hope for your own sake that this goes smoothly," he mutters as he stomps past them.

Kyle follows him out. "Dad?"

Jock turns.

"I'm grateful, okay? And remember, they're not just my kids; they're your grandkids too."

Jock opens his mouth, then appears to reconsider. He takes the measure of his son for a moment, then turns away without replying.

Blackwood follows Jock as he stalks out to the car, a black Land Rover with tinted windows. They both ignore the curious glances of the officers who've gathered to help out. Two armed police officers are already in the vehicle, one in the front passenger seat, one in the back, dressed in tactical gear, each man with a sniper rifle tucked beside him. Jock slides into the vacant rear seat, and Blackwood goes to the driver's side. He puts the address into the GPS and they set off.

The two tactical response officers don't say a word while Blackwood explains what he knows. When he's finished, the one in the back turns to Jock.

"We need to put a wire on you, sir, so we can hear what's going on. And a bulletproof vest as well. We'd give you an earpiece but we're concerned it'll be too noticeable."

"I'll take the vest," Jock retorts, "but you don't need to spy on me. What do you think I'm gonna do?"

"We're not spying on you, sir," the officer persists matter-of-factly. "We're making sure the kidnappers hand over the children without hurting you or them. If there's any indication that things are out of control, we're coming in."

"Won't come to that," Jock says dismissively. "Carmela will listen to me, and I'll talk her round."

Blackwood debates asking more, but he doesn't want to undermine the man's confidence. He can only hope it's well founded.

The officers have studied the layout of the buildings, and the plan is for Jock to appeal to Carmela, refusing to go past the front doorstep before he has proof that the children are alive. They want to lure the kidnappers out so the police can have eyes on what's happening. It's a good tactic in the time frame they've got, but Blackwood is incredibly nervous. In addition to the dire situation, Jock Fisher has proved all along that he can cause fireworks at any moment. Blackwood is praying that, just for once, the man will stick to what they've agreed and do exactly as he's asked.

CHAPTER THIRTY-NINE
ROSE

Rose hardly dares to breathe. Lou and the baby are on the other side of the partition that separates the back seats from the trunk. So close, and yet still so unbearably unreachable.

As soon as the car started to move, she'd become terrified that the trunk would open, exposing her. Since they set off she's been holding on to the underneath of the trunk's lid with all her might, trying to make sure it doesn't slam closed or rattle. Every now and again her fingers get trapped between metal as the car goes over bumps and divots, but she hardly notices the pain, focused only on staying alert. She's hanging on to her composure as precariously as her fingers clutch at the metal above her. Each minute feels like a lifetime.

She'd realized early on that there was little hope of her going inside the farmhouse to subdue whatever was happening, but nevertheless, this is agonizing. She suspects she's in the middle of the final play. Lou is being taken somewhere she'll never be found, along with the baby.

A baby whose life also depends on Rose.

Her throat is swollen with fear. Every moment is critical, and she has to get this right. The best chance she has of overpowering the kidnapper, particularly if he's young and fit, is the element of surprise. She's got that for now, but once he stops the car it's going to be difficult to leap out from her hiding position quickly enough to maintain her advantage. After what happened to Fabien, she knows how this man reacts to someone who interrupts his plans.

She pulls one hand slowly and carefully from holding on to the trunk lid, so she can feel around in the tight space for anything she can use as a weapon. In the tool bag she finds a small wrench, and she pushes it between her knees so she can grab it quickly. Another search uncovers a little screwdriver, which she secures beside the wrench. Otherwise she can only find empty bags and other things too small to be useful. There may be more items behind her, but she can't twist around to see. She wishes she'd paid more attention before she got in.

Nevertheless, these two small tools give her a brief burst of hope; but for now, apart from the car engine and her own breathing, there's only silence. Too much silence. Not even the baby is making a noise. If she closes her eyes she could be anywhere, and she chooses that for a moment, imagining herself back beside Charlie, taking comfort from the safety and support she'd felt in his presence over the last couple of days, and drawing strength for what's inevitably to come.

CHAPTER FORTY
BLACKWOOD

No wonder they'd found no trace of Louisa and the kids, Blackwood thinks as they approach the house. This is a damn good place to hide hostages: extremely remote and with terrible mobile coverage. They'd had to endure a few kilometers of rugged dirt-track driving before they even reached the turnoff, which featured a dilapidated steel postbox on a plinth and the number 204 in faded gold lettering. The long drive-way is horribly exposed, with low grassland on either side. If anyone is watching their arrival, the police are essentially sitting ducks.

Angie is in a van with another load of officers, tailing them about a kilometer behind. Blackwood wishes he could talk to her, and recheck this hasty plan they've devised. There's so much risk he's sure he can feel an arrhythmia kicking in, his heart protesting the constant spikes of adrenaline.

"Remember," he reminds Jock as they get closer, "call out to them. Lure them outside. And be clever in what you say—give us as much information as you can. *Abort* is the key word. You say that, we all come running."

"You don't have to worry, I got it," Jock replies, his irritation obvi-ous. "Let's just get on with this."

On his final words, the house itself comes into view. It's a sprawl-
ing, single-story building, long and low, with half a dozen windows on
this side alone. High brick walls form a perimeter around the house on
three sides and meet at two low steel gates that bar the entrance to the
property. On top of the walls are coils of barbed wire.

Blackwood slows to a stop about five meters away from the gate and
gestures to it. "I hope that's unlocked. When you've gone through," he
tells Jock, "leave it open behind you." He looks at the gravel driveway
leading up to the house. Suddenly this feels like a terrible plan.

"Are we ready to go?" Jock snaps at them all.

Blackwood turns to the other two officers, who nod. He radios
Angie. "Are you in position?"

The radio crackles. "Yes."

"Any news about Rose?"

"Not yet."

Blackwood grimaces as he considers the house, wondering if Rose
is in there too. "Ready when you are," he says to Jock. "Good luck and
be careful. Remember, keep them talking. Say *abort* to get help."

Jock gets out of the car and makes his way to the gate. To Blackwood's relief, they see him pull it back and walk through, leaving it
slightly open.

Jock stops halfway down the drive. "I'm here," he calls, in his distinctive commanding drawl, which resonates through Blackwood's earpiece.
"Come outside and talk."

The man is impressive, Blackwood thinks. It's impossible to tell if he's
nervous. Perhaps he's so used to commanding all the situations he finds
himself in that this is just another spot of tough negotiating for him.

Nothing happens for a while. Jock swings around to look back at
the police vehicle. Blackwood isn't sure how well he can see them from
that distance, but he shakes his head. "Lure them out," he says under
his breath. "Don't go in."

Then the front door opens. Blackwood is expecting to see a man
appear, but it's an older woman, possibly Carmela, holding a little girl
in her arms. She walks carefully down the veranda steps toward Jock.

"Carmela," Jock says, his tone suddenly soft and compliant, as though they are long-lost lovers meeting at a party. "It's been such a long time."

Carmela holds out the child. "Take her," she instructs him, her voice cold. "As a sign of good faith. Give her to them"—she nods at the police car—"then come inside and talk to us."

Jock reaches for the child. "You're trembling," he says. "Why did you do this, Carmela? You didn't have to do this. We could have talked, come to some arrangement."

Carmela says nothing, just turns and runs back up the steps into the house.

Blackwood gets out of the car, his eyes fixed on the little girl who squirms in Jock's arms. They meet at the gate and Jock passes Honey over to Blackwood.

"Try to draw them outside," Blackwood reminds him. "Do not go in. Keep talking."

Jock nods and turns to go back down the driveway. Blackwood races to the car as quickly as he can, with Honey gripped tightly in his arms. He sits her on his knee in the front seat.

"Sir," says Angie's voice through the radio. "We've got a possible problem."

At her tone, Blackwood's insides curdle. "What?"

"We've picked up Rose's phone signal—but it's about twenty minutes from here."

"*What?* I thought she was here?"

"She was."

"What the hell is going on?" He looks toward Jock standing on the gravel driveway. "Hang on, do we know if this family have a car?"

"I can run a check, but surely they must do, living all the way out here."

"Well, there's nothing parked in the driveway." He's thinking fast. "Okay—get one of your vehicles to peel off toward Rose's location. But I need you here. Also, I've got Honey—they handed her over to Jock and he brought her to me."

"That seems a very easy start," Angie replies, voicing exactly what's been worrying him. "Do you want the paramedics to come up?"

"Not yet. She's not in distress and I don't want to distract Jock right now. But I don't like this. There's no sign of Louisa or Kai and they're stalling for some reason. I want your team to move closer. You can get about two hundred meters away from us without the van being seen."

"I'm back," he hears Jock call through his earpiece, and he watches as Jock moves closer to the front steps.

There's no answer.

The little girl on Blackwood's lap is looking up at him with wide eyes—the ice-blue Fisher eyes—compelling him silently to help her understand what's going on.

"Hi, Honey," he says gently. "I'm Detective Blackwood. I know you've had a strange few days, but I'm going to get you back to your mummy and daddy very soon."

Her face crumples into a frown. "I want Lulu," she whines.

"We're going to get Lulu too," Blackwood tells her. "And Kai."

He looks up again to see Jock has moved even closer to the steps.

The front door opens.

Don't do it, Blackwood implores the man silently. *Stay outside.*

"We want to talk to you in private," Carmela calls to Jock. "Come inside. You owe us that much. Then we'll give you the baby."

"Can I trust you, Carmela?" Jock asks softly. "We cared for each other once, remember?"

Honey is tapping on Blackwood's arm. "I want Lulu," she says more insistently.

"We're going to get her for you, sweetheart," Blackwood replies, eyes on Jock and Carmela in the distance, praying he can keep this promise.

"You can trust me," he hears Carmela's voice through his earpiece.

"Okay," Jock says. "Because I'll give you whatever you need. I can take care of you all financially. Forever, I promise. This whole thing has been a terrible mix-up. You'll understand if you give me the chance to explain."

As he climbs the steps toward the front door, Honey points to the house. "Lulu's gone," she says sadly.

It takes Blackwood a moment to register Honey's words, because he's watching in despair, his heart collapsing against his ribs, as Jock ignores all warnings and disappears through the doorway.

As he finally comprehends what the little girl just said, he jolts. "Honey, is Lulu inside the house?"

She shakes her head.

"Is Kai inside the house?"

She stares solemnly at him, and shakes her head again. Opens her mouth and reaffirms his very worst fears. "Gone."

Blackwood looks up at the silent house in horror.

"Before we give you the baby, we thought you should meet your daughter Marisol," a man's voice says through his earpiece.

When Jock speaks again his voice has changed completely. "I . . . I really didn't know she was like this, I swear." His tone is unmistakable: It's the sound of a man begging for his life.

There's no point in waiting any longer. They've lost control. "Abort!" Blackwood yells.

The two snipers leap out, moving quickly and stealthily toward the gate. Blackwood grips the car door handle, steadying both himself and the child on his knee.

Jock's voice comes again in Blackwood's ear. "I'm so, so sorry. I swear I can pay whatever you need to make this right."

"You really think your money can fix everything?" the man's voice scoffs. "It's too late! *Look at her,*" the man screams. "Marisol can barely move; she can't speak, or eat properly, or walk, or dance like she used to. She spends every single day hunched in that chair while Carmela feeds and changes her like a baby. And my son killed a man—because we were desperate, because you wouldn't take care of your own child! You've destroyed our lives, so now all we have left is some Old Testament justice. Do you know what it says in the Old Testament, Jock?"

Blackwood can hear the roar of other vehicles approaching at speed. He clutches Honey tighter, dread filling his lungs.

"*Stop. Don't,*" Jock cries, but each word is riven with fear.

"GO!" Blackwood yells, as a police van screeches to a halt beside him and armed police jump out, swarming across the driveway.

A sudden, earth-shattering bang rents the air, and all the windows in the house blow out in unison, leaving Blackwood's ears ringing. Honey screams, and Blackwood pulls her in to his chest, trying to shield her. In front of him, the armed officers drop their tactical positions and sprint toward the house.

Blackwood jumps out of the car with Honey in his arms, as two ambulances pull up next to the police vehicles. He grabs the arm of a paramedic and hands the child to her. It's chaos ahead of him, more officers and paramedics rushing toward the scene. Prone bodies are being dragged onto the veranda. One, two, three, four. But Honey is right. There's no baby. And the only young woman he can see is definitely not Louisa.

Blackwood walks toward the commotion in a daze. The four bodies on the deck are not moving. Two paramedics are administering CPR to one of them. He doesn't recognize anyone besides Jock. *Where the hell are Louisa and the baby? And Rose?*

Blackwood turns, about to shout more orders, when his legs begin to buckle. The low throbbing through his body that he's struggled with for days becomes a searing pain in his chest. His vision becomes brighter and brighter as the ground comes up to meet him, his head hitting the gravel with a smack.

He hears a yell, "Christ! No!" and then there's a voice close to his face, fingers on his neck. "Oh no you don't, you're not doing this to me now, no bloody way." Angie's hands are moving to his chest, but Blackwood can feel himself floating away. There's no darkness, just an incredible light, and he can hear people shouting but he's not sure who any of them are anymore. All he wants is to go home.

CHAPTER FORTY-ONE
ROSE

The car stops.

Rose had almost been lulled into a stupor as they bumped and bounced over uneven ground, and her hand is a mess of cuts and bruises from being caught repeatedly between metal as she desperately held the trunk open. She's lost some of the feeling in her fingers, but the instant the vehicle's movement ceases she becomes fully alert, listening intently as one door opens, then another.

"Give me the kid," says a male voice that must be Reid. Carmela's stepson. Fabien's murderer.

"Please don't hurt him," comes Lou's reply, her voice shaky and high pitched. She's so close that Rose is sure she could touch her if it weren't for the divide.

"Oh, don't worry, I won't," Reid cackles. "I know people who'll pay a lot of money for him—and they know how to make kids disappear forever. He's worth a fortune. Now get out."

There's a shuffling noise that lasts a while. "Take him and go stand over there," Reid says. "I'm not cutting the cable ties—you can manage."

Rose absorbs Reid's words, making a series of rapid calculations.

She extrapolates the key information. *Disappear. Fortune. Go. Cable ties.* She'll need to judge this correctly to the very last second.

There's more awkward movement outside. The baby begins to wail. "Oh, for fuck's sake," Reid shouts, then, "Give him to me."

And Rose knows this is it.

She pushes the trunk open, quickly assessing the situation. Ten meters away, a disheveled figure wearing dirty jeans and a stained black T-shirt looms menacingly over Lou as she clutches the baby awkwardly, her wrists still bound. He's solidly built with thick, muscular arms: Physically, Lou is no match for him.

And Rose only has one chance to disarm him.

As Reid raises his hand, Rose glimpses a tattoo on his forearm. For a moment she's watching herself twenty years ago, pushing a baby's face into her neck for protection, as a madman with a tattoo shaped like an hourglass comes at her with a blade. She blinks, and her vision clears. This isn't the demon that stalks her nightmares—but *he is Lou's monster.* And Rose will save her daughter, or die trying.

The man lunges toward Lou, reaching for the baby. Lou rears away, screaming and swiping at him with something small clutched in her palm. He roars when it grazes his arm.

With a scorching burst of adrenaline, Rose pushes herself out of the trunk and hits the ground, jumping to her feet so she can gauge their reaction to her unexpected appearance, and be ready for Reid's attack.

Shock stalls the entire scene for a moment. Lou looks dazed, while Reid's murderous expression curls into a snarl. He storms over, grabbing Rose by the collar and spitting into her face. "Who the FUCK are you?"

She doesn't hesitate. The screwdriver is concealed in her fist, the short metal spike hidden against the inside of her wrist. Before Reid can grab her arms and disable her, she twists her hand to reveal the tip, then plunges it, as hard as she can, into his right eye.

He rears back with a scream, pulling at the handle of the screwdriver so that it comes out along with a spurt of blood and ooze. Rose is on her feet and reaching for the wrench, which she'd hidden inside her other sleeve. Quickly, before he can recover, she smashes it against the spot just above his right ear.

She knows the body's weak points from all her training. The weapon connects well. Reid falls forward onto his knees, still screeching with pain. One hand goes back to his eye, coming away covered in blood. Rose aims another blow to the back of his head and he crumples flat to the ground.

In Lou's arms, the baby continues to wail. Rose runs across and drags them both back to the car, watching Reid all the time. She pushes Lou into the front seat, putting the baby between her daughter's bound arms as there's no way of releasing the cable ties. "Where are the keys?" she cries, asking Lou but not really expecting an answer. Lou seems catatonic, gawping at her. Then she croaks out just one word, small and uncertain.

"M-Mum?"

There isn't time to reply, but Rose caresses Lou's cheek for the briefest of seconds before racing around to the driver's side. The keys aren't in the ignition, and so Rose grabs the wrench again, stepping back across to the man's hulking body. The keys dangle from one of his pockets, and she pulls them out gingerly, her heart pounding, half expecting him to roll over and grab her wrist. But those meaty arms remain motionless; the tattoo on his forearm is not an hourglass but an Aztec skull, with empty eye sockets that follow her as she runs back to the car.

Slamming the door closed, she guns the ignition and turns to look behind them, ready to accelerate, taking them back the way they'd come. Suddenly Lou screams. Reid is standing up, his bloodied hands on the hood, his face contorted with rage, one eye a deep red hole. Rose pushes the accelerator hard and the man's expression changes to shock as the car jumps forward, sending him lurching onto the hood. Before they reach the tree line, Rose brakes sharply, bracing herself as the man flies off, his body hitting a solid jarrah tree trunk with a thump, going down again.

Lou screams as the jolt sends her flying toward the dashboard. She automatically shields Kai with her arms, which take the brunt of the impact. To Rose's relief, Kai stays pinioned inside Lou's embrace because of the cable ties, but he still shrieks in fear. Lou's arms must be throbbing, but she immediately tries to comfort Kai, murmuring, "You're okay, you're okay," whispering the words over and over. Rose hauls Lou back onto the seat. She wants to put the seat belt around them, but there's no time; they have to get somewhere safe. She reverses fast, then spins the car around, accelerating down the road with her eyes constantly checking the rearview mirror, as though the man will morph into something supernatural and chase them down.

He doesn't, but she keeps on driving, with Lou and the child both wailing beside her. For a while Rose isn't even aware that tears are coursing down her cheeks too.

She drives for so long that she gets another pulse of fear at the thought she may have gone around in a circle. What if she's taking them back toward danger? She's beginning to lose her mind with dread and disorientation when she hits an open road, and out of nowhere there's a helicopter flying low above her, tracking her journey, staying with her until she realizes she doesn't need to go on.

She pulls over to the side of the road and the helicopter hovers, then lands right in front of the vehicle. Charlie races to Lou's door and pulls it open. Rose can hear sirens in the distance. She watches, exhausted, as Charlie gathers his niece and the baby into his arms, so tenderly, like they are the most rare and precious things he's ever seen.

"Let me take the baby," Rose says gently, and they carefully remove Kai from Lou's arms, only now noticing the blood on her wrists from deep incisions where the cable ties have dug in.

Charlie pulls out a pocketknife and Lou flinches at the sight. "Let's get you free," he reassures her, before slicing the bindings off and throwing them into the footwell of the car.

Rose cradles the baby. His wide eyes watch her intently. His mouth has fallen open in confusion.

There are sirens in the distance. Rose finally lets herself believe it might be over. Her whole body begins to tremble, and she holds on to Kai as tightly as she can.

Lou suddenly goes very still. "Fabien?" she whispers to Charlie.

She is turned away from Rose on the seat, so Rose can only watch

Charlie's face. He pales, his mouth beginning to move but no sound coming out. And Lou knows. She lets out a heartrending wail and slumps forward, all her hopes and dreams shattered, while Charlie lunges toward her, as though if he's quick enough he might catch the broken pieces of her and somehow hold her together. Lou sags against him, sobbing.

The sirens are louder, drawing closer. Kai begins to cry.

"I'm so sorry," Charlie says, rubbing Lou's back as he holds her, his desolate brown eyes locking on Rose. "But you're safe now. We've got you. We're here."

CHAPTER FORTY-TWO
BRONTE

There's nothing Bronte hates more than waiting around, and this week has consisted of little else. She's lost hours to this interminable rescue mission, and she's resorted to constantly fiddling with her phone, reading news articles, and of course checking the stock market. Worst of all, she's spent most of the time stuck in a room with Calamity Kyle and Fretful Frannie, who are suddenly vying to be parents of the year. Kyle is doing the doting-father act, and Frannie is intermittently praying—actually praying, out loud, with her hands together—like she's Mother fucking Mary. Bronte is going to spontaneously combust if she has to listen to much more of their bullshit. The last time she'd seen them before this god-awful week, at Ethan's Easter party, they'd been so shit faced that when Frannie got up for another drink, she'd completely forgotten baby Kai was on her lap. It was fortunate the nanny had been close enough to leap across with hands outstretched and break his fall.

Bronte is still fuming at the way her father had spoken to them before he left on his poorly advised mercy mission. *Sacked, my arse.* When he returns she'll be reminding him of the many reasons why he is better and safer with her and Eddie on his side. He's conveniently forgotten all the dirty laundry they've taken care of over the years, particularly

Eddie's expert eye when it comes to tax issues and company assets. Ethan and Toby can say and do whatever the hell they like, but she won't be standing for any of their dad's crap.

She looks around the beach house, deciding it will be a long time before she comes here again. She's going to buy herself another place, somewhere smaller but with a better view. She'll have to discuss it with Eddie when she gets home. She wishes he were here now. She always feels better when he's around; he's the only person she knows with a quicker and more cunning mind than her father. It's incredible to have a person you can confide in about almost everything, and know that they still love you, for better and worse.

Now, as they wait for news, they've been assigned the most robotic detective on the planet. DS Webster keeps bringing them updates, while a female constable has been making them endless cups of bloody tea. It's so fricking sexist, but for once she can't even be bothered to respond with a snide comment. She just accepts and sips the hot beverages, enjoying the scald in her throat.

At last, they all sense a shift in the detective's posture as he hurries toward them, phone in hand.

"What is it?" Kyle asks, jumping up and standing way too close to the man.

"DS Lennard is on her way," Webster informs them. "She'll be here in ten minutes with an update."

"Come on, man," Kyle insists, his tone and upturned hands reminding Bronte of their father. "You gotta give us more than that."

The detective shrugs. "I can't. I don't know anything else."

Unable to sit still, Kyle disappears toward the front door. A few minutes later, there's a commotion, and Frannie sprints down the corridor too. When she returns, Honey is clutched in her arms, screeching so loud that Bronte winces.

"Where's Lulu? I want *Lulu*!" Honey demands.

"Lou isn't here," Frannie consoles her, casting around desperately as if someone might help. No one moves. Then Frannie's eyes alight on the sofa. "But look, here's Valentine."

Perhaps Frannie does have a smidgen of maternal instinct after all, Bronte thinks, as the little girl wraps her arms around her blue teddy and falls almost instantly asleep on her mother's shoulder.

"Where are the others?" Ethan demands, as DS Angie Lennard strides into the lounge. Bronte readies herself for bad news. The woman looks close to tears.

"Louisa and Kai were separated from Honey, but they're both safe," DS Lennard says. "They're being taken to hospital. Louisa needs treating for shock and wounds on her wrists, and Kai is possibly dehydrated. But they're not seriously injured. We'll take Frannie and Kyle there in a moment, with Honey. But Bob Drake asked me to bring you the news myself."

Bronte watches the skin tighten around the detective's mouth, and gets a curious fluttering sensation in the pit of her stomach. "Where's Dad?"

"There was an explosion at the house," Lennard continues. "A man and woman, and their daughter—the people who took Louisa and the kids—were all killed. It was intentionally set, and meant for your father too. He saved himself by making a last-minute dive toward the front door—the force blew him off his feet, but his Kevlar vest helped him bear the impact. He's been rushed to hospital; the RAC rescue helicopter has taken him straight to Perth. He's not in a good way, but he's alive."

"Right then." Bronte gets up, keen to get to their father's bedside, imagining him suffering, vulnerable. Needing her to take control. "How soon can we get a flight back to Perth?" she asks Ethan.

"I'm on it," he says.

She turns to Kyle. "Are you coming too?"

"No, Lou and Kai have been taken to Bunbury. We'll go and find them first, and meet you up there." He puts an arm around Frannie, who winces as she cuddles Honey, moving slightly away.

Bronte nods, then follows Ethan and Toby to the car. She sits in the front passenger seat, staring out of the window, not even bothering to hide her face when photographers surround the car at the front gates of the estate. Let them get their bloody photo. She looks appropriately hideous, exactly like a grieving daughter and sister. Which is fortuitous, since she feels anything but distress. She's far more excited at what the rest of the day might bring if her father is out of action. She's been preparing to battle Toby and Ethan for control of company assets for years.

She keeps trying to check in with herself, to find the place that isn't numb, to see what emotion might be lurking there, but she can't locate it. She's been this way ever since she found her mother's body beside all those empty bottles, and then listened to her father repeatedly lie to everyone about Trisha's cause of death—a heart attack, he'd announced, when he should have said a broken heart. She suspects he's always known that Bronte was partly responsible for the family implosion—that she was the one who'd overheard him and Carmela, and blabbed about it to her mother—but he's never asked her. Sometimes she wishes he would: Perhaps that would break her out of the block of ice that had frozen around her as she faced life without her only ally in the male-dominated Fisher family.

Her mother had always told Bronte that she was special. The longed-for girl. The only girl. And Bronte had played that card to perfection in her mother's absence, as a way to honor her memory. She's put herself in the center of the Fisher empire, smarter than the rest of them put together, controlling everything, manipulating everyone.

She'd always had one eye out for Marisol, of course. She kept tabs on Carmela's family, and she'd known the girl had come to Perth. But she'd never thought Marisol would be so bold as to ingratiate herself with Kyle's ex, to confront Bronte at a family party, acting so nauseatingly meek and nervous as she'd said to Bronte in a quiet corridor at Kyle's house, "I think I'm your half sister."

Bronte had feigned surprise and delight. "Really?" she'd replied, staring into those all-too-familiar ice-blue eyes. "What makes you think that?"

When the girl tentatively explained her mother and Jock's affair, Bronte laughed. "Oh lord, we knew Daddy was a player, but this is something else. You must tell me more," she'd insisted. "But we need to be discreet. I have to grab a drink. There's a quiet spot on the third floor; meet me on the balcony up there in a sec."

She'd gone downstairs, knocked back a wine, and headed up for the rendezvous, unsure what she was going to do, only knowing that she could keep up a charade for as long as it took to destroy this girl, this pretender, this female bastard come to lay claim to part of the throne. She'd imagined weeks of planning and subterfuge to get rid of her, but when she got up to the third floor, Marisol was on the balcony, looking at the view across the river. Her back was already turned, and it was so, so simple.

Marisol didn't even hear Bronte coming because of the party noise below them. And she had no idea of the bright flash of rage that sent Bronte hurtling toward her, arms outstretched, to push her half sister over the edge.

And that, Bronte thinks, is the one piece of her life that she's never shared with anyone, not even Eddie. Sure, some people might be suspicious, but no one has ever dared to confront her. She'd sworn to herself that she'd die with the knowledge inside her—and she will now, because the girl isn't here anymore. Now Marisol can't ever make a miraculous recovery, which has always been Bronte's worst fear. Now, no one will ever know.

She follows her brothers onto the private plane, and straps herself in. There's a small bottle of Moët in the seat pocket, and she takes it out and pops the cork. "A toast," she says, raising the bottle to her siblings. "May the Fishers live to fight another day."

Her brothers don't have glasses to raise in return. Instead, they both nod at her, with their obligatory smiles—the ones they save for their most important clientele. And then, in unison, they quickly look away.

CHAPTER FORTY-THREE
BLACKWOOD

"You're a darn fool, Malcolm Blackwood, always having to play the hero."

It's not the words, but rather the way Margie is saying them, her lips pressed against his forehead and her eyes watery, that makes him smile. If she keeps talking to him like this, in that tone of voice, she can call him a fool as many times as she wants.

He's about to be prepped for surgery. Since Margie arrived she had lovingly chided him for everything from eating bacon rolls to overwork to caring too much about others and not paying enough attention to himself. But she'd also told him how much she loved him, and that was all he'd been waiting to hear.

"I love you too," he'd replied with a sigh, aware of a long-held tension finally dissipating. "And I'm relieved. I really thought you weren't sure of me again, after all these days without talking."

"Since when did we ever talk while you're on a job? I know I used to check in, but I would barely get a text from you. So I thought you might prefer to be left alone to get on with your work."

Shit, he thinks. *She's right.*

"Perhaps it was just harder this time," he says groggily. "Now I've stopped taking you for granted."

Margie smiles. "Well, you've given me a big enough fright to last me a long time. So let's get you well—again!—and get you retired, and then perhaps we can spend some proper time together."

"Sure," he says. "We can go fishing."

"Mal, you know I hate fishing."

"I'll fish. You can read. I'll buy a boat."

"You're delirious now. I'm going to have to call the doctor if you don't stop this." But he doesn't need to open his eyes to check she's joking; he can hear the happiness in her voice.

"And you can take me line dancing," he adds, in a moment of exquisite generosity.

"Now *that* I can't wait to see," says another bemused female voice.

He opens his eyes a little. "Angie, is that you? Come to take the piss out of my pajamas, have you?"

"Would you expect anything less of me?" she says with a chuckle. "I just came to tell you that, to Webster's great annoyance, I've been unofficially promoted to get this case all tidied up . . . so thanks to you and your dodgy ticker I now get to do all your paperwork, while you take the glory. Which is typical, I might add. I've carried you for all these years; I might as well do it a little longer."

He tries to laugh, but it hurts, so he ends up snorting gently.

"Also, that bloody dynamo Rose Campbell somehow obtained a list of shell companies that point to some nefarious Fisher dealings," she adds. "So we've got a bit more paperwork to do before we can hand it over to the Financial Crimes Squad."

He nods, beckoning Angie toward him, ensuring she can hear. "If you see Rose, tell her . . . tell her . . ." He can't think of how to express the depth of his admiration for her determination and courage. As the words fail him, he closes his eyes.

Angie leans closer. "Already done. However, she didn't rescue everyone on her own. You made some tough calls back there. Drake wouldn't have had the guts, although he's crowing about it already as though he led the bloody tac team response. Jock is going to be okay—albeit with a few war wounds—and those lucky little Fisher kids will never know how much you did for them. But I'll remember," she says in a fierce whisper. "And so will Rose. And Lou. And Kyle. And Frannie." She stands up again. "Now, you know I only brought you back to life because you promised me I could dress up and do karaoke for your retirement bash. So get well soon, then we can go and have a drink and celebrate you properly. You're not ducking out of a big leaving party, you know, even if I have to wheel you there with a tube up your nose."

He snorts harder with laughter this time, causing a sharp twinge in his chest. "Ouch. Go away, Angie," he says.

He feels her squeeze his hand, and he hangs on for just a moment longer, hoping it conveys everything he would dearly love to say.

He must drift off after Angie goes. He wakes up to find the grandchildren have brought him fishing gear and left it beside the bed. Word travels fast in the family, apparently, and although two nets on sticks weren't exactly what he had in mind, it's a start. He can't wait to cuddle those young boys and spend the time with them that he wishes he'd had with his own two lads.

He hears the chime of his phone, and Margie goes to pick it up. "Don't you dare," he snaps, making her glance across in surprise.

"It's Bob Drake," she says, checking the screen. "The man can never leave you alone for more than five minutes. He probably wants to go through your retirement package."

Drake had offered Blackwood retirement three months early, with a generous bonus for what he'd just been through. Although, Margie had added wryly, Drake tended to have ulterior motives for everything. He was probably hoping Blackwood wouldn't sue the force for making him put in so much overtime that his heart valve had burst.

"He can wait," Blackwood says, pushing Margie's hand away gently so that she puts the phone back down. "We've earned the right to say that now, Margie, after our efforts over all these years. From now on, everyone else can wait."

Margie's eyes are glistening as she leans in closer. "Well said, my darling," she replies, squeezing his hand.

CHAPTER FORTY-FOUR
ROSE

As they drive to the airport, Rose can hardly believe it's almost four weeks since she arrived—in some ways it feels like she's been here forever. Trixie has insisted on coming too, and is nestled between Rose and Louisa, her head leaning on Louisa's arm. Charlie's girl is a sweetheart, and Rose has loved getting to know her while they've been waiting for the police and government clearance to make the journey home. Trixie and her assortment of adopted animals had proved the perfect antidote to long hours visiting lawyers and police departments, making statements and answering questions. No one expected Rose to face trial in the circumstances, but there were still a lot of formalities to go through, and not all of them had been concluded. Bob Drake had played a key part in allowing her to go home, but there'd been agreements made that she would return if and when required.

In the front, Charlie and Vee are keeping up a stream of banal conversation. Rose is too tired to join in, and it appears she's not alone. Lou has been staring out of the window for the entire three-hour journey, and Rose would give anything to know what she's thinking. She wishes she could bear some of her daughter's trauma and her grief for Fabien, but for now she'll have to hope that it's enough to be by her side.

After they'd been rescued, Rose hadn't been able to breathe properly until the police caught up with Reid, his body still laid out in front of the jarrah tree. She couldn't bear the thought of him out there in the world and full of vengeance, taunting them both, making them jump at shadows. She'd endured a similar torment while Joseph Burns had been alive, and at times it had felt almost unsurvivable. Still, she'd cried for Carmela and Marisol. The stories that had come out from shocked locals in the nearest town had been all about Gerard's drinking problem and need for control, as well as Reid's violent outbursts even as a youngster. It seemed likely that Carmela had known she was going back into the house to die, willing to concede to a suicide pact with Gerard, perhaps feeling there was nowhere left to turn and not willing to leave Marisol on her own to be put into an institution if they were arrested. But while Gerard had made sure he saved his boy, Carmela had been selfless enough to save Rose's girl, even if she'd given up on everything else. Rose would never forget her.

Vee had arrived to chaos, twelve hours after Rose and Lou were rescued from the lonely country road with baby Kai. She'd made it in time to hold her sister when Rose finally broke down. She'd sorted out everything and found them both a hotel in Perth where Rose could have some space to recuperate. And after a few days, Vee told Rose the truth about Bonnie.

"She left Safehaven the morning after she arrived. I'm so sorry."

Rose swallowed hard, trying to quell the surge of emotion. "What happened?"

"She went back as soon as she'd had a good sleep. Said she'd been tired and overreacted."

Rose sighed. "I wish I could have been there."

"I know." Vee offered her a sympathetic smile. "But you can't save them all. I'm sorry I didn't tell you before, but I didn't want to lower your spirits when you were battling so much here. You needed as much hope as possible."

Rose understood. "We'll get her next time," she reassured Vee, praying they would have another chance. And Vee had smiled kindly, and left it at that.

They'd thought it best to leave Lou alone with Charlie for a while after she got out of hospital. Vee visited them first, and after a few days she said that Lou seemed ready to talk to Rose. So they made the journey to Charlie's, with Rose almost as nervous as the afternoon she'd lain in the trunk of Carmela's car.

Lou was stretched out on the sofa watching *The Big Bang Theory* on her iPad when they arrived. As soon as she saw them she removed her headphones and stared at Rose.

"I still can't believe you're here," she said eventually.

Rose sat down opposite her. "Me neither."

"I thought I was hallucinating when you burst out of the car. It felt like a dream—still does. There are already gaps in my memory. I don't remember anything but that moment, and seeing Charlie."

"You were fighting for your life," Rose told her. "It's natural to block some of it out."

"*You* were fighting for my life," Lou replied. There was a long pause, during which neither of them broke eye contact. "Thank you for saving me," Lou said softly, the words floating away on an extended exhalation, the release of something held deep inside.

Rose hesitated. "You're welcome," she replied, and then kicked herself for sounding so formal. She tried again, knowing how much this conversation mattered, that it might be the bedrock on which their future relationship would form. "I came as soon as I heard you were missing."

"Even though I pushed you away for years?"

"Well, you were hurting, and you'd been lied to for years."

Lou looked pained. "You must have been hurting too. I'm sorry."

At that point, Rose couldn't bear it any longer. "Can I give you a hug?"

When Lou nodded, Rose went over to her daughter, wrapping her up in her arms. Lou had collapsed into Rose, breathing hard and heavy, while Rose stroked her daughter's long, dark hair. When they eventually moved apart, both their faces were streaked with tears.

"I found out a lot about you," Rose told her, "when we were looking for you. And I realized you have a real aptitude for photography. Do you know it runs in the family? My sister Jess works as a wildlife photographer all over the world. She's had photos in *National Geographic*."

"That's amazing," Lou replied, her eyes shining. "I knew a bit about her, but not the *National Geographic* part." Then she smiled shyly, and it was clear she'd been keeping tabs on the Campbell family far more than Rose had realized. It tore at Rose's heart thinking of this girl longing to know her mum and her maternal relatives for so many years, when they would have loved the chance to embrace her too. It was hard not to hate Henry and Evelyn for all the heartbreak they'd caused.

"Have you spoken to your dad?" she asked tentatively.

Lou tensed. "Charlie is my go-between for now."

"Well, I know it might take time, but I'd dearly love to get to know you better," Rose said cautiously.

In response, Lou smiled the kind of smile that reached all the way to her eyes. "I'd like that too. That's why I want to come back to the UK for a while with you and Auntie Vee."

And Rose had smiled in return, gently, so as not to overwhelm Lou, while inside her heart danced with joy.

Later, Charlie had taken Rose for a walk around the property, saying, "Come down to the edge of the tree line with me. I need to check the fence repairs are holding; we had foxes a few days ago and they terrorized the joeys."

They'd walked out over the veranda, down a small set of wooden steps, and headed across the dry grass toward the trees. The further they went, the longer the grass became, until Rose's feet disappeared with each step.

"Don't you get snakes in long grass?" she asked.

"Yep," he agreed, turning to her with a grin. "But they should be in brumation now—which is a bit like hibernation. Anyway, don't worry, I'm a qualified first-aider."

"How reassuring," she murmured, continuing to trudge after him.

"In a couple of months," he told her as they reached a clearer path through the bush, "this area will be full of wildflowers. Pri adored them. They're tiny, but beautiful—just like she was—and I seem to spot more and more of them every year now. I think of them as little gifts she leaves me."

Listening to him, to his sad acceptance of life as it was, and his joy and tenderness in discovering these small, precious things, Rose found her eyes were wet. She brushed away the smattering of tears. The upswell of emotion since rescuing Lou kept catching her off guard. It was overwhelming when she hadn't felt like this in years.

When they'd got to the trees they found a stream running between them, just a trickle of water and some marshy grass on each side. "We call this Wandoo Creek," Charlie told her. "It used to be Settlers Creek, but we don't call it that anymore, since we learned its Noongar name. All of this land here had been turned into horse pasture, and the trees were chopped down as far as you could see. I've got photos of what it was like before, and you wouldn't believe it. Just goes to show it's never too late to start putting something right."

She'd smiled at his unsubtle pep talk—thinking he was encouraging her to keep talking to Lou. Only later on had she realized he might have been hinting at something else.

———

In the airport car park, Charlie pulls the luggage from the SUV and sets it down.

"You don't need to come in," Rose begins, but he holds up a hand.

"We'll see you to the gate, if that's okay."

She relents, and he takes Trixie for a drink while the three women get checked in. They catch up at the coffee bar, and Lou takes Trixie to look at the shops while Vee decides to call home before they set off.

Left alone, Charlie and Rose make small talk about how long it will take to get to London, entertainment on the long flight, and whether Rose will sleep. Eventually, they run out of things to say and fall silent.

Rose takes a deep breath. "I can't thank you enough," she begins. "I feel like we've lived an entire lifetime together these past few weeks."

He doesn't answer her straightaway but holds her gaze. She doesn't flinch, letting him stare, hoping he can see everything else she wishes she could say.

Just as Charlie looks like he's about to speak, Trixie bounds back to the table with Lou behind her and pulls him away, insisting he sees the teddies in the Australiana shop. Vee returns soon after and Rose gathers her things, ready to leave.

When Charlie and Trixie return, they all make their way to the departures area. Trixie starts to cry when she says goodbye to Lou, and Lou gets upset too as she wipes the young girl's tears away. Trixie cuddles her new toy platypus and listens as Lou reassures her that they'll see each other again before too long. Then Lou flings her arms around Charlie. "Thank you for never giving up on me," she says, and Rose understands she's not just talking about the last few weeks.

"We love you, Lou," Charlie replies, his eyes glistening. "You've always got a home here, okay?"

"I know." She smiles. "And I'll be back."

Charlie turns to Vee and hugs her, and then does the same to Rose. "I'll miss you," he says as he steps away.

"Likewise." Rose hesitates, finding it hard to keep her emotions in check.

"We should go, Rose," Vee prompts her gently.

She turns and follows Lou and Vee into the line through to departures. Charlie takes Trixie's hand, and they walk away.

They're just reaching the point where they'll go through the double doors, when a deep voice calls out, "Rose!"

She turns, and Charlie is rushing toward her, pulling Trixie with him. "Come back for a second."

As he gets nearer, he lets go of Trixie's hand, then moves so close that Rose can smell soap and shaving foam and feel the warmth of his breath on her lips. "I don't know when we'll see each other again . . ."

He hesitates, then his hand moves to her face, his thumb briefly caressing the faint silver scar that runs across her cheek. Rose senses the moment passing, and knows what he's trying to say. So she leans in and kisses him.

He responds by pulling her against him, kissing her back as she puts

her arms around his neck and closes her eyes. The busy airport is forgotten for a moment, until they break apart.

Rose is aware of Trixie giggling, of Vee and Lou standing close by,
astonished and amused, but she only has eyes for Charlie.

He rests his forehead gently on hers, smiling. "I've wanted to do
that for a long time," he says. Then, quieter, "Come back to see us again
someday soon, Rose Campbell. When you can get away."

She brushes her fingers gently across his cheek. "Don't worry, I will."

He steps back, holds a hand out to Trixie, and gives Rose one last
deep, warm smile, before the two of them turn away.

"Jesus, Rose," Vee says with a laugh, putting her arm around Lou,
who looks equally shocked. "That was a bit out of the blue."

Rose smiles, and reluctantly turns away from watching Charlie go.
"I'm glad I can still surprise you."

Vee laughs. "I don't think either of us are surprised." She winks
at Lou. "The chemistry between you two is off the charts. But I never
thought you'd actually admit it."

Later, on the plane, Rose's fingers touch her lips, remembering the
kiss, smiling. However, she's also slightly embarrassed, wondering about
Lou's reaction. What must she have thought, watching her estranged
mum kissing her favorite uncle? It was probably very confusing, and
that's the last thing Lou needs. But if she recalls it correctly, Lou had
been grinning alongside Vee. Hopefully that meant she would be okay
with the idea of the connection between Rose and Charlie, when they
got around to talking about it.

Rose glances at her daughter beside her, eyes closed, headphones
in, but her posture too still for her to be sleeping. Then she looks
at her sister in the aisle seat, intent on the film she's watching. Rose
prays with everything she's got that they can build all the bridges they
need to, and that life will be kind to them for a while, keeping them
all safe.

She grabs her iPad and begins to scan through the dozens of emails
waiting for her attention. She's got countless updates from Safehaven,
and the latest draft of the domestic violence report, which means the

team have been working hard. She'll need to refocus soon. The past few weeks have reminded her of just how much her work matters.

However, she has other priorities now too, she thinks, as her gaze drifts back to Lou.

As though sensing Rose's attention, Lou opens her eyes. "Are you okay?" she asks with concern. Rose has noticed this since they've been together: Lou isn't sure how to read Rose's body language yet. But it will come.

"Yes, I'm fine," she assures her daughter. She thinks of showing Lou the photo hidden in her phone case, which she's carried close for so many years—but stops herself. She will, soon, but in a more private place than this. There's no need to rush. They have plenty of time.

"I was just wondering," she says instead. "I have some of my sister Jess's photos on here." She points to her iPad. "Would you like to take a look?"

Lou leans in eagerly. "I'd love to."

Rose picks up the device again, shuffling closer to Lou, making sure they can both see.

"Ready?" she asks Lou.

Lou nods.

And so they begin.

ACKNOWLEDGMENTS

As always, there are an amazing number of people who have supported me during the writing of *When She Was Gone* and another brilliant group dedicated to getting this book into your hands. Without them, I'd be a) much closer to insanity and b) unable to reach you, dear reader! So my gratitude goes to everyone who's played a part in helping this story come to life. As usual, there are a few special mentions. Firstly, my stellar agent, Tara Wynne: always there with support and helping me navigate the industry for nearly twenty years now! Thanks for keeping the faith, Tara, and for always looking out for me. Thanks to Stephanie Koven, Anne Fonteneau, Becca Malzahn, Isabella Bedoya, Brianna Jones, Francie Crawford, and the entire wonderful team at Blackstone for supporting my books and championing *When She Was Gone*. Thanks also to the excellent crew at HarperCollins Australia, with huge gratitude to my publisher, Anna Valdinger, and editor, Shannon Kelly, for giving me advice and time so that this story could be the very best version of itself. To all the sales teams working hard around the country, building bridges between books and bookshops: I deeply appreciate what you do. And to the bookshops, influencers, podcasters, reviewers, and everyone else who adores fiction and puts in long hours to support the books they love, I salute you, and I'm so grateful for your hard work!

Thanks to Dervla McTiernan for the really thoughtful and tough-love early read, which helped me enormously. And to Natasha Lester, thanks for your great feedback and insights and for loving Blackwood as much as I do. Fiona Thorp, thanks for patiently answering my questions—again! I really do owe you a few dinners, you know—or another of our classic cinema nights out. Donna Johnston and Kate Beaufoy, thanks for sharing your beautiful living spaces with me so I could write in peace—and for your ongoing support.

Thanks to all my family and friends, who continue to champion my books and are always my biggest supporters. I'd try to name you all, but I'm scared of who I'll accidentally leave out! I'll be sure to thank you in person.

Hannah and Isabelle: Your creativity and compassion inspire me every day. I used to juggle looking after you with writing these books, and now you're both taking care of me! Thanks for all your patience when the overwhelm hits, for the many dinners and cups of tea, and for listening and caring when I ramble on about my imaginary friends and my long to-do list. I'm a very lucky mum, and I love you both googol.

Finally, as always, thank you to Matt: my champion, my rock, and my sanity saver. Love of my life. I really don't know what I did to deserve you.

READER QUESTIONS

1. Rose is a character who's had to negotiate a lot of trauma. How do you feel about the impact Joseph Burns has had on Rose's life? How do you think this affects her decision-making?

2. An overarching social theme of the book is the different ways that toxic masculinity shows up in people's lives. How does the author expose this, and in which scenes and plotlines can you see its influence?

3. We hear a little of how Mal Blackwood's priorities have changed in recent years. What do they say about his character? Do you think his new priorities make him a more or less effective police officer? Do you think they make him happier? Can he be both happy and effective?

4. How do you feel about Rose's estrangement from Louisa? Do you think they could have tried anything else to reconnect over the years?

5. Another theme of the book is how money and power interfere with procedure, control, and decision-making. How did you see this showing up in the story?

6. What do you think about the choices Rose makes to try to find Lou and the children? How much of these decisions do you feel were made from her own professional life and experiences, and how much from a mother's instinct to save her child?

7. Discuss the different depictions of family in the story, and what the idea of family means to each of the main characters.

8. Blackwood mentions how much policing has changed over his working life. The public, the internet, and the media all have a substantial impact on the investigation, and Blackwood obviously sees this as mostly negative. Do you agree?

9. What do you make of the relationship between Charlie and Rose? Do they have a future?

10. Which character did you warm to the most? And did you change your mind about any of the characters during the course of the story?

11. What do you think will happen to the main characters over the next year? Who will go back to their old lives, and who has changed?

12. Who is most responsible for what happened to Lou and the children? And who else's actions led to their situation?

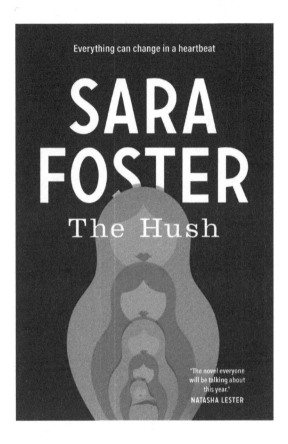

ABOUT THE AUTHOR

Sara Foster is the author of acclaimed dystopian thriller *The Hush* and seven bestselling psychological suspense novels: *You Don't Know Me*, *The Hidden Hours*, *All That Is Lost Between Us*, *The Deceit*, *Shallow Breath*, *Beneath the Shadows*, and *Come Back to Me*. Two of her novels have been optioned for television, and *You Don't Know Me* was adapted into a chart-topping drama podcast series by LiSTNR. Sara has a PhD in creative writing (studying maternal representations in fiction) and lives in Perth, Western Australia, with her husband, two daughters, three cats, Luna the cavoodle, and Sunny the bearded dragon.

 Subscribe to Sara's Substack, *The Resilient Author*, for weekly inspirational posts and a behind-the-scenes look into the world of writing and publishing.

 Sign up to Sara's quarterly reader newsletter and be the first to hear about her books, news, and events.